Praise for *The*

'Zahabi's novel will delight fans of thrilling magic systems and imaginative worlds' *Fantasy Hive*

'The world-building in this fantasy world is unique and yet you can see so many parallels to our own history that you can identify with it immediately' *Broken Geek Designs*

'A brilliant, engaging story, unlike anything I've read before'
The Bibliophile Chronicles

THE HAWKLING

Tales of the Edge: volume 2

Rebecca Zahabi

This edition first published in Great Britain in 2023 by Gollancz

First published in Great Britain in 2023 by Gollancz
an imprint of The Orion Publishing Group Ltd
Carmelite House, 50 Victoria Embankment
London EC4Y 0DZ

An Hachette UK Company

1 3 5 7 9 10 8 6 4 2

Copyright © Rebecca Zahabi 2022

A CIP catalogue record for this book is
available from the British Library.

ISBN (MMP) 978 1 473 23444 4
ISBN (eBook) 978 1 473 23445 1
ISBN (audio) 978 1 473 23446 8

Typeset at The Spartan Press Ltd,
Lymington, Hants

Printed and bound in Great Britain by Clays Ltd,
Elcograf S.p.A.

www.gollancz.co.uk

To Rose,
And to all little sisters.

Chapter One

As with most trouble, it was unexpected. The evening began, as usual, when Isha went downtown, headed for the Coop.

She had grown to love the roaring fire of the tavern, the broth boiling in the fireplace, the apprentices clapping after a duel, slapping each other's backs, encouraging the shyest member of the group to mindbrawl. She was used to the smell of cheap meat and stale beer. Although every surface was tacky, as if the tavern itself were sweating, there was comfort in the poor ramshackle building. It invited everyone in. When she was at the counter, watching Kilian's impersonations of Lady Siobhan, Isha laughed and forgot that nowhere was safe, not even the tavern.

When she arrived that evening, Tatters was already mentoring apprentices. He acknowledged her with a nod from the back of his booth, but he didn't have time to spare. With the threat of war on the horizon, even people who didn't usually visit the tavern wanted some extra training. When it came to her day-to-day life, Isha had found that war involved a lot of paperwork.

She wasn't sure what she'd been expecting. Calls to arms, maybe. Drills in the Nest's courtyard. The bell ringing with news from the Sunrisers every morning. As it was, apprentices were drafted to copy letters and maps, again and again, until their fingers cramped. The Duskdweller Edge and the Sunriser Edge were separated by the Ridge, after all, two countries split apart by a border of stone, so any war between them would be a slow one. An army had to cross the Ridge, through the Shadowpass weaving its way below the mountains, braving the soul-sucking shadows within. Peace had been maintained for centuries because the border was so hard to cross. The sun itself found it hard, rising on the Sunriser Edge, to drag the light-tide across the border to the Duskdweller side.

To prepare against the Renegades, the lawmages enlisted the ungifted's help. There was always a huddle of ten or so ungifted in the courtyard these days, struggling to spell out their names and holding spears awkwardly against their chests. Sometimes an apprentice was required to help copy out name, age, family members, occupation, while the ungifted stood in front of them, stammering the answers and asking whether they thought there was much danger. It was a duty Isha tried to avoid. She didn't know what to say to them, to the fear in their eyes.

The threat of the Renegades aside, life went on. Isha trained with Passerine at the Nest, with Tatters at the tavern. She enjoyed the variety. The Nest was beautiful, but cold. It wasn't made for humans. Its only scents were dust and mites. At the Coop, she felt at home. Maybe it was, as its name suggested, a grimier, smaller, yet more welcoming version of the Nest.

At the counter, she chatted with the innkeeper. He wasn't one to discourage a good drinker.

'Sometimes I fancy I just need you and Tatters to keep this whole place afloat,' he joked.

'He's busy at the moment, isn't he?' Isha said, indicating Tatters. He'd flung his cloak against the back of the bench and rolled up his sleeves. From here, she could only see the back of his head, a dash of red-brown hair, freckled skin. And the collar, of course.

She licked the foam off the top of her cup. The innkeeper had opened a new keg for her, which meant her drink was as much foam as beer.

'He'll only get busier,' said the innkeeper, shaking his head. He turned to serve another apprentice, grabbing several tumblers in one hand, expertly unblocking the wooden tap with the other one. He tugged the tap closed with a grunt before turning to her. 'No offence, kid, but everyone needs people to work their fields and serve their drinks. But if there's one thing the Renegades don't need, it's a bunch of mages sitting on their arses collecting tax. When they get here, it'll not be the city they're after.'

Reading between the lines, that sort of talk could be seen as disloyal. Isha was rather flattered the innkeeper spoke so openly: it meant he trusted her.

'Do you think you'd have a better time with the Renegades? Rather than the Nest? Maybe they'll make you pay less tax.' She drank to give him time to answer, and to hide her amusement at his shocked face.

The innkeeper rested his forearms on the counter. His fingers were glistening with spilt beer. As he pushed his weight into his arms, the fat and muscle swelled between the lines of his horn bracelet. He thought about what she'd said, then shook his head.

'Nah. Forget it. It's be ruled by the mages or be ruled by the khers. Bloodcows think they own the place already.' He smiled. It wasn't often that his grim face broke upwards, or that his lips showed his yellow teeth. 'Not that I like you crazy bunch, but you do keep them off our backs, I'll give you that.'

Isha was too stunned to answer. The innkeeper patted her hand, as if congratulating her on centuries of oppressing khers and ripping horns from their dead. His fingers were sticky.

'Last thing I want is cattle pushing me around,' he concluded.

It seemed like a good time to end the conversation.

Isha went to Tatters and pulled over a stool from a nearby table. She waited, watching the duels that were open to the public, downing the bitter beer. Kilian joined her two hours in. Now that she trained with Passerine, she didn't see him as often – as one of Sir Daegan's followers, he couldn't mingle with her at the Nest. But the tavern was different. It was a neutral ground. She couldn't help but smile at the familiar sight of his rumpled outfit, down to his green shoes, which clashed terribly with the gold of his belt and the grey of his robes. The green dye, though faded, had held up better than expected.

'You've become worse than me,' he said by way of greeting.

'Shut up and get me another drink,' she said. 'Put it on my tab.'

'You've even got a tab!' He rolled his eyes. 'What have I done? You were an innocent apprentice when you got here.'

I've got a tab because I win enough duels to wipe it, she thought. She was proud of her achievements in mindbrawl.

Tatters waved them both forward. He freed places on the bench next to him, pulling a platter of bread and cheese close. He invited them to eat and tell him the latest news. Isha took her knife out of the small sheath on her belt, cut a slice of cheese, and handed it to Kilian.

'Look at what you've done to her,' Kilian said, taking the cheese. 'It's terrible. She's always mindbrawling and drinking now.'

'The best way to live a life.' Tatters smiled.

The cheese was hard and sour. This was a good trading period for Tatters; Isha hoped he wasn't inviting too many apprentices out, but instead hoarding the money for later, the time that was bound to come when business would be slower.

'How is Arushi?' she asked.

'Sulking, I think,' Tatters said. His own knife, bone-handled and worn, lay on the table between them. 'I don't see much of her at the moment.'

'But you're not thinking of horn-humping, are you?' asked Kilian.

Tatters and Isha exchanged a glance.

'If you think I'm the first man to have the idea,' Tatters said, 'or the first kher, for that matter, you lack imagination.'

Tatters broke off a chunk of bread with dirty hands. Since she had been living at the Nest, Isha's skin had lost the roughness she'd gained through farm work. Tatters' hands reminded her of her foster father, and what her own hands would have looked like, had she stayed at home.

'I always tell him he lacks imagination,' she said. 'That's why his mindbrawl's so poor.'

'You're one to brag!' Kilian threw back his head, pretending to be offended. He flung his blond hair dangerously close to the torches.

'She is, actually.'

Tatters turned to Isha, and her heartbeat picked up as she realised he was about to ask her to duel. But before he could, the door of the tavern was slammed open. Conversations across the room died down to a hush, as if words were candles that the cold wind blowing from the door had extinguished.

Isha spotted blue robes. Two ordained mages.

The innkeeper rushed to greet them. The men were draped in the night-sky blue of recently ordained mages – not high mages in control of the Nest, but not apprentices, either. Tatters' mind shut down, although he sat poised, with the alertness of a dog sniffing the air. He pushed himself behind Isha and, intuitively, she sat on the edge of the bench, so she would be hiding him.

The innkeeper freed a table for the mages, chasing off a group of apprentices, who were then left stranded, holding their beers, scratching their noses, watching their feet. They looked uncomfortable but unwilling to run for it just yet. The mages talked to the innkeeper, who shook his head and spread out his hands. Unsatisfied, one of the men stood up.

'I know you're here, Tatters.'

The silence thickened. A few apprentices cleared their throats. A few others, conveniently placed close to the door, made a swift exit. Kilian seemed to long to be part of them, but he was wedged against the bench by the heavy table and the cheese platter. The mage spoke again:

'I am not here to close this place down, but I could. Make yourself known.'

Isha's heart was beating hard. She didn't turn to Tatters, but she sensed that other apprentices were, or were about to. Tatters sighed, his shoulders sagging under his mismatched rags. He got up.

'Long time no see, Ninian. It is Ninian, right?'

The mage turned to him. 'Give the man some space,' he ordered. As Tatters squeezed past Isha, he picked up his knife. She let him pass and didn't follow. It wasn't as if she could help.

The crowd cleared a way for Tatters, who took his time to reach the mage, making a show of sheathing his knife. The gold of his collar glowed.

'You've been here before, haven't you?' Tatters asked in a performer's voice, so everyone could hear. 'You were an apprentice yourself, Ninian. I hope you haven't forgotten.'

'We are all friends here,' said Ninian. 'I didn't come to cause trouble.'

Tatters touched wrists with both mages. He stood in sharp contrast: he was smaller, lankier, less well groomed, with messy hair, a messier beard, traces of age and wear across his features. They had chubby cheeks where he had only lines of hunger.

The innkeeper brought them three tumblers of amber-coloured mead, not the dregs of beer he sold the apprentices. Kilian would have used the opportunity to make himself scarce, Isha supposed, if she hadn't picked up the cheese and changed tables.

'What are you doing?' Kilian hissed.

She didn't answer. She placed herself behind Ninian and his friend, so that Tatters could see her but it would be more difficult for the two men to spot her. Kilian hesitated, then sat down next to her; they had to squeeze in, as the table was already full of apprentices.

'You're going to get in trouble,' he whispered.

'Or maybe I'll get Tatters out of trouble,' she answered.

She tugged her stool sideways, trying to find an angle from which she could study the ordained mages. When Ninian drank, he scrunched his nose and made a disparaging comment on the quality of the brew. Tatters didn't drink. Sitting before the two intruders, he crossed his hands on the table.

'What are you here for?' asked Tatters.

'You're in a hurry,' said Ninian.

Tatters shrugged. 'I don't know if you can feel it, but you've rather spoilt the mood.'

From where she was eavesdropping, Isha didn't have a good view of Ninian, but she did have a good view of Kilian, who pulled a face to express how inappropriate Tatters' behaviour was. There was a brief conversation between Tatters and Ninian, which Isha missed – they were speaking too low, and the apprentices, gathering courage, were talking again.

After downing his tumbler, Ninian handed it without a word to the innkeeper, who went to fill it again. The other mage,

Ninian's companion, was playing at running a finger along the wooden rim, staring across the room. Both mages were closely shaved, their hair washed and oiled, their clothes uncreased and cleaned.

'I want to duel you,' said Ninian, loud enough for the room to hear.

Someone gasped, earning themselves a glare from Ninian's friend. This wasn't what Isha had been expecting, but it didn't mean it was better.

Even Tatters seemed taken aback. He picked up his tumbler and gulped down its contents. When he put it down, he smacked his lips before answering. 'Are you sure about this? I'm always happy to mindbrawl apprentices, but an ordained mage is a different business.'

Ninian leant across the table. Isha didn't hear the full sentence, but she thought he might have said: 'I've always wanted to be you.' Or maybe it was: 'I've always wanted to *beat* you.' Ninian lifted the rim of his blue robe, squeezing it between finger and thumb, and whispered something else, but she missed the words that matched the gesture.

The friend turned around to scan the room, so she pretended to be engrossed in her cheese. Beside her, Kilian was nervously tapping his fingers against the table.

'Who's the settler?' Tatters asked. He caught Isha's eye, as she'd placed herself in his line of sight, but didn't smile. Caitlin, his usual settler, wasn't in the tavern tonight.

Ninian pointed to his friend. 'But you can pick a second settler, if you wish.' Two settlers, one for each duellist, helped prevent cheating.

Again, Tatters' gaze drifted to where Isha was sitting. Even though she might have misread his intention, even though her throat was knotted, she nodded. He hesitated, but in the end he said, 'I'm fine with just the one.'

'It will be an open duel.' Ninian addressed the whole tavern. 'You are welcome to place bets as you always do.'

Tatters crossed his hands behind his neck, stretching backwards.

'All right.'

The bustle of the tavern picked up again as apprentices crowded around the counter. Tatters set up two chairs face-to-face, in the centre of the room. Isha pushed through the throng of people to join him, Kilian trailing behind. She helped prepare the reduced stage where they would battle.

'I've never seen you lose,' she said quietly. He had been beaten before, or so she'd heard, but she had yet to see it happen. Tatters kicked a tumbler aside, and it rolled under a bench.

'Will you lose this one?' asked Kilian.

Tatters smiled. 'Of course. I'm not an ordained mage.'

Isha glanced at him. There was something about his cheeky, confident smile.

You think you can win, don't you? she mindlinked.

I don't think. It's overrated.

Kilian must have sensed they were excluding him from their conversation. 'Come on guys, it's just insulting,' he complained.

'Get used to it, Isha's too smart for the both of us,' said Tatters. 'She'll always be hiding stuff from you.'

Isha would have echoed Tatters' smile, if he hadn't been so close to the truth. She felt uneasy knowing that, even when bantering, he always hit his mark. She followed the two men to the counter. Kilian placed bets on Ninian; she refused to bet.

'Mindscrew the arrogant bastard,' growled the innkeeper, as he took Kilian's bet and jotted it down, scratching the numbers in his wax tablet.

'You do realise it's a crime if I attack a mage?' asked Tatters.

The innkeeper mumbled something unintelligible, then said, 'Yes. Right. But mindscrew his ass.'

'That's not how mindscrewing works,' laughed Tatters. 'But I'll do my best.'

'You'd better.'

The innkeeper dipped a glass in a bucket of soiled water with a layer of grease shining across its surface. He rubbed it with a soaked rag in an attempt to wash it. Isha tried to ignore the fact that this had probably already happened to the tumbler she'd been drinking out of.

'Don't bet any silver on me,' Tatters warned.

The tavern was hot and packed with bodies, a slit of night visible through the half-open door. Ninian's friend seated himself a few minutes before the duel was supposed to start. Isha spotted him squeezing Ninian's fingers, planting a quick kiss on his lips. Because of the trust it required, it wasn't uncommon for lovers to work as settlers for each other. The Nest didn't much care who slept with whom, as long as it didn't prevent people from serving the high mages.

The Temple had taught her, at the farm, that Raudaz, the lightborn of war, and Byluk, the lightborn of death, were two male lightborns who lived a married couple's life. Unfortunately, their union was sterile, breeding only battlefields.

Eyes closed, Ninian's lover was preparing the arena. His breathing slowed, until he could be dozing or dying.

Ninian and Tatters positioned themselves face-to-face. Tatters let himself drop back into his chair, but Ninian didn't.

'Ordained mages fight standing,' said Ninian.

Tatters shrugged, as if he couldn't care less. 'Let's do that, then.' He got to his feet, legs apart, arms crossed before him. He closed his eyes.

Isha didn't join the mindbrawl immediately. The background sound of conversation died down. The apprentices closed their eyes, grew still. Only the innkeeper stayed wide awake, leaning on his counter, frowning at the silent figures, trying to second-guess what could be happening. *It must be alien for the ungifted*, Isha realised. *A whole room of people standing eyes closed, doing nothing, until one of them collapses.*

She tucked her legs under the hewn bench. Resting her head against a beam, she mindlinked to the arena.

The mind of Ninian's lover was crowded, but accommodated everyone easily by creating a fake amphitheatre in which they could sit. Isha naturally drifted next to Kilian, known minds recognising and attracting each other. They were sitting together at the front of the coliseum. Everyone, Isha suspected, perceived themselves in the best seats, while perceiving the others around the top of the arena.

'It's good settler work,' said Kilian approvingly.

'If you could do stuff like this, you could become an official duel settler,' she said.

'Always better than fighting the damn things.'

The warmth of the tavern, the scent of spilt beer faded. The circle of white sand where Ninian was standing grew more tangible. His blue robes billowed around him. His pale skin seemed cut out of the azure background, as if his hands and head were floating, detached from his body. The long thin fingers were still; his face was like marble. His hair was a dusty brown, which he polished in mindlink until it glowed like copper.

Tatters was still in rags, still collarbound. There was something humbling about the simplicity of his outfit.

Isha knew the tricks of the trade. Mindbrawl was a balancing act between looking shabby and overworked. If you changed yourself too much, you seemed more fragile, as if you were overcompensating. What did it reveal of your weakness if you couldn't even show yourself as you were?

'This is going to be good,' said Kilian.

'It is,' agreed a young female voice.

Isha and Kilian both turned. Lal was sitting next to them.

She was a young girl shaped from mist, with a see-through quality to her, but dressed like a young man, with a shirt and a shoulder-cape. Before Isha could say anything, she interrupted, 'Don't worry, I don't think the settler has noticed me.'

Isha opened her mouth and closed it again. In the end she said: 'Isn't it a bit risky talking to us and getting ready to fight at the same time?'

Lal shrugged. 'Almost makes you think I'm not a projection but a real person, doesn't it?' Her tone wasn't entirely friendly. Isha was surprised by Lal's admission. She knew Lal was Tatters' younger sister but, as far as she was aware, Kilian simply thought she was a mental double created by Tatters. It was risky to be so open in his presence. Or maybe Lal didn't think enough of Kilian to care.

Kilian focused his attention on Tatters and Ninian – because of how mindlink worked, although he didn't move, he disappeared from their conversation. Isha supposed he was trying to understand what Lal was for; he would return soon.

Lal was on the cusp of outgrowing childhood, with long limbs, an easy smile. Tatters' red hair, dishevelled but longer. His sister. Isha had to force herself to remember it. The ghost of his sister. Was this what she looked like when she died? Or what she would have looked like, had she lived?

'We need to talk,' said Lal. 'You've been keeping secrets from us.'

Isha wondered if Tatters could hear this conversation or if he was too focused.

'You've been keeping secrets from me,' Isha answered. She thought she was only being fair, but Lal had a wicked little leer on her wicked little features. The worst was her voice, soft and childlike and threatening.

'I'll get the truth out of you,' said Lal.

Isha gritted her teeth. She had been training hard for a reason – she had been preparing so that, when her enemies made themselves known, she wouldn't back down. She would fight.

She glared at Lal's hazel eyes.

'You can try,' she said.

To her surprise, Lal smiled. 'Tatters and I are always here. The invitation to duel is always here. What are you waiting for?'

Kilian reappeared beside them, brimming with excitement. 'It's starting!'

Ninian's first attack hit before anyone noticed he had crafted it. Suddenly Tatters' collar grew to encompass his shoulders, then shrank slowly. Isha watched, a sickly feeling in the pit of her stomach; Ninian must have prepared for this fight by studying exactly how collars manifested during their first use. The circle grew smaller and smaller, but when it reached Tatters' neck, he didn't seem worried. He let the crushing reality of becoming a collarbound encircle his throat and settle there.

'Seen it all before,' he joked.

Ninian reacted with a wealth of images which, even from her distance as a witness, burnt across Isha's retina. They were discordant, incoherent, as effective as a nightmare. *Someone's wet kiss crushing your lips, and the lick of blood as their mouth was shattered by a bolt fired from a crossbow, and gore and teeth and skin splashed your face, and the only person you ever loved died. The realisation that the crossbow was in your hands.*

The searing pain as you planted the knife through your hand and then, methodically, carved out the ligaments. Moving the torn hand towards your eye, pushing the fingers underneath the eyelid. The rubbery texture of the eyeball as you tugged it out of its socket. The blurred vision as you ripped it out of your face. The touch of clear, cold goo running down your cheek.

Next to her, Kilian made a sound as if the air had been knocked out of his lungs.

'This is good,' he whispered.

Lal was gone. Maybe she had decided the fight was worthy of her attention after all.

Isha nodded. Almost everything was contained in the sense of touch, and the deep, gut-wrenching dread Ninian threaded inside his visions. It was powerful enough that people observing the duel could taste blood in their mouths.

Ninian stopped. Tatters was still standing, head cocked to one side.

'To be fair, I never did any of that before,' he admitted. 'Now I know what it would feel like.'

Ninian waited, on the defensive, but nothing happened. As far as Isha could tell, Tatters wasn't doing anything. Tapping his toes against the settler's floor, he gave the crowd a derisive smile.

'Why won't you fight?' snarled Ninian.

'Oh, I wouldn't dare,' said Tatters.

The ripple of the blow went through Isha. *Figures huddled below the gates of the Nest. The empty glaze across their eyes. And there, amongst the wan faces, someone you recognised, someone lost but loved. You knelt before them before realising who they were.*

It was you. You were the lacunant begging before the gates.

This was the fate all mages feared – this was what they would all become, from the bushy-tailed apprentices to the hardened mindbrawlers. They would die empty husks.

Yet Tatters remained unfazed. Maybe because Isha was focusing on the duel once more, maybe because he had been searching for her, Kilian manifested beside her. Isha knew spacing was an illusion when they were in someone's mind, but she had never met a settler who could accommodate this illusion like Ninian's lover – sense of perspective and the layout of the arena remained, but people's places inside it shifted at will.

'You're very good,' said Tatters, in his tutoring voice.

When he took a step forwards, Ninian raised his mental defences immediately. Tatters drew a flower on the floor, imagining precise veins down the leaves, pistils within the centre.

'You think like a swordsman. When you're fighting, get your hardest hit out there first. You want to kill the opponent as fast as possible, not make a good show.'

'Why aren't you following your own advice, then?' Ninian sounded more startled than angry; more exhausted than challenging. Even from her removed position, Isha could tell how trying his visions had been both to make and maintain.

Tatters went on, ignoring Ninian's intervention, 'But if you notice you're tiring yourself and your hits are more effort to you than pain to the other guy, then maybe you should change tactics.'

They waited in silence. Isha could taste the strain on Ninian's mind in the air. If Tatters was tired, he was concealing it well.

Now that the intensity of the fight had dulled somewhat, Lal returned. Kilian nudged her with his elbow.

'Are you the big finale?' he asked.

Lal shook her head. 'I'm not getting involved.'

Ninian pounced on Tatters again. The imaginings were achingly precise, with the patterned details of a spiderweb. Isha could taste and breathe and touch them. But Tatters didn't seem affected. It wasn't like anything she had seen him do before – rather than try to avoid or deflect what was thrown at him, he allowed it to reach him. It was as if he couldn't feel what Ninian had created, like a poorly-made imagining from an apprentice, badly executed. But the visions were precise enough that they should hit their mark.

'If he did this all the time, no-one would ever touch him.' She was thinking out loud, but in mindlink, the difference between thinking and talking was flimsy at best.

'He won't use it with you,' said Lal. 'He shouldn't use it now. Do it too often, and people will work out what the trick is.'

Kilian watched Lal with interest, still expectant. 'Why do you talk about yourself using "he"?' he asked. 'Does it help?'

Lal smiled. 'Keep telling yourself that.'

In the arena, Ninian backed down. He spat on the floor in rage. His mind was at the end of its tether. It shivered like a sheet of fabric being pulled at both ends, fraying down the centre.

'What now?' he shouted, and Isha could hear the fear in his voice. 'Shall we get down to punches?'

'How about we call it a draw?' asked Tatters.

Ninian didn't acknowledge the end of the fight. He left the arena.

'What an idiot.' The harshness in Lal's tone surprised Isha.

Although she wasn't on Ninian's side, Isha felt the need to say, 'He was pretty good.'

'I'm talking about Tatters,' said Lal. 'Now he's shown everyone he's dangerous.'

The child shook her head and vanished. Troubled, Isha left the settled mind. Inside the tavern, the air felt heavy, as if there were particles of fat floating around, sticking to her lungs, making it difficult to breathe. She swallowed stale saliva.

Ninian was nowhere to be found. He must have gone outside. The apprentices, rubbing their swollen eyes, were emerging from mindlink. She sipped her beer, focusing on its taste to bring herself back to the present. She had pins and needles down her arms and legs; she tapped her feet on the ground to bring some sensation back into them.

Tatters stepped out from mindlink and went to lounge on the seat prepared beforehand. He didn't brag, and his mind was closed. The audience crowded around the bar area, discussing the duel which had just taken place, expressing frustration at the lost bets. Isha waited for Kilian to join her in the real world. His face was surprisingly serious, a tense expression across his round features.

When he opened his eyes, she handed him his beer.

'That was ... something,' he said, shaking his head from side to side.

At first Isha thought he was shaking it to help himself leave mindlink; then she realised he was shaking it in disbelief, staring at Tatters.

'By all the underworlds, who is this guy?' he whispered.

It's only now that you think of asking? She'd put the question to Kilian a thousand times, and he'd brushed it away, saying people came from everywhere, that Tatters could be a Sunriser despite the pale skin, or maybe a village mage with parlour tricks. Obviously the parlour trick theory was null.

Isha observed the settler as he collapsed his mind. He was the last to do so, as his role required. When he surfaced, he stretched, ignoring his lover's absence. Rather formally, he cracked his wrists, his ankles and his neck. He turned to Tatters and said something, but Isha couldn't make out the words.

'Let's talk to him.' She was about to get up when Kilian placed a hand on her forearm.

'I know you like him, but this isn't normal.' Kilian lowered his voice, as if Tatters could hear him through the din of shouting, talking, and banging tumblers. 'This shouldn't be possible.'

The settler got up and left. It was too late to catch his opinion on what had taken place.

'You told me Tatters was good,' Isha said. 'You brought me here the first time.'

Kilian rubbed the stubble of his first beard with one hand, keeping the other on her forearm. 'This is different. He, you know, could have wrecked an ordained mage. From the Nest.'

'Only he didn't,' she said. *So maybe he couldn't.*

For the first time, Isha considered the possibility of Tatters being under a ban from his collar. She was nearly sure, from the glow of the collar, that it wasn't active. It reacted erratically, so it might be broken. But if it wasn't, there must be orders he had to submit to, and not attacking a mage seemed like something a conscientious master would include.

Despite his concerns, Kilian followed her as she made her way towards Tatters. The innkeeper brought him a glass to celebrate his officially-not-a-victory.

'A draw? Really?' The innkeeper asked, handing Tatters his drink. 'I mean, it's still good money. But if you'd won, we could've made a small fortune! Might even have been able to afford a servant, for a change.'

'I told folks not to bet on me.'

The innkeeper scoffed. 'You don't want to share your room with someone doing real work around here, that's all.'

Tatters downed the beer. Kilian stood too close to Isha, and she wasn't sure whether he wanted to protect her, or secretly hoped she would protect him.

'An impressive duel,' she said.

Tatters' smile was sad. He was sitting back to front on the chair, with his arms and chest pressed against the backrest, his legs spread out on either side. He held his glass loosely – foam seeped from the top and ran down his fingers.

'What did the settler say?' she asked.

'Ninian is being sent to the Shadowpass. Apparently none of the refugees are making sense. Nobody can tell the high mages how they crossed – they're all too damaged by the crossing. He's being sent to investigate.'

Tatters drank some more, letting beer run down the corner of his lips. 'That's why he wanted to duel me today. To know if he was ready for what he might have to face out there.' He wiped his mouth on his sleeve before concluding. 'I've failed you all.'

There was a silence, for want of something to say.

'What?' Kilian stuttered at last, as if they could have misheard. Tatters sighed.

'I taught Ninian. And I let him go and be ordained and believe he was good.'

He looked at his beer, as if he hoped to find answers there. He shook his head, not liking what he saw.

'As a teacher, I shouldn't have let him believe that. I shouldn't let any of you believe that. What are you going to do when your enemies are fighting back?'

Isha watched as he licked the foam off his fingers.

'You told me I was good,' she said. 'Was that a lie too?'

'No, but you're really good,' said Kilian. 'Right?'

Tatters gave her a wary look.

'You're special,' he answered, matter-of-factly. 'Surely you've noticed by now.'

Isha thought about what Lal had said. She thought about secrets and lies and birds of prey embroidered on red flags.

'Do you think we should fight?' she asked.

She pretended not to notice Kilian's horrified look.

'Let's say part of me would like to duel you,' Tatters said. She could tell he was picking his words carefully. 'And part of me would rather we were friends.'

She didn't like the turn the conversation was taking. They drank together. They ate together at the khers' house. He walked her home at night. 'Aren't we friends?' she asked. *Is that why you didn't want me to be your settler?*

Kilian was glancing from one to the other, the way a child might between two parents fighting, not sure which side to pick, smart enough not to intervene.

'I don't know,' said Tatters. 'You tell me.'

She was standing, arms crossed, and he was crouched around his chair, hugging his beer. He rested his chin on his forearm, pushing his head backwards to be able to hold her stare.

She was alone.

It was like noticing a wound she hadn't known she had, and suddenly realising that she was in pain. There was Kilian, but there was much he didn't understand. There was Tatters, but he followed his own agenda. There was Passerine, but they weren't close.

There was no-one she could tell about a hawk branded on flags and faces.

She hadn't known she was going to say it until she did:

'I would like to know who my friends and foes are.' It sounded plaintive, even to her ears.

Tatters finished his drink, his Adam's apple moving as he gulped the dregs of his glass, head thrown back, as if he would never need to breathe again. When he put his beer down, he inhaled like a man breaking the surface after a long swim underwater.

'Don't we all,' he said. 'Don't we all.'

'I don't get it,' said Kilian. 'I thought we were all friends?'

***

20

Tatters waited for the Coop to quieten before leaving. After Ninian's departure, most apprentices had followed suit, Isha and Kilian included. When only the heavy drinkers remained perched at the counter, he grabbed his set of keys, hung it on his belt, and waved the innkeeper goodbye. Outside it was drizzling; he pulled his black stana over his head to protect himself.

Make sure no-one follows us, Lal said.

Who do you think I am?

He was cautious while passing through the city, attentive to the way the shadows and minds moved around him. The shops were closed, wooden shutters hiding the wares; the front doors were locked. Rats were hunting for food in the gutters. The only humans outside were ungifted, refugees or locals, either sleeping across porches or building fires on the pavements for warmth, with the odd scuffle or argument taking place. A merchant even threw a bucket of water out of their window to shush a group of noisy beggars, as one did to separate fighting cats.

Tatters crossed several of the mages' borders. Each time, he felt the ripple of past minds, like a splash in a puddle. In the moonlight, the bowls of mercury glinted on their stands. The emotions trapped there echoed with lonely calls, reaching out into the night. The rain rolled off the heavier metal, which shimmered at the touch of water.

Not only were the city gates closed at night, but the security had been reinforced since Mezyan's visit – for all the disdain the mages showed a half-kher, his message from the Renegades, his threats and flashy speeches, had not gone unheard. More patrols, several guards at the door, a metal glint above, where archers were defending the walls. Big wooden planks which could be drawn across the gates, to better resist a battering ram. The miscellanea of a city bracing for a fight. Tatters bribed the guards, under the pretext that he needed to catch up with an apprentice headed for the Nest.

Which is nearly true, Lal pointed out.

The guards waved him through; they'd had drunk apprentices shuffling past all night, and couldn't care less about Lady Siobhan's infamous collarbound.

The high road linking the city and the Nest was muddy. Taking into consideration the low light and the slippery grass, Tatters walked slowly, concentrating on every step. In the distance, the Nest emerged from the ground like a ragged piece of cliff, its high walls streaked with rain. The giants' gates, like the rusted ribs of a long-dead monster, loomed before it.

It was a long, wet, chilly walk – but Tatters always had company.

Why did you go and spook Isha? he asked.

He felt Lal shrug. *We agreed to make a stand. So, we should start with the easy prey. Isha is the best Renegade for us to target. If we can break her mind, we can pillage any of the plans they were dumb enough to let her know about.*

Are we sure she's on their side?

We're sure she's Hawk's daughter, Lal said. *That's enough.*

If possible, Tatters would have avoided a direct confrontation, to spare Isha any violence. He would much rather spy on her mind, to unearth her secrets, than go digging for them with a pickaxe.

We've done it your way so far, and where has it got us? Lal wasn't impressed.

Tatters continued to pick his path without answering, confident Lal could sense his reservations. There was no point in arguing: they had other worries for tonight. As he reached the bridge, the clouds parted enough for the moon to peek out. The huge chains embedded in the earth, tethering the Edge to the mainland, glinted in the dull light.

One day, those rusted chains will give way, said Lal. *And everything we know will be swallowed by the void.*

Tatters gazed at the links, each thicker than a man. *But not in our lifetime.*

After the bridge, he left the main road for the marshier area south of the Nest. To the north were the Temple, some woodland, and the higher grounds used for festivals. At the moment, it served as a place to assemble trebuchets and other siege weapons, anything to throw at the Renegades from the other side of the chasm. The wooden machinery lurked like bulky, sleeping beasts. To the south, where the river curved, was an area where the horses were brought out to graze, with low shrubs whose only use was to be eaten by sheep and ponies.

The stables, which were in the inner courtyard of the Nest, hugging its walls, had an exit on this side of the castle. It was too narrow to be an entryway for an attack – at least, that was the reasoning – but was large enough for horses to be led out in pairs. Horses were rotated in and out of the stables, into the pastures, during spring and summertime. Now the colder months had started, they mostly stayed inside.

A wooden awning jutted out of the walls, protecting a sodden area of beaten earth. The hay thrown upon the ground did nothing to soak up the puddles, and it was rotting. When Tatters reached the relative cover of the awning, the side-door leading to the stables was already open. Caitlin was waiting for him, her skin golden under the light of her torch.

'You took your sweet time,' she said.

'May you grow tall too,' he answered, pulling down his stana. She only frowned. 'Don't bother turning on the charm, it doesn't work on me. And if you try anything shady, you can walk back to the Coop,' she warned.

'I wouldn't dream of it.' As he counted out the coins, he tried to see if he could spot a figure behind Caitlin in the warmth of the stables. He couldn't see anything. The smell of hay, of the bodies of horses, drifted through the entrance. As did the flies, which even in winter never left the stables.

'Do you do this often?' he asked, as he handed over the sum. 'I imagine lots of ungifted want the chance to make a wish to the lightborn. You could line your pockets with gold.'

'That's none of your business,' Caitlin said. 'I'm doing you a favour here, Tatters.'

He'd been keeping a close eye on her thoughts, so he perceived the twinge of guilt. This was a regular hustle, then. Well, he could understand. Caitlin would be making some money on the side, milking her master's assets for her own profit.

'You were always ambitious,' he said noncommittally. Maybe Sir Daegan trusted her with the lightborn because he felt his collarbound needed a female guardian to help with women's troubles.

Caitlin glared at him. 'Tatters, you have your favourites and people you protect. You have your master and people to protect you.'

As if, Lal snorted.

'But if I don't look out for myself, no-one else will,' Caitlin concluded, letting the coins slide from her fingers to her leather purse.

She waved to someone in the depths of the stables. The lightborn stepped into the light cast by the torch. The collar around her neck was a dull shade of gold. Her blonde hair had been braided, but he could tell it wasn't a labour of love. It had been done roughly, for practical purposes only. She was wearing the blue dress he had seen before: long-sleeved, delicate and gauze-like, utterly inappropriate for this weather. At least it had stopped raining.

'May you grow tall.' He gave her a low bow. She didn't show any sign of recognition.

'I'll leave you to it,' Caitlin said, in the tone of voice of someone who knows exactly how an event is going to unfold.

Tatters moved away from the disciple, leaving her at the threshold, leading the lightborn outside. As soon as she was outdoors, she went to the edge of the awning, her eyes searching upwards to meet the stars, which could barely be seen wrestling for space with the clouds. It was hard to tell, from her expression, if this was longing, or for want of anything else of interest to look at.

'It is a pleasure to meet you,' he said, 'even though I wish we'd met in happier circumstances.'

She didn't answer. Usually, he wasn't one to stay silent, but there was nothing he could say to this serious, closed face. He searched for a suitable topic to share with her, but the only obvious common ground was servitude. He didn't want to ask her how long she'd been a collarbound, how she'd been caught, what she missed most. He hadn't wanted people to ask him those questions.

He settled for: 'What's your name?'

Caitlin was alert, leaning on the stables' doorframe, close enough to study their movements, but too far to hear them. No doubt people before him had tried to draw the lightborn into conversation, and failed.

She will answer us, Lal thought confidently. *We're different.*

And she had perceived that difference, he hoped. Although for a moment he believed he had failed too, and the lightborn wouldn't answer.

'My name cannot be translated,' she said at last.

Tatters hadn't even been sure she could speak the Duskdweller tongue until then. Understanding orders coming through the collar was one thing – the collar had a way of pressing meaning into your soul – but he was impressed to hear her speak clearly, albeit hesitantly, with a lilting accent that he couldn't place.

Too excited at having received an answer, he spoke fast, his words rushing out as if there was too little time to say everything. 'You can give me a false name, if you want. Or an idea of what your name sounds like. It would be great to be properly introduced.'

She was staring at him with calm, unreadable features. He wondered if he'd spooked her. In an attempt to be friendly, he added, 'I'm Tatters.'

She had golden-hazel eyes, the colour of her light. Again, she turned them towards the sky. Her voice wasn't so much dismissive as neutral. 'I've heard your slave-name before.'

So much for killing the conversation, thought Lal.

He forced himself to think of something to say. She had no-one else. It didn't matter whether she made this easy for him or not – what mattered was that she was alone in this strange place that wasn't her home, enslaved to men who weren't her people.

'Is there anything I can give you, anything you want?' he asked.

'My freedom,' she said, without hesitation.

Of course, he thought, cursing himself. Out loud he said, 'That's not something I can do.'

'Then you have nothing I want.'

The silence was speckled with sounds, the distant rumble of the river, the wind through the grass, the horses sighing in their stalls. Flies crawled on the manure visible in the patch of light.

You didn't have a nice word for anyone, when Hawk bound us, Lal said. *Why would she have a kind word for you?*

You're right, he answered.

From the doorway, Caitlin was gawking. She must have heard the soft whisper of voices.

He studied the lightborn's profile. Her eyes had changed colour, it seemed, maybe because of the dark hue of the moorland. They were now a deep shade of green, an echo of the underbrush.

'I am sorry,' he said.

He was sorry, for the existence of the collars; for the fact that here they were, miserable, in the cold, huddled under low mists gorged with rain, beneath fortifications of sandstone; for the fact that she was bound to tread mud, rather than travel the skies.

Her tone lost none of its hardness. 'Your pity will not break this collar.'

You should say to her what you wished Mezyan had said to you. Lal's advice was, for once, unjudgemental, maybe even gentle.

'Nothing I can give you now will break it,' Tatters said. 'But I will try. I just wanted you to know that you are not alone. You have someone on your side.'

At first she didn't say anything. Then she pushed herself away from the awning. She placed her feet carefully, one in front of the other, curving her body sideways, keeping her toes pointed in front of her. She lifted her arms in two graceful arcs. She stood, poised, holding the pose, and Tatters stared, conscious of Caitlin behind them. The lightborn looked like a bird prepared to take flight.

When she moved, each gesture was as precise as a line of writing. It was a brief spin, a half-circle, a dip, an arching of arms and legs. It was the step of a dance, Tatters guessed. It was too graceful to be anything but movement for the sake of beauty.

She glanced at him expectantly.

When he didn't answer, stumped, she said, 'My name.'

He wasn't sure he understood. She must have gathered as much, because after a brief pause, she went through the motions again, more swiftly this time.

'My name.' Although the way she repeated herself made him think she must be surprised, her face didn't show any shock. She didn't shake her head, or move her mouth and lips, or narrow her eyes.

For the first time, he wondered if maybe facial expressions were not something she understood. That might explain why she seemed so aloof – maybe she didn't know how to use nonverbal cues. And why should she? She had only been in human shape for a couple of weeks. Maybe she didn't have the same instinct as children, who immediately knew what a frown or a smile meant, and how to use them.

'I'm sorry,' he said again. 'I don't understand.'

Caitlin was too close; the dance had made her inch nearer. Tatters drew the lightborn further away – into the marshland, over broken shrubs – to avoid being overheard.

'The dance is a connection,' she said. 'It is speech.' She was articulate, with the slowness, carefulness, of someone unfamiliar with a language. That must be the collar's doing. If ordered to learn, however difficult the task, a collarbound would. 'Where humans rely on sounds to indicate meaning, lightborns use movement. There are no sounds up in the air.'

'Really?' said Tatters. 'Sounds are new to you?'

She nodded.

Lal pointed out the nod. *So much for your theory about body-language.*

Maybe she picked up nodding, but not the rest. If you used dancing to communicate, you might miss small facial expressions, but understand touching wrists, nodding, shaking your head, things like that.

'It is similar to human writing,' the lightborn said. 'But you write with your soul. Dancing together means…' She took a deep breath, bracing herself for something, but then she sighed, letting the air hiss through her teeth. 'Our souls take the shape of our words. We are what we have said. What we spell is what we become. We don't lie,' she explained. 'Unlike humans. Language creates kinship, not chains.'

His thoughts were spinning with this new information. A language without lies. A way to share truths as you spun across the skies.

'Why don't humans dance?' she asked.

'But we do,' Tatters said. 'We just don't dance in the same way.'

He wondered if the human dances, the ones they performed at the Temple on festival nights, were remnants of a time when humans and lightborns could communicate. Did those dances have meaning? If so, what were they trying to say, what call were they sending out into night?

He would need time for this to settle. There were so many implications, for her, for the Temple, which he still wasn't able to process. No sounds? Did that mean she had never heard music? And no lies? Did that mean that a conversation was always a heart-to-heart?

You would have trouble speaking a language with no lies, sneered Lal.

They were both mulling over what had been said. The light-born emerged from her daydream first.

'The sigil for my name means a small light, seen from afar, bright even from a distance.'

She spoke so low, and sounded so fragile, that Tatters wasn't sure what to answer. Once upon a time, her mother had cradled her in her light, had watched her grow, and had called her daughter *my small bright light, my faraway star*. Now here she was, amongst enemies.

'We can find a human equivalent,' he found himself saying before he'd had a chance to think about it. 'You could choose Sunshine. Or Astra? Celestia?'

The small star. Starling, said Lal.

'Starling,' Tatters repeated out loud, trying out the word.

She didn't say anything at first, her head tilted upwards, gazing at the sky. Her braid fell sideways across her shoulder, touching her cheek.

'It literally means a small star,' he explained. 'But it's also a bird. A black bird flecked with white spots, like a starry night.' He thought of the feathers of a starling, of the pinpricks of white painted on dusty brown, and how it echoed the night around them, yet could never do it justice.

'Starling,' she said. 'It is short.'

'Most human names are short,' said Tatters.

'Starling,' she said again, as if tasting the sound. 'Yes.' There was resignation in her voice, more than joy. 'Before I thought it didn't matter. But I suppose I need a human name, after all.'

She tore herself away from the sky, levelling her stare so it didn't lift above the moors.

You have given her a slave-name, said Lal.

The lightborn didn't look at him. Maybe silence would have been kinder, after all.

Caitlin bridged the distance between them, frowning, trying to hide how troubled she was and doing a poor job of it. Her thoughts reeked of worry and bafflement.

'All right, that's enough.' She placed herself protectively beside Starling, shooing her aside. The lightborn fell into step without even glancing at the pushy disciple. 'How did you do it?' Caitlin asked. Her tone was unfriendly.

Tatters shrugged, spreading out his hands. 'Do what?'

'You think I'm an idiot,' she hissed. 'But it can't just be the collarbound connection.'

'Don't fret about it, Cat.'

She can't tell anyone about us, anyway, thought Lal, *without admitting the part she played.*

He turned to Starling. 'I'll be back as soon as I can,' he promised. He pulled his stana up, heading further out into the moors. He could see the two women, framed by the light, but he was already deep enough into the darkness to be nearly out of sight.

He left with the buoyed feeling of having bested the Nest twice that night.

Chapter Two

Isha was reading in a corner of the library. In winter, with frost licking at the high windows, she needed a woollen blanket across her lap as well as her apprentice's robes to be able to do so without shivering. This was a place of learning, not entertainment, yet she enjoyed the austere atmosphere. Reading was as new and exciting as mindlink. It was also, Isha had found out, sometimes just as dangerous.

One of the books was open on display. The volume was about Isha's height, and her width if she spread out her arms. Its pages were threadbare with use. In the past, it had been loved and thumbed often, until the cover was worn, the spine showing the threads sewn to hold it in place. Its engravings were abstract, flowing lines, incomplete patterns bursting in gold leaf and vivid hues across the page. All giant art was similar, from the windows, the wrought iron grates and balustrades, down to the painted floors: everything was drawn in a swirl of interwoven shapes.

She was reading a human-sized volume at one of the tables when she heard a commotion. A cat's shriek, a startled Kilian muttering an apology, the rush of tiny paws getting out of the way. He must have walked on one of the library cats, kept around to prevent mice from eating the vellum. He turned a corner, still checking over his shoulder. When he caught sight of her, he smiled and made his way towards her.

'Do you want to come to the cloth market with me?' he asked after greeting her. 'It's for the lightborn.'

He took a seat beside her, resting his elbows on the rough wood.

'The lightborn hasn't got any outfits,' he said. 'Save one dress. Sir Daegan told me to buy some cloth so a tailor can make her more stuff.'

'And you can't do that on your own?' Isha asked.

Kilian pouted. 'I don't want to walk all the way to the city alone.' He slumped over his arms, resting his forehead against the table as if mentioning it was enough to exhaust him. 'I asked Caitlin,' he added, his voice muffled, 'but she told me to get lost.'

Isha raised an eyebrow at that. 'So I'm your second choice?'

'I mean, I know the cloth market isn't your idea of a fun time,' Kilian admitted, propping his chin against his arm. 'That's why I asked her first. But you might find it's not so bad, once you're there. Plus, you get to choose what a lightborn wears. If that's not incredible, I don't know what is.'

'If you insist,' Isha relented. She didn't agree so much for Kilian's sake as for the lightborn's. She still felt guilty about her fate. She owed her some new garments, at least.

Isha put her book away, squeezing it into a gap between the thick volumes. The brown bindings with gold and copper lettering stood side-by-side, silent shapes loaded with words.

'Any luck?' asked Kilian.

She had been leafing through old mindbrawl techniques, some illustrated, trying to determine what Tatters had used against Ninian. She hadn't found out.

'No,' answered Isha. 'But I'm fighting him anyway.'

Lal was right. The invitation was there. She had studied

long enough. What was she afraid of? He had cheated with Ninian, she was sure, but he wouldn't cheat against her. He would give her a fair fight.

You're special. Surely you've noticed by now. Special. From a different species. She nearly wished she was a half-kher. Had she been linked to the iwdan, at least she would have known whose side she was on.

An ordained mage fighting a mindbrawl in a tavern wasn't something they could discuss openly. They spoke in low voices as they left the library, sticking close to the walls in the wide corridors.

'You're mad,' Kilian said. 'He'll trash your mind to pieces if he wants to.'

He put a hand on her shoulder.

'But I'll be betting on you.'

They chatted all the way to the textile market. It was a colourful array of shops, with hagglers calling out to each other, rolls of cloth spilling off stalls, and tailors fitting clothing as they talked to their clients, their mouths full of pins. There were thick bundles of fabric on wooden rolls, and bored old women finger-knitting wool as they waited for buyers. A couple of younger women were sewing leather armour for the soldiers, as part of the mandatory war effort.

And, of all people, there was Tatters, wrangling over a long piece of velvet. Isha hesitated.

'Want to risk it?' Kilian asked, looking uneasy.

She considered avoiding Tatters – in the crowded market, it would have been easy enough.

'Let's see what he's up to,' she decided.

They joined him as he finally managed to agree on a price with the seller.

'May you grow tall,' he said when he spotted them. 'You're looking sharp for folks who've been drinking.'

'I'll return you the compliment,' said Isha. They touched wrists while he waited for the shopkeeper to cut his square of cloth. Kilian pretended to watch the wares, staying behind Isha.

'I couldn't find the shop Uaza mentioned, but she asked me for cloth last time I visited, and I wouldn't want to vex a kher matriarch,' said Tatters. 'I figured a nice bit of velvet would do the trick.'

'And he made a great choice,' added the shopkeeper, a middle-aged woman with a wrinkled face. 'Look at this beauty!'

She handed Isha the fabric. Dutifully, Isha brushed her fingers against it. It was soft, a deep shade of green. Although Tatters had only bought a modest piece, which could be used as a small shawl, maybe, or added at the bottom of a dress to decorate it, it must have been expensive. It was probably worth most of what he had won on bets yesterday. But another fight with odds as biased as his duel with Ninian wouldn't happen again. It was rare for *everyone* to bet on the wrong outcome, making the innkeeper the true winner of the evening.

'That's your savings gone,' said Isha.

'All green is half-price after the festival!' argued the shop-keeper. 'It's worth three times that, but I've been good to your man.'

His interest piqued, Kilian bent over to touch the velvet. He made a sound which was neither agreement nor disagreement.

'I believe you,' Tatters told the shopkeeper. He turned to Isha with a glint in his eyes. 'Haven't you been listening to what the Nest teaches? You can't ascend with material riches anyway.'

He smiled as the shopkeeper handed him the folded velvet.

'Your man is right,' she said. 'It'll only weigh you down, love, if you want to take flight.' She said it as if she didn't quite believe a grubby apprentice would ever ascend. Maybe she was religious and didn't believe anyone was destined to ascend.

Tatters thanked her warmly, admiring the cloth as they moved away from the stall.

'I thought you weren't seeing much of Arushi at the moment,' Isha said.

'I'm hoping to change that. Plus, I've never had that kind of money. I don't know what else to do with it.'

'You could give it to me,' Kilian said. 'I'd know what to do with it.'

Tatters laughed. He lifted his purchase to the sun; the velvet was dark and light in patches, like sunshine through fern leaves. He sighed happily, his sinister mood from the night before forgotten.

As if he were reading her thoughts – which he might have been, although Isha suspected she would have noticed – Tatters said:

'I'm sorry about yesterday. I was a bit on edge. Ninian reminded me the Renegades are only getting closer.'

Isha nodded. 'It's worrying.'

'That's because you worry too much,' Kilian said.

Tatters tucked his velvet under his arm. 'I don't think you realise how dangerous the Renegades are.' He glanced at Isha. 'But you do, don't you?'

Pulling her cloak tighter, she didn't answer. The sky was white with clouds. It was growing colder by the day.

They walked together, their strides matching. More Sunrisers filled the streets than usual – not as many as in the poor quarters, where they lived sunk in doorways and gutters. Here were the Sunrisers who had money left after the crossing. Although the Shadowpass stole from people, it wasn't much interested in gold: they had clung on to goods but hadn't been able to hold on to memory. Their fingers curled around trinkets that no longer had any emotional worth, only a set price. The Sunrisers were buying warm coats, new tablecloths, curtains – as if they could refurbish their new lodgings with the pieces of the life they'd left behind.

Isha could make out different groups amongst the refugees: some wore knotted, unstitched cloth that showed their arms, and they were generally taller, with lankier silhouettes; some had sewn tunics, driftwood baubles hanging from their belts, brown hair bleached by sunlight; only a couple were as dark as Passerine, with curly hair, which the women braided with nasivyati to create beautiful, colourful headdresses.

They reached the end of the textile market.

'We'll have to turn back,' said Kilian. 'We still have to order cloth.'

'What do you want to buy?' Tatters asked.

Isha wondered if telling him counted as gossip. 'We need to buy something for a dress.'

Tatters cocked his head to one side, as he did when he was thinking, or when he didn't believe a lie. 'They won't let you wear it, you know.'

'It's not for me.'

'It's for the lightborn,' said Kilian.

A tender expression passed on Tatters' face. 'What price are you looking at?'

'Expensive.'

Isha indicated the purse tied to Kilian's belt. Tatters chuckled. 'Ah, the whims of mages. Shall I introduce you to someone who can help?'

Kilian was reluctant. 'I shouldn't leave the market. He's given me specific instructions.'

'In that case, give me half the money,' Isha said. 'If there's anything good, I'll buy it for you.' Clearly sceptical about the whole proceedings, Kilian handed over some of Sir Daegan's money.

Are you sure about this? Kilian asked her in mindlink. *You'll be all right alone with him?*

His protectiveness annoyed her. *I thought I was the one who worried too much. Plus, he can probably hear us, you know.*

'I can. But go on, pretend the old guy isn't here, I don't mind,' teased Tatters. 'I'll bring her back in one piece, I promise,' he added, shooing Kilian away.

He brought Isha to a residential area with rundown buildings, before knocking on the door of a small house stuck against the city gates. It might have been an old barracks that served the guards patrolling the gates, before it crumbled on itself. It had been hastily repaired with thatch and mudbrick.

The door was opened by a kher – a male kher, armed with a dagger. That was unusual. But if the kher was a surprise to Isha, an apprentice and a collarbound were a shock for the kher. He pushed them back outside and asked for their names. Tatters obliged, adding he knew the owner. The kher glowered at him before shutting the door.

'People are always slamming doors in my face.' Isha wasn't sure whether she was complaining or making conversation.

Tatters patted her shoulder. 'It's part of the fun, I'm afraid.'

The kher opened the door again. As they entered the musty room, Isha realised that, although doors were often barred, she always managed to get through. Never alone – never without help. But Passerine had helped her inside the Nest. Tatters had helped her inside the Pit. Even Kilian had helped her get into Sir Daegan's class and inside the tavern. If she didn't have the power to break the lock, friends were keys.

It turned out Tatters had brought Isha to a pawnbroker. The owner was a stooped woman, her shawl wrapped so tightly around her head there wasn't much of her to see, beside two beady eyes and a mouth of gold teeth. The kher was twice the size and weight of his employer.

There was nothing in the main room but a desk and cheap linen in a pile. Tatters pointed out the linen to Isha, saying it was for clients to wipe their tears as they pawned away their soul.

'Don't be stupid, Tatters,' grumbled the old woman. 'People pawn their soul without a sob. The damn thing's too light, they don't even notice it's gone.'

She eyed him with an expert's quick, mean eye.

'Brought me something sweet?' she asked.

Tatters shook his head. 'We're here as buyers. And it's for the girl.'

The old woman turned her attention to Isha, who explained that she was looking for a dress. The pawnbroker nodded to herself as Isha talked, then lifted a bony finger and promised to be right back.

The woman scrambled down a staircase into the cellar underneath the house. The kher, Tatters and Isha waited. Motes of dust were floating in long lines in the air. The place smelt of damp. The kher brought his fingers to his mouth, trimming his nails with his teeth. He spat the nail cuttings across the room.

The old woman huffed back up, an armful of dresses under one hand, the other holding up her skirts. She placed the clothing on the desk.

'I've got just what you need,' she said. 'Might be a bit narrow, mind.'

'It's not for me,' said Isha.

When the pawnbroker shook a dress, a cloud of dust rose from it, making Isha's nose itch. It was a scarlet robe with lacing at the front. Tatters looked at it critically and, before Isha could say anything, he intervened:

'Visible shoulders and back? I know what job the owner of *this* dress was doing. Come on, you must have better than that.'

The old woman grumbled that she wasn't made of dresses, but Tatters wouldn't listen.

'You're telling me you haven't had one rich noblewoman fallen into disrepute? Someone with a bit of class?'

'Noblewomen fall into disrepute every evening,' said the old woman. 'Doesn't mean they give me their clothes.'

'Who else would they give them to?' answered Tatters.

The old woman argued some more, and showed Isha two other outfits, but Tatters wouldn't let her consider them. The pawnbroker reluctantly packed her bundle into a corner of the desk before disappearing downstairs again.

The kher finished biting his nails. He moved on to putting some ochre on his horns. It could have been threatening, if he hadn't needed to refer himself to a rotting mirror on the wall, twisting his neck this way and that to check the end result.

When the old woman came back, she unfurled three pieces of cloth on the desk. It was a Sunriser nasivyati, an ensemble composed of three unsewn squares of fabric. Passerine had worn these, so Isha was familiar with each piece and how to fold it. The first was a deep shade of blue, to wrap around the hips to form a skirt; the second was a lighter shade, an azure stana to fold across the shoulders and forearms; the last piece, much longer than the other two, akin to a scarf, was bleached white. It could be worn around the neck or as a wimple.

A couple of silver pins, uncommon for Sunriser clothing, were placed beside the nasivyati.

Tatters mindlinked to Isha. *My guess is, that's the best she's got.*

Isha touched the fabric. Wool. The scarf had strands of silver woven into it.

'Good thing with a Sunriser dress, it's never too tight,' the pawnbroker said, untactfully. 'You can grow fat in them.'

'That's very considerate.' Isha tried to keep the sarcasm out of her voice.

Tatters picked up one of the pins, which had a silver bird with a blue gem for an eye.

'Is this from the convent of the Winged Maidens?' he asked.

The old woman threw her hands into the air. 'What would I know?'

'Come on,' Tatters insisted. 'The Wingshade who brought it to you, was she a woman? A recent refugee, for example?'

'I don't talk about my clients,' she snapped. 'You of all people should know that.'

Tatters didn't insist, but he pulled a face, dropping the pin back on the desk as if it burnt his fingers. Isha ran her hands over the smooth fabric. The silver thread enhanced the blue dye. She imagined a woman who had been powerful, fleeing her convent by foot, crossing the Shadowpass, her most precious possessions on her back. Would she take out the bird pin at night, to give herself courage? Maybe kiss it for good luck?

'So the Renegades are good for business, are they?' Tatters asked.

The old woman shook her finger under his nose. The kher turned away from the mirror in case this meant trouble.

'Don't put words I never said in my mouth! Those Renegades have unholy practices. I'll have no part in it. They do orgies, I've heard, where humans and khers do such things together as would make a young lady's ears drop off if I spoke of it.'

'Sounds fun,' said Tatters.

41

The old woman slapped his wrist, as one would an unruly child. 'Ah, for shame!'

She turned to Isha, still shaking her head.

'He's bad, that one.' Then, without transition or time to pause for breath: 'Do you want it or not?'

She paid the woman. Tatters argued the price was too high, but Isha didn't want to haggle, and anyway the money wasn't hers. Kilian hadn't only given her coin – for high sums, coin wasn't practical. There were silver and gold trinkets in the purse; the woman took a gold ring and two silver bracelets. Thankfully, it didn't contain any baina. Now that Isha knew the mage's money was carved out of kher horn, she was reluctant to own and spend it, even where it was the only accepted currency.

They left the pawnbroker's shop. As Tatters escorted Isha back to the textile market, they spoke little. They watched the Sunrisers wincing as they got up from their places on the floor to go begging for food. Isha broke a flimsy silver bracelet in four and gave each chunk to a different refugee. A woman heavy with child, with thin arms and legs, was struggling to walk through the busy roads, helping herself by leaning on shopkeepers' stalls. Isha hoped she hadn't fled on her own. It would be hard enough to give birth in this foreign city, amongst uncaring folk.

When they found Kilian, he didn't comment on the price of the dress – if anything, he seemed impressed they had succeeded in finding a full piece at such short notice.

'It is nice,' Kilian admitted. 'The tailor will need to stitch each bit together, obviously, but the silver is good.'

Tatters shook his head, chuckling. 'Stitches in a nasivyati, you unbeliever! Ah well, as long as the lightborn likes it. I'll leave the rest to you.'

He was about to leave when Isha stopped him, placing a hand on his arm.

'We should pick a day.' She paused. This was difficult, but she had to say it. 'For our duel.'

Kilian made a sound between a gasp and a laugh. 'Puffin, you've got guts.'

Tatters gave her a quizzical look. 'Is that a challenge?'

She nodded. He passed a hand through his hair, ruffling his red locks. His cloak hung in shreds around him. As winter grew, it wouldn't be enough to keep him warm. The rags stood in stark contrast to the lovely green velvet in his arms.

'I hope you haven't been pushed into this by ... bad advice, let us say.'

Isha shook her head. She was ready. She had been ready for a while now. She was answering Lal's provocation, but only because she thought she had a good chance of success.

'Well, I've got people to see tonight.' He lifted his present, the piece of velvet, and smiled. 'But tomorrow, if you want to, we'll fight.'

* * *

On the way back, Kilian and Isha caught up with a procession. A group of priests and believers were heading for the Nest, recognisable from their threadbare clothes, and from the absence of belts, shoes, or hats.

'It's rare for them to leave their Temple,' Kilian said, curious but unworried.

They passed the believers, a larger group than Isha had imagined at first, including a priest whom she vaguely recognised, his eyes sunken with sleepless nights. Then she remembered: he was the one who had insisted on her purifying herself and painting her face with blood during the Groniz festival. Osmund.

He had told her, once, that he would vouch for her if she ever wanted to pray at the Temple.

The believers stayed at the sides of the path to let the crowd of servants and mages through, but there wasn't humility in their eyes; it was something harder, akin to anger. They carried woven religious symbols, threaded grass and straw knotted into little characters, golden and green, to symbolise Groniz and Gelhwos. This wasn't unusual, but they also had threads dyed red, and spirals painted in ochre on little stone tablets, which celebrated Raudaz.

Isha felt uneasy at the sight. Why would they need the light-born of battle, supposedly the leader of war, to bless them?

'We should speed up,' she said. 'Let's get to the Nest before them.'

But Kilian was tired from the long walk, and they were laden with cloth, so despite her insistence they made slow progress, staying in front of the procession without being able to leave it far behind.

'I don't think it's worth running,' was Kilian's excuse. 'What can they do – pray at us?'

A second cluster of believers was waiting by the side of the track, in front of them. Isha tried not to feel trapped between the two, but it was hard to ignore that, together, they would make up a crowd of nearly forty people. In the second group, she noticed a small figure: the Doorkeeper.

She was thinner than when Isha had seen her at the festival, old age sagging the flesh around her neck, tiredness rimming her eyes and blueing her lips. Isha wondered if she was the only one to have this creeping sense of dread, this chill that wasn't from the wind running down her spine. Only a grave event would have brought the Doorkeeper out of her Temple.

More symbols for Raudaz could be seen: red string inter-twined between priests' fingers, or tied into locks of hair. Isha and Kilian overtook this second group, but behind them, the believers mingled into one large march.

They arrived at the gates together. Priests filled the entrance, but they could have been mistaken for beggars with their hag-gard faces and worn, hole-ridden clothes. The procession fanned out across the threshold.

The lawmages and kher guards eyed them cautiously, letting Kilian and Isha pass, asking the priests to state their business. Ungifted lined the inner courtyard, recently enlisted folk receiv-ing weapons and instructions. Grooms were preparing horses and coaches to support the areas around the Ridge that would most need help against Hawk. As was custom to bring fresh produce to the mages, merchants had set up stalls along the arches of the courtyard. A few people paused to stare at the unusual visitors.

'I'll bring this cloth to Daegan's tailor now,' Kilian said. 'Thanks for the help!'

Isha only nodded, her attention elsewhere.

A guard was sent to announce the Doorkeeper, who was invited to wait in the courtyard in the meantime, with her people. Isha tucked herself to one side, beside the stables, perched on the horses' water trough. She had a good view of the yard, but she was away from the centre of attention. She was partly hidden by a coachwoman, who was busy harnessing two heavy horses to a cart of supplies.

As Tatters had taught her: keep your eyes and ears open, but stay out of trouble.

The ungifted who worked for the mages – the enlisted force, the servants, the stable hands – came to pay the Doorkeeper their respects. A few bowed, a couple more devout people threw a button at her feet. But they all recognised her as someone they obeyed not out of fear, but out of faith. A few servants, who had been inside the main hall, also came outside to greet her. It was becoming a tight fit. The priests, if they spread out, could fill the area completely.

After a few minutes of waiting, a coterie of high mages arrived, clearly disgruntled at having been dragged away from lunch. They waded through the crowd, shooing people out of their path. Lady Siobhan was in the centre, leaning heavily on her malachite cane, her other hand resting on Sir Daegan's arm for balance. Amongst the mages, the collarbound lightborn stood out, the only person not wearing black.

When the lightborn appeared, most believers knelt to touch the ground, and Osmund bent over to take some soil, rubbing it onto his forehead. Some of the servants, who didn't usually bow to her, followed their priest's example. The coachwoman beside Isha briefly crouched to press her fingers to the earth. The horse beside her snorted.

'Forgive us,' the Doorkeeper said. The believers repeated this, and soon a chorus of whispers echoed around her. *Forgive us, forgive us.* They muttered a name too, without raising their voices: *Gelhwos.*

Gelhwos was the ruler of all lightborns and the bearer of light. Gelhwos was supposed to be both male and female, thunderstorm and sunlight, summer and spring. They were golden, symbol of the first light. By flying across the sky, they broke the first winter and brought the first thaw.

The lightborn didn't seem to notice, or care much, for the believers. Maybe this was just one more bizarre human behaviour among many.

Lady Siobhan reached out, her mind unthreatening, inclusive, polite. *May I invite you inside?*

But the show of goodwill didn't soften the Doorkeeper, who shook her head. 'Outdoors is good enough for my people, so it is good enough for me.' She took a step forward, a faltering step, which betrayed aching bones and painful knees. Sitting down to talk wouldn't have been a luxury, but comfort wasn't part of the Temple's teachings.

'Lady Siobhan, you have failed us,' the Doorkeeper announced.

The crowd was silent as a kher grave. Every person within earshot went still. The ungifted being enlisted, Isha couldn't help but notice, were armed. Lightly armed, with weapons they didn't know how to use, but armed nonetheless, and they had a strong motive to dislike the mages.

The Doorkeeper continued calmly, as if unaware of the storm she was brewing: 'Are mages the foes of true believers?'

Lady Siobhan seemed too shocked to react. Sir Daegan spoke for her, out of turn.

'Of course not,' he said placatingly.

The Doorkeeper, like Lady Siobhan, had a voice frayed with age, and, like Lady Siobhan, she could speak as quietly as she willed, for everyone would strain to hear her words. 'It is criminal of you to keep a lightborn bound to your bidding.' When addressing Sir Daegan, she was all venom. 'One for the eyes: you display her as one displays wealth, but she is not yours to claim.'

Her accusations cracked like a whip. Everyone was watching for the lightborn's reaction. Even the coachwoman glanced up and, catching Isha's eye, smiled, maybe to show she agreed, maybe to reassure her that nothing would go wrong.

'One for the hands: you bind her as one binds the powerless, yet she burns with a higher power than yours.'

Mutterings now, from the ungifted all around, muted 'hear, hear!' and 'shame' as one would during a trial. And the Doorkeeper was a severe judge: she lifted her walking stick with difficulty and, wavering on her feet, pointed it towards Sir Daegan.

'One for the heart: you are burdened with arrogance and envy, and burden her in turn, with the mantle of your arrogance and envy.'

She let her staff thump on the ground.

'Unbind the lightborn,' she said. 'Only then can we be considered allies. You enlist my people for your war, but we will not fight in the name of enslavement, we will not die for your vanity. Unless you free her, we will resist you.'

Isha was conflicted: at least, at last, someone other than Passerine acknowledged that what had happened to the lightborn was a crime. The Temple, the same religion which despised and banned the khers, was stating that collars were wrong. But had she been human, the Doorkeeper would have let her live out her days as a collarbound. Isha should be elated for the lightborn, but she could only feel a dulled, confused sort of anger.

The murmurs swelled before petering out as people waited for the mages' answer. Isha sensed mindlink crackling between the supreme mage and Daegan, as they decided how to react.

At last, Daegan bowed, but although the gesture was meek and recognised the Doorkeeper's authority, his answer did not. 'We are sorry you feel this way. Unfortunately, we are unable to satisfy your demand. The lightborn may win us the war against the Renegades, may ensure your safety. You should consider—'

His speech was lost as a ripple disturbed the crowd, a movement like the tide. Osmund called out for the believers to tighten their ranks. He acted as the Doorkeeper's bannerman, able to shout and run when she could only whisper and totter, and he served her well. People rallied to his call, until a part of the procession had curled around the mages, barring their way. The courtyard was brimming with priests and believers, including

48

ungifted who were on the fence, not quite ready for violence, but unwilling to leave the Doorkeeper undefended.

The surge of people made the animals nervous. Beside Isha, the heavy horses jerked their heads, trying to tug their reins out of the coachwoman's hands. Their ears were flattened against their heads, disappearing into their manes. Despite their handler's efforts to shush them, they stamped the ground, and if not for the heavy chariot, Isha suspected they would have bolted already.

Mindlink emanated from the mages, attempting to hold back the ungifted – but although praying opened the mind, faith sometimes protected it, making it harder to influence. The mental barrier of belief was in place.

Furious, Daegan shouted, 'What is this? Are these men under your orders?'

Isha nearly missed the Doorkeeper's answer: people were calling out to each other, apprentices were running for cover, merchants were hurriedly pulling back their stalls, and some of the believers had started chanting in low, rumbling voices.

'I am the Keeper of the threshold between the world of the living, of Groniz, and of the dead, of Byluk. I am not the Keeper of the door between the Nest and the outside world. If others want to bar or enable your passage, that is not my concern.'

Her aged face was severe.

'Unlike you, I know how far my authority reaches.'

Suddenly a group of people pushed to one side, creating a mess of elbowing and stamping, shrieking and crying as ungifted were dragged apart. Isha had to jump behind the water trough to avoid being trampled.

Careful! This was Lady Siobhan, but she was addressing Daegan, who was trying to part the waves of people. Taking control of the minds within reach, he forced them to turn away

49

from him. But by doing so, he only caused unexpected shifts in the mass of bodies and, if anything, brought the already-fraught believers closer to the high mages.

One of the heavy horses panicked and kicked, forcing people to scramble out of its way. At the same time, the other one lurched forward, forcing the chariot into a half-turn, its wheels screeching. When the crowd got too close, the mages thrust the ungifted back, sending grown adults tumbling into one another, into the coachwoman, into the horses. Thankfully, Isha could huddle further back, against the wall of the stables. Not everyone was as lucky.

A woman fell to the ground; people walked over her hands and legs before she managed to get to her feet, bruised and stunned, gasping like someone drowning. A man clung to the horses' reins as he slipped, tugging them out of the coachwoman's hand.

In front of them, Osmund motioned for the believers to interlink their arms, in order to create a human chain, more difficult to untangle for the mages.

'Set the lightborn free!' Osmund bellowed. He set the pace for a chant, which the believers soon copied: 'Your war, our light! Your war, *our light!*'

We don't want to shed blood. Lady Siobhan warned her mages with loud, clear mindlink, which the ungifted weren't privy to. *Let me handle this.*

Lady Siobhan extended her hand for the lightborn. Daegan must have confirmed her gesture with an order, because the lightborn carefully took the older woman's hand in hers.

Lady Siobhan, delicately holding the lightborn, still resting on her cane, wobbled closer to, not further from, the commotion. Her mind expanded around the ungifted like mist. She crafted a soothing, soft sensation that enveloped every thought, calming the horses, dampening the fiery tempers. It was hard to feel threatened by a slim young collarbound helping an older woman who was too frail to walk unaided. Throwing stones at a rich, plump, sneering figure, such as Sir Daegan, was different from facing two women, their dresses gathering dust in the messy courtyard.

Reverently, the believers parted for the lightborn. Some of Osmund's martial attitude deflated. As the pair reached him, he seemed to hesitate as to the proper greeting. Kneeling before the supreme mage would be admitting she was right, but not showing proper respect to a lightborn would be an act of ego. In the end, he went for a compromise, dipping into a low bow, brushing the ground with his fingers. It was a miracle no-one tripped on his hands.

The lightborn knew what was expected of her or, more likely, she was following Sir Daegan's instructions. She extended her wrist for Osmund as he rose.

'I am so sorry,' he said, returning her greeting. 'For the collar. It shames us all.'

He turned to address the crowd.

'We are blessed to be in the presence of Gelhwos!'

The chant expanded like a river with a broken dam. Isha recognised the prayer. It was usually sung at dusk, to beg lightborns to fly lower and cast their eyes down on suffering humans. The idea was that, when dawn broke, the lightborns would have solved the problems during the night.

It was such a well-known tune, everyone could follow, priests and townsfolk alike. The song filled the air. Men and women stamped their feet in rhythm. The Doorkeeper half-closed her eyes, humming the baseline in a higher key.

I understand your anger. With words woven with emotion, Lady Siobhan extended her address, and her influence, like a fisherman casting a wider net in a riverbed. *But don't think of the necklace as a bit in a horse's mouth. That is not its purpose. Think of it more as a saddle. We do not control where the lightborn goes or what she does. But we harness part of her energy so that, as she travels upwards, we are carried with her.*

A necklace. Of course. One of those pretty things which could easily be removed. Lady Siobhan might seem friendly, but she was lying through her teeth, knowing full well the sort of abuse a collar entailed. She might be frail, but magic swathed her like a stink, and a smell of rot was engulfing the people around her. It was a subtle sedative: each word she shared with the ungifted was part persuasion, part power.

In the same way alcohol could be diluted in water and become more palatable, thus was Siobhan diluting her mindlink. But the ungifted would become drunk and pliant just the same.

Behind her trough, Isha hardened her mind, shielded it, with images of the lightborn struggling in her cage and khers caught in the pillories; with the violence she had witnessed, which Lady Siobhan had allowed. The two horses were hanging their heads low, eyes lidded, lower lip relaxed. From the effect on the animals, it was easy to guess the control being applied on the humans.

We don't choose the path, but the lightborn helps us follow it, Lady Siobhan declared.

The lightborn delved deeper into the throng, touching people's wrists as she went. They encircled her, trying to kiss her fingers, some going as far as stroking her hair. Isha wasn't sure how the collarbound stayed so calm: she would have hated so many hands trying to clasp her, like ants creeping across her skin, small, six-legged crawlers trying to get into her clothes, as if she were a corpse with maggots trying to infest her.

We are blessed that Gelhwos is with us. They will help us through these difficult times.

One old woman started crying, and the lightborn wiped the tears off her cheeks, as tenderly as a daughter. But she didn't smile. She cast a strange, untouched gaze on the humans. She didn't sing the tune. She probably didn't know it.

The prayers would have melted a harder heart. *Bring my husband back from the war. Save my child from her fever. Bring us peace. Protect us from the Renegades.* When had hope become this painful, Isha wondered, like something digging through her lungs?

Lady Siobhan understood the ungifted she ruled over. She gave them what they wanted – something sacred, something beautiful to hold on to. But in return, she wanted them to obey.

The protestors had settled by the time Lady Siobhan reached the centre of the blockade. The Doorkeeper deigned to open her eyes. Her humming stopped. She watched the supreme mage through grey, thinning eyelashes.

'You are a woman of principle,' Lady Siobhan mumbled through damaged teeth. This small effort apparently exhausted her, because she swapped back to mindlink. *I expect you to hold me to high standards, and I am pleased you visited today. Will you trust me that this is a necessary measure to face the Renegades?*

They were two old women who had held the city together for over forty years. From the long gaze they exchanged, Isha suspected they knew each other's tricks, and weren't deceived by pretty words, even though they were skilled at giving them. When the Doorkeeper spoke at last, it was with a lucidity that belied her status as an ungifted who should have been more easily manipulated.

'Set Gelhwos free. If lightborns wish to pick a side in the war, they will. If they want to bless us, they may, but we should not presume that they must.'

In war, people who suffer, suffer more. Lady Siobhan's mindlink was enticing, like good wine, sweet on the tongue and warm in the throat. *Without the lightborn, the fight will last longer, more lives will be lost. Without the lightborn, Renegades might invade your Temple again, letting khers pillage your sacred grounds.*

They had similar silhouettes, the same bend to their spines, though Lady Siobhan stood taller, clothed with gold and black dye and silver jewellery, whereas the Doorkeeper hadn't even covered her knobbly, veined feet with shoes.

As soon as the war is over, we will set the lightborn free, Lady Siobhan promised.

The Doorkeeper paused. Maybe the mindlink was finally taking hold, or maybe she realised her people had been pacified and would be hard to whip back into anger. Maybe the fear of another Mezyan in her Temple, stamping on the mosaic floors, overruled her wish to protect the lightborn.

'Supreme Mage, you are a woman of peace,' she said at last. 'We will trust your judgement.'

The danger was over. The crowd dispersed. Isha felt light-headed, as if she had held her breath for too long.

But as the coachwoman soothed her horses, as life resumed, Isha couldn't help but wonder what would have happened if Lady Siobhan had been a worse negotiator, or if she hadn't been skilled at mindlink, or devoted to maintaining the peace. A compromise would only last so long.

***

Tatters' excitement at the idea of showing off his present was dampened when he reached Arushi's house, only to stumble into an argument between the two sisters.

'It's not stealing, it's getting back what's ours,' Yua was saying.

54

Tatters pushed the beaded curtain aside. The sisters ignored him. Arushi was clenching her hand around her belt with fingers like claws.

'You have no idea of the danger you're putting us in!' she snapped.

At a glance, the room was empty: the children had fled. The ashes were cooling in the firepit. The pots were hanging from the ceiling and around the chimney. In the corner, the old kher Uaza was pretending to sleep with her chin against her chest.

He was about to step out of the house again and wait for some steam to blow off when Arushi noticed him. Her glare pinned him to the spot.

'Your friend Mezyan has put dumb ideas into my sister's head, and now she is being reckless,' she said.

So much for bringing a peace-offering.

Yua was having none of this. She shoved Arushi's shoulder, like children do when gearing up to a fight. Despite being the younger sibling, she was a longlived, clearly not used to being ignored. Arushi gripped her belt tighter. Her sword slapped against her thigh.

It was the first time Tatters had heard Yua raise her voice: 'Trying to fight back isn't dumb!'

Fighting the mages is the worst idea she's had, said Lal. *She'll get herself killed.*

Aghast, Tatters found his voice to say, 'I never said we should fight the mages…'

If anything, Arushi seethed more. 'No, I know *your* theory, it's even more stupid.' Yua, braced as if for a physical struggle, wasn't lowering her eyes. 'Everyone plays nice and everything gets better. Thank you for your contribution.'

'But surely it's good for you to know that not everyone thinks iwdan are at the bottom of the pile?' Tatters said weakly.

He moved his bundle of velvet from one hand to the other, not sure what to do with it now. 'That people do believe we are equal.'

'And that we can live in harmony,' Yua added. 'All of us together.'

Harmony hasn't worked out so far, has it? said Lal.

Arushi aimed her furious stare – and the point of her horns – at her sister.

'Harmony? Why are there refugees in the streets, if the Renegades bring harmony?' Her head whipped around to confront Tatters. 'Why are all these people fleeing your free, equal world?' She spat the last words as if they burnt her tongue.

Tatters could feel the soft, irrelevant fabric under his fingers. *Your.* She had called it *his* world.

'There are no iwdan.' Yua's voice had dropped. She was quiet now, but firm. She put a hand on her sister's forearm. 'Did you notice?' When Arushi turned towards her, Yua held her gaze, searching her face. 'There are no iwdan refugees.'

Of course there aren't, thought Lal. *It doesn't mean the Renegades have got harmony. It only means the khers have got revenge.*

Arushi shrugged off her sister. 'I need to think.' She pushed past Tatters and through the curtain. He followed.

At first it seemed as if Arushi was going to snap at him to leave her alone. But then she let him fall into step behind her, leading him through the streets of the Pit. They were narrow, with the walls leaning towards each other, bumpy where cracks had been filled with mud and straw. Some had paintings – oxen and dogs, cockerels and vines, fruit trees and robins – drawn in ochre on the limewashed surfaces.

Arushi reached a back-street between two houses, a dead end cut off by a chicken pen. A child was playing with pebbles, sitting on a long stone that served as a bench.

'Why don't you scarper and come back when your horns have grown?' said Arushi. The child ran off.

Arushi let herself drop on the stone, rubbing her forehead with the flat of her hand. The sun cut across her cheek, showing the shadows under her eyes, the lines of tiredness down her face.

Tatters handed her his present. 'I didn't come to talk politics.'

She unfolded the velvet. She didn't speak at first, but held it up to the light, as he had done.

'Thank you,' she said.

They sat in silence, side-by-side. Arushi brought the velvet to her cheek and brushed it against her skin, but without smiling, mechanically, as if her mind were elsewhere. She lowered it and let it rest in her lap. Tatters looked at the precious fabric between her hands. As he had hoped, the green was deep enough to underline a kher's red skin, adding a glow to it.

Arushi sighed. The velvet lay limp against her fingers.

'I don't trust the Renegades,' she said.

And you shouldn't, said Lal. *We trusted them. See where that got us.*

Tatters cleared his throat. 'I don't agree with the Renegades.'

Saying it out loud was strange. He had never disavowed the Renegades. He had never needed to. They knew what he hated about them; he had made it abundantly clear. He had argued with Hawk like he had never argued with anyone since. He had run away. Sometimes he forgot the ideas he shared with them, how similar they were. Other people saw the resemblance, though.

What did you call it? he asked Lal. *Ah yes. Hawk's legacy.*

'If you don't agree, why were you one of them?' Arushi didn't sound angry, only exhausted. She undid her belt so she could sit comfortably, without her sword sticking out against her leg.

'I'm no longer with them. That's what's important,' he answered.

Closing her eyes, Arushi tilted back her head, to drink in the last rays of sunlight. She didn't stir. Tatters let her rest. He stayed beside her and closed his eyes. The sun was warm. He could see orange shapes against his eyelids.

It had been a hot day when they had returned to his home village. The memories lifted like the heat radiating from the earth. It had been the first time he'd argued with Hawk.

It was during the first thrills of victory, when the Renegades realised they could overturn a convent, that Hawk's mind-brawling techniques worked. She had asked which village they should go to next. Tatters had given the name of his hometown in the Pearls. It had seemed like the right thing to do – bring freedom to his family, break the yoke of the mages weighing down on them. He was drunk, like they all were, on blood and success.

His siblings hadn't been as glad to see Tatters as he had hoped. His mother was dead. She had died in childbirth, as they had expected, as she had feared. Still, it was a shock to return and find her gone.

The Renegades hanged the mages who resisted. Milinda was Tatters' elder sister. Half-sister, to be accurate. He had never been as close to his other siblings as he had been to Lal, but she was still family. She had worked as a handmaid for the head of the convent. She walked with Tatters to the scaffold where the bodies were displayed, including her former master. The old man's eyes were bulging.

Milinda reached out to stroke his foot, making the body rock in the breeze. She was older. There were webs of wrinkles at the corner of her eyes.

'He was such an old softie,' she whispered.

She started crying. Tatters didn't know whether to hug her or not. This was his fault, his and Hawk's – they had killed him. He looked away.

'How is he going to ascend?' Milinda was crying harder.

The Renegades burnt the bodies. They couldn't allow the professional mourners to take them. Like the Duskdwellers, the Pearls believed in throwing their dead over the Edge, although they made do with the Eastern side, where the sun rose, as a graveyard. But there were too many corpses, for one thing. And it would have given away the Renegades' position.

'That was all he cared about, you know.' Each of Milinda's sobs cut through Tatters like a knife. The pain was sharp, unshareable. 'Ascending, and his cats. But if you burn his body, how is he going to ascend?'

He looked at her then. She covered her face, like children do, and wept inside her cupped hands. The tears trickled down her wrists. She had outgrown their shared childhood, the narrow hips, the sticky knotted hair – she was now taller than him. They had lived apart for years. But it was only now, standing side-by-side before the hanged men, that they lost each other.

Tatters was wearing a black stana. He had taken it off one of the corpses. Not the dead of this village, no, but did it matter which mage it was who had died for Tatters to wear dyed cloth?

When Milinda had collected herself, and wiped her cheeks, and apologised for her outburst, saying that of course he was right – he was with the conquerors who had taken over the village, after all, she couldn't afford to say he was wrong, but every word broke his heart a bit more – Tatters went to see Hawk.

She was sitting on a stool of tanned hide and wood before a table that had been stolen from the convent, dragged outside for her, below a tree. She liked the air and the sun. The branches' shadows patterned the plundered maps and scrolls. A fallen leaf from the tree had got caught in her hair without her noticing.

Hawk didn't glance up from her reading.

'Either you believe it's good, and you do it. Or you believe it's evil, and you don't,' she said. 'You can't make exceptions. Exceptions are moral weakness.'

Afterwards, it seemed such an obvious answer. Hawk never changed. She never yielded. She never forgave. He should have fled, then, the moment she stormed through his village, the moment she showed she could be merciless. What good was a leader who wouldn't allow for weakness? Humans were flawed. Humans were weak. If she couldn't grant them mercy then, she wouldn't ever give them any.

If he had told Hawk this at the time, she might have smiled. She might have admitted the truth – that he was right.

They built the pyre. The smell of human flesh, like roasting pork, was thick in the air. People wandering too close to the fire could breathe in the grease from sweltering bodies.

On the same day, they inscribed Lal's name beside his mother's on the family shrine.

'Why did you come back?' His brother avoided Tatters' eye. He focused on carving Lal's name on the shrine. 'I could've imagined you were happy. I could've imagined she was alive.'

Tell him about me, said Lal. *Tell him I survived.*

Tatters didn't. *He will think I'm mad. Let him grieve.*

Although he couldn't say it, although he tried not to think it, Tatters grieved too. He grieved for a time when Lal was alive, flesh and blood and bone alive, not a shadow inside his mind.

A hand touched his cheek and wiped the tears away. Tatters looked up into Arushi's tender face. He should have felt more confused. For a moment, he didn't. It seemed natural for Arushi to sit beside him, on the rough stone bench next to his home.

It took him time to realise his brother, the shrine, the familiar objects were gone.

'You're crying,' Arushi said.

She was right. When Tatters rubbed his eyes, he found them wet. *I was mindrambling. Again.* He tried to hide how frightened he was. Lal wasn't fooled.

This isn't good, she said. *You can't tell the difference between past and present.*

He didn't want to listen to her. She was right. It meant his mind was breaking.

'It's nothing,' he told Arushi. 'I'm fine.'

Arushi wasn't fooled either.

'Of course,' she said. 'You look fine.'

But he didn't want to talk, and she didn't want to push. They sat in the dead end until the sun had set.

***

They returned to the house for the evening meal, which went as well as could be expected. Uaza fawned over the piece of velvet, speaking of how she would cut it up into several pieces and thread it into the clothes of the family, as a pattern along the neckline, maybe, or around the cuffs of the sleeves. All the children came to touch it, eager to have something so fine stitched onto their usual linen tunics.

When he tried, Tatters found he couldn't speak to Arushi. Her family was in the way: Ganez with his grievances, Yua with her revolutionary speeches, Uaza repeating the same opaque, metaphor-riddled stories.

Tatters stayed beside the fire long after the children had fallen asleep on the carpet around them and thick rugs had been piled up for Uaza to sleep on. He stayed after Ganez huddled on the floor, his bedding beside the children's. He stayed after Yua excused herself, her current lovers following her upstairs, into the attic which contained two private rooms. As far as Tatters understood it, the rooms were reserved for the leaders of the household. Since the matriarch found the rope ladder too much to handle, that meant the rooms were Yua's and Arushi's.

The embers were glowing, with only Tatters and Arushi beside the fire. He knew it was time to leave, but he couldn't bring himself to. He listened to the breathing of the sleeping khers – children, older men, the even older woman. Someone was snoring.

Arushi said something, in such a hushed voice that he didn't hear. But he guessed from her gaze that she had spoken.

'What did you say?'

'Would you like to come upstairs?' she repeated.

Lal had objections before Tatters could even consider it. *You can't be serious about this. We have bigger problems. That's what we should be focusing on.*

Tatters thought about the lacunants in front of the gates, with bleached clothes, hugging their begging bowls and rocking them like the babies they never had – a picture of what his future would be, of who he would become. Between the enemies on the outside and the enemies on the inside, it was a question of when, not if.

All the more reason to indulge, he thought.

Am I allowed to puke? asked Lal.

He reached out to take Arushi's hand and squeezed it, enjoying the silence inside his mind, the feeling of belonging only to himself.

'Thank you for the invitation,' he said. 'I'd love to.'

He had to let go when they climbed the rope ladder that led upstairs. Arushi's room was sober, simple: a mattress of packed straw, a shield pushed up against the wall. The smell of oil and leather made him dizzy. It reminded him of the Renegades' camp. It reminded him of Hawk.

Arushi closed the door behind them.

'Are you all right?' she asked.

He hugged her. When he held her against him, the memories faded. He nestled his nose against her neck to breathe in her smell. She was smaller than him, despite the horns. They pressed against his cheek; cold, hard. She was nothing like Hawk.

'Yes,' he said.

Arushi lifted her face to kiss him. They took their time. He let his hands run along the shape of her, as if he were moulding her out of clay, while she threaded her fingers through his beard. They didn't speak much, or only in whispers. They undressed each other in slow, careful gestures, lifting the heavy cloth with gentle hands. Arushi touched his forehead lightly when she pulled his tunic over his head, stroking his brow as if to find his horns.

Tattoos snaked across her arms, her chest, her thighs. He hadn't realised she would have patterns running down her hips, across her breasts. He followed the black lines, planting kisses along the ink.

'Would you like us to fleshbind?' she asked.

He hadn't realised it was an option. For him, fleshbinding had always been a way to avoid torture, not a skill to enhance pleasure. It wasn't something to accept lightly: fleshbinding lasted for life. Once two people had shared blood, they would always be linked. Only distance could prevent fleshbinding – and even then, ability and intimacy influenced how far the connection could be stretched.

But caution had guided Tatters too often.

'Happily,' he answered.

She slid one hand behind the nape of his neck and kissed him deeply. She caught his lower lip between her teeth, but when she bit him, it was tender. He tasted blood in both their mouths.

They shared sensations. It was a shock; painful, almost, like drinking strong liquor that burnt his throat but left him warm and humming.

The fleshbinding made every gesture more intense. He felt desire rising inside him until it was impossible to know whose craving longed to grab and hold and squeeze and lick. Every caress was felt again and again, her hand his skin, her skin his hand, until he couldn't tell where his body ended and hers began, or whose fingers were sinking into the small of his back, nails catching skin. Everything seemed to expand, his heart, his lungs, and they turned into one long, writhing creature with a thousand limbs, hands and tongues and lips aching for touch; hot, halting. The coarse hay of the mattress, the slickness of her sweat. Her teeth left marks along his shoulders.

Afterwards, as they lay together on her bed, the fresh air against his chest made him shiver. Where her legs were intertwined with his, her flesh was warm. There was a lump of hay in the small of his back.

Her face was peaceful. He ran a finger along the horn closest to him. Normally khers didn't let humans touch their horns; the connotations of baina were too strong. He counted the annulations as his finger bumped over them before pressing the tip of his thumb against the point at the end. It was strange to think of her age when watching her body – lean, youthful, despite the muscles. She appeared much younger than him, yet she wasn't. He wondered if, to her, he looked old.

Arushi rolled over. This close to her, Tatters noticed for the first time the fine hairs running down her ears and jawline, the colour of rust, different from the jet-black of her hair. She rested both her hands against his temples.

'It's strange,' she whispered.

'What is?'

She shook her head, laughing self-consciously.

'Tell me,' he insisted.

'Where are your horns?' she asked. 'No-one who's a proper age doesn't have horns.' She brushed her fingers through his hair, her eyes full of wonder. He understood. There was a strangeness to being together now, although it had felt right. It had felt more than right: it hadn't been like anything he had experienced before.

'I was thinking the same thing,' he said. 'By human standards you look so ... young.'

'I'm old.' Her tone was flat.

'I'm old too.' He kissed her neck. 'But not too old for this.'

It was growing cold. Tatters got up to fetch the cover flung against the door. He tried to ignore Lal as she awakened. She made it easy by staying at the back of his mind, sulking.

I don't even want to know what happened, she grumbled. As he retrieved the rough fabric, he talked, maybe to drown out anything Lal might add.

'I've never used fleshbinding while making love,' he admitted. 'It's ... confusing.'

Arushi chuckled. 'If you think five is confusing, you should wait until the Sar festival, when everyone gets involved.'

He stopped. *Five?* He stood there stupidly, holding the cover in one hand. Arushi pushed herself up on one elbow. Her hair stuck out at odd angles; it changed her face, softened it, took away the stern authority of the guard she usually carried around her.

'Five,' he repeated out loud.

Arushi was still smiling, albeit hesitantly, obviously sensing something was amiss. 'Yes,' she said. 'Five giving.'

Lal laughed. It wasn't an inclusive laugh. *You forgot khers share everything. Absolutely everything.*

'Say that again.' Tatters knew he should give her the cover but, frozen to the spot, he couldn't bring himself to. 'Who was sharing the fleshbinding we did right now?' It had to be people within range, probably inside the house.

Instead of answering, Arushi frowned. 'I don't understand,' she said. She stood up, stretching as she did so. She retrieved the cover, their fingers briefly touching as she threw it across her shoulders, to stop the cold that was seeping in. 'You said that you were happy to do some fleshbinding.'

I hope you really like Yua. Lal was on a roll. *Five giving, but how many taking, do you think? Old mum? Ganez?*

His head was spinning. 'I don't think I can stay.' He bent over to retrieve his tunic. Arushi gave him a look as if he had punched her.

'What in the underworlds has got into you?' she asked.

'I think I misunderstood the question.' It sounded absurd, but he wasn't sure what else he could say.

'And I thought your friend Mezyan had explained the basics of kher culture to you,' she answered, crossing her arms. She was starting to sound annoyed. 'Look, it's not like it's someone you don't know. It's just Yua and her lovers.'

It's just her sister, after all, said Lal. He could tell she was enjoying his dismay in a vicious, jealous way. *What's the big deal?*

He couldn't explain it. 'I need to think about this.' And, because Arushi looked forlorn and hurt, and because she didn't seem to understand why he was upset, he added: 'I'm sorry.'

He left the house. Outside, he felt stunned and sick.

A lover's hangover, said Lal.

Chapter Three

The evening of Isha's duel with Tatters, the Coop was crammed with curious apprentices: Sir Daegan's followers, Tatters' regulars, everyone far and wide who had heard about the tattooed girl's unusual story. People knew that she was impudent yet had been tolerated by Sir Daegan; that she was a disloyal apprentice who had changed masters; that she had created a mindlink double which even Tatters was impressed with. She had built up a reputation.

'Did you bring your own audience?' laughed Tatters, apparently enjoying the attention.

'They'll be betting on me, I'm warning you,' she joked.

'I hope so. All the more profit for me.'

She smiled, but only with her lips. Despite her bravado, her stomach churned with nerves. She would have preferred the Coop half-full, with a half-interested crowd.

Kilian was at the counter, his pale hair seemingly golden despite the grimy light, debating with the innkeeper. It was a relief to hang out with him; it soothed her.

'I swear, the Inner Sea has foam,' Kilian was saying. 'It's like a lake, but with foam.'

'Ask your Sunriser girl,' the innkeeper said, waving to Isha. 'She'll tell you that's nonsense.'

Isha had never seen the Inner Sea. She pushed herself up onto one of the stools, taking the beer mug Kilian slid her way.

'I believe the Inner Sea is normal water, but with salt,' she said.

The innkeeper wasn't impressed. 'No, that's not right. The fish would die.'

'And foam,' insisted Kilian, intent on not being proven wrong. 'I saw a painting. It has foam on top.' He took a long gulp from his drink. 'But maybe it doesn't have fish,' he conceded.

'You should ask a refugee,' Isha said. She already felt more relaxed. This was what she had needed: to discuss something irrelevant. *There is a world*, she thought, *in which my most important problem is to assess whether a body of water I will never see has foam on top.*

When Tatters announced their mindbrawl, a queue formed at the counter. The innkeeper wrote everyone's bets on the wax tablet hanging from his belt. He counted the money twice and accepted baina, even though it was illegal for an ungifted like him to handle that currency.

Tatters placed two chairs face-to-face in the centre of the tavern. Caitlin would be the settler.

'We need a stage name for you, puffin,' she teased. She had a way of staring at other women as men did, with eyes not quite stopping on their faces but taking in their figures.

'My own name is enough,' Isha said. She certainly didn't need to be called puffin.

'Maybe,' agreed Tatters. He was sitting on his chair, but he'd turned it the wrong way round, so he could cross his arms over the backrest, legs spread out on either side. He tucked his chin in the crook of his arms. 'But a second name is like a mindbrawl double. It can do great stuff for you, if you find something that fits.'

She already had an alias, as weighted with meaning as her tattoo. It wasn't one she cared to use. Unfortunately, Tatters must have been attuned to her thoughts – they were about to fight, after all.

'Go on,' he said. 'You've got an idea, I can tell.'

She would never escape the person her mother wanted her to be. 'The eyas.'

Caitlin smirked. 'The eye-ass? There must be a story behind that one. Although not one for children, I bet.'

Tatters frowned. He didn't seem amused in the least. Something about the way he gazed at Isha sent a shiver down her spine. *He knows what an eyas is. What the name means.*

But he only asked: 'What is an eyas, then?'

They were interrupted by the innkeeper shouting that the bets had been taken and they could start.

'We're in your hands, Cat,' said Tatters, thankfully dropping the subject. His settler smiled, throwing her thick hair over one shoulder. She closed her eyes. Tatters followed suit, not changing his posture on the chair to a more formal one. Lastly, Isha sank into her seat, breathed deeply, and joined them.

Although Isha had never fought there, she had attended duels in Caitlin's arena before. She recognised the high stone steps that delineated it, the lovely summer sky that shone down upon it. The ground felt bouncy and soft; maybe it was supposed to be some kind of clay.

Tatters was waiting for her, his usual mindbrawling self – slightly taller, his rags better arranged, his belt glinting as if oiled. He looked better fed than he was, less grubby. But he still wore the collar.

Isha could summon her bird-self, her eyas, at short notice now. Shifting from tattoo to shadow, the black bird of ink detached from her cheek to take flight. Tatters crossed his arms, cocking one foot against the ground, like horses sometimes do, when they half-lift one hoof. Isha focused on keeping her mind split in two. But before she could coordinate an attack, Tatters moved against her.

Tatters never struck first: he must have decided she was a threat.

The black bird flew in a circle, turning to face her. For a confusing moment, Isha wondered whether it was possible to lose control of parts of your mind. Then she realised this was Tatters' projection, a fictional copy of her double.

The bird dripped, as if the ink shaping it were melting, until it had swollen and morphed into a second Isha. This copy of her placed both hands on Isha's shoulders and stared through her with empty, all-black eyes.

'You're nothing,' she hissed, in a voice that was too much like her own, and yet unlike it. 'You think there is anything behind the tattoo? You are me. You are what is written on your face.'

The arena shifted like quicksand, and Isha found herself trapped inside a constructed memory. It was simple and effective. A man was sorting through horses – mares, Isha knew without needing to be told. As with all of Tatters' imaginings, it was exquisite. She could smell the horses. She could feel the heat of their bodies.

The handler gave names and duties out loud, to no-one in particular. To do so, he referred to the symbols branded across their rumps. He patted their necks, checked the mark the hot iron had left in the coat, before moving on to the next. The last of the mares had a stylised bird of prey spreading across her croup, and the man read out her name and her role as an apprentice from the scar.

Someone would ride this mare, and she would obey the orders coming through the bit.

And Isha could feel the crushing certainty, growing from her core, that she would never be anything more than her tattoo. The branded daughter. She wouldn't be anything else. She couldn't be.

She struggled to contain her mind. She wouldn't go down with the first hit – her pride would not allow it. She dragged herself back into one entity, trying to ignore the pity Tatters felt for horses, which pervaded everything he projected towards her.

Tatters let go. He was stepping back, which annoyed her more than it should. If he'd wanted to take her down, if this had been a fight for their lives, he would have won. The crowd was tense as she untangled herself from his mindlink, reshaping herself further in Caitlin's arena.

Her double had dissolved. That must have been what Tatters had wanted to achieve.

'If the double weakens you, don't call it forth.' He was using his teaching voice, but cautiously, without dropping his defences. 'Or if you do, use the element of surprise.'

'And the tattoo is the weakness people always go for, I know,' said Isha. She tried to keep her frustration from her tone.

What made Tatters so good at mindlink was that he knew, always, which blow would hurt most. He could have insulted Isha by mentioning how the tattoo disfigured her – but she didn't care about looks. He could have used the halfbreed connotation – but she didn't mind being associated with the khers. What she did mind, what tore at her heart, was knowing that her own mother had marked her as nothing more than her daughter. The eyas, the hawk. She was who she was, not thanks to something she had done, but because of what had been done to her.

At least Tatters was similar in that regard. They both carried something they hadn't chosen but now had to submit to.

Or maybe not. Not being able to choose was terrible, of course. But what if you had the chance to choose – and chose wrong? Wouldn't that be worse?

She glanced at Tatters, who was waiting for her, frowning, guarded. She could tell he was expecting her to hit hard. Well, she wouldn't disappoint.

People never got the collar to work with you. But maybe I can.

She attacked.

She crafted the image of a faceless figure in front of Tatters, then she filled the figure with the sense of 'master', although she didn't know what that would be. She infused it with authority and parenthood, for want of a better sense of what a master would entail. She gave it something of Sir Daegan and Passerine, something of the high mages who could ban apprentices from their presence. Truth thickened the precision of her creation.

She also gave it the shape and smell of Hawk. It was a guess, but it was better than nothing.

The figure handed his collar to Tatters. It was a slim circle of gold, like a coronet.

'Can I be your master?' it asked.

Tatters was very still. It was the intense, sudden stillness of an animal before it bolted. He didn't try to parry her imagining.

The figure smiled, as if an agreement had been reached. It placed the circle of gold on Tatters' forehead. The collar started glowing.

To Isha's surprise, Tatters didn't fight back. It turned out he couldn't.

There was a sound like a pouch ripping open and water pouring out. The thundering of a waterfall, too loud to be anything but white noise. Isha felt Tatters' mind weakening like she would the earth splitting under her feet. She strained to keep her balance as his thoughts undammed.

Soulsplintering was always disturbing to witness. It was as if Tatters were bleeding, but it was a mush of emotions that poured out of him, tainting the arena like ink, blocking the audience, hiding the blue sky, spreading in a tide until it reached Isha. It enveloped her, a bubble or a boil growing around her, cutting her off from the outside world, as thick and raw as if blood had, indeed, been spilt. It enclosed them together, leaving the audience stranded, trapping her in Tatters' shattering mind.

Despite her efforts, she slipped away from herself. She became Tatters.

It was the same military encampment as before, on a sunny wintry day, with cold-sharp air, a brilliant sun. Blue sky. He was wearing several layers of furs and a lovely stana that had belonged to a high mage. He stamped his feet on the frozen ground to stave off the cold. All the trees had silver bark, without leaves.

From the corner of his eye, Isha saw movement. Men and women milling around, some of them kindling the morning fire to prepare breakfast. A kher sat with his back to them, kneeling on the ground to milk a goat. His horns were longer and sharper than those of the animal. Tents stood in a circle around them, their cloth billowing like beating hearts as wind pumped inside them.

The warriors of the encampment were a mixed lot, humans and khers, all Sunrisers; the only white-skinned person was Tatters. White Sunrisers came from a small ethnicity in the Pearls and were uncommon but not unheard of. Isha knew, without needing to be told, that they sometimes called him Milky. He didn't mind the nickname.

Her mother stepped out of her tent. If it was a shock to see her, the greater shock for Isha was the person behind her. He was younger. He wasn't wearing robes but pieces of studded leather armour with large curving shoulder-guards that fell down to his elbows. When he breathed, white vapour rose around his mouth.

It was Passerine.

Although Isha was startled, Tatters wasn't. She sensed only a vague excitement as he headed closer.

'Want to see this beauty?' Hawk asked. Her voice was a string instrument plucking its lowest chord. Passerine stood beside her.

The collar was smaller than Tatters expected. It was a crown of gold, with no decorations, no carvings, nothing but hair-thin threads of metal braided together. Hawk let him hold it. Despite the cold, the metal was tepid. When he squeezed it between his fingers, it seemed as if he could snap it in two.

Power radiated from the collar. He could practically taste it.

'And this will work?' He sounded youthful; this was a much younger version of Tatters. Isha could perceive Lal within him, like a low hum, an inner song.

'We'll see, won't we?' Hawk smiled with her eyes, revealing crow's feet lines.

Tatters nodded, to himself or to the people before him. 'Here goes nothing.'

He lifted the collar above his head. It shone more strongly than before, enough light to fill a room. Some members of the encampment stopped to watch. The kher rested one hand on the goat's back and held his bucket of milk with the other as he stared. Passerine had a slick, expressionless face as he stood beside Hawk.

The collar grew in width. It floated down to rest above Tatters' shoulders, letting out heat and light, burning with inner fire.

'Is this normal?' He hid his worry behind a scoff. 'That'd be just like you, to give me a broken one.'

Hawk shook her head, chuckling. She lifted her hand, fingers outstretched. 'Ready?' she asked.

The memory was tinged with horror. Part of him knew this shouldn't happen, should never have happened. Part of him screamed.

Hawk placed her fingers on the rim of gold. 'I am your master,' she said.

The collar shrank. Its light dimmed. Soon it rested against his skin, pressing against his neck. When he swallowed, he felt it like a too-tight scarf.

Lal screamed.

Her high-pitched shriek speared him ear to ear. *It's doing something to us! Take it off! Take it off!* Pain, acute, as if a knife was being pressed against his temple. Dapples of black and blue flashed across his eyesight. He stumbled forward, an arm out for balance. Hawk – his master – caught him.

'It's all right,' she whispered. 'It might...'

'Take it off,' he croaked.

'We decided on this together,' she said.

'Take it off!'

Lal was howling. It was like having a wildcat inside his skull, hissing and spitting and sinking its claws inside his head. Her terror was contagious. It ran through his veins like blood, each beat of his heart spreading it further. All he could see was the ground, frosted grass that snapped when he stepped on it. He watched the broken blades of grass and heard his own spine snap.

The scene brutally stopped, with a shock like a lurch, a missed step.

Before Isha could find her footing, Caitlin flung her out of Tatters' mind. Caitlin must have been overtaken by the memories too. Her role as a settler was to ban Isha as soon as Tatters

75

weakened, if Isha didn't step away of her own accord. But Isha hadn't had a chance to decide to leave his mind – she'd been overwhelmed. She suspected Caitlin had only just regained enough control to shove her away. Although these scenes had lasted what felt like a lifetime, in mindlink they could have been the length of a heartbeat.

Isha only realised it when she opened her eyes. She had won. She should have felt victorious. Instead, she felt sick.

My mother. She branded me, she branded you. Maybe that was why Tatters' collar had reacted so strongly when she'd touched it. Did it recognise her? Or the blood inside her? *We are so similar – why did neither of us know about the other?*

We both belong to the same woman.

She touched her neck, half-expecting to find gold there. She glanced at Tatters, who hadn't fainted. He opened his eyes as if waking from a nightmare. They gazed at each other. There was too much to unpack in his expression. He turned away first.

The innkeeper, who couldn't know the outcome, stood between them.

Still not looking at her, Tatters lifted his hands and clapped. He kept his head bowed, his elbows on the chair's backrest. Apprentices opened their eyes, blinking away from Caitlin's arena, and cheered. They would have only caught glimpses of the soulsplintering, the silver bark, maybe, the sense of dread, at a stretch, the figures milling about the encampment. Caitlin was different. As the settler, she would have had as clear a picture as Isha.

Some members of the audience hooted, and Kilian patted her on the back, and the innkeeper laughed a raucous laugh and said you should never underestimate a pretty girl. Winking, he promised her good money for her fight.

'Well done,' was all Tatters said.

Isha wasn't the only person to have won a mindbrawl against Tatters, but she could tell she had hurt him. It was the difference, maybe, between disarming an opponent and cutting off their hand.

Nothing much happened. Tatters went to sit in his usual corner to talk to apprentices. Isha was given her earnings. People congratulated her. Sir Daegan's apprentices weren't impressed: after all, what more could one expect from some low-class mage? People who knew Tatters were impressed, especially those who had witnessed the duel against Ninian. They listed previous winners to Isha, while beside her Kilian boasted for them both, with such earnest pleasure that she couldn't be upset with him.

'With how hard you trained, you deserved to win,' he kept repeating.

She smiled and nodded and small-talked and waited for an opportunity to speak with Tatters in private.

She didn't get it. When the flow of admirers thinned somewhat, Caitlin asked her if she could spare a minute. Kilian invited her to sit beside them, but she only shook her head.

'Just the two of us, outside,' Caitlin said. Her voice was terse, unfriendly. It was an order.

Isha nodded; she'd had enough battling in front of an audience for one night. When she got up, Kilian pouted.

'Now you're a big name, you don't want to hang out with me,' he complained.

She laughed at how beside the point he was. On impulse, without quite deciding to, she hugged him, a quick squeeze of the shoulders.

'I'll be back in a minute,' she promised.

She followed Caitlin outside. The alleyway in front of the inn was narrow, with two gutters running down either side. This was where the tenants threw their garbage and the contents of their chamber pots. To access the tavern, clients used a plank thrown above the gully. The stench of human and animal waste didn't seem to put the apprentices off their drinks. In any other part of town, this would have been crowded with homeless people sorting through the rotten food in the ditch, idlers bullying cats, or prostitutes counting their change. But because of the number of apprentices who came to the inn, ungifted steered away. No-one wanted to end up mindscrewed.

Caitlin stood at a distance from the tavern door, beside a steamed-up window. Her rust-coloured hair matched the thatched roof.

'What do you think?' she asked.

Isha shrugged. 'You tell me. You brought me out here.' She was behaving like Tatters, as unhelpful as he often was when sharing information, but she couldn't help herself.

Caitlin sighed. 'What we saw. We both saw it. His master.'

My mother. Isha had expected Caitlin to ask about Passerine, but maybe she hadn't spotted him.

'What about her?' asked Isha.

Caitlin flicked one perfect russet curl over one perfect shoulder. She was taller than Isha. Maybe that was why Isha always got the impression Caitlin was looking down on her.

'Look, I was working with him long before you came into the picture,' Caitlin said, as if she were addressing a child being unreasonable about a pet. 'This is something else. I always assumed his master was some high mage who didn't need him in the evenings and this was how Tatters made his spare money. But that woman ... She wasn't even a mage.'

You assume she wasn't a mage because she didn't have the cloak. All that proves is that she isn't from a legal convent. Isha kept her thoughts to herself. She was careful to repress them as much as possible, as Caitlin wasn't above spying.

'You're reading too much into this,' said Isha. 'So his master isn't a mage. What does that change?'

Caitlin crossed her arms. 'You know it's more than that. They were all Sunrisers. And what's the Nest's biggest threat right now?' It was a rhetorical question. 'Sunrisers! Don't you think it's too much of a coincidence? That place looked like a military camp.' Caitlin lowered her voice to a whisper. 'He might be spying for the Renegades.'

Isha maintained a neutral face and dulled thoughts. She suspected, but she didn't want to tell Caitlin, that Tatters wasn't working for Hawk anymore. From the way he behaved, it looked more like he was hiding from her than obeying her orders. It was difficult to know which side he was on, but as far as Isha was concerned, that had always been the case. She remembered her dream. *What does his bind look like?* That wasn't the question of someone who was sure they could get their slave to come to heel.

Tatters, like her, had fled the Renegades. Like her, he had to conceal his past allegiance from the Nest.

'We don't know how old that memory is,' said Isha. 'He might have been bought and sold since. Whoever his master *was* doesn't say much about who his master *is*. In any case, I wouldn't take the memory of an underground mindbrawl at face value.'

Caitlin cast her a disapproving look, which didn't so much say 'I don't believe you' as 'we should be on the same side.' Isha held it quietly. She didn't owe Caitlin anything.

But she might owe Tatters something. She wanted to talk to him more than to his suspicious settler.

However, by the time Isha went back inside the tavern, Tatters had gone upstairs to bed.

* * *

Tatters sat down on an empty barrel, resting his skull against the underbelly of a wooden beam, folded forward, his forearms on his thighs. He felt drained. Lal was seething.

That's the second time she's invaded our thoughts! We have to do something about it!

The first time I let her. Although he didn't know at the time what letting Isha touch the collar would entail. *And this time she earned it.* With the most straightforward mindbrawl technique possible – hitting the weak spot. It had been a lucky guess on her part, assuming that he had chosen to be a collarbound, that he could have avoided it. And she had been right. To this day, he hated himself for his lapse in judgement. Knowing he'd had the opportunity to say no to Hawk still left him raw, brittle. *What do you expect me to do about it?*

Lal refused to calm down, trembling inside his mind with small bursts of emotion. He felt like water brought to a boil, the bubbles shivering through it, without the water having a say.

Isha played fair, Tatters argued. *As long as we don't know she's our enemy, we do the same.*

He tried to stretch and failed; there wasn't enough space between the barrel and the roof. He cracked his neck instead, rolling his head across his shoulders.

Instead of getting any information out of her, we've revealed our hand, Lal said.

Or not, said Tatters. *If she is close to Hawk, we are probably old news to her.*

He was trying to be reassuring, but even he wasn't convinced. What had happened today shouldn't have happened, and Lal was right, it was dangerous. It put them in Isha's power. It also meant he was losing it and that, no doubt, was the most alarming. He shouldn't have fallen for that attack. He should have expected it.

She's learning to hurt us, learning to control us, said Lal. *The next step is, she brings Passerine to us, reels us in like a fish. And guts us like one.*

After that grim prediction, Lal sulked. Tatters tapped his fingers against the barrel. He drummed a tune and listened to it for a while.

Tatters wanted to speak to Isha, but Lal would hate that impulse. And maybe she was right. It might be naïve to hope they were on the same side. In any case, the damage was done. He was too exhausted to leave tonight, or to make a sound decision. He would have to wait, braced for the worst, but hopeful that Isha's behaviour would prove him right, and reveal them as unlikely allies. After all, if she wanted to harm him, she'd had a perfect opportunity – which she hadn't abused.

Tatters jumped off the barrel. He rolled up his cloak into a pillow, then packed the straw of his bed. Maybe a lightborn would fly above as he slept and solve his problems for him. Throwing off his belt, he crashed down and closed his eyes.

Unwittingly, the memories rose, like mist from the Edge.

He saw himself in Hawk's tent. It was his first evening wearing the collar.

He was lying on her makeshift bed, the weight of the gold heavy around his neck. Lal was silent. It was night. The roof of the tent let a glow filter in from the stars, and cold filter in from the breeze. He watched the cloth move like a sail and listened to the wooden posts as they creaked. It had worked, but he felt no sense of victory. He was sore. Although he had succeeded, he hadn't won.

Hawk was sitting beside him, on the same bed, working on her poetry. He could hear the feather scraping the paper. It was a small, grating sound. She hadn't noticed he was awake.

'Take it off,' he said.

His voice was rough. He coughed.

'You're awake.' She turned to him, put a hand to his brow to check his temperature. Her fingers were coarse. Tatters stared at her, unblinking. His chest heaved.

She stared back. He didn't need to repeat himself; she knew what he was thinking. She didn't need to say anything, either. The fact that he was still wearing the collar was statement enough.

They had decided on this together, but he didn't have the power to undo it.

He pushed back the blankets. He wasn't sure how long he had been unconscious – clearly long enough to worry her. His head hurt. He couldn't hear Lal. He felt too hot, feverish, even when he scrambled to his feet. Hawk didn't try to follow him. Instead, she stayed on the bed, still holding her quill, and watched as he draped his cloak around his shoulders.

As he was about to leave the tent, she whispered, 'Wait.'

It struck him like walking into a shock-cold river. His teeth ached. He stopped in his tracks, shackled to the spot. Hawk wasn't used to the collar yet. He knew now, although he didn't realise it then, that she hadn't meant to use the collar's magic. It was too powerful to wield gently. If the master gave an order, the collarbound obeyed. That was what the collar was for. It didn't understand nuance.

Hawk picked up one of her scarves. It was deep red, long enough to fall to her hips if she knotted it loosely around her neck. As she handed it to Tatters, she said, 'Take this.'

He didn't have a choice.

The scarf was soft. Hawk smiled, but her eyes were sad. 'What you did today, no human has ever done.'

He gripped the scarf without putting it on. He could guess why she had given it to him – to hide the collar. But he would tumble into the underworlds before he did anything she wanted, or rather, anything she wanted but didn't order him to do.

'I guess that proves I'm not human,' he said.

She shook her head but didn't deny it. 'I'm proud of you.'

He left her tent. It was that or screaming.

Outside, a few Renegades were drinking around the fire, including Mezyan and Passerine. Five or six soldiers, male and female, iwdan and human, were sharing mugs of warm beer. The smell of hot alcohol drifted from the cauldron hanging over the firepit, now nearly empty. They stopped talking when they spotted Tatters. He noticed they kept their eyes away from the collar, as one would avoid staring at a scar.

'Congratulations, Milky.' This Renegade was a stubby stubborn kher. She lifted her glass to him. 'You did us proud.' She downed her drink.

'Yes,' said Mezyan. 'One of Hawk's plans actually worked – who would've thought?'

Some people laughed. Passerine didn't. The woman leant forward and scraped at the dregs of beer inside the cauldron with her cup. A tall man, half his face damaged by a sword-cut, nudged Passerine with his elbow.

'The new recruit has beaten you to it!'

Tatters wondered if he was the only one to see Passerine wince.

'Tatters is always beating us,' said someone else.

The tall man guffawed. 'You've seen nothing yet! Now he'll be twice as good.'

Tatters didn't sit with them. He studied their faces glowing in the light of the fire. No-one mentioned the collar. He stood there, holding the scarf, feeling the gold around his neck like a dagger slitting his throat. The Renegades' words and laughter

83

didn't sound human. The more he listened, the less he heard, until it turned to mindless squawking.

Mezyan was asking him a question, gently but firmly, tethering Tatters back to the here and now.

'You've had it rough. Why don't you sit down?' Mezyan repeated. 'Have a drink.'

And in a few minutes, Hawk would join them, and they would share a beer like old friends. Mezyan was always the peacemaker.

Tatters turned away from the fire. He couldn't care less for the Renegades calling him back as he strode out into the forest.

It wasn't long before he slowed. The woods were pitch-black, the glimmer of the moon hidden by the foliage. The Renegades always set up camp beside a water spot, but Tatters wasn't sure he'd be able to locate it, and he weighed the wisdom of walking without the faintest idea of how to find his way back.

Mezyan caught up with him, holding a torch which he must have lit at the fire.

'Hey,' he said. 'Want some company?'

Tatters shrugged. At least Mezyan had some light.

They walked together towards the stream. The flickering torch helped them climb over roots and avoid low branches. After some time, Tatters' eyes adjusted to the night. Everything had dim grey outlines.

They picked a fallen tree, in the cool air close to the river. Although the wood was rotten, it was sturdy enough to hold them. Mezyan planted his torch in the muddy bank before climbing up the trunk, placing himself high enough to be able to swing his legs. Tatters scrambled up beside him. He stared at the fire, reflecting silver lights on the stream's surface, until his eyes stung.

'It's going to be all right,' said Mezyan. 'It will take some getting used to, that's all.'

84

Tatters wondered what his face betrayed of his feelings, considering Mezyan couldn't mindlink. He glanced at the halfbreed. Not for the first time, Mezyan reminded him of a sheep, what with the curly hair, the circular white horns, and something about his face, the roundness of it, the depth of his eyes, which gave him the same pensive expression.

'So you think what she did was all right?' Tatters asked. His voice wasn't as sharp as he expected. He was still in a state of shock. Fury would come later, when he was stronger, when Lal had returned. She had been wounded, not beaten, by the collar. She would find ways to survive despite the giant's magic.

Sighing, Mezyan rested his hands on either side of his legs, gazing down at his feet.

'I'm not saying I agree with it. But I get it. I think she's frightened, and—'

'Oh, she's frightened?' Tatters interrupted. 'You know who else is frightened? Want me to give you three guesses?'

Mezyan looked away. 'I'm just saying I understand why she did it.'

Something inside Tatters' chest caved in. 'You do?' He wondered if he sounded as hollow as he felt. 'Very well. I'm listening.'

Mezyan shook his head. 'You're not really, though, are you?'

Tatters fought the urge to shove Mezyan off the tree. 'The agreement was that we would try the collar, see if it worked, and take it off afterwards.' He found himself raising his voice. 'She broke her word!'

Mezyan took the scarf from Tatters and played with it, coiling it around his hand, running finger and thumb along it as if to test the thickness of the fabric.

'Look at it this way,' Mezyan said, his eyes still on the cloth. 'With what you've done today, we can change the world. We can finally make a difference. But you've learnt everything you could from us. You don't need our protection anymore. What happens if you leave?'

They couldn't hold each other's eye, so instead Tatters watched the torch leaning sideways in the mud. He wondered if he should straighten it, but he didn't budge. 'So it's about trust.'

Mezyan shook his head. He let the scarf fall on his lap and tucked his hands under his thighs, maybe for warmth. He kept swinging his legs, as if they were wings, and if he beat them enough he could leave the ground.

'No. It's about our only chance at change.'

Tatters' heart sank. He should have expected it. When Hawk had needed an army, she'd created one. Now she needed a slave, so she'd got herself one.

They didn't speak. The torch was sinking, now lying nearly horizontally in the mud. The stream giggled and spluttered.

In the end, Mezyan wrapped the scarf around Tatters' neck.

'It's not about the collar,' he said. 'It's about the cause.' Maybe he thought Tatters could forget the thing existed by hiding it from sight. Maybe that's what Hawk thought, too.

Mezyan jumped down to retrieve the torch, which made a wet noise when he pulled it out of the riverbank. He wiped the sludge off his hands on the log where he'd been seated.

Tatters followed him back to the camp.

In retrospect, Mezyan should have told him something else, something more obvious. Hawk wouldn't back down. If he tried to fight her, it wouldn't end with a battle – it would end with a war.

But we won that war, said Lal.

Maybe, thought Tatters. *Or maybe it isn't over.*

Chapter Four

Tatters woke with the first lights of dawn. He retrieved his cloak, shaking some life back into it. He rinsed his face with cold water from a wooden bucket by the door. After relieving himself, he tipped the chamber pot through the window, sloshed the water from the bucket into the chamber pot, and threw that out of the window too. He was about to head downstairs when Lal sprung to life inside his mind.

He's here, she said.

If Tatters had been drowsy a moment before, he wasn't now. *Are you sure?*

I can taste his mind.

There was no doubt who she was talking about. Passerine had found them. After all, it had only been a matter of time.

This is Isha's doing, I'm sure, Lal snarled.

Tatters glanced around the attic, trying to work out if there was anything he needed. He buckled his belt around his waist, then flung his stana over his shoulders. Should he run down the staircase and out of the front door?

Passerine is a front door person, said Lal.

Which left the window. It was unlucky that he'd just thrown a rather unsavoury mixture out of it. Well, it couldn't be helped. He stepped onto the window-ledge. The tavern's wall, irregular at best, was wattle and daub, thickly built. It was streaked with urine and worse, without many foot-holes in the roughcast surface. Because it was a back alley, the road below was beaten earth. Still, it looked too high to jump.

He's close, Lal hissed.

Tatters unsheathed his knife. He planted it in the rammed earth, turning himself so he faced the wall, his feet scraping against the edge of the windowsill.

Here goes nothing.

He let his feet drop. The knife couldn't sustain his weight, and it cut through the dry mud. Tatters fell from his window, but it was a controlled fall, with the jagged shock of the knife tugging at his arm as it sliced through the earth, until it jammed against the stones of the ground floor. Tatters jumped down unharmed – but he had left a distinctive line from his window to the street.

He wiped his knife clean and slipped it into his belt. Dawn was breaking, spilling yellow and white across the sky, as he pulled his stana over his head.

Tatters knew mages could follow a trail of emotion – fear, faith, fury, all left a faint scent in the air. If he wanted to shake off Passerine, he needed to find a way to blur that trail.

Busy streets, advised Lal.

Tatters tried not to run. Running attracted attention. People would remember a fleeing hooded figure, and they would point the lawmages in the right direction. He tried to hide the fear from his face, but keep a set, serious expression, as if he were on an errand for his master. He strode down the street, staying close to the buildings, not turning back.

The town was quiet. The main roads had a few early-risers, mostly shopkeepers and grooms, or servants. The stench of fresh excrement rose with the sun as people emptied a night's-worth of chamber pots out of their windows.

There aren't enough of them to hide me from Passerine.

Heading for the outskirts of town, even attempting to leave the city, was too dangerous until they knew for sure whether Passerine was acting alone or had involved the lawmages. The prayers that filled the Temple would cover his mental imprint, so it could be a decent hiding-place, but it was a dead end. Once at the Temple, if Passerine caught up, the only way out was over the Edge. A knife wouldn't soften that fall.

No, not the Temple, said Lal.

Only one solution bore scrutiny. Even Lal begrudgingly admitted it was the only way to escape at short notice.

Tatters abruptly changed direction through a side-alley. When there was no-one to see, he ran.

***

Isha's stomach twisted when Passerine knocked at the Coop's door. While he waited for an answer, he took a step back to study the building's façade, his profile cut out against the sky. His face, unreadable, could have been carved out of ebony – he might have been the figurehead of a ship.

She heard the innkeeper unbolt the door. He opened it, wearing only an undertunic, his thick body hair visible through the fabric. When he saw her, he grumbled about the Coop being closed, and she of all people should know this was no time to wake him up. Then he spotted Passerine.

He stood gaping, mouth half-open. His eyes went from her to him. She sensed his fear, and his thoughts, shiny and sharp as knives. *Did she sell me out? The kherbitch! She wouldn't. Would she?*

Passerine graced him with a curt smile. Isha was sure he read as much as she did in the innkeeper's thoughts, if not more.

Why isn't he wearing his kher horn? she wondered. It would have protected them both. Maybe he didn't wear it to sleep.

The innkeeper apologised for the delay and said he would be with them right away, before slamming the door shut. When he opened it again, his thoughts were unreachable, and the horn bracelet was firmly screwed around his arm.

He invited them in. Passerine had to stoop to cross the threshold. He scanned the main room and, although she knew it by heart, Isha did so too, noticing how different it looked by day. It was empty, with the chairs placed on the tables. The ground stuck under their feet and their shoes made a sucking sound when they unglued from the wood. The morning light showed the cracks between the floorboards, the dust above the kegs. The place struck her as cramped and poor.

'Do you live alone?' asked Passerine.

The innkeeper glared at Isha.

'I rent the room upstairs, sir,' he said. 'There's just the one tenant. Nothing fancy.'

Passerine nodded. He studied his surroundings as he would a painting, soaking up every detail. 'May I?'

'He'll still be sleeping,' said the innkeeper.

'Maybe.'

Without waiting for further permission, Passerine crossed the tavern. He reached the steps behind the counter, one hand holding back his cloak to prevent it from touching the furniture.

Isha gave the innkeeper an apologetic smile as she rushed behind her master. Her heart was pounding inside her throat. When she swallowed, the spit stuck.

Passerine pushed the door to the attic open. Isha had never been there before. It was full of barrels, with hemp rope and dirty sheets hanging from the ceiling, the smell of dust, flax, and stale air pervading everything. The morning breeze wafted in through the open window.

Tatters was nowhere to be seen.

Passerine didn't seem surprised. He leant out of the window, checking the street on both sides. Slowly, as if there was no rush, he turned on his heels to head back down the staircase. He didn't acknowledge the innkeeper as he left.

Isha followed like a smaller, paler shadow. Passerine walked at an easy pace, but he moved with purpose. Tentatively, she tried to expand her mind, to reach out.

Passerine was scouting the area in front of him with his mind. She could sense him like one can taste the tang of something rotting when walking beside an orchard in late summer. It was slight, but it hung in the air. He was using the lawmages' technique of following someone's trail of thought. Isha retreated before he could find her prying. She didn't want him to ask her if she knew anything, because she wouldn't be able to lie.

Tatters had once told her mindlink was all about lying. She wasn't sure whether protecting him was the right thing to do – but she wanted to keep that choice open.

Maybe a good way to do that would be not to think about Tatters. She tried to discipline herself. His head cocked backwards to soak up the sun, Passerine strode with a smile playing on his lips.

Isha recognised the path they were taking. It wasn't the shortest way, but it was bringing them closer to the Pit by going through a number of narrow back alleys with washing hanging from the windows above and beggars sleeping in groups on the floor, sighing as the mages crept by. Isha tried to avoid putting her feet on people's hands, while Passerine let the hem of his cloak brush over their closed eyelids.

As Isha had expected, this roundabout route brought them to the Pit. Although it was unusual for khers to bother guarding it in the small hours of the morning, there was a silhouette striding towards the gates. Arushi. Isha's heart expanded, filling up her throat, preventing her from breathing.

Passerine arrived at the threshold before Arushi could reach him. But as he crossed the gates, she planted herself before him, feet apart, blocking his way forward. She gave him a toothless, lipless smile.

'How can I help you, sir?' she asked.

Arushi was half-dressed, wearing trousers but no belt, her guard's shirt but not the leather jacket. She didn't have her sword, and her horns were duller than usual, as if she hadn't been able to polish them. Isha spotted a faded notch in her cheek where her pillow had pressed against her skin.

Passerine gave Arushi an up-and-down gaze, from the tip of her horns to her toes. The mudbrick houses and night-time tents stood silent around them. Although no-one was out in the streets, the tents packed the road, crammed wall-to-wall with the kher families who couldn't, or wouldn't, own a house. Isha spotted a few hens under a wheelbarrow, squashed together for warmth, their feathers puffed out. A few opened their beady eyes. Like the Coop, the Pit seemed more rundown by dawn.

'I have reasons to believe a collarbound might have come here this morning.'

Arushi's glare was like a punch. Isha didn't need mindlink to know Arushi was having the same thoughts as the innkeeper – did the flatface betray me? Would she?

'You didn't happen to see him, by any chance?' asked Passerine. His voice was liquid; it ran down Isha's spine like cold water. It was framed as a question, but it wasn't one.

92

'No, I didn't,' said Arushi. 'This is too early. No-one is up yet, except for you.'

'You are,' said Passerine.

Arushi gave him another smile. They were smiling at each other like dogs snarl before a fight, sniffing out the opponent, deciding when to go for the throat. Passerine was much taller than her, which meant Arushi was forced to push her chin backwards to hold his gaze. Isha knew this would be uncomfortable for her as it meant her horns were pointing behind her – the wrong way.

'I'm the head of guards. Being alert while other people sleep is my job.'

Passerine turned away from Arushi to give the Pit a proprietorial look. His mind permeated the place, stronger now that there were no other thoughts to distract from it. His words were like stones dropped in a well: 'I don't believe it is forbidden for mages to visit your area of the city?'

'Nothing's forbidden for the mages,' said Arushi. The sentence could have been servile, but her tone wasn't.

This scene reminded Isha of another night, weeks ago, when Sir Daegan had ordered her to bind his lightborn. Isha wasn't sure she would ever forgive herself for placing the collar on her and forcing her into servitude. Today, Passerine was using her to find Tatters. It had all happened once before.

He would walk her around the Pit, like one does when dowsing, until her mind reacted, until he sensed from her thoughts that this was the place to hunt further. Tatters might be able to hide his presence by being close to the iwdan, but Isha didn't have that option.

She had already helped masters bind collarbounds one time too many.

On impulse, she touched Arushi, as if they were familiar friends. Her mindlink shut down, so the scent that radiated

93

around Passerine disappeared. Arushi tensed as Isha passed her arm across the kher's shoulders and leant her weight on her.

'How about you escort us while we visit?' Isha asked. 'Your duties as head of guards must include protecting mages in the rougher parts of the city.'

Arushi frowned, but didn't resist. To Isha's relief, she didn't angle her horns downwards either.

'I'd be happy to give you a tour,' she said. 'If that's what you want.'

Passerine nodded. Isha wasn't sure if he was answering Arushi or conceding a point. There was something playful in his gesture, like a bow you would give a rival. His smile didn't change. His eyes were holes that sucked in the light.

Arushi knew what a mage touching her meant, so she must realise Isha had consciously locked down her mind to prevent Passerine from intruding. She didn't push the apprentice away, but let her fawn over her, like an exuberant friend, or maybe like an enemy who wanted to prove you couldn't afford to show you disliked them. Isha herself wasn't sure which part she was playing.

As they walked around the Pit, Isha fumbled for her pouch, taking out a baina coin, trying to keep her gestures subtle. Once the baina was tucked inside the palm of her hand, she let go of Arushi. No doubt Passerine wasn't fooled. What remained to be seen was whether he'd confront her.

They were drawing whispers from bleary-eyed adults who were leaving their tents for a morning piss. The sight of a high mage and an apprentice brought a couple of men closer. The certainty that had guided Passerine up to now was gone, proving Isha had been right. He ambled behind Arushi and studied the khers who peeked out of their homes. His smile faded into a neutral expression as he followed his guide.

Arushi brought them to the central square with the murals, stopping at every possible opportunity to slow their progress. She found details to point out in the houses around them, decorations that khers had hung, sculptures they'd made in the wooden pillars holding up their shambled homes. Obviously, she was trying to buy time. From the distant expression on Passerine's features, his mind was elsewhere, searching for Tatters.

'As you can see, there isn't a collarbound around,' said Arushi, once they'd reached their destination.

Passerine didn't answer. Of course a collarbound could still be lurking in the Pit, hiding inside a house or a tent – and of course he was. Probably in Arushi's home, Isha guessed. Her fist tightened around the small shard of baina, the only barrier protecting her thoughts from intrusions.

A male iwdan crossed the square towards them, careful to step between the tents strewn on the ground. He was a broad-shouldered, tough-looking kher: Ganez. About four other men followed in his wake. Maybe they had been the ones to fetch him and tell him his sister was in trouble.

Passerine returned from wherever his mindlink had taken him. Isha squirmed as Ganez and his friends formed a semi-circle in front of them. She couldn't hold their hard gazes, the accusations they held, recognising her as someone who had shared meals with them, yet now stood beside a high mage wanting to invade their homes.

'What's your business here?' Ganez asked gruffly, belatedly adding, 'Sir.'

Passerine ignored the male kher, speaking over his head, addressing Arushi: 'I would like to check a couple of houses. I trust you will cooperate?'

Arushi and Ganez exchanged a glance.

'With all due respect, sir,' she answered, speaking through clenched teeth, 'do you have the lawmages' permission for this?'

When Passerine didn't answer immediately, Arushi saw her chance. She ploughed on, growing in confidence: 'I would need you to either be accompanied by a lawmage, or to have an official warrant from the Nest.'

Ganez added in a low, threatening rumble, 'If not, I'm afraid your visit stops here.'

Isha fidgeted. Her hands were sweaty; the baina felt slippery inside her fist. She wasn't sure what Passerine would decide, and she feared a fight. They were facing half a dozen khers, including Arushi, who although unarmed was still a trained soldier. As morning light continued to fill the Pit, more and more iwdan were leaving their tents. If there was violence, the onlookers would quickly decide whose side to pick. They wouldn't choose the mages'.

Passerine couldn't mindlink the khers. But if they laid a hand on him, the Nest would hang the ones responsible in retaliation. This stalemate only had bad outcomes.

'Thank you for your time,' Passerine said, backing down. Isha could have collapsed in relief. 'I would hate to make you late for work.'

He gestured to Isha. When she fell into step behind him, she felt Arushi's stare as if it were tangible, as if a fly had stung the nape of her neck. She followed him out of the Pit as the first few iwdan folded up their tents and the female guards left to relieve their colleagues from the night shift.

Isha hoped Passerine would drop the matter. She should have known better.

He turned to her. 'Shall we get breakfast in town?'

It sounded like an invitation, but it was an order. She was gripping her coin so hard it hurt.

'I would like to talk to you,' Passerine said.

***

'You'd better have a good explanation,' said Arushi.

Tatters sat huddled beside the chimney, kindling the fire. Most members of the household were up now. A woman Tatters didn't know was breaking up equal shares of bread for the children, which they dipped in soft goat's cheese and scoffed in seconds. Uaza was in her usual corner, grumbling that she needed warm milk. The milk was on the pot, above the burgeoning flames.

'Well…' mumbled Tatters.

Before he could finish, Yua climbed down the rope ladder from the room above. She jumped when she was halfway down and landed gracefully. Ganez was waiting beside the door, already dressed. Male iwdan had to get up early to travel to the fields surrounding the city, offering their services as hired labour. They often walked leagues from farm to farm, only to come back without work or coin at the end of the day. A couple of khers, a mix of friends and family, were standing beside Ganez. One of the older children gave the men a bag filled with bread and cheese, which Ganez flung over his shoulder.

Yua said offhandedly, 'The way you left us the other night was an insult to me, and to my family. And I hear you're already creating new trouble for my ucma.'

'Yua is right, collarbound,' said Ganez. 'If you have come to apologise, do it quickly. I have work to do.'

Yua and Ganez waited. Tatters stayed crouched beside the fire. The children stopped quarrelling to listen. The only sound was the crackling of wet wood. The room smelt of tepid milk and smoke.

If we're staying here, you need them on your side, said Lal.

Tatters got up. Although this was only a guess, from what he'd seen other khers do and from how they used their horns, Tatters

97

bent his head backwards as much as he could. He had to put one hand behind his skull to hold it. The position revealed his throat. It felt vulnerable – because Yua's horns were pointed in that direction, and there was little Tatters could do if she pushed them closer, but also because the collar was obvious in ways it wasn't when hair fell across it.

He'd seen iwdan do this as a submissive gesture, much in the same way humans bowed. Like bowing, there were gradations – the curt throwing back of the head, or the full leaning backwards version. He was doing it as far as his head would go. He hoped it sent the right message.

'I'm sorry,' he said. 'I didn't mean to offend.' Because he was standing on the opposite side of the room from Ganez, it seemed as if he was addressing this to the whole household. Maybe he was.

The silence stretched on for too long. Tatters' neck ached. It was hard to tell, from the khers' expressions, what they thought of his plea.

If they want you out, what then? asked Lal. *We try the gates? The Temple?*

Ganez grunted. 'That's enough,' he said. Tatters took a more natural position, rubbing his neck. The collar felt hot, more so than usual, making it difficult to swallow.

'You should apologise to the women. They're the ones who make decisions in the hearth.'

With those words, Ganez shouldered his bag and left the house. The kids started eating again. Uaza squinted at Tatters with wet red eyes.

'What happened?' Yua asked. Her no-nonsense tone indicated that, although the first hurdle was cleared, this wasn't over.

Arushi crossed the room, avoiding the central carpet where the food was on display, to sit down beside Tatters. He busied himself with the fire, using the poker to mess around with the twigs.

'There was a high mage looking for you,' she said. 'I lied to him. This could cost me my job.'

Tatters sensed Lal's amusement. *You silly cow. This could cost you your life.*

Don't, he begged.

If you want to hide here, fine. But you're putting everyone in danger.

I need time to think this through.

Arushi put a hand on his wrist; Lal was snuffed out like a candle.

'Look at me,' she said. 'Tell me the truth.'

Tatters met her gaze. He was aware of Yua beside them, as she stood stirring the milk for her mother, and it was clear she was listening. The fourth woman, the one he didn't know, was still tending to the children. What he said to Arushi went up to Uaza, then became communal knowledge for the rest of the household. Khers shared everything – pain and pleasure, public outrage, and secrets.

'The high mage was a tall Sunriser, wasn't he?' Might as well check.

She nodded, one hand still pressing against his forearm. 'High mage Passerine,' she said. 'You mentioned him in front of Mezyan.'

Surprised, Tatters assented. He hadn't expected Arushi to remember the name. Yua poured the milk from the pot into an earthenware jug. 'Want some?' she asked. Tatters hadn't eaten breakfast. He wasn't hungry, but this might be his last hot meal in a while – if he decided to leave the city, or if the khers decided to throw him out.

'Please,' he said.

Yua poured him a glass, while Uaza protested that she should serve her elders first. 'Surely it's guests first, mother,' argued Yua.

'Pah! He isn't a guest.' Uaza did a gesture of dismissal, swift despite her old age. 'He's family now.'

Tatters stared at the fire, cheeks burning hot, but not because of the flames. He tried not to imagine what the old kher knew of his relationship with Arushi. The idea that she might have shared Arushi's sensations... Whether it was true or not, it felt incestuous. It was bad enough to know Yua had been a part of it. Now it was as if Uaza had licked his skin and her tongue could remember the tang of salt on his shoulders.

'You're embarrassing him,' said Arushi.

'I'm inviting him into our home,' answered Uaza. When she took her cup from Yua's hands, her fingers trembled slightly. Her voice was hoarse as she pushed on it to address her daughter from the other side of the room. 'It looks like he needs a home.'

Tatters grimaced. 'Thank you for your kind offer, but I need to tell you more before I accept such generosity.'

'I agree with that,' Arushi said.

'You're too picky,' said her mother. She sipped her milk. It left a white line on her upper lip. 'No iwdan was good enough for you, and now that you've at last found someone to share your hearth with, you want to throw him out? So what if he's human? Ganez will come around.'

Arushi raised her voice. 'Seshaq, I don't care about Ganez! You have no understanding of the politics of the Nest, and the trouble this might...'

'And you have no idea of the politics of your own people!' Uaza's voice was startlingly loud. Everyone fell silent. The children buried their noses into their food. Uaza wiped her upper lip on her sleeve, squinting with leaking eyes at her milk. Her horns were near-perfect circles, with no tips to aim at foes, but she still lowered her face in Arushi's direction, like rams do before colliding. 'Be silent, tawa. After all those years, that's still all you are. You are always acting in the mages' best interest, neglecting family, lovers, friends. Neglecting your tiyayat.'

Even Tatters knew that was unfair. Arushi's mouth twitched, as if she were about to snarl.

'Very well.' She let go of Tatters' arm.

What did I miss? asked Lal.

Arushi stood up to face Uaza, keeping her back towards Tatters and the fire. The children all but cowered before her; they flattened themselves on the carpet, keeping their faces averted so she wouldn't catch their eyes, or sticking bread in their mouths and pretending to munch on it. The iwdan Tatters didn't know made the wise choice of leaving before the storm; the curtain of beads briefly shimmered as she slipped outside.

'Let's take in a runaway with no information whatsoever about what he's done or who's after him,' growled Arushi. 'After all, you are the best person to decide what is safe and what isn't, aren't you?'

Uaza's voice was hard. 'Don't forget your place.'

Arushi took a deep breath, bracing herself to say something. Uaza put down her cup, the clunk of the wood on the floor as ominous as the click of a crossbow firing.

Yua placed herself between the two of them, still holding her jug with both hands.

'If I may?' she said.

Arushi kept her chin low, but nodded. The old kher spat that it wasn't as if anyone listened to her anyway.

'It can't hurt to ask Tatters what this is all about,' said Yua, 'or what he wants to do. And it can't hurt to remind him that he has friends here.'

The three women shifted their attention to Tatters.

Time to shine, said Lal. For a moment, Tatters wondered whether it was worse to live with your family inside your flesh or inside your head. Maybe sharing sensations with her mother was as natural to Arushi as sharing a mental space with Lal was to Tatters.

But they're not your family, said Lal.

How do you know?

You're about to lie to them.

Lal wasn't wrong.

'I'm afraid I can't tell you much,' said Tatters. He held his cup of milk in his palms but didn't drink it, enjoying the way the warmth from the wooden goblet seeped into his hands. 'If I try, the collar will stop me.'

He studied their reactions to estimate how successful his lie was. It was as if everyone had suddenly remembered he was a collarbound. In the polished surface of a hanging pan, he caught a glimpse of himself. The collar shone with new light as the fire caught it, reflecting gold.

'But this is about Nest and Renegade politics, and it is...' He hesitated. Even he wasn't sure how bad the situation was yet. 'It is *very* dangerous. Of course, I'd be very grateful if you let me stay here. But there is a real risk for all of you. The mages won't take kindly to it.' *Or the Renegades, for that matter.*

Yua laughed, a crystalline noise that echoed across the room. It relaxed some of the tension: the children's shoulders loosened, Uaza cracked a smile. But Tatters clenched his drink harder. Yua didn't take anything seriously – and so she dismissed this warning like everything else.

'Is that all?' When Yua shook her head, the beads in her horns sang like bells in the wind. 'An enemy of the mages is a friend of mine. You know that, Tatters. Anyway, what is life without a bit of risk?'

Uaza picked up her milk again. 'I have already told you what I think.' She finished her cup and handed it to Yua for a refill. Smiling, Yua helped her mother to a second glass.

But then there was the person who mattered most, and she hadn't spoken yet. Arushi stood staring at him, with the hearth between them, and her emotions moved across her face with the flames. He wished he could reach out with mindlink, but even without magic, he felt close to her, as if their fingertips were touching. Even without, he could read her.

She was torn. This was about the safety of her household. She worked for the mages because no-one else in her family could feed themselves, so she served people she despised, but she had grown to understand them, and she recognised them as powerful foes. She was probably the only kher in this room who could read human emotions well enough to know Tatters was worried.

She fleshbound with him. She shared the pit at the bottom of her stomach. She shared the tension knotting the muscles of her back. And she said:

'You're welcome to stay.'

***

Passerine found an inn for travellers, crammed with Sunriser refugees of the richer kind. Clients could pay for servings of porridge that had been simmering in a pot several hours, with a bored servant beside the cauldron topping up oats and milk as required. Passerine bought breakfast – which included boiled eggs, hard bread, fruit – and requested a private room to eat in. The innkeeper unlocked a room upstairs with a small table and a bed. Passerine piled the food on the table, pulled two chairs over, and kept the key. Isha didn't want to linger on why the innkeeper thought they needed a bed.

They sat face-to-face. Isha watched the motes of dust hanging behind Passerine. He poured them each a glass of ale from the jug before cutting thick slices of bread. Too tense to eat, she tried to sip the ale.

They could hear noise through the floorboards. Chattering voices like birds at the morning chorus. Chairs being dragged across the room. Food sloshing, plates clattering, cutlery being dropped. Yet the room in which they were sitting was filled with that particular silence born of two people not speaking to each other.

Passerine picked up a boiled egg and tapped it against the table to crack it. Isha tried not to jump.

'I would rather not use force against you,' said Passerine calmly, as if they were discussing the weather. He peeled his egg. 'I could make you drop that baina, if need be.'

She had a mouthful of ale, which she forced herself to swallow. *How did this happen? How did I find myself in this situation?*

'So, what does he call himself at the moment?'

When she didn't answer, Passerine glanced up. He shook off the eggshell sticking to the tip of his fingers.

'Let's see if I can guess. Maybe he didn't even change name. Is it Milky?' He studied her. 'Tatters?'

'Yes,' she said. There seemed no point in trying to deny it.

Passerine went back to his egg, removing the eggshell, but also the white membrane that hung like skin between the egg and its shell.

'I'm glad he offered to teach you some of what he knows, because he knows a lot,' said Passerine. 'Do you know where he learnt it? Did he tell you?'

He sounded affable enough, but she wondered how much choice she had. He had made it clear she couldn't walk out of this conversation.

She shook her head. 'He didn't tell me, but I know. He was a Renegade.' *Those who love you will know you. And those who wish you harm will know you too.* She had to decide who to trust, and she had to decide now, but her thoughts were a herd of scared sheep, confused and bleating, bumping into each other as they scampered away. Could she trust the man who had saved her if he also threatened her?

She picked up a slice of bread, for want of something to do. She didn't eat it.

'You met him when you were a Renegade,' she said.

'Yes. But as you know, I left the Renegades. In part because of what they did to you.' Passerine removed the last piece of shell from his egg. Instead of eating it, he put it aside.

'To her credit, Hawk didn't want to raise you in a military encampment,' he went on. 'That was why she placed you in a foster home. The only reason she tried to take you from your foster parents, I think, is because she felt that it was time to cross the Shadowpass. Maybe she wanted you to rule the Wingshade convents while she waged war. Maybe she would have sent you all the way to the south of the Inner Sea, back home. Maybe she wanted you safe, or maybe she wanted you by her side. Who knows?'

Isha waited as Passerine bit his egg, chewed, and dabbed his lips with the napkin beside his plate.

'Do you think she'll come for me?' she asked.

'Maybe.'

The motes of dust danced, slowly spinning in the air.

Passerine sighed before correcting himself: 'Of course she will. Hawk will want you on her side of the battle.'

She couldn't help it: she touched her tattoo. *My eyas.* Memories wiped and muddled, past life in pieces. Why would any mother do this to her daughter?

'I doubt she wanted to hurt you,' Passerine said. He could read her, it seemed, even with the baina. 'It was a miscalculation. She planned on you coming without a fuss.'

Isha busied herself by tearing the bread to shreds, starting with the crust. She didn't dare use her left hand, as she had no other way to keep the baina against her skin. Passerine was dithering out of kindness for her, but the questions would circle back to Tatters. Passerine truly didn't want to hurt her; she believed that, at least. But he might care more about finding Tatters than he did about sparing her.

'Do you know what Hawk wants? Why she's doing this?' she said, hoping to delay the confrontation.

Passerine was drinking his ale; he finished his cup before answering. 'She wants to rule. She thinks she will do a better job of it. To be fair, she might. She wants the iwdan to be equal to mages, mages to rein in their power, ungifted to be treated better. It all works in theory.'

'And in practice?'

She studied his profile as he looked out of the window at the street below. 'In practice, there is a lot of blood,' he said quietly.

They were silent. She gathered the crumbs she'd made into a pile, uneaten.

'Won't she want you back?' Isha asked.

Passerine smiled at that. 'No,' he said. 'I tried to take you out of her reach. She will never forgive me for that.'

It lay unstated, but she heard the words he hadn't said. *She will never forgive me for saving you.* Isha pictured her mother, the possessive, intransigent soldier, and tried to match that image with someone wanting to build a better world. It didn't work. She couldn't bring herself to believe that Hawk would want her back out of love – what kind of love involved branding her own child with a war banner?

'I believe Tatters is a dangerous foe, but a useful ally,' said Passerine, pulling her out of her daydream. 'If we can get our hands on him, he might prove to be a great help against Sir Daegan and, when she reaches us, against Hawk.'

When he focused on her, his attention was like a spiderweb on her skin – a touch as light as silk, but somewhat sinister; slight, sticky lines.

'Now tell me where he is.'

She imagined Tatters hoarding knowledge, like monsters sit on gold and eat travellers to add their bones to the pile. She could see him in her mind's eye, scaly, with wings and many eyes, coiled around his rotting pile of shields and swords, coins and skulls. And Lal like an evil bat perched on his shoulder.

But she didn't agree with Passerine.

'You don't need to fight him for this,' she said. 'You both want the same things.'

A crack showed in his patience, a sliver of annoyance. 'What you believe you know about him is irrelevant. He is an astute liar.'

As astute as you? She was relieved the baina still hid her thoughts. But it wouldn't save her. Passerine was right. He could take it off her easily. When he spoke again, his tone indicated he was no longer negotiating. He had grown stern.

'Tell me where he is, or where he's gone by now.'

She had a feeling of losing her footing, of free falling. Her hand was cramped from holding the baina so tensely, for so long. She wasn't sure the innkeeper would come if she shouted.

'I can arrange a meeting,' she blurted out.

Isha spoke so quickly she wasn't sure he could understand the jumble of words. 'If I ask him to speak with you, on neutral ground, you can meet up without dragging the lawmages into it.' She forced herself to pause for breath, to let her brain catch up with her mouth. 'You're both trying to stop Hawk.' Which she really hoped was true. 'I'll vouch for you. He trusts me. We can do this without any violence.'

There was a pause. Although it must only have been brief, it felt long to Isha, as Passerine considered what she had said, poured himself some more ale, drank slowly. He wanted this done privately, she was nearly sure, otherwise he could have found another, more secure way of confronting Tatters. She prayed she'd guessed right.

'Very well,' he said. 'I would rather do things peacefully.'

Her relief was short-lived.

'You have one day,' Passerine said. 'I can't grant you more: Tatters is too slippery. If by tomorrow morning we haven't been able to meet up, I will do things my own way.'

Chapter Five

The day went past in a blur. Tatters was alone with Uaza most of the time, so they traded tales, listening and narrating in turn. He shared some of Mezyan's stories, and she was suitably impressed. An uaza who knew the old legends and the meaning of every tattoo, who could tattoo in turn or read the lines inked on someone's skin, was a powerful iwdan.

'But you need to know a hundred stories before you are an uaza,' she said. 'And a hundred for each god, if you want to be a great one.'

'I'm far from a hundred,' Tatters admitted.

He was restless despite the calm setting. He spent each story focused not on what was being said, but on what he could hear outside, all the while crouched more than seated, ready to bolt. If Uaza noticed this, she didn't comment. She was content talking as she waited for her sons and daughters to return. Grandchildren moved in and out of the house, coming inside to nap on the rugs, or listen to a tale, or watch the collarbound, before going to play outside again.

Arushi was home first. It was only late afternoon; she must have left the guard tower early. She entered the room in a huff, dumping her leather jacket in one corner. Hands on her hips, without removing her belt or her shoes, she turned to Tatters.

'Shall we talk?' she asked.

Tatters warily rose to his feet. He hadn't been looking forward to this conversation.

As Arushi pulled back the curtain for him, Uaza said, 'Why do you need to leave? Talk here.'

When Arushi shook her head, her mother frowned.

'What does it change?'

'Humans,' said Arushi. She managed to make it sound like an insult. 'They like their secrets.'

Outside, the low sun was too bright for Tatters' eyes, which had got used to the shade inside the house. He put a hand over them and squinted down the road. His heartbeat quickened, even though he couldn't see anyone wearing a robe, nor sense a hostile mind.

Would you be able to feel a mage in the heart of the Pit, even if there was one? said Lal.

'Are you all right?' Arushi asked.

Tatters nodded. 'Can we find somewhere...' He wondered how to put it. Somewhere less exposed. But Arushi had sounded sick of humans and their habit of secrecy.

She waved his concerns away. 'I get it. Come on.'

They made their way towards the centre of the Pit. Tatters hadn't felt this nervous in years. He kept glancing over his shoulder, half-expecting Passerine to be there. They reached the central square, where the mural towered above them. Iwdan were everywhere, calling from one household to another to borrow food and spices, shooing the children out of their way. There were mostly women, talking and laughing, sitting in the streets where the men would soon be, below trees and on porches, enjoying the last rays of sunlight and the chance to play a final game before the evening meal.

At one end of the mural, which was painted directly against the city walls, stood a metal gate that Arushi pushed open. It led to a courtyard, still encircled by high walls, but unkempt and overgrown. Wooden statues were placed at regular intervals. With a shiver, Tatters guessed what this was. The kher cemetery.

The wooden statues represented horns and marked the graves. Each piece was a work of art, made to copy the annulations and curve of the dead kher's horns, varnished to stand the test of time. Tatters trod uneasily. He didn't like the idea of rotting bodies beneath his feet. As far as he was concerned, the proper place for the dead was over the Edge.

Arushi knelt, placing one hand on the ground. Breathing deeply, she took a handful of dirt and looked at it, as if she could find what she wanted to say in the soil. She threw the earth away as she stood up again.

'No-one will bother us here, or eavesdrop, if that's what you're so worried about,' she said.

Tatters gave her a weak smile. Arushi wandered around the planted horns, but she didn't seem to share his disquiet. He looked at the lacquered wood, which loving hands had patiently carved. Despite the care put into them, the oldest statues were marked with woodworm, and some had the tips broken off.

'Is there anything I should do?' he asked.

He meant: *to honour your dead.* But Arushi placed her fists on her hips and said:

'Now you mention it, care to explain why you left me for no reason, then came back with a high mage after you?'

We haven't got time for this, said Lal.

Tatters wondered if Arushi could have chosen a worse place. Khers might share everything, but sex and death weren't topics he was comfortable mixing.

'Can we talk about that here?' he asked. 'Wouldn't it be disrespectful?'

Arushi snorted through her nose. 'What's disrespectful is the way you're treating me. You won't even talk to my family, even though they took you in.' Tatters couldn't disagree. He took a step forward, not sure what he wanted to do, hug her maybe, touch her arm at least. But she took a step back, swiftly. 'I'm not doing this alone,' she said. 'If you won't talk in front of my elders, then you can talk in front of my ancestors.'

Tatters tried not to imagine the flesh disintegrating, the maggots, the bones covered in earth. It was somehow more disturbing to think that Arushi had come here not to be alone. It made him more conscious of what he was standing on.

We have more serious problems than this, said Lal.

'It's difficult to explain,' said Tatters.

Arushi didn't seem fazed. 'Take your time.' She went to lean on the wall of the cemetery. It not only put distance between them, but also a small forest of blackened horns, twisting out of the ground like hands of drowning men trying to reach out for air.

'I left the other day because…'

Because sharing sex with your siblings is gross, said Lal.

Can you let me do this? It's hard enough without you butting in.

You shouldn't be doing this in the first place, grumbled Lal.

'Because?' Arushi repeated.

'Because I wasn't expecting Yua and her lovers to be involved,' he said. 'It was a shock.'

He studied her face for a glimpse of understanding, but he didn't find any. She frowned. 'That doesn't explain why you left.'

Ah, the pleasure of interspecies relationships, said Lal. *Are you done yet?*

He wasn't. He wanted to close the gap between him and Arushi, but it didn't feel right to walk over the graves. Gingerly, he inched forward, trying not to put weight in his toes, giving the horns a wide berth.

'You're underestimating how much of a shock, I think,' he said.

'And you're underestimating how much of an insult it was to leave,' she snapped.

'Maybe.' The sun was setting behind Arushi, which meant it was difficult to make her out. Everything glowed, bathed in red light. 'Can we agree that, as a human I was shocked, and that as an iwdan you were insulted, but that neither of us wanted to do that to the other?'

When he took another step forward, she didn't back away. He could see the tense set of her shoulders through her shirt.

'Thank you for giving me shelter today,' he said softly. Uaza was right. He needed a home. He hadn't had one in years.

Her shoulders sagged as they relaxed. 'There's being angry with you, and there's letting you get arrested,' Arushi said. 'Contrary to what most mages think, I'm not a monster.'

He leant next to her, against the wall. They weren't touching. Shadows streaked the courtyard, each pair of horns drawn twice over, once growing out of the ground and once as a shadow, creating a chequered pattern.

'I might need to go into hiding tonight,' he said. He longed to embrace her, but knew it would be unwelcome. 'I wouldn't want to leave on a misunderstanding.'

'The lawmages haven't put a price on your head,' she said.

That was good news. Passerine was acting alone. Still, watching the graves made him wonder whether his enemies would give him the decency of a flight over the Edge, or whether they'd let his body decay beneath the ground.

Passerine wouldn't kill you, said Lal. *He'll use you, which is worse. What do we do now?*

Run, said Lal. *Hide. Pick fights we're sure to win.*

'I don't want to leave.' As he said it, he realised it was a mistake. Saying it made it worse. He shouldn't give anyone – not even himself – a choice. He should go while he still had the chance. Lie low for a couple of months. Return when he was certain his trail had grown cold. Brew a plan in the meantime.

He hoped Arushi would ask him to stay, but she kept her gaze fixed ahead of her, not meeting his eyes. When she spoke, her voice was stern.

'What about Isha?'

'I'm torn,' he admitted. 'She might be Passerine's pawn.' The high mage had come to the Coop straight after their fight, after all. 'If so, it's getting too much for me to handle.'

When Arushi turned to him at last, he didn't find what he had yearned for in her features. She was severe, guarded. She was still beautiful, of course, but distant. He could see the lines of her tattoo through the linen of her shirt, climbing up her collarbone, and he could imagine the rest, snaking down her chest to her hips.

'Today Isha went out of her way to keep us safe. To keep you safe, actually.'

How can you be sure it wasn't a trick? Lal asked.

'Are you certain it wasn't some complicated ploy?' he said out loud, echoing Lal's concerns.

'When I saw her, Isha looked frightened. And lonely. And lost,' said Arushi. 'She took a risk going against her master.'

He sensed that Lal was doubtful. But Tatters couldn't challenge Arushi's assertive tone. She watched his face, searching for something there, in the same way he had searched for something in hers.

What if we've got it wrong? he asked Lal. *What if Isha isn't Hawk's ally, but her victim? She doesn't wear her tattoo with pride.*

She always reacts to the idea of branding in mindlink. Maybe Passerine didn't bring her here of her own free will. Maybe she is under his orders.

'I don't know about humans,' Arushi went on. 'But in an iwdan hearth, it isn't the children's role to protect the adults.' Her eyes were as black as the rising night. 'Everyone has a duty in life, and you should think about yours.'

He only noticed he'd been cold when her warm fingers curled around his. Although he should be used to this, although he knew khers used touch more than humans, still he couldn't help the way his heart leapt when she squeezed his hand.

Something like fear coiled around him as he realised how much it mattered, this small thing, this hand holding his. He hadn't cared this much in a long time.

'You need to speak to Isha,' Arushi said. 'Tell her the truth, even if you won't tell me.'

'It would be a risk.' Tatters heard the uncertainty creeping into his voice.

'Isha took a risk too,' Arushi answered curtly. Her touch was firm, like that of a friend pulling him out of the water to solid ground.

He should break contact, so he could hear Lal's thoughts on this, but he couldn't bring himself to.

'I'm not sure I can trust her,' he said.

'Trust is a gift. You can never be sure.'

He wanted to believe her. Lal would hate this, would call it gambling with their safety. They had trusted before. It hadn't ended well.

But maybe, at last, it was time to trust again.

***

You are a hard-headed fool, and you will die a hard-headed fool.

Tatters didn't answer, in part because he couldn't help but agree with Lal. He should have left town at dusk, during the change of guards, while no-one was watching the gates closely. He should have been on the road by now, on a hired mule, making his way along the Edge towards an isolated village.

But Arushi had sounded so sure. He was a teacher, after all. He'd been a guide, helping Isha map the city, the Temple, the Pit. He couldn't leave her without a word of explanation.

Only you can. And you should, said Lal. *You owe her nothing.* She was like an insect buzzing inside his skull, stinging the underside of his head. *You certainly don't owe her your life.*

Tatters focused on the paved road under the soles of his shoes, on the irregular flagstones pressing against his toes. *If you live only for yourself, there is no point in living.*

It was final. Lal yielded at last.

It was strange to hear the tavern before he saw it: a shriek of laughter, the roll of voices flowing like the tide, regularly breaking and picking up again. From outside, the thatched roof glowed auburn in the moonlight and the rickety sign that hung over the Coop, depicting a couple of crudely drawn hens, creaked in the wind, its paint flaking.

A refugee was dozing opposite the entrance, a nest of covers around him. Only his dusty feet poked out. Above him, someone had scratched in the stone 'Renegades are Rebirth'. The letters were drawn with a flourish, and the artist had spent some time decorating their contours with reddish clay. Because it couldn't hurt to be cautious, Tatters checked the refugee's mind for a trap. The man was sleeping soundly.

The door of the tavern was open, so Tatters stepped inside.

It was like entering a familiar dream; he recognised the scents, the heat, the faces, the grain of the tables. A few apprentices noticed him, some waving, others greeting him loudly from their end of the room. He tried to smile to everyone.

He caught the innkeeper's eye from across the tavern. Immediately, the man put away the drink he was serving and wiped his hands on his stained apron. While the innkeeper was making his way towards him, Tatters glanced across the room. He found Isha where he normally sat, in his booth, beside Kilian, Caitlin and the usual crew. Isha seemed relieved to see him; the others seemed surprised.

He gestured for her to stay where she was, but still she pushed past the person seated beside her in the booth. He reached her as the innkeeper reached him, and they found themselves standing together in the narrow space between the tables. Isha tried to put down her cup of ale but couldn't find a place to do so.

'May you grow tall,' Tatters said.

Isha echoed his greeting, but the innkeeper didn't.

'You've got a nerve, coming back after this morning,' he said, shoving his chin towards Tatters.

'He won't look here twice.'

A group of apprentices joined them for a closer look. Some wanted to eavesdrop on the conversation and some, Tatters hoped, genuinely wanted to know where he had been.

The innkeeper thrust his thumb towards Isha. 'He'll be here soon enough, if she tells him.'

In his mind, Lal swore. A sense of foreboding, which he'd been trying to ignore, rose inside Tatters. As the apprentices crowded closer, closing in on him, he felt as if a noose was being pulled tighter.

'She brought him here the first time, didn't she?' said the innkeeper. Isha had grown pale.

'Are we talking about Sir Passerine?' Kilian asked, too eagerly for Tatters' taste.

'Is it him you were running from?' added Caitlin, her intelligent eyes focusing on him.

It was a trap, hissed Lal, *and Arushi fell for it. Get out of here!*

Tatters forced himself to clamp down on the panic trying to take hold. He ignored Lal.

'I know Isha is his apprentice.' He kept his tone soothing, but he wasn't sure whether he was trying to convince the innkeeper or himself. 'I still think we can work this out.'

The apprentices were listening, their interest sparked.

'Yes, that's exactly what I was hoping,' answered Isha. She had pleading eyes, but her expression was obscured by the tattoo, making it difficult to untangle truth from lies. 'If we just take the time to talk it through—'

Tatters never heard the end of her sentence, because at that moment, several mages entered the tavern behind him. Their boots, shod with metal like horses, clanged on the worn floor. He perceived they were mages instantly; their presence was as tangible as a stench.

He turned to face them. Undyed belts glowed white against the fabric of their robes. Lawmages. Five of them. They were between him and the door.

The room went still. Without actually moving, the apprentices leant away from Tatters as if he had the rot of leprosy on him. The innkeeper blanched, his eyes darting from side to side before concluding, like Tatters, that the only way out was past the lawmages.

The Coop needs a back door, said Lal.

I'll be sure to point it out to our landlord, said Tatters. *If we survive.*

Alternatively, if he could make it to the counter and up the steps, he could maybe jump out of the attic's window. Again. The throng of apprentices obstructed that direction. They would slow

him down at best; at worst, they would become the lawmages'
tools in arresting him.

A small lawmage, smaller than Tatters, with a thin wiry neck
and jutting bones, was the one who spoke:

'Are you the collarbound they call Tatters?'

No, wrong man, answered Lal. *Nice try, better luck next time.*

Beside this emaciated figure was another lawmage, of squarer
build, with a face damaged by smallpox, and beautiful, lush hair
the colour of ripe wheat. Of course.

'Ah, if it isn't my good friend Goldie,' Tatters said.

'I told you to keep away from the Nest, Sunriser.' Goldie was
smiling, showing his yellow teeth. He was wearing kher horn,
so his mind was sealed off. 'But now we have you.'

Beside him, Tatters heard Isha's sharp intake of breath.
Absurdly, she squared her shoulders, moving closer rather than
further away, as if to help.

The question is who she's going to help, said Lal.

Tatters sensed the minds around him tense as they prepared
to pounce, like one can see the lines of muscle in a crouched cat.
There had been a time when he could fight five mages at once.
He wondered if he still could.

'There is more than one collarbound in this city,' he said,
trying to stall for time. 'And more interesting ones than me.
Apparently, there's even a bound lightborn.'

'I asked you a question,' said the head lawmage. His tone was
sharp. Behind him, his men and women spread out, unfolding
like a fan, drawing a half-circle; they were physically blocking
the space inside the tavern, as well as mentally. Goldie casually
crossed the room, giving Tatters a wide enough berth to not be
threatening, not yet. But he placed himself close to the staircase,
cutting off that retreat. The apprentices stuck close to the walls.

The thin lawmage folded his hands in front of his chest, his elbows sticking out; he was all bones and taut skin. 'If you do not answer, I will assume you are the person we are looking for, and that you are resisting arrest.'

'It's him,' snarled Goldie. 'All his chatter won't save him.'

'Don't you have to accuse me of something first?' said Tatters. He glanced at the kher horn around the innkeeper's arm. It was tightly screwed around his wrist, which meant it would be too slow to twist it off him.

Your name.

The two words split the air – the lawmage's lips squeezed shut, twitching. The apprentices backed away further, including Kilian, who was pulling Isha by the elbow so she wouldn't stay near the centre of attention. Tatters briefly caught her eye; she looked grief-stricken. If it was only acting, then she was an excellent liar.

He did an exaggerated bow. 'I am Tatters. May you grow tall.' He straightened. The lawmages' expressions didn't change. No smile broke their severe features. Goldie, by contrast, was smirking.

The windows? asked Lal. Tatters checked, but there was a lawmage standing before the glass. Plus, they were too small to jump through, and crawling might mean getting caught in the frame.

The head lawmage picked his words and spoke them with distaste, as if they were crawling insects that he held in his mouth reluctantly: 'You are accused of spying for the Sunriser outlaws called the Renegades, practising illegal mindbrawl, depraving apprentices, illegal gambling and assault on an ordained mage.'

He forgot petty theft and horn-humping, said Lal. *This is Isha's doing.*

If it is, where is Passerine?

'You are required by law to follow us back to the Nest,' said the head lawmage. In the tavern's light, his balding head had brown patches, like sweat stains on old cloth.

'One way or another,' added Goldie.

Running. Lal's cold hand. Bruises. Branches whipping his face. Lacunants with holes in their minds still seeping pus like eyes burst open with a knife. Tatters shifted his weight into his heels, bracing himself.

As often with mindlink, it happened fast.

The lawmages sensed his change in posture. Before he had closed down his mind, they attacked.

Images and sensations and smells hit him. He focused on his body, on the warmth of the tavern, and closed the gap between him and the closest lawmage. The apprentices scrambled out of the way with shouts of surprise. They hadn't expected him to use force. Mages didn't move when they brawled.

Their loss, growled Lal.

As Tatters shoved people aside, four lawmages stood dumb – only Goldie swore and waded through the crowd towards him. Goldie would be the fighter, then, the only lawmage able to use his fists, which was why he was wearing kher horn. The horn would protect him from mindlink, but it would also be impossible for him to use his gift.

Tatters reached one lawmage and smashed his elbow into the man's stomach. When he folded over with a gasp, Tatters used his weight to push him over. The man rolled on a table, falling heavily off the other side, his head hitting the floorboards with a loud thud. Apprentices scattered. Tatters swung to face the next lawmage as their mindlink increased in violence. Two women tried to overwhelm him mentally, never moving an inch. Visions flashed before his eyes; he gritted his teeth. The head lawmage stumbled back with something unexpected on his face: fear.

He was too close, and his old bones wouldn't withstand one good punch.

Tatters used Hawk's technique, a simple, effective little trick. *This isn't real.* He bit the inside of his mouth until he tasted blood. *This isn't real.* He fleshbound with Arushi, although she was too far away to feel anything, relying on the kher magic to dull the lawmages' power. *This isn't real.* It had worked with Ninian; it could work now. If you convinced your mind it couldn't bleed, it wouldn't. Mindlink was all about lying. And Hawk had discovered you could lie to yourself. *This isn't real.*

One down, four to go, said Lal. Two women, Goldie – who was drawing closer – and the head lawmage.

Apprentices were clogging the way, so Tatters jumped on a long wooden table and ran towards the head lawmage. One woman broke formation. Lawmages weren't used to mindlinking and fighting; their concentration snapped when he charged them. There was a mad dash for the door as everyone tried to get out. The head lawmage was stuck, the apprentices blocking the exit. For a wild moment, as he leapt off the table to reach him, Tatters thought he might win this fight.

The woman who hadn't lost her nerve threw herself in front of him. Maybe she was hoping to become a fighter, like Goldie. Tatters punched her. He was out of shape, but not so out of shape that she could fend off his hits. The first swing should have landed on her side, but she blocked it. The second one caught her nose. Blood ran down her face. The apprentices shrieked at the smell and sight of it.

Three left, Lal said.

He hadn't trained properly in ages, so his balance between physical and mental combat was weaker. As he was wrestling the woman out of the way, the head lawmage mindlinked with such brutality that Tatters stopped, fists lifted, in the middle of his struggle.

He saw a slave being beaten. A dog with a muzzle. He felt leather around his mouth, shackling down his teeth. A silhouette hanging from a tree, but around their neck, in place of rope, was the red cloth of the Renegades' flag.

I'm on it, said Lal.

She thunderbolted out of his mind. There was little to see: she left no trace, not even a shimmer in the air. Still, it was painful, like splitting bone apart. She flung herself against the head lawmage, turning the images he had crafted upside-down, pulling the characters inside out, leaving lumps of flesh and bleeding sinew.

The remaining woman, the one who wasn't picking herself off the floor, joined her mind to her leader's, shielding him from Lal's onslaught. Behind them, Goldie was closing in, swearing colourfully at the apprentices barring his way.

I can't move while you're doing that, Tatters warned. It was hard enough to keep the images from overwhelming him, let alone fight back.

His hands were shaking; his joints hurt. Blood pooled inside his mouth. He couldn't keep this up.

You only need to get to the door, said Lal. *Then we're clear.*

He took a step, focusing fiercely, trying to walk with his spirit cleaved in half. The door was only a couple of feet away. Once he was past the threshold, Lal would return, and he could run.

Then Goldie caught up with him.

The lawmage's blow struck the nape of his neck, hard enough to send Tatters staggering forwards. Lal was forced to drop her offensive. Goldie grabbed Tatters' shoulder, spinning him around. As Tatters lifted his arms to parry the inevitable hit to his face, the two remaining lawmages attacked.

Their mindbrawl caught him from an unexpected direction –
an image of his childhood, his mother stroking the hair out of
his eyes. She was disappointed, but she loved him. She kissed
his forehead and asked him to be good from now on.

He wanted to say, 'I'm sorry for what I did to Lal.' Before he
could, his mother whispered, 'I know.'

It's not real!

Lal's call brought him to his senses. He was dizzy. Maybe
Goldie had landed a couple of punches while he was mindrambling. Even inside the tavern, the nightmare continued – the
walls twisted, the floorboards lifted and sank like waves. He
could see his sister Milinda with Isha's tattoo on her face, and
a hunchback Passerine climbing down the chimney. Pieces of
himself were being torn apart. Like hounds shred a fox, the
lawmages were clamping down on parts of him and ripping
them off. He couldn't remember the name of his mother. He
couldn't remember the colour of the sun when it sets. He could
see a kher guard who wore a green shawl, and he didn't know
who she was, or why she was important.

Lal held him together out of sheer strength of will. *You are
my brother. You are real. They aren't.*

We have to surrender. The thought floated to the surface like
wood during a wreckage. *We have to surrender now. They're
winning.*

He remembered the last time this had happened. The sense
of the sky opening above him. The stars, the stars, so many stars
above his head. Past and present and potential futures crashed
together. There was a time when he could have shaken off five
opponents – but he was older now. He had been shackled since.

Tatters surrendered.

* * *

It stopped as abruptly as it had started; Isha's teeth still ached. Tatters was standing, swaying on his feet, as blood dripped from the corner of his mouth. His eyes were glazed over. Two of the lawmages stood with their eyes closed, while the third had slumped against a table leg. The one Tatters had called Goldie was still holding him. The last one took a handkerchief to wipe the blood from her nose and beamed at the gathered apprentices, albeit shakily. When she clapped her hands together, the sound was like a slap.

'Please keep your distances inside and outside the criminal's mind.' Her voice was muffled by the blood clogging up her nose.

'Or I'll be the one dealing with you,' Goldie added gruffly.

The lawmage crouched beside her collapsed friend. With short, efficient gestures, she fussed over him, helping him sit down on a chair, asking the innkeeper for something to drink.

'And bring me your permit for that kher horn,' she added. She was polite and brittle. The innkeeper ran to serve her.

Isha pulled her sleeves over her hands to hide that they were shaking. Passerine had lied to her. He had sent the lawmages in to capture Tatters. She breathed hard so she wouldn't throw up.

'Is he a lacunant?' asked Kilian.

Caitlin shook her head. She looked less surprised than the others.

'He managed to surrender,' said Caitlin. 'Not a lot of people can do that *after* the lawmages strike.'

Because it means fending off the attacks long enough to settle your mind. Isha observed the wounded lawmage. Her handkerchief was scarlet as she pressed it against her face. The friend she was tending to wouldn't speak, and hardly drank the ale being pushed past his lips. They were five against one, but as far as Isha could tell, Tatters had hurt them more than they had hurt him.

Some of the apprentices had closed their eyes, their faces set in concentration. Isha realised they were mindlinking.

'Shall we have a look?' said Kilian. Excitement flushed his cheeks.

'I don't know,' said Isha. 'It feels wrong...'

She watched as the woman lawmage asked the innkeeper for hot water, towels, some bread dipped in milk. She unknotted a pouch of salts from her belt and brought it to her friend's nose.

Isha caught Caitlin glancing in the same direction. Their eyes met.

'He is dangerous,' said Caitlin. It was the way she said it, the defensiveness in her voice.

'You did this?' hissed Isha. *Tatters is going to think it's me who betrayed him! And Passerine is going to be livid.* She wasn't sure the situation could be any worse.

Caitlin gave her a cool stare. Her eyes were the colour of clay along a riverbed, sucking at people's shoes as they walked across it.

'I told them what I'd seen, that's all. You should have done the same.'

Kilian waited, his head cocked to one side, blond hair brushing against his forehead. When it was clear neither of the girls were going to explain anything to him, he shrugged.

'I'm going to have a look,' he said.

His graceful features closed into a frown. Unsure whether this would help, at a loss what else she could do, Isha followed him. She heard her body gasp when she reached Tatters' settled mind.

It was a library, a maze of high shelves with book upon book stacked in neat rows. Some of the books were worn leather as high as a giant's manuscript; some were made with green and blue binding; some had padlocks across them. At the centre, there was a large wooden table and a few chairs.

The head lawmage was seated there, a few manuscripts open before him. Isha could glimpse engravings and pictures, cursive writing, a loose sheaf of vellum with verses written down its side. An orange light, like the sun at dusk, bathed the room. There was no need for candles.

The other lawmage was guarding Tatters' mind, preventing the apprentices from opening any of the volumes – not that any had dared. Where the library ended, there were no walls nor ceiling, only darkness: black ground black skies black mist. It resembled Passerine's settled mind in its bleakness.

Tatters was nowhere to be seen because he was everywhere. His thoughts and experiences and memories were consigned here, in no specific order, on the shelves. Isha had never seen an undefended mind, which offered up everything it held for someone else to see. It was exhilarating – so much power, so much knowledge, complete control of another human at her fingertips – and at the same time she was afraid, disgusted, as if she were seeing a half-dissected body, the bones and nerves and veins bulging as the skin was peeled off.

Kilian's smile had worn off. 'It's very strange,' he whispered. His words echoed in the silence. With a shiver, Isha realised that everything they said or did could be perceived by Tatters. A few apprentices were milling across the space, reading the covers and titles, keeping their hands to themselves.

Kilian and Isha walked side-by-side. The library was smaller than it had appeared at first; a few modest rows, a central space. As they went past the books, Isha tried to read what was written on their spines. Most of them didn't have a title, but some had gold lettering against their thick binding.

At one end of the library stood a circular pedestal. It was carved out of white stone, with a gold rim of intricate patterns. Its size and shape reminded Isha of a bird bath. On top were several old parchments, rolled and bound together with ribbons. When Isha moved closer, she noticed the glass encasement above the pedestal, which prevented curious minds from prying.

A lawmage was stationed beside it. She tapped the glass with her fingers, but it wouldn't yield. When she placed her hand against the glass, the rim of gold shone brighter. The lawmage pushed against the glass, and the gold increased its light and heat, until even Isha could feel its power pulsing towards her. The lawmage removed her hand. The glow dulled and died.

'Leave it,' said the head lawmage from his table. 'It is not our place to meddle with the collar.'

Kilian and Isha glanced at each other. He mouthed the word 'collar?' to her. She pointed to the gold, not unlike a coronet, which circled the top of the pedestal. This was a part of Tatters' mind which no-one could access – giants' magic shielded it from the lawmages, and maybe even from Tatters himself.

Kilian seemed satisfied with their brief peek and was ready to return to the tavern. But Isha wasn't. Where was Lal? If she was an independent entity, distinct from Tatters, she should manifest in the library somehow.

'Don't you think Lal should be there?' asked Isha.

'Lal?' repeated Kilian.

Isha cursed herself. 'Tatters' double. The little gi— child.'

Kilian shook his head. In mindlink, his movements were more controlled, and his hair moved as if under the effect of a breeze, elegantly framing his face.

'Believe me, it must be hard enough surrendering,' he said. 'I doubt he's got time to create a double.'

But that was the point – she wasn't a double. It should be hard to hide her from prying lawmages. And Lal wasn't under a ban from the collar, otherwise Isha wouldn't have been able to talk about her with Tatters. If she wasn't on the pedestal of gold, and if she wasn't in the library, where was she?

The more Isha studied the settled mind, the more suspicious it became. Where was the damage she had sensed within Tatters, the fear, even Passerine? Where was the long rift of regret and grief which should be running down this mental space? Where was his little sister, who had found a corner inside him where she could live, long after she should have joined her ancestors over the Edge?

'I think something's missing,' said Isha.

Kilian shrugged. 'Tatters is missing. That's because the books are him.'

Isha stared at the formless mist which limited the library. 'I'm going to go explore.'

Kilian followed with an indulgent sigh, the one adults use to humour an impatient child. They stepped outside of the library and into the shapeless night beyond. Isha advanced with her back to the library, straining her mind's eye. Everything was flat. Everything was even. The sky and the ground were the same polished black.

'We won't find anything here,' said Kilian. His voice was muffled by the mist, in the same way snow swallows sound.

Isha pushed forward, Kilian still behind her. She wouldn't have admitted it, but his presence reassured her. The emptiness was eerie. This was what a dead mind must feel like – blank. Absence where there should be presence. This space was like the unseeing eye of a corpse, in that it felt as if it should glimmer, but it didn't.

Until it did.

A light flickered in front of them. Her heart beat harder while she hurried forward, tugging Kilian by the wrist. 'Look!'

As they came closer, the light grew stronger, and they started to make out shapes – people, walls, books on high wooden shelves. It was the library. They had come back to their starting point.

'It's a circle,' said Kilian, obviously relieved. 'I guess wherever you go, you find yourself back inside the library.'

Isha wasn't going to drop the matter so easily. 'I'm trying again,' she said.

'If the lawmages didn't find anything, you won't,' said Kilian.

He was right. But they didn't know there was something more to find.

'You can wait for me here, if you want.'

She hoped he would insist, but he nodded. 'All right.'

She turned her back to Kilian and the library. She stared into the black mist. With a deep breath, she waded inside it.

The same phenomenon happened several times. Whichever direction she left the library from, she found herself back where she had started. It was convincing, as if Tatters didn't have a closed mind, but one which slowly slipped into unconsciousness. You could step up and down the gradients to and from self-awareness.

Isha knew there was more to him than this. The fourth time she left the library, she waited until the light it shed was as big as a candle. She kept the light on her right as she explored. She made sure she didn't lose sight of the glimmer, but stayed alongside it. That way, she knew she wasn't walking towards it. She wasn't walking away from it, either. She was trying to find the centre of the circle.

The night of Tatters' mind grew colder, until Isha found herself shivering. She rubbed her arms. The library was still on her right, but the texture of the darkness had changed. It pricked her with pins of cold. Frost climbed across her skin, drawing its fern-like patterns against her flesh.

If the mind was growing hostile, it meant she was nearing something important. She clenched her jaw to stop her teeth from chattering and ploughed on.

The more she moved forward, the more tempting the warmth of the tavern, the idea of stepping out of mindlink into the smells of brew and broth. She could escape this empty world for one with cosy seats, hot food, colour. The light of the library kept appearing in front of her, and she had to turn again and again to avoid returning towards it. Her head was spinning as if someone had forced her to go round and round on the spot, a blindfold over her face.

And then she found them.

Lal was standing with her arms and legs spread apart. Tendrils of smoke coiled underneath her nails. Her hair fanned out around her, floating, its bright red turning dull brown then black, before spreading around her. The hair and smoke drifted slightly, like foam at the surface of a lake. Where it rippled and shimmered, Isha saw silhouettes behind it, hidden by the thick material. It was as if a curtain of black silk had been pulled across Tatters' mind – what was on the other side was barely visible, outlines of projected shadows.

Isha tried to understand the technical aspect of such a mind-link trick. Did you have to convince yourself you didn't exist? Or you repressed aspects of your personality, pushing them into dreams, unconsciousness, ingrained fears and reactions? Even if you pulled off such a trick, how would you ever find yourself again? How would you know when you were complete, if the magic consisted in forgetting there were shards of your soul missing?

Maybe this was when having several names helped. You gave the lawmages Tatters the slave, while the real you, the person linked to your true name, was elsewhere. Maybe it was similar to what she had done against the Renegades, suppressing her eyas self. But that had nearly destroyed her.

Lal opened her eyes. Isha saw the tension in her face. For the first time, she tasted fear inside her mouth. She had never seen the child look so forlorn, so frightened. Behind Lal, she guessed at a shape, taller than his sister, nearly invisible behind the barrier of her willpower. He too was afraid.

'What are you doing here?' Lal asked. Before Isha could answer, Lal blanched. She buckled under an invisible weight; her knees faltered. 'Leave us! You are attracting their attention!'

Isha looked at the ghost of the child.

This is when you know whether you are Tatters' friend.

The thought caught her off-guard. If she told the lawmages, this would be the end of his secrets. She watched Lal, her slim jaw screwed shut, the veins in her eyes strained red.

She returned to the library. When she reached the rows of volumes, she felt shaken. She wondered if she was the only one to notice that the books were see-through, that their words only served to hide what was written between the lines.

'So?' asked Kilian.

He was standing beside the pedestal, studying it with interest. The lawmages would assume any information they couldn't find was contained inside the collar, which meant Tatters could hide most of his self from them.

'There was nothing,' she found herself saying. 'It's a circle.'

'I told you so.' Kilian lost interest in the pedestal. 'Shall we leave him in peace?'

Isha nodded. She blinked, forcing herself away from Tatters' mind.

Inside the tavern, her mouth was thick with spit. There was gunk in her eyes which she rubbed clean. The innkeeper was wan and obedient. The wounded lawmage was recovering, as his friend placed damp bread between his lips. Goldie was keeping Tatters in an iron grip. The Coop didn't give out warmth and safety anymore. The crude items, the stink of cheap beer, the young faces covered in acne – everything seemed smaller, meaner. Isha wondered whether Kilian felt the same. The tavern was a shell she had outgrown.

The apprentices left Tatters' mind. As they recovered their footing in the real world, some of them left, while others stayed to watch the end of the show. Caitlin was nowhere to be seen. A thick silence smothered the tavern, like curdled milk.

At last, the head lawmage, with marks of old age across his skin, unhooked a pair of manacles from his belt. They were black. It took Isha some time to realise it was because they were carved out of kher horn. They were too small for Tatters' arms, and would cut into his skin. He snapped them around the collarbound's wrists anyway, locking them with a thin metal key.

No-one spoke. Isha could perceive the lawmages discussing something through mindlink, but their messages were subtle enough that she couldn't hear their content.

When Tatters moved, it came as a shock – he had been as still as the dead. He wiped the blood that had trickled down his chin. He struck her as old, with lines down his mouth and brow that hadn't been there before. His eyelids were bruised. When he tried to rub them, the short chain that leashed him to Goldie didn't allow him to lift his hands. He let them fall back before him, held together as if in prayer.

'Our work is done,' said the head lawmage. The innkeeper bowed, thanking him profusely. The lawmages gathered around their leader, forming the same threatening semi-circle as when they had entered.

When they were about to leave, Tatters turned to stare at Isha. She stood, tongue-tied, trying to read his expression. He gave her no sign – no smile, nod, or word. She wondered if he knew she hadn't given him up, if he understood she hadn't wanted this to happen, if he was furious with her.

A lawmage tugged at his bonds and he – at last, but too late – turned away.

Chapter Six

Tatters picked at the horn shackles around his wrists, letting the sound of his nails scratching against the keratin wash over him. He had never been bound with kher horn before. It cut off Lal. They had put him in a small individual cell, with a slim slit of light close to the ceiling, where the top of the cell met the Nest's courtyard. It was too thin an opening for his fingers, blocked with earth and weeds. The sickly light was green.

He tried to forget he was cold. Rats were scuffling about, mangy creatures that came too close, even when he stamped his feet to fend them off. The oak door closing off his cell also enclosed the smells of sweat, urine and fear that had stewed down here. His hands were bound close together, making them difficult to use. The lawmages had also taken away his belt and his shoes, so his tunic hung loose around him, letting the damp seep into his bones.

He hadn't slept. Instead, he'd listened to life running its course in the courtyard. He was cut off from the other prisoners, but he could hear the daily activity of the Nest through the ceiling. When the guards came in, it was only because he was seated against the door that he heard the echo of their boots down the stone corridor.

As they neared his cell, Tatters struggled to his feet without the help of his hands. It was Goldie who opened the door, holding a torch. The damaged, pockmarked face grinned; his hair shone gold in the firelight. Behind him, there was a lawmage of higher rank, young despite the bone cane tucked under his arm, breathing through a silk handkerchief pressed against his nose.

The richer lawmage took a step forward to study Tatters. There was a coldness in his eyes, something reptilian, the kind of man who didn't feel warmth unless it was given to him by someone else.

The lawmage removed his handkerchief.

'Do you know who I am?' he asked.

Tatters shook his head. 'I don't have the honour.'

The man smiled. He was what mages aspired to be: young and already successful, square-jawed and masculine, tall, lean – without too many muscles, to show he was a man of the mind, not the flesh. A young lion in a world of wolves.

'Sir Leofric. I am in charge of these prisons.' He pressed his handkerchief against his nose once more and inhaled deeply, before tucking it inside his belt. 'And it takes an exceptional prisoner to bring me down here.' He motioned towards Goldie. 'Normally Varun takes care of things.'

Sir Leofric. Tatters knew the name. He had a reputation for cruelty. No-one became head lawmage at his age by being kind. Lal might have been able to tell him more, but as it was, that was all Tatters could remember.

His hands free, Sir Leofric held his cane loosely, not letting it touch the ground. He tapped its tip against his thigh.

'Bring the light closer,' he ordered.

Goldie brought the flame near Tatters' face, forcing him to squint against the fire while trying not to flinch. Sir Leofric looked at the collar closely. When he leant forward, he brought a whiff of perfume with him; a pungent, herbal mix.

'Be careful with that one, he's vicious,' Goldie cautioned.

Sir Leofric lifted his hand and, as casually as he would touch a lover, he tapped his nail against the gold binding. The collar gave out a sound like a spoon against a crystal glass. Despite himself, Tatters winced. The touch was intrusive, as if someone had put their fingers inside his mouth.

The ring reverberated across the cell and inside Tatters. Sir Leofric listened with interest.

'The collar is active, I believe?' he said. He stood unmoving, too close, even when Goldie moved the torch backwards to hold it at a distance.

Tatters nodded. If they believed the collar was working, they would think of him as property – and a mage wouldn't break another mage's toy, or at least, not without a reason. As long as they thought he was a slave, he was safe.

'I thought so. Who is your master?' Sir Leofric's voice was quiet, carrying the simple threat of power.

Tatters bit his lips. Without Lal, decisions were more difficult to make. 'My master is Lady Siobhan.'

All he could hope for was that the old woman was too much of a lacunant to deny this. Goldie snorted in scorn. Twirling his cane between his hands, Sir Leofric said sweetly:

'Haven't you heard? Lady Siobhan is dead.'

Tatters' mind went blank. He felt the mud against his naked toes, felt himself sinking into the dirt of this place.

He pictured the last time he had seen the supreme mage, her stooped silhouette, the sound of her cane on the sandstone. The way the sun had caught her white hair. In this cell without a sky, it was hard to imagine her gone.

At last, Sir Leofric took a step back. 'The collar stops being active when the master dies, I would imagine.' It wasn't a question. He was stating a fact. 'I will ask again. Who is your master?'

When Tatters didn't answer, Goldie caught him by the shackles, tugging at them. Tatters slipped on the wet earth, and his head came level with Sir Leofric's cane. He felt a sharp sting as Goldie kicked at the back of his knee – he crumpled to the floor without being able to soften the fall with his hands. He bit his tongue to stifle the short, involuntary sound of pain.

'Answer!' barked Goldie.

No answer came to mind. On his knees, the ground was colder, harder. The grime of the cell stuck to him, traces of old blood, of other prisoners thrown down against the same ground. Sir Leofric petted Tatters' forehead with his cane as he would a dog.

'You think we can't hurt you, don't you?' Sir Leofric only smiled.

Tatters shook his head, trying to clear the dizziness out of it. There was a dull ache in his knees.

Sir Leofric brushed at the corners of his mouth with his fingers. Every gesture was elegant and sparse. Movements one would use at a ball or during a political dinner, unsuited to the coarseness of the prison. When he spoke, his voice was creamy:

'Think carefully. There might be a ban in the collar preventing you from speaking your master's name. But you can work around binds. You can even fight them, if you're ready to attempt challenging the collar's magic.'

Beside him, Tatters could make out Goldie's boots, thick leather hugging his calves, stained with mud.

'I would like to make a case that the pain of resisting the collar will be lesser than the pain we can inflict.'

It was his softness which spooked Tatters most. He didn't threaten so much as he advised you on the best course of action – for your own sake, of course.

'We should talk less,' Goldie complained, 'hit him more. People open up after a couple of punches.'

'Don't be impatient,' Sir Leofric answered. He took a step forward, pushing his cane under Tatters' chin, forcing Tatters to lift his face and meet his gaze. His irises were green. They were the kind of eyes girls would fight for; sparkling, playful.

When he tapped his cane against his prisoner's jaw, Tatters felt it in his teeth.

'You are a mage, aren't you?' It was a rhetorical question. 'As long as you can still mindlink, you are in working order.'

Sir Leofric smashed the tip of his cane in Tatters' chest. He aimed just above the stomach, where the bones meet at the solar plexus. He hit like one would with a spear, point forward.

It knocked the air out of Tatters' lungs. He crumpled, reflexively, as if he could close in around the pain and hold it. He tried to breathe, but the air was blades. He gasped, struggling like a man drowning, and for a terrifying moment he thought he wouldn't manage, that he would choke. He gulped in small hissing breaths which hardly filled his lungs. He pressed both his arms against his chest, but the pain only burnt brighter, spreading across his ribcage, licking his bones.

He coiled in a ball on the floor, his head against his knees. His pulse was ringing in his ears so loudly that he barely heard Sir Leofric chuckle.

'I'll let you think about it,' Sir Leofric said. He bent over and, nearly fondly, ruffled Tatters' hair. 'You're going to be with me for a while, I suspect. We'll get to know each other.'

He stepped out of the cell. Goldie closed it behind him. The darkness engulfed Tatters; he had got used to the torchlight.

He listened as their steps thudded and faded against the stone.

***

Lady Siobhan's death had been announced during the night, while Isha had been tossing and turning in bed, kept awake by concern, then by the relentless ringing that tolled until dawn. The bell was too big for humans, like everything else inside the Nest, and it produced a deep clang that shook the walls. The seagulls had taken flight and circled the castle like noisy ghosts, shrieking shapes in the clouded sky.

Like the birds, the mages had chattered all night, gossiping about who might be their new leader. Most often, the head of the Nest would leave the decision of who should rule to their peers, but sometimes counsellors were chosen, when the supreme mage was whimsical or wise. Lady Siobhan was reputed to be both. The deceased's last wishes would be read out loud by a priest at their funeral. That was when the mages would discover whether Lady Siobhan had chosen an heir and, if so, who it might be.

Isha already knew Passerine's place at the Nest was not secure. The next supreme mage might not be as generous as Lady Siobhan towards refugees. Passerine owned no land. Aside from her, he had no apprentices. Sir Daegan had ambition and a lightborn; he would make good use of both.

Now it was morning. The sky was heavy and low, thick with mist. There were no birds. The quicksilver river drowned all other sounds.

Passerine had requested her presence beside him during the funeral, so Isha stood at the front of the procession. She was one of the only apprentices amongst the group of high mages waiting at the gates of the Nest for Lady Siobhan to be brought out. Isha glanced up at Passerine's profile. His irises were as black as if his pupils had bled inside his eyes. He caught her staring at him. Maybe he misunderstood her expression, because he said:

'Don't worry. Our time has not come yet.'

It wasn't for herself that she was worried.

The bearers carried the body through the gates. Isha had often seen them; they walked the lands far from the Edge and helped the bodies make their way to temples, where the dead could take flight. Wrapped in her death shroud, Lady Siobhan was so light that two men were enough to lift her, at the head and tail of the funeral stretcher.

The shroud was white, embroidered with gold, with the spires of the Nest on a bright blue background at the centre. Death shrouds were unique, woven by relatives or servants. Loved ones worked on the fabric long before the life was waning. As Lady Siobhan's death had been looming for a while now, her shroud had been lovingly detailed. The rich cloth flowed around the body, on the carriers' shoulders, poured over the road like the train of a dress, with ordained mages holding it to prevent the soft material from gathering dust.

Isha thought of Tatters in the carved manacles. There wouldn't be a funeral for a collarbound; they would dump his body over the Edge with a group of other misfits. Had anyone worked on a death shroud for Tatters? And if they had, would the priests use it?

The high mages waited for the bearers to take the front of the procession. Passerine moved as if he had attended the funeral before; he knew all the steps. He walked in the wake of the veil, Isha beside him as they slowly left the Nest and headed for the Temple. The khers wouldn't attend the funeral, but they formed a guard of honour around the gates.

The death shroud stood out on the moor, a pale shape floating above the heather. The high mages behind, black following white, were like the shadows cast by clouds. Isha listened to their steps – soft sticky sounds of mud, turning to dull thumps on the stone path.

The heather gave way to sparse woodland, indicating the start of the Temple grounds. The priests were waiting for them, men and women with shorn hair, undyed clothes. The professional mourners paid for the occasion started crying at the sight of the body, their wails echoing the seagulls' night-time screams. The mourners were wearing blue – the colour of the sky, the colour of death, the colour of Byluk.

The priests took Lady Siobhan from the bearers. The gestures were slow and ceremonial. Handing over the body without getting entangled in its long shroud required time. While the rites were being performed, the mourners threw themselves on the ground in a fit of tears, slapping their chests. Isha had never seen professional mourners, although she understood they were a sign of status. Mages, who were especially reluctant to show vulnerability, often relied on their services. There was something inhuman in their complete abandon, in the grief of their howling. One woman was ripping clumps of hair from her scalp.

None of the mages cried. Yet such a deep sadness seemed to well from the mourners, from the priests, from the few ungifted who had somehow made it to the front of the procession, that Isha couldn't help but feel shaken. She hadn't known Lady Siobhan. She had barely seen the supreme mage. But she noticed a servant wiping his cheeks, and a priestess lifting a hand to comfort him as he wept quietly, solemnly.

Once the priests had shouldered the body and taken the train from the ordained mages, the carriers stepped back. Their work stopped here. They didn't enter the sacred areas reserved for Byluk, the Taker, because it was considered bad luck. They were here to carry the dead away – people didn't want them to bring death back.

Now that they were officially on Temple grounds, the mages removed their shoes. Isha untied the leather buckle at the side of her ankle, watching Passerine from the corner of her eye, noticing the pale underside of his feet. Others followed suit, from the highest mage to the lowliest apprentice, and it was touching, Isha thought, seeing these feet that were always strapped in gilded leather and furs, now naked in the cold, suddenly equal.

The priests set off towards the Edge, the mages in tow. Isha felt the lush grass beneath her feet, the wetness of the ground. The crowd rippled with noise, a river of black and grey waters. Like the river, they were headed towards the end of the world.

As they walked towards the Edge, the cliff seemed to expand, until the whiteness of the sky was all Isha could see, and the rocks she was standing on appeared sandy and friable, about to crumble. Holding the body high above their heads, the priests started singing.

As during the Groniz festival, their song echoed inside Isha. But Groniz was the Giver and lightborn of life. This was a song about a spark turning to ash, about being left behind when a loved one was torn from your embrace. The priests, broad-chested, hummed deep notes, which resonated as if from within a well; the priestesses' voices were akin to wooden instruments, polished with practice, hollow.

Young novices were scattered along the procession, handing the mages paper lanterns, as yet unlit. Isha held hers tentatively, afraid her sweaty hands would crumple the delicate paper.

The priests finished their song. The wind answered with a song of its own, hissing and spitting, tugging at the procession, pulling clothes and hair and bodies closer, as if trying to draw them to the Edge.

They reached the area where the dead took flight. It was a dip in the cliff, leading downwards, around which the high mages could assemble. The Doorkeeper was waiting for them, as frail as Lady Siobhan had been. Although she was as thin as a bird, the wind didn't ruffle her. The procession spread out along the Edge, to watch the death shroud fill with wind. Beside Passerine, Isha had a good view of the whole proceedings. The priests placed the body at the mouth of the decline, lying her down respect-fully. The people holding the veil arranged themselves above and around the slope, raising the shroud. Isha held her breath.

At first, the wind wasn't favourable. The priests waited. Isha had heard stories of failed funerals, the shroud failing to lift the body; or the knots being too loose, letting the corpse tumble while the shroud flew. The worst tale she had heard had been about a flight where the wind had carried the deceased back to land, rather than into the mist. It was a terrible omen: a ghost refusing to leave. She wondered, throat tight, whether Lady Siobhan would keep her bony fingers clasped around the Nest, even after Byluk should have claimed her.

At last, the wind turned. The death shroud unfolded, the silk expanding and filling with air, shaping itself into a large circular sail to travel the underworld. The Doorkeeper gave the signal: the priests let go. Isha heard Passerine's intake of breath – or it might have been the wind, gasping at the present it had been given. The body soared. Lifted above the Edge, it floated down-wards with the slow grace of a leaf falling from a tree. The veil streamed behind, its colours vivid against the pale mist.

They waited as the shimmering fabric sank out of view. Then the first high mage joined the Doorkeeper, descending the uncertain slope, until he was standing on the last large rocks jutting out over the rim of the world. She helped him light his lamp and send it after Lady Siobhan. The wind caught the blue paper immediately and ripped it out of the high mage's hand, carrying it out of reach.

Each mourner performed the same ritual. Not all funerals were such formal, fastidious affairs, but it wouldn't do to rush the departure of the supreme mage. Isha watched as Sir Daegan handed his lamp to the Doorkeeper, who struggled to light it against the fierce wind, and set it over the Edge for him. His collarbound, the expressionless lightborn, copied him by handing over a lamp that glowed against her slender fingers. Another mage, a woman, followed in their wake. More high mages. A couple of faces Isha didn't recognise, but which represented power.

Then came Passerine's turn. Isha stayed back as he gave his lamp. The wind snatched it away, greedily stealing the warmth it was given. When Passerine started back up the slope, Isha climbed down into the dip of the dead. It was gritty against her naked feet. Its rough surface was a pale grey, only slightly more solid, slightly less see-through than the sky. Her hands were trembling.

She reached the Doorkeeper. The woman was wearing undyed cloth, worn but not torn. Her face was sallow; she looked like an undead spirit herself, with an otherworldly smile.

The Doorkeeper lit the lamp while Isha held it. She let go too early; the wind snuffed out the flame, but she couldn't catch the lamp in time – it was already gone, swallowed by the sky, joining the other blue specks dappling the ether like tears.

She returned to Passerine's side while the mages concluded the ceremony. When the last lamp was set loose, the Doorkeeper left the Edge for the front steps of the Temple. The procession curled around her to listen. She revealed a thick roll of parchment, sealed with Lady Siobhan's personal heraldry. She broke the seal to unfold the parchment; two novices helped her, shielding the skin-thin paper from the wind. The will had to be read out loud, so the departed would hear, and would know her wishes had been followed.

Behind the mages, further along the Edge, the ungifted were sending out lamps and throwing gifts to Lady Siobhan. They were still mourning. The mages, however, were already focused on her legacy.

Isha shivered while the Doorkeeper read through the will's opening formalities. Without her shoes, she was freezing. The mages fidgeted, straining their ears.

'I bequeath the Nest,' said the Doorkeeper, and the murmur of voices was so loud that she stopped and waited for silence before continuing, 'I bequeath the Nest, and the responsibility of protecting it and loving it, fighting for it and dying within it, to the one man who has proved that he will protect, love, fight and die there.'

The Doorkeeper paused. She squinted at the name on the vellum. Behind her, the blue lamps devoted to Byluk were fading, their fire gone, eaten by the Edge.

'I bequeath the Nest to Sir Daegan.'

Isha felt her stomach drop as certainly as the body had. Passerine's hand pressed against her shoulder; he was supporting her, to prevent her from faltering. His hand was firm through the fabric of her robes.

She was only an apprentice. A man who despised her, who hated her protector, was now in charge of her home. She turned away from Sir Daegan. She didn't want to see what his face would reveal.

While the clapping covered the sound of their voices, Passerine leant forward.

'We will do this together,' he whispered. There was no surprise or hesitation in his tone, only cold certainty. She hadn't yet told him about Tatters.

As Passerine straightened, Isha heard the voice of Arushi's mother. She saw Uaza sitting beside the chimney, her eyes bloodshot, the half-washed plates in a pile in front of her. The memory was uncalled for, but it stuck. *You will be a ruler and a leader of the flock. You will change how mages fly.* It overlapped with the sound of cheering, the hungry smiles, the grief-blue lamps as they floated away.

Afterwards, the procession dwindled. The formal part of the ceremony was over. Some stayed to pray and honour Lady Siobhan. Some made their way back to the Nest. The clouds were thick, tangible, as if the sky were made of tougher stone than the cliff. The ground was hard, the branches leafless. Isha's warm breath added to the whiteness around her.

She had lost her shoes. It seemed such a trivial thing, but she couldn't find them. Passerine retrieved his and waited, but there were rows upon rows of leather soles, some thrown against each other in disordered piles, and she hunted through them in vain, clenching her jaw to prevent her teeth from chattering, conscious of the grass and dirt sticking to her toes.

'Go ahead without me,' she told Passerine.

He nodded. 'We can talk in my chambers.'

She dreaded that conversation, as she knew she wouldn't be the bearer of good news.

Once he'd left, she combed through the area where she'd left her shoes. Her feet were soaked up to her ankles; her toes were numb. As she searched, a priest came to greet her. She only recognised him when he was close: Osmund. As always, he looked as if he hadn't slept in weeks.

'May you grow tall,' she said, out of habit.

'I don't need to grow tall,' he answered. 'I am not so proud as to presume I will ascend.'

She wasn't sure how to answer that. Unprompted, Osmund said, 'Would you care for an Unburdening?'

The last person to have offered to do so was Tatters. She felt such an ache in her heart at the thought, such longing, that she nodded.

'I knew you were an apprentice to be relied upon,' he said.

Walking towards the shrine was like walking through a memory, following a man who was nearly a stranger to a frail, fragile, suspended place.

It already sheltered two people Unburdening. They waited outside in silence. Glancing away from the shrine, towards the Temple buildings, Isha noticed that more people than usual were milling about the sacred grounds. She spotted Sunriser refugees, but also Duskdwellers, people who had left their land in the countryside – the undefended fields that supplied the Nest with food – and had come to the city for the safety of sturdy walls. These people must have failed to find a place in town and chosen the Temple instead. It wasn't as well guarded, but it was welcoming. It was also a home the Renegades couldn't reach without alerting the mages.

Only when the men stepped out of the shrine – two ungifted, from their livery two of Lady Siobhan's servants – did Osmund invite Isha to step inside. She remembered the shrine without fondness, its moving structure like a boat in a storm, the gaps between the pillars that showed the void below, the hard benches, the ice that seeped into her bones, the faded paint.

Like last time, fear of heights clenched her lungs, made her dizzy. She sat down, crossing her legs rather than letting them dangle as was the custom. Osmund joined her, gazing out to where the clouds were blotting out the horizon.

'Shall we ask questions?' Isha asked tentatively, when Osmund didn't speak first.

He shook his head. She wondered if he was old, or only worn. His features were heavy, but there was no white peppering his hair.

'Questions frame the words we answer. Unburdening is about letting the truth come forward, not trying to capture it.'

She nodded, although she wasn't sure she understood. They sat together in silence, side-by-side but without looking at each other, staring into the abyss. After a while, Isha had to admit the shrine was strangely soothing. She felt light-headed, as if stunned or half asleep. The wood rocking in the breeze lulled her.

When Osmund spoke, his voice and presence startled her. He had been so still, she could have been alone.

'One for the eyes. Scenes I have seen.' He had a deliberate, rhythmic way of speaking, as if he had held the words close before letting them loose. 'I overheard two maids talking of Lady Siobhan's death. They said she had fallen from her bed in the night. She had slipped on steps in the dark. But they were doubtful. They said she knew the steps by heart. The bruise blossomed across the side of her face, like the aftermath of a blow.'

Osmund didn't accuse anyone, but Isha's heart was hammering inside her chest. Was this a test of faith? Why would a priest tell a mage that there were rumours Lady Siobhan's death wasn't natural? Unsure, she reached out to sense his thoughts – and what shocked her was his trust. He trusted her; or at least he trusted the sacredness of the shrine. He wasn't speaking for political purposes, but because he had heard this rumour, and it had worried him, and he wanted to tell someone who would not repeat it. He was speaking to Unburden himself.

His face was languid as he stared far beyond the shrine. It was her turn.

'One for the eyes. Scenes I have seen.' She hesitated. 'I saw a young man weeping for his father's death.' She pictured Ka, bleeding under the whip's blows.

hed.

ty.

.ned.

. Osmund spoke
with more ease.

'One for the hands. Deeds I have done,' he said. 'I begged the Doorkeeper not to let Sir Daegan onto the Temple grounds. I went down on my knees and said it would be a sin, but she refused my plea.' His tone betrayed this was a painful truth, one he tried to keep far from his heart. 'Mages bound the land, the animals, the khers and the people, those you call the ungifted. But what arrogance brought a mage to bind a god, I do not know.'

Isha swallowed. Although Osmund had shaved, she could see stubble along the top of his jaw, close to his ears. He clenched it, grinding his teeth against the emotion welling inside him.

'One for the hands. Deeds I have done,' she said. Beyond Osmund's face, the sky was uniformly white, as if a curtain had been drawn across the shrine. The world felt flat. 'I ran away from my mother, and now I don't know who it is I left behind.' The words stuck against her mouth. They tasted of bile.

Osmund knotted his hands together and placed them on his lap. They were skeleton hands, bone showing under the skin, hands wrought from long hours of fasting.

'One for the heart. Feelings I've felt,' he said. 'When Sir Daegan, the binder of lightborns, was proclaimed Supreme Mage of the Nest, I felt hatred.'

She didn't read hatred in his thoughts, though, only a deep weariness, akin to despair. He rested his head against a beam of the shrine – his matted brown hair caught against a splinter. He didn't seem to notice.

'One for the heart. Feelings I've felt,' Isha echoed. 'I...' She wasn't sure what to say. More than one emotion boiled inside her. She felt powerless. She didn't know how to make a change, and it ate through her like moths through cloth. She felt grief.

150

For Lady Siobhan, an old woman whom her own people didn't weep for, too focused on tearing each other apart. She felt guilt. For Tatters, who she'd lost, maybe completely, who she hadn't warned about Caitlin early enough, whose downfall, unwittingly, she'd caused.

'Take your time,' said Osmund. 'Let it come to you.'

She closed her eyes. She took a deep breath of cutting clear air, intoxicating and pure. She found the word that had been waiting inside her.

'Rage,' she said. The answer surprised her. It was the sort of anger that could burn places to the ground, could soak shirt cuffs with blood. 'I feel rage,' she repeated, stunned to find this twisted, hateful thing inside her. She looked at her hands, watched them clench and unclench, imagining the talons of a bird of prey, imagining she could rip and tear, claw and cleave. She could have broken a lawmage's wrist and felt nothing but grim glee.

'I am so angry, I don't let myself feel it most of the time,' she whispered.

Osmund didn't nod, he didn't smile. He didn't judge. The ritual, now it had been performed, resonated with Isha in unexpected ways. For once she had given something without expecting something back. For once she hadn't lied.

'Why me?' she asked.

Osmund's gaze was lost beyond the Edge. 'Who are you? You are a stranger who knows my name.'

Maybe that was what ungifted had that the mages lacked. They didn't read other people's thoughts, but at least they knew their own.

***

The Unburdening hadn't sorted her shoe problem.

As she was rummaging through the collection of discarded footwear, she spotted a flash of green, and realised they must be Kilian's shoes. Passerine and Sir Daegan hadn't walked far apart in the procession – maybe her shoes would be with Sir Daegan's followers.

She found them. She had never been so grateful for Kilian playing with dye.

As she knelt to wipe her feet with the bottom of her robes, she heard a familiar voice.

'My toes are about to fall off, puffin.'

'Mine too,' she admitted.

Kilian grinned, dropping into a crouch beside her. 'I want these green beauties to feature on my death shroud,' he said as he pulled them on. Behind him, she spotted more of Sir Daegan's followers. Lowering her gaze, she kept herself busy rubbing some life back into her feet.

Kilian fell silent. He seemed to realise, belatedly, that although the announcement had been good news for Daegan, it was bad news for Isha.

'See you around,' he muttered, squeezing her shoulder briefly, before he slipped away.

On the way back, Isha stamped her feet on the path, where mud had frozen into potholes. The kher guards, bearing Lady Siobhan's personal heraldry on their shields as a homage, were still standing around the Nest's gates as Isha approached. Their positions were less formal, and they bunched into small groups rather than keep to their rigorous lines.

Arushi peeled off from the group. The kher wore her shield slung across her back – it slapped against the back of her legs.

'What happened to Tatters?' she asked. If her voice had ever been friendly, it wasn't now. It was a wonder she hadn't yet heard the news; as the head of guards, she would be made aware soon enough. Maybe Lady Siobhan's death had delayed her other duties.

Isha forced herself to say, 'He was arrested by lawmages.'

They stared at each other across the brown, bleak landscape. There was no point in saying she had nothing to do with it. Arushi wouldn't believe her; she wouldn't have believed herself, had the roles been reversed.

'I told him to go to you,' Arushi whispered. The broken trust in her eyes cut like broken glass. Isha tried to find words that would bridge the gap between them, the rift she could feel growing, splitting ground.

Before she could, Arushi laughed, the mirthless laugh of someone who got the joke but didn't find it funny. A few snowflakes drifted down and settled on her shoulders. 'You're everything the Nest stands for, and I told him to go to you.'

You're everything the Nest stands for. Baina. Horns torn out of dead fathers. Grieving sons sent to the pillory. Tithes taken from ungifted. A giant's home colonised by parasites.

Arushi must have sensed Isha was about to speak, because she lifted a hand to shush her. 'I've heard enough.' When she left, her steps were strong, decisive, although her expression had been wounded, lost.

Isha lifted her head towards the sky, and saw the twirling flakes as they tumbled down, thicker by the moment.

The first winter snow was falling.

* * *

The crack in the ceiling helped keep track of time, which was how Tatters knew it had only been a day before the lawmages returned. When he heard the key turn in his cell's lock, he got up, bracing himself for what came next. If they wanted to get information out of him, they would. Lal was right. He'd gone soft. He wouldn't be able to resist torture.

He wasn't planning on having to.

When he saw a flash of green fabric, he felt a mix of relief and fear. Give him Goldie any day – the man was much easier to deal with than his superior. But on the other hand, Tatters' idea would only work if Sir Leofric visited in person.

Sir Leofric strolled inside the cell, smiling cheerfully when he saw Tatters, as if greeting an old friend. Goldie followed; squat, glowering.

Well, there was no reason not to be pleasant. Sir Leofric and Tatters agreed on that, at least.

'May you grow tall,' said Tatters. Not that he wanted the lawmage to ever ascend, but it wouldn't be the first lie he'd told.

Goldie's smirk distorted his face. 'Pleased to see us, are you? We can change that.'

He placed his torch in a sconce on the wall – Tatters hadn't even seen it before. It cast a faint, yellowish light. Enough to see the white of people's eyes, but not to catch their expressions.

'Now, now,' said Sir Leofric. He lifted his hand. Tatters noticed he was wearing pale velvet gloves. 'Maybe our friend has decided to cooperate.'

Tatters shook his head. 'No such luck.'

All he could do was hold on as long as possible and hope that Arushi made up her mind to save him. She would know what had happened soon enough. As a guard, she must have the keys to the prison. Had Lal been present, he imagined she would've had some snarky comment about the fact that Tatters needed rescuing. But she wasn't. And, as a matter of fact, he did need rescuing.

Sir Leofric let out a small sigh, which he tried to hide as a sigh of disappointment but was obviously a sigh of delight.

'Such a shame,' he said. 'You could've been out of here today.'

'I can take it from here, if you want,' Goldie offered.

Sir Leofric frowned at that. 'Please, Varun, be quiet.'

Goldie cracked his knuckles. He didn't do it in the threatening way of a guard about to break someone's jaw. He did it in the blasé way of people who are used to breaking jaws, and who get a bit restless when no bone-snapping is happening.

'Where to start?' wondered Sir Leofric out loud. He had a dreamy, faraway look in his green eyes. When he took a step closer, Tatters made a conscious effort to unclench his fists. The man made his skin crawl.

'Do you know, I've always wanted a collarbound?' Sir Leofric went on.

He closed the gap between them. Goldie stayed one step behind, with the bored expression of someone who knows the drill. If anything, he seemed a bit irritated that Sir Leofric was taking over his prisoner.

How cute, Goldie's the jealous type, thought Tatters.

No-one answered.

Tatters felt very alone.

Sir Leofric took off one glove. It was a long, fussy business. He held his glove and tucked his cane under his arm, in the way of a gentleman preparing to touch wrists. He lifted the other hand towards Tatters' face. Tatters tried not to shy away. He didn't like being treated like a wild animal, one you invited to sniff your fingers before you tried to tame them.

Sir Leofric cupped Tatters' chin in his hand. 'You're surprisingly docile,' he said. 'How long have you been a collarbound?'

'A long time.' He forced himself to stamp down on his pride.

He shouldn't care whether the lawmage had his fun. Any time during which they weren't ripping out his nails was worth taking.

'Is it a side-effect of the collar? Does it make you more submissive? Although apparently you put up a fight when they took you in.'

I pick my battles. Tatters gave Sir Leofric a tight smile. The man was speaking to himself. There was no need to answer.

'Absolute power over someone,' Sir Leofric said. His green eyes were bright and lively. 'I would love it. Such a shame the collars are so rare.' He let go of Tatters' chin. 'Would you like it, do you think? Owning a collarbound?'

Tatters took a moment to realise the question was addressed to him.

'I don't care for collars,' he said.

'Really?' Sir Leofric let out a polite, conceited laugh. 'Not even if the places were reversed? Wouldn't you like to be able to bind your master with one word?'

Tatters had never given it much thought. He'd never had the power to break Hawk. He wondered what he would have done if he had. Probably not much. Stopped her from starting a war, maybe. He wasn't one for revenge. Revenge was a messy business.

'Power isn't really my thing,' he said.

'Oh, but it is,' said Sir Leofric. 'Otherwise, you wouldn't be a mage. Or you wouldn't be a good one. And I was told you were very good.'

Sir Leofric was standing uncomfortably close. Tatters could see how the routine, or whatever it was – the game – would put prisoners off. He nearly wanted the straightforwardness of someone thrashing him. It would be less insidious than what Sir Leofric was trying to achieve.

The lawmage placed his free hand around Tatters' neck. He did it casually enough, but the touch of his skin against the gold of the collar was like fire. Suddenly the collar felt tighter. The contact was more than unpleasant – it was intimate, private, taboo. It was as if a door at the bottom of his soul had opened and Sir Leofric was staring inside.

Sir Leofric brought his face closer, close enough that his breath brushed against Tatters' cheek.

'You hate this, don't you?' He couldn't hide his glee. 'I don't know why, but you hate it.'

When Isha had touched the collar, the shock had been immediate, and it had stopped as violently as it had started. Now, Tatters felt as if something was crawling up his back, a snake coiling around his spine. As if, somehow, Sir Leofric was infesting the collar, was imprinting himself into the binds that were holding Tatters into place. It was as if the man was pinning him down, the weight of him increasing.

Soon.

Sir Leofric smiled his youthful, charming smile. 'I'd love to have a collarbound. But given a choice, I wouldn't have picked you.' He lowered his voice. He pressed closer to whisper in Tatters' ear. 'Let's face it, I would only bind someone I would fuck.'

Now.

Tatters bit Sir Leofric. He bit him as hard as he could, on the cheek. Sir Leofric jumped back with a scream – of surprise as much as pain. Tatters didn't let go. A piece of skin stayed caught between his teeth. He spat it out, wincing at the tang of someone else's blood in his mouth.

Goldie was between them before Sir Leofric had even had time to pull away. The head lawmage lifted a hand to his face, touching the ragged cut across his cheekbone. He watched the blood darken the tip of his fingers. For a moment, he looked more incredulous than angry.

Goldie caught Tatters by the neck, his fingers digging into the tender flesh where the jawline met the throat. Tatters focused. He fleshbound with Sir Leofric.

The lawmage clutched at his neck, choking. His lovely eyes bulged. Tatters sensed nothing but a slight discomfort, a slight rasp in his breath. He heard Goldie roar something in his ears, but the words didn't make sense. He was concentrating. Goldie slammed his fist into Tatters' stomach.

It was strange. Tatters folded over, but he didn't feel the hit. By the way Sir Leofric stumbled, nearly falling to his knees, it was a good thing he didn't.

'Varun!' Sir Leofric gasped. 'Stop!'

Goldie froze, his arm already raised to land the next blow. It obviously wasn't Sir Leofric who was supposed to beg for it to end.

Tatters could have forgiven Hawk, then, for everything else. Skies, the things that woman had taught him. Without fleshbinding, he wouldn't have survived this day.

But then, without her, he wouldn't be here in the first place.

He missed Lal. She would know whether to curse or bless Hawk for what had happened.

Goldie let go of him and turned to his superior. Gingerly, Tatters let some of the pain filter back to him – no more than an ache in his throat and his chest. He didn't want the recoil to be too much of a shock, once Sir Leofric was out of reach. He rubbed his throat. He would have bruises there.

'Is something wrong, sir?' Goldie asked, helping Sir Leofric to his feet. Sir Leofric clutched his arm, wincing, wheezing. The bitemark on his cheek was an ugly thing that broke the symmetry of his face.

'Ah . . . I . . . you brute,' muttered Sir Leofric. Goldie only looked confused. He glared at Tatters, conscious that he was missing something.

'I told you not to get too close,' Goldie concluded grumpily. 'I could have dealt with him.'

Sir Leofric fumbled inside his sleeve for a handkerchief. He had a soft white one that he pressed to his face. It was soon stained red. He seemed to be recovering his breath, although amazement had ruffled his composure. He was flushed in the face, still panting. Tatters swallowed tentatively. His throat could do it, at least. And it was someone else's blood he could taste.

Sir Leofric bent to retrieve the glove he had dropped. The mud had tainted it brown.

'Fleshbinding,' said Sir Leofric. 'He must be a mongrel.'

Goldie, still holding Sir Leofric's arm, didn't look convinced. 'Mongrels can't mindlink.'

'This one can. Of course. He had to have some special talent. Who would bother binding him otherwise?'

'It wouldn't be for my good looks, as you so nicely put it,' said Tatters. He shouldn't have spoken, but he was giddy with relief. Lal would have chided him for being careless.

Sir Leofric pulled himself to his full height, grimacing. He handed Goldie his handkerchief and glove so he could rub his thorax. Goldie took them with bad grace, holding the bloodied piece of cloth at arm's length.

'May I point out that a fleshbinding link lasts for life?' Tatters said. He kept his expression as neutral as he could manage. This wasn't bragging; it was a threat. 'I think this is information you might be interested in. It never fades.'

Sir Leofric's veneer of calm briefly cracked, like varnish splitting after drying in the sun. Goldie took over immediately.

'Don't be cocky,' he warned.

'No, no, let him,' said Sir Leofric. His control had returned. 'He deserves it.'

Sir Leofric gave Tatters a long, admiring look. It made Tatters squirm. It wasn't what he had hoped for.

'Please,' said Sir Leofric, 'do enjoy this moment. Enjoy it to the full.' He took his handkerchief back and dabbed at his cheek again, hissing through his teeth at the pain, before crumpling the silk into his fist. 'You won't be able to enjoy it again.'

Chapter Seven

After the funeral, Isha joined Passerine in his chambers. His room had been a giant's alcove, and its ceiling arched, growing narrower the higher it went, ending in a pointed tip. The furniture was expensive but impersonal: a rug as thick and beautifully crafted as a piece of kher artwork, a huge bed, a wardrobe with carved lions on the drawer handles, a desk with ink bottles and vellum spread across it.

But the only sign that Passerine lived here was his research. His papers were covered in strange, curling lines, indecipherable squiggles that could have been the result of doodling, if not for how intricate they were. He seemed to sketch more than he wrote.

The study was bleak. The window, added by humans, was too small to light the vast space the giants had built.

'This is unfortunate,' Passerine said, without preamble, 'if predictable.'

Isha shifted uncomfortably on her feet. Passerine went to open the window – beyond, she could see the ragged cliff of the Edge and the mist rising from it, still dotted with blue, the last lingering lamps.

'After the proper mourning period, Lord Daegan will become our new supreme mage,' said Passerine. 'Before then, we need a way to prevent him from starting a war he can't win and, more urgently, we need to speak to Tatters.'

He turned to face Isha. The room was shades of greys and whites, snow falling outside, grey clouds, black robes. Even the rug seemed drained of colour.

'He's in prison,' she said. 'There was nothing I could do.'

To say Passerine frowned wouldn't have encompassed the way his whole expression turned to ice. Isha told him most of the story: how the last time she had seen Tatters, he was being taken away by the lawmages, in kher shackles. She didn't sense Passerine inside her mind, but he would be monitoring her thoughts closely, hunting for a lie. She stuck to the truth.

When she was done, he didn't answer her immediately. He closed his hand, keeping his eyes on his fingers. She could feel the coiled tension inside him as he slowly formed a fist.

'I should have gone to him when I could,' said Passerine. He opened his hand, as slowly as he had closed it. Each finger was taut. 'It is not your fault,' he added. 'It is entirely mine.'

She had expected a more explosive display of anger. As often, as always, Passerine was one step ahead of her.

'I apologise,' he said. 'I was wrong to drag you into this.' He crossed the room towards her and extended his hand. After a moment of hesitation, she took it. He clasped her fingers in his, awkwardly, with the lack of grace of someone unfamiliar with human touch. 'I am sorry,' he repeated. 'I should never have threatened you.'

He squeezed, before letting go. She was stumped by this admission of vulnerability, as small as it had been. She had never heard a high mage apologising, ever, for anything.

'Of course, I would never hurt you. It's absurd. I don't know why I ...' Passerine paused. He seemed torn. 'Tatters brings out the worst in me,' he concluded.

He went to stand beside the window, resting his back against the cold stone of his chambers, while she stayed at the centre of the room, her shoes sinking in the soft carpet.

'What are we going to do?' Isha asked, not daring to hope, yet. Shouldn't a high mage be able to get anyone out of prison?

She was right not to be optimistic. 'This makes matters very difficult,' Passerine said. 'The lawmages are out of my control.'

'But,' mumbled Isha, 'he knows you're here. You're the only high mage who knows about him and who could help.' She whispered, even though they were the only people in the room. 'He might ask the lawmages whether you can vouch for him in a trial?'

Passerine smiled thinly.

'*If* he has a trial. And even then, I doubt it. You are under the illusion that we are – or were – friends. I doubt Tatters would be pleased to see me.' His voice was like stones at the bottom of a lake: cold, still, deep.

Isha didn't know what to answer. She wanted to argue in Tatters' favour, but she didn't know enough about their relationship, or even about their place in the Renegades' camp. She let out a frustrated sound, hissing through her teeth.

'Well, it can't hurt to try,' said Passerine. Isha's head snapped up. As always, his expression gave nothing away. 'Let's see what the lawmages say.'

At the door of the prisons, everyone was reluctant to give a clear answer. Passerine had to ask a couple of kher and human guards before anyone agreed to call a lawmage who might be able to share information. While they waited, a group of ungifted soldiers were being taken through drills, pacing the hard, ice-packed ground. Isha watched them idly as they ran through defensive and offensive positions, mimicking strikes and shield walls under the supervision of a mage.

The man who finally came out of the heavy, iron-strung door was neat enough to attend a fancy ceremony. He certainly didn't fit with Isha's idea of a prison warden: he was tall, trim, smiling, with bright green eyes and a cloak to match. He was dabbing at his cheek with a handkerchief; an uneven wound marked his cheekbone.

'May you grow tall.' His tone was smooth and warm, like melted sugar. His attention barely flickered towards Passerine before landing on Isha. 'Ah, Lord Daegan's little rebel,' he said. 'I've heard about you. You do find yourself in the most interesting places...' He let his sentence hang, unfinished.

'Isha.'

'Isha,' he repeated, as if tasting the name.

Only then did he seem to notice Passerine standing beside her. 'But where are my manners!' The lawmage let out a laugh as he extended his wrist. 'Sir Leofric.'

Passerine and Isha touched wrists with him. She squirmed under his intelligent gaze.

'What can I do for you?' Sir Leofric asked, and for a moment, he seemed so open that Isha thought they might be able to do this without a struggle.

But as Passerine explained that he'd heard about the arrest of a collarbound, Sir Leofric's smile faded faster than snow at the thaw. The lawmages were independent from the high mages, to a degree. Belatedly, Isha realised they cherished their autonomy. Of course. All mages fought fiercely for any scrap of power they'd been given.

'I will stop you right there,' Sir Leofric said, lifting a gloved hand to shush Passerine. He waved his bloodstained hand-kerchief. 'This has nothing to do with you. It is only polite to defer to those whose business it is to deal with criminals.'

A glint akin to hunger filled his eyes. Sir Leofric dropped into a conspiratorial whisper. 'Unless it does have something to do with you? The timing of your arrival at the Nest is awfully convenient, and Lord Daegan has asked me to root out any Renegade spies.'

His attention moved like that of a snake, flitting from Isha to Passerine, as if deciding which person to strike. She closed her mind, protecting it with thoughts about the funeral, about Daegan, about the arrest at the tavern, about anything and everything as long as it was not something he could use against her. Despite the biting cold, the rush of fear heated her body like a fever. Her hands were damp with sweat.

'If you have something to tell me, I'm all ears,' Sir Leofric concluded. 'I'm always happy to talk.'

Passerine held himself very straight. He had crow's feet at the corner of his eyes. Compared to the lawmage, young and polished, he seemed old.

When he spoke, it was like his posture; stiff, unfriendly. 'I doubt we'll be able to help.'

'No, I didn't think you would.' The smile had returned, teasing now, superior. Sir Leofric dismissed them as he would have some cheeky apprentices begging for a favour.

Passerine and Isha crossed the courtyard in silence. Once they were far removed from the door, out of sight, Isha wiped her hands on her robes. Her heart was still beating wildly.

'I suspected as much,' Passerine said.

'But he thinks we are...'

Don't even say it, he mindlinked softly. *It was only a threat, nothing else. But we cannot go back to him. We mustn't give him a reason to doubt us.*

Swallowing, Isha nodded. For the first time, the reality of what had happened to Tatters, and its implications, were sinking in. They weren't safe. With Sir – no, Lord – Daegan in charge, they were one step away from being thrown into the cells, let alone getting anyone out.

For the lawmages, we need either the power to coerce them, or something they want and that we can give them, Passerine said, sticking to mindlink. *I'll see what other solutions I can find, but I can't make promises.*

Isha knew he spoke not only about freeing Tatters, but also protecting her from Lord Daegan, from the Renegades, from the upcoming conflict between the two.

***

If Passerine couldn't do anything yet, she needed to speak to Arushi.

It was not a conversation Isha was eager to have, but it wasn't one she could walk away from. Whatever Passerine planned in order to weather the storm that was about to shake the Nest, Isha wouldn't have time, then, for apologies. And maybe, just maybe, Arushi and Isha could think of something together to get Tatters out of prison. With thorough preparation and a high mage's help, they might even succeed.

She tried to hide how nervous she was as she reached the Pit. To her surprise, the guards didn't move to block her way. One of them glanced at her and nodded in recognition; the other one didn't even lift his head. She crossed the Pit's threshold, feeling light-headed. She had been bracing herself to force a door open, only to find it unlocked.

She gritted her teeth. *You have opened gates for me. I will open this one for you.* She hadn't even known that she was on Tatters' side until now. She still wasn't sure she trusted him. But she would do this for him, if she could.

The Pit was lively. It was early evening, and female iwdan were gathered in the streets, trading stories and food. The men hadn't yet returned from whatever work they had found in town. It was snowing steadily, as it had since Lady Siobhan's funeral. The khers were cleaning out spaces between the tents, brushing the snow aside, making piles of brown sludge along the walls. Dead leaves from the trees, orange, red, brown, were turning into mush on the ground. The livestock was being herded by the children inside half-crumbled buildings. The Pit was preparing for winter and foul weather.

Arushi's house dominated the nearby tents and rundown dwellings. Isha rubbed her hands together for warmth, waiting to see if Yua or someone else would come up and spare her from having to knock. When they didn't, she took the time to steady her breathing before tentatively rapping against the hard wood of the doorframe.

While she waited, snow continued to fall. Flakes settled on her sleeves like small, intricate pieces of jewellery.

She heard sounds inside the house. Heavy boots hitting the floor, and a voice calling out: 'I know it's a human, because only humans knock! Seshaq, haven't you got horns?'

Arushi strode out, still addressing someone over her shoulder, which meant she pushed through the bead curtain before she spotted Isha. She was halfway through swapping her uniform for more casual clothing, wearing a shirt, untucked from her trousers; her boots, not yet unlaced; her trousers but no belt.

The curtain chimed behind her. Her eyes turned sour.

'It wasn't me, I swear I didn't tell the lawmages anything,' Isha rushed to say, hoping to get her story out before she was interrupted. 'It was unlucky timing. They were watching Tatters following a fight between us.' From the way Arushi's frown deepened, this was not the right thing to say. Isha tried to explain: 'A mindbrawl. We did a mindbrawl, and the settler found it suspicious, and the lawmages were already keeping an eye out for him when he came to the tavern and...'

Without forewarning, Arushi slammed her fist against the doorframe. Isha jumped. She might have continued speaking nonetheless, but Arushi hit it again, breaking the wood, splinters cutting into her fist.

Arushi stared at her hand as blood pooled around the shards of wood. Isha shut up.

For a while Arushi only breathed, heavily, wrestling control out of her anger. When she turned her attention to Isha, it was impossible not to blanch under her glare.

'You're a fantastic liar. I'll give you that, kid. You don't even need mindlink to control people.' Isha was about to protest, but Arushi shook her head. 'No. Listen.' As Arushi spoke, her voice grew steadily more furious. 'Tatters was running from something. You brought a high mage to the Pit, hot on his trail. He was safe here, but when he left, to see *you*, to speak with *you*, he disappeared.' By now Arushi was shaking.

Someone inside the house shouted something, and she answered:

'Give me a break! I'm coming. Just finishing this.'

Her jaw was clenched, her fists held so tightly they trembled, her anger so overwhelming it overwhelmed even pain. The same powerless anger Isha had felt against Lord Daegan, against people she could never fight back.

She wanted to say something, but she was rooted to the spot, her mouth stuck shut. Arushi leant forward, her clenched fist red as a bruise, one blood-drop hanging from her wrist.

'I don't even know where he is now. I can't find him, or traces of him, anywhere. He isn't on the prison register, none of my iwdan guards have seen him. If the humans have, they're keeping quiet. For all I know, he's dead. If you've killed him, do you think I care that you didn't do it on purpose?'

With those words, Arushi went back inside. The frame was stained with her blood.

At first, Isha couldn't move. But the prospect of being found by another member of the household, and having to go through this again, was too much to bear. She retraced her steps back to the gate, wondering what had made her think she would be able to explain herself. She could have gone down on her knees and begged Arushi to believe her, but she doubted even that would have dented the guardswoman's resolve.

Arushi's words twisted in her stomach. *If you've killed him.* If the head of guards couldn't find Tatters, it did not bode well.

But they wouldn't kill him. They can't. Her thoughts sounded desperate, even to herself.

This was probably her last time in the Pit. Isha made a conscious effort to lift her face and look around her. The half-built houses, patched with cloth, and the tents drawn between them, threw colour across the muddy ground. A young child was tottering after a goat, trying to pet it. A female kher, with curvy horns that grew close to her skull, entangled with her hair, was painting a wall. Her fingers were tinted with ochre; she lightly dabbed at the picture, ignoring the snow steadily covering the bottom of her artwork.

And Ka was walking towards Isha with a slow, easy step, his hands loosely holding on to his belt, an arrud across his shoulders.

'Tidir, eyas.'

His face was guarded. He didn't seem to feel the cold.

'Idir,' said Isha, remembering her gendered greetings.

169

'What are you doing here?' Ka asked. He stood in front of her, looking down, unsmiling.

'I tried to talk to Arushi,' she admitted. 'She made me understand I wasn't welcome.'

'Why would you be welcome?'

Ka loomed above her, staring with unblinking eyes. She thought about him trapped in the pillory, how much smaller he had seemed, more vulnerable. It was vaguely threatening to notice the thickness of his forearms, the width of his shoulders. He was stronger than her, there was no doubt. And mindlink wouldn't protect her from him.

She knew what Ka was implying. All the khers must know by now. 'I am not responsible for what happened to Tatters,' Isha repeated. 'Arushi got it wrong.'

'Is that true?'

'Yes,' she said.

Nothing lightened his features; no sneer, no show of sympathy. His words were stern. 'Why did you come, then?'

She wasn't welcome in the Pit, but it didn't matter. She was never welcome anywhere. She could do this anyway.

'I am looking for people to help me save Tatters,' she said.

He stared at her, no doubt trying to gauge whether she was telling the truth. She held his gaze. The patterned wool distracted from the stiff set of his posture, from the way his horns stood above his head in sharp points. But the arrud couldn't quite hide the whip scars at the top of his shoulders, lapping at the nape of his neck.

'Haven't you got any other clothes?' he asked.

The question took her off-guard. 'What?'

They were both still standing in the middle of the street, under the snow. Isha was cold, wet, uncomfortable. Snowflakes were covering Ka's arrud, dulling its brightness.

'The robes.' He crossed his arms. 'Why do you wear something that says you hate us?'

There were no words to answer that. Weakly, Isha mumbled, 'It's a crime for me not to wear the robes.'

'Isn't it a crime for you to come here?' Ka asked.

Isha shook her head. But Ka had a point. It wasn't illegal for her to come to the Pit, but it was frowned upon, probably as much – if not more so – than not wearing the Nest's robes.

'Come back with different clothes.' His voice was hard, and it was difficult to tell if this was a warning or a piece of advice.

He turned away, abruptly putting an end to the conversation.

* * *

Isha arrived at the Coop at the end of the afternoon, well before the start of the drinking hours. She tried to hide how uncertain she felt as she walked inside.

The innkeeper was wiping the tables clean. He looked up, stopped, the rag still in his hand, and asked curtly:

'What do you want?'

'I want to use Tatters' room,' she said.

That stumped him. He didn't answer, clutching his dirty cloth. Isha noticed a bucket of water on the floor, and that the ground was glistening where he had washed the wooden boards.

'I will pay you for it,' she said, 'but I'm not renting it to live. Only for occasional use.'

She pointed to the bucket. 'I can help with that too. I haven't got much money, and next to nothing that isn't baina.' She took a deep breath. It was shakier than she would have liked. 'You've been saying that you need a servant for a while now. Well, I'm not a servant, but I can pour drinks and carry them to tables. Unlike most apprentices, I don't think I'm too good for it.'

The innkeeper frowned, looking her up and down, his rag slung over his arm. She spotted his kher bracelet, shining with grease.

'You cheeky brat,' he spat. 'You'll spy on me, then you'll bring the lawmages down on me again.'

'I didn't tell them anything,' she said through clenched teeth. 'That was Caitlin.'

'And your fancy Sunriser lord?'

When Isha hesitated, the innkeeper coughed something like a laugh and turned away from her.

'No, wait,' pleaded Isha. 'I need a place where I can change from my robes into something less conspicuous.'

The innkeeper froze. His face turned red, with white splotches on his cheeks. When he bared his teeth, they were lined with yellow.

'You want to bring more trouble, do your dirty meddling in my house?'

She noticed that he had raised his voice, but she noticed, also, that he wasn't trying to throw her out. Without Tatters, with the threat of the lawmages, he would lose most of his income. She wondered if the apprentices had grown wary of the place yet. In time, mindbrawl would move away to safer, more secret spaces.

'You need to attract new clients, refugees maybe,' she said. People who wouldn't mind the dirt and the poor beer. 'And a half-Sunriser, or at least someone who looks like she might be part Sunriser, is a good advertisement. It means refugees will trust you.' Isha struggled for more arguments. She needed this. Passerine had said he couldn't help; the khers were her only chance. She set her pride aside to say: 'I'm a curiosity. You can make this the tavern where that tattooed girl works. It means people will remember the Coop, if nothing else. And I can't cause you trouble without causing trouble for myself.'

The innkeeper stared at her. She stared back – she had out-gazed Sir Passerine and Sir Daegan; another middle-aged man, with more raw force but less power, wouldn't scare her.

'You're stubborn as a goat,' the innkeeper said at last. 'You sure you've got no hornblood?' Gritting her teeth, she didn't answer. After weighing his options a moment longer, the innkeeper thrust his rag between her arms. 'Show me what you're made of, and I'll consider it.'

She didn't thank him. And he didn't thank her, not after she finished cleaning the main room, not as she brought mugs of beer to the clients, not when she swept away the mess at the end of the night, scrubbing the glasses clean until her hands were raw. It was exhausting work, which she was unused to, which left her sore and sweaty. But when she had finished, and the innkeeper was locking up, he threw her a key on a ring.

'Take this. Keep your mouth shut and work hard, and we've got a deal.'

Isha's heart leapt when she recognised the rusted ring – it was Tatters' key.

'I will,' she said, because she was relieved, because she was grateful. And then, because she was a mage, because she wasn't a servant to be bullied and spoken harshly to, she added: 'And we'll both keep our mouths shut about this.'

***

They came to an agreement: Isha helped two days a week, and the rest of the time she could come and go inside the Coop as she pleased. Chores she was required to take on for the Nest had to be done in the morning, before she spent the afternoon on her knees scrubbing the floor and the evenings rushed off her feet carrying drinks.

It meant she had people staring at her tattoo, and commenting on her figure, and sometimes even trying to pinch her. But she had mindlink on her side. She could sense a lustful thought towards her and quell it before it came to fruition; if not, she could turn the thought to guilt, or fear. Sometimes an apprentice dropped by, and mocked her for degrading herself, but nobody called the lawmages. Or if they did, this was too minor a slight for them to intervene. Inside the Nest, she was known under many unflattering names, no doubt, and considered a feral apprentice with a master who didn't know how to keep her in check.

With any other teacher, this would have spelled trouble. Passerine, however, hardly required an apprentice. If he noticed her absences, they were too rare for him to bring it up with her. If he heard the rumours, he either didn't care, or he trusted her choices.

Outside the Nest, she cultivated a reputation as the untouchable, slightly sinister, but certainly intriguing halfblood girl. Amongst ungifted, being a halfblood protected her. It was common knowledge halfbloods couldn't mindlink.

In return, she could take off her mage's robes and, for the first time since she had arrived at the Nest, roam the city mostly unnoticed.

Today she pulled on her dress, tightened a leather belt around her waist, and fastened her travelling cloak across her shoulders. In preparation, she had bought a piece of pottery, a painted vase, and she tucked it under one arm.

She headed for the Pit.

By the time she'd reached the Pit's gates, she was shivering. The ground, thick with sludge, dampened the bottom of her dress and sucked at her shoes. A weak, wet snow was falling, easily mistaken for rain. The two khers at the gates had pulled a piece of cloth over the entrance and were huddled under that cheap protection, poking it from time to time with a stick to get the snow off it. They barely shot her a glance. With civilian clothes and a tattoo, she was as much one of them as a halfblood could be.

Inside the kher quarter, she faltered. The streets, packed with mud-streaked snow, were empty. People were inside their homes, so chances of stumbling upon Ka by chance were low.

She turned back to the gates and called out: 'Do you know where Ka's house is?'

The guard chuckled. 'What a fancy word! You mean his tiyayat, his hearth.' He pointed her in the right direction.

She trudged through the snow, which was more heavily packed here. Although the Pit was empty, it wasn't quiet. Isha could hear chatting, animals bleating, even chicken cackling, from inside the tents. They squatted like colourful toads, with smoke drifting out of the hole at their summit. Warmth and laughter spilt from within, but Isha had never been in a kher tent – she was only familiar with Arushi's house, and she wasn't sure how to find Ka's tiyayat, if that was what it was called.

The tall trees were leafless. Isha brought her cloak closer, but she couldn't stop the sludge from filtering into her clothes. After wandering in vain for a while, she gave up and picked a tent at random. She couldn't knock, and she didn't know what the proper greeting for making herself known should be. She tried coughing and shuffling on the spot, but the people inside were busy so no-one heard her.

In the end, she gathered her courage – her feet were growing frozen, her toes were hard blocks of ice – and she unlaced the tent's flap. Opening it, she poked her head inside.

A household of khers were gathered around a central fire, rugs thrown about the floor with hay underneath for insulation.

Goats were lying at the edges of the tent; hens were roosting on the right-hand side of the entrance. The whole family fell silent when Isha appeared. An array of faces stared, all seemingly as young, but with horns of different lengths.

The heat warmed Isha's face instantly, and she hoped her longing wasn't too obvious.

'Tidir. Idir.' What was the proper way to greet a group? 'I am so sorry for bothering you, but could you please tell me where Ka's...' She struggled with the unfamiliar word. 'Ka's tiyayat is?'

The family was surprised, but not unduly so. A woman turned to a child and said, 'Show the taniybu the way.' Isha wondered if it was an insult. It was better than soulworm, at any rate.

The child reluctantly joined Isha on the threshold and tiptoed outside into the snow. Scowling at the sludge sticking to her naked feet, the young kher observed the surrounding tents, before indicating one of them.

'There.' She looked over Isha quizzically. 'What was your great deed?'

Before Isha could think of an answer, the matriarch snapped: 'Don't bother her unless you're inviting her inside.'

The child retreated, leaving Isha feeling lost. She was missing too much of the language, too many of the social cues. She closed the flap of the tent, fastening the laces which held it in place. She had to put the vase on the floor to do so.

Teeth chattering, too cold to care about whether she was welcome, she went to the designated tent. She begged silently that Ka was there and that he wouldn't mind letting her in. She thought of Tatters. *Power is the number of thresholds you can cross.* And helplessness is being stuck outside to brave the winter alone.

She unlaced the front of the tent's flap before lifting it. The scene inside was similar to the previous home: hay on the ground, woollen rugs on top, a fire in the centre. Animals were relegated to an area near the entrance – two dogs with shaggy fur, a sheep, a rooster with beautiful blue crest feathers. About half a dozen children, as many men, and twice as many women were inside. Cooking utensils were hanging on a rack at the back. The colours inside the tent were orange and gold, the colours of the khers' skin, the colours of sunset.

The conversations stopped at her arrival.

'Tidir. Idir,' she said again.

To her relief, Isha caught Ka's eye as she glanced across the tent. A sheep skin was wrapped around his shoulders, giving the impression that his clothes were lined with fur. He frowned at her.

'I, erm,' she faltered. 'I am a fr...' Maybe not a friend. An acquaintance? Before she could finish, an old kher – not as old as Uaza, but with horns dangerously close to her forehead, the tips scratching at the skin on top of her eyebrows – interrupted her.

'I remember you.'

It was the woman who had knelt beside the body when they had sawn off the old man's horns. Isha remembered her trying to talk with the lawmages, to explain that Ka was upset, that he just needed time.

'You look frozen, taniybu,' said the old kher. 'Come inside to speak.'

Isha gratefully stepped inside. The heat from the smoky fire and the animals' bodies was better, in that moment, than the giants' hearths at the Nest. She could feel her toes thawing.

'Sorry for intruding,' she said. 'I believe I was invited by Ka but, if I misunderstood, I will be on my way.' As an afterthought, she lifted the vase. 'I brought a gift.'

The old kher, who was probably the head of the household, addressed Ka in iwdan. He answered her swiftly, in a rough voice. His sentences were short, curt. Some sort of argument began, but it only involved the women – the men stayed silent. When Isha visited in autumn, men left the household as dinner concluded. Now that it was too cold to lounge outside, they remained inside, even if the price was to submit to the women's rule.

During the long-winded debate, she stood awkwardly beside the sheep. One of the dogs lifted its head to sniff at her legs; the other one, sleeping on its side, didn't wake up.

Something had been decided. Ka joined her at the entrance. He gestured for her to leave the vase with one of the children. Then, to Isha's dismay, they both stepped outside, back into the dreary cold.

'What do you think you're doing?' Ka asked, as soon as he'd closed the tent's flap behind them.

He didn't seem pleased to see her in the least.

'You said I could visit if I changed clothes,' she answered sharply. She was fed up with walls and locks and barred homes. 'You shouldn't say it if you don't mean it.'

Because she'd raised her voice, he raised his. 'That's what makes you think you can barge in and ask to be treated like a guest? A change of wardrobe? If I wore grey, would I be allowed inside the Nest?'

They stood in the Pit, as they had last time, stuck outdoors, as that seemed to be the only place they could talk. Her anger filtered out of her. She was shivering again, sick to the bone with failing. This had been a terrible idea. She shouldn't try to belong; she never could.

Ka was right. Tatters had been invited to the Pit by Arushi, but she had never been a guest, only his unwanted companion. She missed him, then, his easy laugh, his way of distracting attention away from her when the kher household became too pressing, his teachings, his help.

She missed him, and she couldn't get him back. This was the only place where she could find allies, yet even here, she was making a mess of things.

After a pause, Ka added, 'You're not even taniybu.' He said this as if it were an accusation, as if she had tried to trick him. 'You're human, aren't you?'

'Yes.' She tried to memorise the word for future use. 'I am not a halfblood, if that's your question.'

His frown was drawing deep furrows in his forehead.

'I thought you wanted to talk, so here I am,' she said softly.

'You don't speak iwdan,' he said. 'You couldn't talk with my tidewran even if you wanted to.'

'If you want me to leave, I'll leave.'

He hesitated. Maybe he could tell that she was exhausted, or maybe he was tired of fighting as well. Maybe it was the cold which numbed them both. Gruffly, he guided them away from the tiyayat, through the maze of roads criss-crossing the Pit, towards one of the empty houses.

She recognised the building with a sinking heart. It was where Yua and Isha had carried his father's body. Today, it was empty. It must be the kher equivalent of a funeral temple, to prepare bodies before their last voyage. In contrast to the warm colours and warmer fire of the tent, the place was dusty, barren. It was spiderweb grey. The hearth at the centre held ash and blackened wood.

Still, it was better than outdoors. They sat on either side of the hearth, on a brown-black rug. Ka drew his sheep pelt tighter around his shoulders. They let the silence settle.

Isha poked at the half-burnt logs. After a while, Ka helped her assemble the wood into a pyramid. At least they both agreed the room could do with a fire. They prepared the kindle, but neither of them had a lighter. Isha sat back down on her haunches, rubbing her forearms, wondering if it would be worth getting up to hunt for flint.

Ka pushed one leg out, resting the sole of his foot against the fire grid, and rolled up his trousers to the knee. He seemed to have decided something, so she waited. He revealed a circular tattoo, not unlike a bracelet or leather band, at the top of his calf. Isha couldn't quite make it out: there were stylised circles; someone lying down between the decorative bands, horns growing upwards from their brow; something complicated, maybe a bird, maybe a fountain of water, maybe a plant, above the horns.

'You know tattoos start at the wrist or waist?' Ka asked.

Isha nodded. Uaza had mentioned as much.

'All good deeds go upwards from there,' said Ka. 'Everything we do that makes us who we are, which we are proud of, we draw across our back, shoulders, waist, arms.' He took a deep breath. 'Everything we do that makes us who we are, which we are ashamed of, which we wish wasn't a part of us, we draw across our thighs, knees, feet, hands.'

He paused. 'Hands are often where we draw grief.' His hands were unmarked, though, despite his father's recent passing. Isha pictured Mezyan's hands, the circles like nooses around the knuckles, and wondered what sort of grief was so permanent as to be tattooed across each finger.

Ka pressed his palms against his calf. 'But my shame is deeper than hands, so I wanted the tattoo to be lower.' At last, the lines across his leg started to make sense: they were layers of earth. The silhouette must be his father, under the grass, then grit, then soil, which now enclosed him. She still wasn't sure what the shape hanging above his father's horns was.

'What is it, above the ground?' she whispered.

'A scavenger,' Ka said. 'A carrion bird.'

Of course. Isha swallowed thickly. A crow, that circle for its beady eye, that splash of ink for its wing, that curved line for a cruel beak.

'I have another one under the other knee,' said Ka, rolling his trousers down again. 'To match. The mark of the falconer, with the birds I tend to. Because I'm working with those who hate my people.'

He patted his trousers down, smoothing them around his ankle. 'The two birds on my body are birds of shame. What makes you think you deserve a bird of pride?'

He looked up, but not at her – at her tattoo. This explained some reactions she'd received when khers had seen her. Why had she got a tattoo on her face, as high as tattoos could go, as if it were something to be proud of? *What is my great deed?*

It wasn't her great deed. It never had been.

'My mother has done a lot for iwdan,' she said.

'And have you?'

She shook her head.

Restless, unable to hold his eye, Isha got up and hunted through the house for something to start the fire. In a woven basket with linen, dried lavender, bone needles and small household utensils, she found a wrought metal striker and a piece of flint. Sitting back down in front of Ka, she struck the metal with the stone until sparks flew. Keeping her hands busy helped. The flicker of warmth helped.

'I hear what you're trying to tell me,' she said at last. 'But you cannot blame me for a tattoo that was given to me as a child. You cannot blame me for what humans did before I was born.'

Ka brought his hands over the fire. The smoke curled around his nails; his fingertips glowed red.

'You couldn't have done anything before, no. But you can do something now.'

She had never viewed the tattoo that way: something to live up to, rather than something to constrict her. A promise to achieve, rather than a bind to break.

She rubbed her forehead with both hands. She wasn't trembling now, but she felt drained. The cold and the confusion had left her hollow, as if her bones had been emptied of marrow and filled with snow.

'What do you need me to do?' she asked.

Tension lifted, as if her words had dispelled a curse. Ka's shoulders relaxed. He went around the fire, poking at it with a stick to help it catch. He crouched beside her; bulky, broad, smelling of wet sheep.

He spoke nearly, albeit not quite, jokingly. 'Learning iwdan would help, for starters.'

'I'll learn iwdan,' she promised. 'But I'll need someone to teach me.'

Ka nodded. 'It's good that you came, eyas.'

He yielded a smile at last. It was a tentative, small smile; a tentative, small peace between them.

'We'll make a hawk out of you yet.'

Chapter Eight

As Isha no longer trained as part of a group, she was half-starved for mindlink – anything, even basic concentration exercises – until Passerine at last decided on a training session.

He brought her to one of the training rooms, where she hadn't been since her last daily sessions with Lord Daegan. The room felt too big for two people, even though it was smaller than the one she was accustomed to. The walls were painted with the heraldry of the Nest.

'Let's do some work,' said Passerine.

Isha didn't want to question him, but she didn't understand this change of heart. Since she'd left Lord Daegan, he had encouraged her to study by herself. He hadn't wanted to tutor her when she had arrived at the Nest, either.

'I am sorry you feel I've neglected you,' said Passerine, casually answering her thoughts out loud. 'I have been busy, and I am not a teacher by nature. But I will do my best.'

Annoyed, she kept a barrier of white noise and useless thoughts at the forefront of her mind.

'Better,' said Passerine. 'But you need to do that all the time. I am sure you realise that Sir Leofric, or another high mage, might be tempted to spy on you. You cannot, under any circumstances, let slip our link with Hawk. From now on, we will meet here every morning.'

He strode to the centre of the room, motioning for Isha to stand before him. He was taller than her, but he didn't use his size to belittle her like Lord Daegan used to. They stood well apart.

'You are going to conceal information from me,' he said. 'For example: what have you eaten for breakfast this morning? Hide this memory away.'

Isha had no idea how to do so. She had eaten porridge for breakfast – she always did. It was a recurring action, one that she performed often enough for it to be embedded in other memories, of conversations, of banter with Kilian, of lonely times in the mess, sitting beside the giant's chimney.

'We will be talking as you hide,' said Passerine. 'Are you ready?'

She nodded, focusing on the limestone wall behind him. Passerine asked her a few questions, about her day so far, the situation with the Renegades. His mind circled hers, but she didn't feel him trying to invade, like in mindbrawl. She was slow to answer his questions, her conversation stilted.

'Try to be natural,' said Passerine.

She did her best. About a minute later, he lifted one hand to interrupt her. 'Found,' he said. He mindlinked her memory of eating this morning, sharply defined, like a painting taken in the spur of the moment.

'I didn't feel you,' she said, frustrated.

Passerine didn't smile, but his features relaxed somewhat, as if he were amused by her reaction.

'You were trained by Tatters,' he said, 'and Tatters is anything but subtle. He doesn't need to be. He has Lal to protect him.'

She tried to hide her surprise at the fact that Passerine knew about Lal; of course he knew, she reasoned. He had known Tatters longer than her.

Passerine was still speaking: 'Don't get me wrong – Tatters is a powerful mage. But that's part of the problem. He has enough raw power to push through people's barriers. But sometimes it's easier to steal without being seen, to avoid a direct confrontation.' His lips curled into a thin smile. 'Win before the mindbrawl starts.'

'Tatters says that too,' Isha said. She wanted to speak up for him, to be fair to his teachings.

Passerine became serious. The brief smile disappeared, and his face had his usual stern expression, washed from emotion, as impersonal as the walls of the room.

'We will try once more,' he said.

* * *

After her training session, Isha headed for the mess, hoping for warm gruel. Several fires burnt within the large hall; the heat was so strong all the windows were covered in condensation from the temperature gap between both sides of the glass. Servants manned the pots, and the food was richer, meatier, than anything one could find at the Pit. Despite the growl in her stomach, Isha didn't fetch herself a meal immediately. She wandered around the room, went to touch the high iron grates of the only firepit which wasn't lit, wondering whether the giants had been like humans – each their own table, each their own tribe – or if they had been like khers, sharing everything.

Kilian was in line for a bowl of soup, drawing an animal in one of the windows to kill time. His yellow belt stood out starkly.

Isha hesitated. Now that she was affiliated to Passerine and apprentices avoided the Coop, she hardly ever spent time with Kilian. They had exchanged a couple of words, hasty greetings in the corridors, nothing like a proper chat. It was difficult to sit and speak when their belts marked them out as enemies. Their neutral ground had been taken from them.

It seemed such a shame that she shouldn't speak to people she had grown fond of. Maybe she was being naïve. Maybe she was lonely.

She found herself ambling towards Kilian, telling herself she would just greet him briefly. He had eyes as blue as the winter sky, but they were anxious rather than pleased.

'May you grow tall,' she said. She pointed to the silhouette he'd drawn on the window. 'I like the cat. Dog. Whatever that thing is.'

She managed to make him chuckle. 'I'm not going to be an artist, am I? At least you could tell it's got four legs.' He added chunky whiskers. 'A cat it is, then.'

'How are you, anyway?' she asked.

'I'm doing fine. And you?'

They barely had time for small talk: Kilian glanced at something beyond Isha's shoulder, and she turned to see Caitlin striding close, lips pursed. Her usual pack – a couple of apprentices who hung on to her every word, eager to please – followed. As soon as she was close enough, she snapped the kind of warning a dog would, when preparing to bite.

'Ah, so the puffin is back at the Nest. And here I was thinking you spent all your time drinking at the tavern and shagging khers.' Caitlin flashed Isha a smile that was all teeth. 'I see you got the most out of Tatters' teachings.'

Despite herself, Isha bristled. She focused on keeping her voice quiet.

'Tatters is probably dead because of you.' She wanted to speak without emotion, but a crack found its way into her words. 'They probably flung him off the Edge, without a funeral, without telling anyone.' The queue was moving on, but she ignored it. 'Do you think his ghost will hang around?'

Caitlin had paled, but she held her chin high. 'I don't believe in ghosts.'

No-one spoke up. They had all known Tatters, they had all bought him a drink, but they wouldn't say a word for him now. Isha looked at the circle of faces, and she could remember who liked drinking until they were dizzy but not until they were sick, who didn't like the people who got up before the bell and ate all the apples in the mess, who was homesick, who had a crush on an older mage.

She caught Kilian's eye. He gave her a smile and a shrug, something which was trying to defuse the situation, as if this was a lot of fuss over nothing.

'You're such hypocrites,' Isha spat. *No-one is ready to stand up for Tatters. No-one is ready to stand up for anyone but themselves.* 'And cowards. All of you.'

Isha looked across the room, at the tables varnished with sweat and oil, at the blackened pots, at the worn tiles glowing in the firelight. Everything seemed far away, as if seen through a veil of mist. She could only think of Ka, of the tattoo circling his leg, of the idea of inking his skin with birds of shame.

'I fail to see how you're so much better than us,' said Caitlin. 'For all your big mouth, you're still following a second-rate mage. How different are you from us, really?'

What makes you think you deserve a bird of pride? Although Isha hated herself for agreeing, Caitlin had a point. Her words meant nothing. They hadn't protected Ka from the pillory. They wouldn't get Tatters out of prison.

Still, they were not the same.

'I am not bound to obey. I can make my own choices. And the man I follow doesn't rely on weaker people to do his dirty work.' Isha held Caitlin's gaze. 'That's the difference between us.'

The difference was that she wanted to change.

She left the mess without eating. She wasn't hungry anymore.

***

Contrary to what Tatters had hoped, no kher guards worked in his part of the prison. He would have been able to speak with a kher, to convince them to take back a message to Arushi, but this place was only staffed by humans.

They gave him food and water once a day. It was tasteless, gritty porridge, probably with more woodcuttings than oats in the mix, going by the texture. The water was clear; it must have come from the river. It was more effort to find stale water to give the prisoners, obviously, than it was to send servants down to the riverbank.

It had grown steadily colder as the days went by. He couldn't sleep the time away. He was sick of sleeping; when he lay down on the stones, the insidious chill crawled into his bones. And the rats got cocky and walked over his hands. He couldn't see them, but he heard them, snuffling and searching. For the time being, they hadn't bitten him, although sometimes their rough pelts brushed against him. He tried to kick them when they came close. Once he caught one, but it barely skidded away. He was surprised at the weight of it; it must be as plump as a cat. It wasn't a comforting thought.

Worse was the gloom. If he glanced upwards, all he could make out was a thin glow. He couldn't see his hands. He couldn't see his food. He couldn't talk to Lal. With the kher horn against his skin, even his dreams were devoid of company.

It was dark and he was lonely.

But, he reminded himself, dark and lonely was much, much better than dark, lonely and in pain.

Despite knowing this, relief overwhelmed him when his door opened and light filtered inside. It was only a flickering torch, but he had to shield his eyes. At first, he could only make out two figures, before he adjusted to the details.

'My dear, you are in a state,' said Sir Leofric mildly. 'Varun, if you would be so kind.'

Goldie entered the cell, torch in hand. Tatters got to his feet too fast, with too little food inside him. His head spun, his vision blurring for a few seconds, which meant he didn't pull away fast enough when Goldie grabbed his arm. The lawmage gripped his elbow to drag him out of his cell.

'This is new.' Tatters couldn't help speaking out loud. It was a relief to hear his own voice. He could still speak. He was still human.

'I am trying out a theory,' said Sir Leofric, amiably enough. 'This might prove or disprove what we know about you.'

His eyes were as brilliant as before, a vivid green that matched his cloak. A small, nearly elegant scar ran down his cheek. It was barely visible; it looked like a thorn-scratch, nothing more. But it was still there.

Sir Leofric set off down the corridor, and Goldie followed, hauling Tatters along. Tatters noticed Sir Leofric was careful not to outpace them or to give Goldie cause to hold him too roughly. Tatters hadn't walked in weeks. After a few steps, he was out of breath, his legs weak beneath him. He watched the doors on either side of the corridor as they went past. He wondered if he would find his way if he were groping against the walls, trying to get out by himself.

They went up a staircase, into an area dimly lit by the winter sun filtering through low windows. Here, visitors who had come to beg for a family member's release were assembled, presents for the guards in their laps. He was obviously kept in a more secret part of the prison. What a reassuring thought. Lal would have something smart to say about it, no doubt, when he was free of these manacles.

A few people bowed when Sir Leofric passed, tried to push gifts into his hands, begged for indulgent treatment. He brushed them away as he would insistent midges. Still the crowd followed, mothers holding up young children – 'It's his father, sir, you wouldn't do that to a babe?' – and adults dragging their elderly parents behind them – 'See how old she is, it will kill her if you are cruel.' Sir Leofric left the hopeless figures behind without a second glance.

After one last flight of steps, another twist and turn of the corridor, they were outside. Everything was white. Tatters stared at the small courtyard, covered in a thick layer of snow. The roofs and turrets of the Nest were capped, and there was frost along the giants' coloured windowpanes.

How long have I been down there? He hadn't been expecting snow. It felt as if the world had shapeshifted while he wasn't looking, growing this white pelt, this new, sharp, breathtaking cold.

The first step in the snow bit into Tatters' skin. After two steps, his naked feet throbbed. Without breaking his stride, Tatters fleshbound with Sir Leofric. He had the satisfaction, at least, of seeing the high mage stumble, if only briefly, immediately catching himself.

The snow crunched as their small group made their way across. It was a side-garden, not the main courtyard. A private area. Tatters forced himself to take deep breaths. He had heard rumours about the hidden spaces where the Nest conducted their executions. He might be left here to die of cold, hunger or despair, whichever came first. Or maybe Sir Leofric was going to try to find out the range at which Tatters could fleshbind, the sweet spot where he could hurt his prisoner and be safe.

'What's the theory?' Tatters asked, trying to keep his voice carefree.

Sir Leofric merely smiled. 'No, no, that won't do. I will tell you afterwards if this proves to be conclusive.'

Mages were waiting at the end of the courtyard. Lawmages, the odd apprentice, one high mage. In a line, shoulders squared, legs apart, the lawmages sprang to attention when Sir Leofric came closer. Tatters also noticed prisoners: three of them, chained together. Two were dressed like ungifted, one was an apprentice. They were all wearing gleaming black manacles carved out of kher horn.

Kher guards stood on either side of the prisoners. Heart pounding, Tatters looked at everyone, but no-one caught his eye. It wasn't anybody he recognised.

They stopped. The ice around his ankles was melting, but Tatters remained comfortably numb. Sir Leofric, however, stamped his feet a couple of times, sighed through his teeth, then turned to Goldie and snapped:

'For skies' sake, get the man some shoes.'

Goldie was clearly put off by the request, but he handed Tatters to a kher guard and, grumbling under his breath, went to fetch some footwear. Everyone waited, at Sir Leofric's beck and call, without daring to question him.

Tatters wanted to talk with the kher, but he didn't dare give himself away. The iwdan woman holding him kept a neutral face, gaze locked straight ahead. However, as they waited in the quiet cold, she squeezed his arm. It was a brief, conscious gesture, a reminder that he had friends, after all. It was so quick it should have been impossible to notice.

But he had been fleshbinding. Sir Leofric slapped his wrist, as if he'd been bitten by an insect. Afterwards, he kept a close eye on Tatters and the guard, with the attentiveness a butcher might give an animal, when working out how to carve up the meat.

'Do you know, you are *such* an interesting prisoner,' Sir Leofric mused. 'I am sorry it took me so long to catch you.' Despite the foul weather, he didn't seem disgruntled. If anything, his expression was expectant, hungry.

Goldie returned with shoes, which Tatters pulled on, grateful for this small mercy. At last, the scene was set to Sir Leofric's liking: the prisoners in a line before them, Goldie by his side, Tatters close at hand. No-one but mages and guards as witnesses.

His heart sank as Tatters realised what was about to happen.

'No need to be so tense,' said Sir Leofric. 'We won't harm you. You're too valuable to waste on a quick execution.'

'You shouldn't have told him,' said Goldie. His voice was softer than Tatters remembered. He'd imagined it gruff, animal-like, but it was the normal voice of an adult man. 'He could've fretted throughout.'

Sir Leofric shook his head. 'For this to work, he mustn't be thinking about saving his skin. He must know there's no reason to be frightened.' He smiled at Tatters. 'So don't be,' he added, so pleasantly that it was impossible not to feel afraid.

Sir Leofric removed a pendant that had been hanging from his neck. It was made of wrought silver, encasing a glass capsule. Inside, Tatters could see a thimbleful of mercury.

'Let us begin,' said Sir Leofric. He waved to the kher guards. They seized the apprentice and dragged him forward, forcing him to his knees in front of the line of lawmages. Tatters stared at the young man's face, wondering if he knew him. Had he already seen these emaciated, terrified features? Maybe in the tavern, lounging at the back of the room, downing cheap beer?

He watched as the apprentice struggled against his guards. With a shudder, Tatters realised the apprentice was clinging to the iwdan as they tried to remove his manacles, begging them to let him keep them. Better that than the alternative.

But the khers removed the shackles. The high mage who had been waiting to the side took this as her cue. Her hair was tied back, revealing stark features, into a ponytail falling in one line down to her hips. Her belt was bleached white, the tips dyed red.

'May I talk to the prisoner before you do this?' she asked Sir Leofric.

Either he was in a good mood, or he was always enthusiastic before a punishment. 'Please do,' he said, waving her over with a flourish.

When the mage walked, her long ponytail danced from side to side. The young man knelt on the ground as she approached, pressing his forehead in the snow. Tatters couldn't hear what he said. But he heard the mage's answer – she spoke clearly, addressing the small audience as much as the apprentice.

'You disgraced yourself, you disgraced the Nest. And you disgraced me. Was your betrayal worth it?'

The apprentice shook his head. He was crying.

'I didn't think so.' The mage spoke with disgust, not pity. She extended her hand. Still crying, the apprentice removed his belt – white tipped with red – and handed it to her. She pulled it out of his unresisting hand. When she turned away, she didn't look back.

Sir Leofric took over with the practised tone of an actor. 'Young man, you are charged with harbouring sympathies for the Renegades and encouraging other apprentices to consider their shocking practices, despite knowing full well that they have declared war on the Nest. This is an act of treason.'

Tatters felt colder, suddenly, but not because of the snow. It was as if he had swallowed a block of ice and, rather than melt, the block was sitting at the bottom of his stomach. He couldn't remember all the charges laid against him, but he was pretty sure they included spying for the Renegades.

Sir Leofric stepped back. 'I do wish we could take off your manacles,' he told Tatters, 'but you are too dangerous. Still, you will understand what is happening.' He lifted his hand and snapped his fingers. 'Even ungifted do.'

Tatters did understand what was happening, even though there was nothing to see.

The line of lawmages didn't move. Maybe their breaths quickened. Maybe their eyes glazed over. Maybe Tatters only saw this because he wanted to see something.

The apprentice howled. It was the kind of sound that was expected from a vixen, not a human. Tatters winced as it increased. If it was possible to rip out his throat through screaming, the apprentice would have. He clutched at his clothes, at the snow, at the air. The line of lawmages barely shivered. There was nothing to see, because everything was happening inside the apprentice's mind.

They were tearing him to shreds, destroying his sense of self. They were taking away what had kept him up at night, what he had believed in, what had given him pleasure. They were taking what was intimate, never to be shared with anyone. They were taking what had been public, a source of pride he told everyone.

They were making a lacunant.

He would be given a bowl, afterwards, carved out of crude wood. He would be left to beg in front of the gates. And he would never think of running, never consider that he might have lived another life, never understand there was something before this slow death sucking at dew and raindrops.

Sir Leofric was wavering on his feet, as if his body had to find its balance on its own, without a mind to guide it. He was clutching his pendant in one hand, the mercury glinting within. Was he stealing a strand of the apprentice's memories to keep as his own, sealing it away in the quicksilver? It would be like stealing someone's teeth, or hair, after breaking their neck.

The screaming stopped. The apprentice gazed around like a babe just born, wondering at the marvels of the world, not knowing what the world had done to him. When he started kneading the snow with his hands, like a cat kneads a cushion before lying down, Tatters knew it was over. The apprentice didn't seem aware of the people around him, even as the kher guards picked him off the floor, took him away, brought the next prisoner forward.

Tatters turned away the second time. He couldn't watch.

'You're not enjoying the show?' asked Sir Leofric.

Each time his eyes caught the pendant, balancing at the end of its chain between Sir Leofric's fingers, Tatters imagined a man after being hanged as he was brought down from the scaffold. The blue of his face, the thick tongue choked in his mouth, the bulging, bloodshot eyes. The nail scratches down his neck, deep enough to draw blood. And then Sir Leofric kneeling beside the body, picking out a lock of hair and cutting it with a silver pair of scissors. He couldn't shake off this image.

'You're stealing their souls,' said Tatters. He wished it was a question.

Sir Leofric smiled. 'How very dramatic. This is a keepsake, nothing more.'

He placed a hand on Tatters' shoulder and leant in closely. He whispered with the contained excitement, the soft intimacy, of loving words. 'I take their last memory. When they know they are going to die, when hope leaves them. The very last moment of every life that ends here.'

Without letting this sink in, flitting to another subject, he asked, 'Do you know what makes a good mage?'

The third prisoner was being yanked forward. It was a woman, charged for hiding that she had the gift. She hadn't wanted to come to the Nest because she wanted to care for her family and, yes, maybe use her gift now and then to smooth things over. Nothing big. But using mindlink without telling the mages was worse than robbing them. They didn't take to it kindly.

This was what Tatters would have been killed for, had the Renegades not found him.

'Three things make a good mage,' confided Sir Leofric. 'One is wanting power. One is having imagination.' He patted Tatters' shoulder. 'I'll let you think about the third one.'

As the khers were removing the manacles, the woman raised her voice: 'Let me hang, like all decent folk! I'm not a mage. I never was. You are bullies, and thieves, and murderers. Grave-robbers!' There was spittle flying from her lips. The khers backed away from her, warily but without fear. As soon as she was free, she stormed up to Sir Leofric, lifting her skirts above the snow, her knees red with cold.

'If you are going to kill me, do it,' she snarled. 'But don't make me into one of those ghoulish creatures.'

She inhaled, lifting her chin high, ready to curse more – but then stopped abruptly, mid-stride. Her eyes winked in and out of focus, as if she were struggling to see.

And then the screaming started.

It lasted much longer than the apprentice; she must have been stronger. Tatters gritted his teeth and didn't even notice he had bitten his tongue. When she stopped struggling, his jaw ached.

He swallowed blood. The sound of her voice was still ringing in his ears. He only realised he had stepped forward, in a pantomime attempt to help, when Goldie pulled him back in line.

Sir Leofric was watching him, toying with his pendant, rubbing its precious content between finger and thumb. He stroked his cheek, maybe to dull the pain he shared with Tatters. Rather than discomfort, it was fascination that lit up his eyes.

'You're an interesting colour,' said Sir Leofric, as the woman was taken away. He was still massaging his jaw, maybe even savouring the sensation.

The audience, now officially dismissed, was dispersing.

'He hasn't got the stomach for crime,' said Goldie. 'No wonder he's a slave.'

Ignoring him, Sir Leofric addressed Tatters. 'Have you thought about it?'

Tatters couldn't breathe. The winter air was too cold. The winter lights, the greys and blues and whites, were too bright, too pale, too bleak.

'What was the question?' he asked.

He couldn't tear his eyes away from the woman. She took the begging bowl the iwdan handed her as meekly as a lamb. As they ushered her away, she gnawed on her hand, pushing four fingers in her mouth.

Sir Leofric tapped his cane against Tatters' cheek to get his attention.

'I expect you to listen when I'm speaking,' he said, politely enough, although Tatters could hear the control it took for the lawmage to stay calm, the slight slip of emotion at the edge of his words. 'What makes a good mage? A drive for power. Imagination. And?'

Tatters shook his head. The sky above was overcast. It would snow again during the night.

'Empathy,' said Sir Leofric.

He lifted his pendant. Tatters shuffled uneasily, trying not to show how much he disliked the thing. Judging by Sir Leofric's expression, he failed.

'You see, I was trying to understand where your power stems from,' said Sir Leofric. 'And now it's clear why you are a talented mage. You are good with people, I bet. Good at talking to them. Good at getting them to like you. Good at knowing what they want, what will hurt them. Sometimes you know them so well, you like them – even the miserable ones. Am I wrong?'

Tatters' tongue hurt. He tried not to lick his lips, cracked by the cold, to avoid leaving red smears across them. 'And you're terrible with people,' he answered. 'Everyone pretends they like you, every girl you court seems to love you until you try to kiss her, everyone laughs at your jokes. But you know they whisper curses behind your back. And you hate them, even the wonderful ones.'

Goldie seemed on the verge of slapping him, but Sir Leofric lifted his hand.

'Gloat,' he said. 'Please. I am listening.'

Tatters shook his head. He was tired. He ached for Lal's company. He thought of the apprentice's face and wondered if he'd ever shared a drink with the boy, if he could have forgotten him.

He thought of the woman. Maybe a helpful family member would collect her, later, when the mages weren't looking.

'Very well,' said Sir Leofric, after a pause. He slipped his pendant around his neck and wiped the snowflakes which had landed on his sleeves. 'It's a shame, really. This was your last chance to feel powerful. It's my turn.'

He lifted two slim fingers. 'I know you empathise with people, whether you want to or not. And I know you are friends with khers.'

His green eyes never left Tatters' face, and they creased with a genuine smile when he spotted the truth in Tatters' discomfort.

'Bearing this in mind, I have found a way to torture you that means you are not able to use fleshbinding,' Sir Leofric concluded. 'Isn't that wonderful?'

The lawmages were waiting to be dismissed, chatting, joking, as if nothing out of the ordinary had happened. Tatters shook his head, trying to focus his thoughts.

'Do what you want,' he said. 'You cannot hurt me unless you kill me.'

Sir Leofric clapped his hands together like a child, grinning with such obvious pleasure that one could forget, for a moment, what it was he was smiling about.

'We're not going to be hurting *you*.'

Chapter Nine

Isha found herself slipping away to the Pit more and more often. Much more could be learnt with Ka than within the confines of the Nest – or at least it felt that way.

She picked up that every tiyayat was organised around the female bloodline, and that male concubines had ranks depending on whether they were casual lovers or long-term members of the hearth who helped tend to the children. A male could be a lover to more than one woman, but only the father to one set of children.

Isha also studied the iwdan language. Ka taught her scraps of sentences. Once in a while, he invited her into his tiyayat, in which fewer people spoke the human tongue fluently. She learnt by pointing at items around the house and asking what the word for them was, or asking for translations of words which were repeated often. The children were happy to indulge her.

She was told that 'the Pit' wasn't, as she had assumed, a derogatory term. It was short for 'the Firepit', a literal translation of tiyayat. It meant this was the hearth of all khers in the city – the Home would have been a better translation.

Today, Isha found Ka waiting for her at the Pit's gates, leaning his weight against the wall, the tip of his horns scratching lines in the soft mudbrick. He'd invited her on an outing, without revealing where he wanted them to go.

'Tidir, eyas.' He eyed her new outfit as she came closer. 'I imagine it's easier to move around now,' he guessed.

The dress she'd worn at the farm wasn't suited to snow, and Isha had wanted breeches to run in if need be, so she'd decided to purchase winter clothes. The tailor had taken time – and a good part of the monthly money Passerine gave her – but it was worth it. The tunic and shoulder-cape were brown, with birds in yellow thread embellishing the sleeves and the hem. The colours were subdued, but the embroidery was fancy, and the fabric thick enough to fend off the cold.

'You look like a merchant human,' said Ka. 'Someone rich.'

It was difficult to tell if he was mocking her or not. He was smiling, but not in an inclusive way.

Isha tried not to sound defensive. 'I will wear my old clothes when I'm working at the tavern.'

Ka made a derisive sound, blowing air out of his nose. 'And one Isha goes to work, and one to the Pit, and yet another to the Nest. Into how many bits do you want to split yourself?'

'Just say you don't like them.'

'I like them, rich girl.'

He pushed himself off the wall, nodding his goodbyes to the guards before heading confidently down the street, leaving his quarter behind. Having never spent time with him outside the Pit, Isha couldn't help but worry about the ungifted around them, about their reaction to a kher and a human strolling together.

Ka might have sensed this, because he leant closer to ask: 'Embarrassed, eyas? Do I spoil your nice outfit?'

Now his tone was definitely unfriendly.

'No,' she lied.

She avoided a puddle, which brought her closer to the

merchants selling wares – late autumn harvests which, despite the cold to keep them fresh, were starting to let out the sick-sweet smell of rot. She felt hemmed in, by Ka on one side, and by the stalls on the other, where children stood with too-little money and hungry eyes. A few refugees were haggling with a shopkeeper, shivering in their flimsy nasivyati, unsuited to the Duskdweller climate.

'Apparently the Sunrisers are loaded with golden trinkets,' Ka said, following Isha's gaze. 'Magical ones, even. Shame for them they can't eat their gold.'

There wasn't much sympathy in his voice.

'I wouldn't listen to street gossip,' Isha answered. She picked the rumour Ka would be least inclined to believe as an example. 'I've heard iwdan are beating up refugees to steal from them.'

They had to stop to let a cart pass the narrow street; its wheels threw up slush. The horse was wearing blinkers, and jerked its head left and right, snorting. Ka patiently let it through, not taking offence at her comment. This lack of reaction, more than anything he might have said, worried her.

'It's not true, is it?' she asked.

'Sunrisers are slave states,' Ka said, dodging the question. 'With iwdan slaves.'

That was not the answer she had been hoping for. 'Not all of them,' she said. 'And even so. If you were begging for food on the street, would you deserve having what little you have left taken from you?'

Ka heard the hardening in her tone, and his temper flared in turn. 'You're the one saying we shouldn't listen to rumours. Take your own advice.'

A lot of their conversations ended this way: with the sharp snap of long-tried patience. After that, they walked in silence, their feet making wet sounds on the pavement, listening to merchants calling out to each other, to the beat of horses' hooves, to the songs of women sweeping their front steps clear of snow.

She followed Ka out of the city. They started towards the cliff where the Nest perched.

'They won't let you in,' she said, although he knew this already. She was growing nervous. It was one thing to discard her apprentice's robes in town, quite another to brave the crowd coming to and from the Nest.

'We're not keeping to this road for long,' he promised.

They soon turned off the main track to pick a small, over-grown path running south-west towards the cliff. The ground was soggy. Mud sucked at their feet, while patches of grass which seemed solid suddenly gave in.

'You were better off wearing your servant's clothes,' Ka noted.

'Next time I will,' grumbled Isha.

They followed the curve of the river from afar, towards an uninhabited patch of moorland south of the Nest. As the distance to the Edge grew shorter, the illusion that the clouds were a continuation of the ground grew stronger. She had the impression that the bumps of bushes below her feet and the nebulous shapes of clouds were one and the same: green grass giving place to white.

'If it'd been snowing today, we wouldn't even notice if we stepped off the Edge,' she muttered.

Ka smirked. 'Don't tell me you're afraid of heights. Aren't you supposed to be able to fly?'

'With my mind,' Isha said. 'My body never promised anything. It's more of the dropping-through-the-underworlds disposition.'

She couldn't see the cliff; the fall beyond could have been a puddle reflecting the sky.

To her discomfort, Ka brought them closer and closer to the Edge. When she glanced back, the silhouettes of mages and servants along the main road were as small as insects. She saw the tall gates of the city through a cloud of mist and spray thrown up by the river. The sound of the waterfall was deafening.

'Where are we going?' Isha asked.

'Over the Edge,' said Ka. She glared at him, but he only laughed. 'I am serious, eyas. If you don't know how to fly, I hope you're a quick learner.'

The wind lifted as they got closer to the end of the earth. Isha's shoulder-cape fluttered, buffeted like a sail. When the Edge was a few strides away, Isha stopped. Ka went down into a crouch. There was more stone, less mud, but it didn't make the ground any less slippery. The rock surface was slick, with clumps of moss. The wind pulled at her with its long, invisible fingers.

Ka scrambled towards the cliff.

'Are you coming?' he asked.

Isha shook her head. 'What for?' She had to shout to be heard. They were far from the river, but it was all they could hear.

Ka rolled his eyes. He sat perched on the Edge like a large red mountain goat. He was holding on to the rock with one hand. Drops of water like dew were caught in his hair.

'I'll show you.' His grin was vicious. 'Are you afraid I'll push you?'

Isha knelt, cursing herself for yielding to provocation. She crept forward, on her hands and feet, gripping the moss, conscious that it would easily rip from the stone if she pulled too hard.

She joined Ka at the Edge. She peered over. Underneath it was white and grey, each cloud a different shade of colourless. The wind numbed her cheeks.

'Enjoying yourself yet?' Ka asked. 'I'll go first.'

With those words, he let himself drop over the Edge.

Isha had to stifle her scream. Ka held on to the cliff with both hands and flung his legs into the emptiness. He hung there for a moment before letting go. A flock of seagulls took flight suddenly at the spot where he had fallen, the sound of their wings and their squawking filling the air. He disappeared, swallowed away from sight.

The wind howled.

'Can you hear me?'

Trembling, Isha answered: 'Yes.' He was somewhere below her, out of sight. She lay flat on the ground, trying to ignore the wind, to forget that it gripped at her as if to lift her off the cliff. The moss was wet, and soon her new clothes were soaked; her hands were muddy. She couldn't care less.

'Come closer!' Ka entreated.

Tentatively, she crawled forward. She put her head over the Edge, as far as she dared, clinging to the cliff with the rest of her body. She wanted to push her hair out of her eyes, as the wind kept swiping it across her face, but she couldn't spare a hand to do so.

Below, there was a platform on the face of the cliff, the mouth of a tunnel maybe, or simply of an alcove. Ka was standing there, fists on his hips, proud. He chuckled when he saw her.

'You're not going down headfirst.' He motioned with one hand. 'The other way. Feet-first. I'll catch you.'

'Are you out of your mind?' she asked. 'How are you going to get back up?'

He shrugged his careless shrug. 'I've done it before.' He stepped closer to the end of his platform, either not noticing or not caring about the way the wind tried to trip him, hissing at his ankles. 'Anyway, the Temple says I don't have a mind, so I can hardly lose it, can I?'

Isha took a deep breath. It smelt of earth, of the black mud that could be scraped between tree roots, of something slightly rotten. The wind was everywhere; in her hair, under her clothes, shaking her hands. Backing away from the Edge first, she then did as Ka advised and started towards the cliff feet-first. It was one of the most frightening things she had ever done: sliding backwards, not knowing when the world would end.

Her foot met emptiness. She let it down, very carefully, over the Edge. One leg first. And then the other, when she heard Ka's words of encouragement, when she was certain her hold on the rock with both arms was strong enough.

'Lower yourself slowly,' Ka said.

She didn't know how. Her left foot scraped against a piece of the cliff, but below her there was a gap, the alcove where Ka was standing, and she couldn't hold on to anything there. Her right leg hung loosely in mid-air. She was stuck. She couldn't go further down and she wasn't sure she had enough strength in her arms to hoist herself back up.

Big hands caught her ankles. She felt more relieved than she should have at knowing someone else was holding on.

'Nearly there,' he said. 'Come closer.'

She wasn't a good rock-climber; it wasn't a skill apprentices were taught at the Nest. Lowering herself, she placed her feet on Ka's shoulders, reassured by the fact that she was now standing on *something*.

Ka's hands went higher, caught her waist and, to her horror, pulled. She shrieked as he lifted her off the side of the cliff – for a moment she feared the wind had ripped her off the Edge. He hugged her to his chest, turned, and placed her down effortlessly beside him. She felt solid stone under her feet, stone behind her back. She collapsed onto the floor. Too focused on recovering her breath, she barely noticed that they were at the mouth of a cave.

Ka knelt beside her. 'You did well.'

She would have nightmares of missing her footing.

'Never do that without warning. Ever. Never ever ever ever,' she said. 'I nearly kicked you. I nearly fought back. It would have killed us both.'

'But you didn't,' he said. 'And here we are.'

She relented long enough to take in her surroundings. To her left, there was a piece of rock opening onto the cliff-face. Beyond was a sight Isha had never seen – the sky without a horizon. As far as the eye could see, there were clouds, and sky, and space. No earth. No Edge. No line dividing the ground from the ether, the living from the dead.

Staring out made her dizzy. She turned to her right. The hole was large enough for someone to stand. Old birds' nests clung along the sides of the cave, with the seagulls that hadn't been spooked huddled close together in the crannies. The ground was sprinkled with dried bird droppings.

A storm lantern lay on the floor, its shutters rusted, its handle worn. Ka picked it up and lit it, his swift movements betraying how often he did this.

'You've been here before,' Isha said.

Ka didn't look up from the lamp as the wick caught. 'I visit from time to time,' he said. 'Sometimes I bring some more oil, or a blanket. If there is a war, I'll bring my tid-idewran here to hide.'

Isha now knew that idewran were relatives through the male bloodline, while tidewran were relatives through the female bloodline. Tid-idewran included both. Greetings could be used in the same way: tid-idir was used to address a group of women and men.

'I hope it won't come to that,' she said. It might be safe, but what a gloomy place to hide a family, with the seabirds for food and the gaping void for company.

Ka closed the lantern's shutters against the wind. He was working quietly, bent over his task. It was only when he got up that she thought to thank him.

'Thank you for showing me this place.'

'It's fine,' Ka said. 'If you change your mind and join the mages, I'll just have to kill you.'

'I'd like to see you try,' she said. 'But still. Sekk iss.'

Ka snorted. He lifted the lamp to chest-height before starting down the cave. Isha followed, frowning.

'Am I using it wrong?'

'It can be used as thanks,' said Ka. 'But your accent is weird.'

The cave, rather than becoming narrower, grew larger as they headed inward. What had been rough sides of stone, sloping downwards, became smoother. Isha was glad for the small talk; it took her mind off the cold rising from the underground, like the earth breathing.

'Sekk iss,' she said again, trying out the words on her tongue, to copy Ka's pronunciation. Sekk iss, *May your horns grow*, was a strange set phrase, which fitted any number of situations. It could mean, as Isha understood it, either thanks, good luck, or farewell.

'Sekk iss,' he corrected her.

The cave was full of their whispers, like the tongue of snakes.

Ka guided them down an unexpected slope – a slab of stone cutting downwards, slippery with damp, yellow lines striating the rock surface. Fungus was growing down its sides, pale brown and beige, thick and creamy to the eye, yet hard to the touch. Ka manoeuvred easily, finding eroded footings that he seemed to know by heart, placing the lamp down when he needed both hands, retrieving it as soon as he was past the obstacle.

Here the tunnels weren't manmade, Isha could tell. She hadn't been sure before, but the heavy stalagmites squatting on the ground were natural, as were the thin, wavy, cloth-like veils of stone on the ceiling. Stalactites like needles hung suspended.

'Tawa sar,' sighed Ka. *Child of stone*. 'I know you are a bird, eyas, but isn't this beautiful?'

When he turned to her, the lamp turned with him, throwing shadows that lengthened the stalagmites, casting a light that petered out before it reached the ends of the cave.

'To tell you the truth, I'm more comfortable here than near the Edge,' Isha admitted.

Ka stopped. He breathed in the underground smell – a clear scent, like water over earth. The rocks were streaked with brown and yellow and orange, sometimes ochre, sometimes red. She came to stand beside him. The silence was eerie. It was a silence that had stayed, undisturbed, long before humans and khers could speak their names. It was a silence that would stay, uncaring, long after all humans had taken flight and all khers were buried.

'It is beautiful,' she agreed, in a hush. The stones seemed to listen, to soak up their words.

'This links to the tunnels the giants built.' Ka pointed, but Isha couldn't see much past his arm. 'It leads to large square tunnels, sometimes even with carved decoration along the centre of the walls.'

'That I would like to see,' she said.

Ka shook his head. He placed the lantern down on a stalagmite, his hand cupped above it, to catch the drops before they fell on his light.

'It's too dangerous to go there,' he said. 'I think they might also be used by the mages, for what they do below the Nest.'

Isha went to sit on the floor; the ground was cold, but she hugged her cloak closer. Her clothes were damp in places – along the shins, down the torso. She listened to the drops of water landing with a muted sound in Ka's palm.

'Mages use tunnels below the Nest?' This was news to her. 'What for?'

When Isha looked up, she saw that his face was closed, his lips pressed into a thin line. 'As an extension of the prisons, I would imagine,' he said.

Isha stared at their lantern, this flame protected by metal and glass, burning to keep the dark at bay. Like the wick, her heart lit up, with the lonely, bright fire of hope.

'Is there a way to check?' she asked. 'To explore at night, maybe, when nobody is there?'

Ka angled his hand so that the water would trickle to the floor. Although he was frowning, she sensed him not angry, but worried.

'Why do you think I brought you here?' he asked.

'This might lead us to Tatters,' she answered.

Ka didn't speak at first. At the Nest, there was always the river churning, the birds screeching, the distant sounds of the city adding their clunks and neighs and barks to the mix. Underground, Isha couldn't hear the river. The absence rang in her ears louder than the crash of water. If she strained her hearing, she could make out drips and drops, and Ka's breathing.

'Tatters helped me when the lawmages had me,' Ka said at last. 'I want to be the one to help him now the lawmages have him.'

'We don't even know if he's alive,' Isha whispered.

'Yes, we do,' said Ka.

Her heart leapt into her throat. 'What? How? Are we sure?'

He ran his hand along his horns, a gesture that Isha had seen khers do before, as often as humans bit their nails or tugged at their hair.

'He was spotted by one of the guards. Arushi had everyone keeping an eye out for him, and Tara saw him. It was a while ago now, but it didn't look like the Nest wanted him dead.'

'No-one told me,' Isha said, crestfallen.

She got up to stand beside Ka, by the lantern. When she placed her hands beside the glass shutters, the heat from the candle was a small, tangible thing, a piece of light cut out in the fabric of darkness.

'We only have your word that you didn't have a hand in Tatters' arrest.' Before she could defend herself, again, he said, 'It's enough for me. But not for Arushi.'

It hurt to hear it, but she was not surprised. She placed her fingers against the lamp's shutters until the heat stung. 'I understand.'

'We're lucky Tatters can fleshbind,' Ka went on. 'If he really is down those tunnels, it will help us find him.'

Isha shook her head. 'That's impossible.'

'Whether it is possible or not, he can. I experienced it firsthand.'

She wasn't sure how to answer that, so she focused on the matter at hand. 'Whatever his powers, if we can find a safe way to explore those tunnels, we might be able to find him.'

Ka nodded. His half-lit profile, like the fire, kept flickering between moods; it was hard for her to know when their relationship would be easy or conflictual.

'Any decision to go against the Nest would need to be voted for, at the Pit. I have a plan I could submit to the vote, but it requires a mage.' Ka granted her a sidelong, self-derogatory smile. 'Unlucky, right?'

There was only one answer she could give. 'I want to help.'

He placed his hands around hers. Touch wasn't easy between them, but it was essential between khers. It was a sign of trust.

They were both uncomfortable, Isha suspected, but despite this, the gesture was important.

Holding hands underground, in silence, was a promise.

***

All Passerine said when he met Isha in the library was, 'You will want to hear this.' After a couple of strides, he added, 'The Renegades have made their move.'

Her heart clenched in fear. He wouldn't say anything more. She had shorter legs and was forced into a half-run to keep up with him.

She knew the path they were taking, even though this was a part of the Nest she had never visited. Passerine took her to one of the spiral staircases the humans had built. There were four in all, in each corner of the Nest, and they were used when mages needed to reach the top of the castle. Parts of the old staircases built by the giants had crumbled and fallen, especially closer to the top of the Nest, and rather than repairing the outsized steps, mages had built their own.

They started the ascent, Isha soon gasping for breath. The passage was steep, unforgiving. When she pressed her hand on one wall to help herself up, she found that there was a line worn out in the stones, made by generations of mages who, like her, had rested their hands there. Under her palm, the stone was cold as ice. The further up they went, the cooler the passageway became, until Isha could believe she was climbing a snowy mountaintop, not a tower.

For the most part, the spiral staircase was made of sandstone. Passerine climbed up the steps swiftly, Isha struggling behind. As they neared the top, however, creamy-coloured marble, and what Isha thought might be alabaster, appeared. The last few steps, polished white, led into the council room.

She heard the wind before she felt it. It howled like wolves celebrating a hunt.

The council was the highest point of the Nest. It didn't have walls, nor a ceiling. In many ways it was like the Temple – only it wasn't the Nest that had copied the priests, it was the Temple that had copied the giants.

It was a circle of stone, a balcony of sorts, encased in pale winter sky. Along its outer ring stood tall slabs of stained glass, all of various colours – they were too large for humans to ever replicate them. Isha marvelled at one continuous panel of bright-red glass, two fists thick, enough for it to be nearly opaque. The glass created complicated galleries that prevented the wind from reaching the centre of the chamber. It served as a wind-catcher.

There was knowing it, and there was seeing a wind-path of coloured glass, like frozen lightborns caught in flight.

On one side of the circular roof, a few steps still clung to the stone where the giants' stairway had given way. When Isha glanced down, her heart plunged and soared, like a bird dipping from the roof. She could see everything – the Temple, the Nest's courtyard, the high gates like a monster's ribcage, the moorland dappled with brown and white.

'We're late,' Passerine said.

The wind screamed through the pathways but, when they stepped into the centre of the council, it was eerily still. A circular mosaic of abstract art decorated the floor, its colours echoing the glass panes. Lord Daegan and several other high mages were already there, assembling around a table. The round table seemed small and mean, its legs hiding the centre of the mosaic – a late addition. An apprentice was brushing the snow off its polished surface.

Legends said that this was where the giants had taken flight. Because of this, it was a hallowed place. Despite the biting cold, mages made important decisions here. Isha spotted Sir Cintay, placed not far from Lord Daegan. He was not the only Wingshade refugee, but since he had given Daegan his convent's collar, he had a place of honour at his side. Isha also recognised the unmistakable green cloth of the head lawmage, Sir Leofric. And a couple of Sunriser mages who had been invited to attend. Everyone was warmly clad.

'At last, you grace us with your presence,' Lord Daegan said.

Beside the supreme mage there was his collarbound. Her pale hair had been plaited; the braid circled her forehead like a crown. She was wearing the bright blue fabric with silver strands that Isha had bought for her, the sacred nasivyati pieces stitched together, as Kilian had predicted, to form an overdress and skirts, long sleeves, even a sort of creased ruff around her shoulders. A thick coat and fur boots completed her outfit.

The collarbound looked at Isha over the heads of the assembled mages, something like recognition in her eyes. Isha wondered if she remembered the human who had bound her with a collar, the one she should hate. But when Isha clumsily nodded towards her – trying to convey *something*, at least, how sorry she was, some basic human decency – the woman turned away.

A couple of apprentices were present, standing behind the most eminent high mages. No ungifted servants were permitted in such an important place. Ill at ease, she stuck close to Passerine.

As soon as Passerine reached his seat, however, Lord Daegan snapped:

'What makes you think you can bring your pet to our meetings?'

Passerine brushed the snow off his chair. 'You bring yours,' he said.

Isha had enough sense to shut her mouth.

'Only mages of high status are allowed to bring servants,' Lord Daegan said. 'Which you are not.'

'I am a high mage,' Passerine countered. 'Unless you are denying me that title?'

Like clouds heavy with lightning, tension lifted between both men. Isha was on the verge of apologising and leaving the room when Sir Leofric waved a bejewelled hand to catch Lord Daegan's attention. Silver rings littered his fingers.

'I'll have the girl,' he said. 'She isn't a threat.' From the way he glanced at Passerine as he said it, he might have been mentioning the master, not the apprentice. 'Apparently Wingshade girls make the best servants,' he added, his smile as bright as his rings.

One of the refugee mages – an older woman with a severe, lined face – scowled at Sir Leofric's words, but she didn't intervene. After a moment's hesitation, Lord Daegan relented, crossing his hands in front of his stomach, his face impassive. 'Do as you will. If you want her, she can serve you.'

Passerine clenched his jaw but nodded his thanks to Sir Leofric. Even more uneasy than if she'd been forced to leave the room, Isha went to stand beside the lawmage. When he didn't sit down, she realised she was supposed to clean his chair. She didn't have anything to wipe the snow with, so she used her sleeve. He watched her, faintly amused, as she prepared his seat, held it for him, helped him sit down.

Lord Daegan waited until the high mages had made themselves comfortable, ignoring the sidelong glances they cast him and his lightborn. Not wanting to provoke him, Isha stood behind Sir Leofric's high-backed chair and tried to lie as low as a tattooed apprentice could.

215

Lord Daegan signalled to an apprentice, who was standing respectfully aside now that the table was wiped clean.

'Bring in the messenger.'

After bowing, the young man faded behind the glass, his silhouette visible for a moment like a purple shadow. The high mages waited in tense silence while the wind sang.

Two silhouettes, at first only fudged outlines behind the coloured glass, emerged from the wind-paths. The way newcomers went from coloured shapes to grey, colourless people when they reached the council reminded Isha of how the lightborn had smoothly transitioned from a ray of light to human form.

The messenger was an ordained mage, his hands and face hastily washed, the rest of his demeanour indicating he was weary of travelling and hadn't had the time to rest. His robes were splattered with mud; he smelled of horse-sweat. At first Isha didn't recognise him, until she realised she knew his gait, albeit without the limp; she knew his features, albeit without the grime. It was Ninian. He nodded towards the members of the council, his eyes lingering on the collarbound before he cleared his throat to speak:

'The Renegades have started crossing the Shadowpass.'

Across the council, the same expression of astonishment passed on people's faces – Passerine was the only exception. He had been expecting this. Maybe she had also been waiting for this to happen, because Isha didn't feel any strong surprise, only a gaping emptiness, as if the roots of the world had given way.

'An army cannot cross the Shadowpass in one go,' said Lord Daegan.

'They aren't trying to,' said Ninian. 'They have built a temporary fortification around the Duskdweller side of the Shadowpass and are crossing in groups of twenty or so, every day.' He glanced at Sir Cintay, rubbing his hands together – either because of the cold or out of nervousness. 'They are using the refugees as a shield.'

He cleared his throat. 'When they cross the light-tide, the Renegades leave refugees in front of and behind their contingent. If anyone starts growing mad because of the night-tide, they can adapt their pace – if people behind start raving, they need to go faster. If people in front start raving, they need to slow down.' He swallowed. 'Canaries down the mine. Only they do it with humans.'

Ninian mindlinked an image to the council, which Passerine shared with Isha. She held on to the high-backed chair with one hand to steady herself as the pictures flooded her mind.

It was one of Ninian's own memories. Like all mindlink, it shared not only visions, but sensations. He was talking to a woman bundled in layers of rags, wearing all her possessions on her back. She was a Sunriser, with yellowed teeth and bright, feverish eyes. Each piece of clothing was a different thickness, making her look like a shaggy dog with patchy fur.

They were in a small town, probably not far from the Shadowpass. She was leaning against the wall of a shack, while other refugees were on the floor, lining the street. None of the others seemed fit to speak.

'They take volunteers, sir,' she explained. 'They say, you want to be free? You're sick of us? You can go, but you have to cross the Shadowpass. And then you can be free.' The woman pulled her sleeves over her bony fingers. She tugged at the fraying fabric, undoing the loose threads. 'So they let us come with them. But we have to walk in front, just at the edge of the shadows, where you can hear the noise they make...' The woman's eyes glazed over. 'Have you ever heard the shadows, sir?'

Isha was conscious of Ninian answering the woman by shaking his head. He was standing a few feet away from the wall, to keep himself apart from the Sunrisers.

'They...' The woman made a vague gesture with her hand, back and forth, to imitate waves lapping at a shore. '*Shik shik shik shik*. Like brushing glass off tiles. *Shik shik shik shik.*'

The woman was lost in her description, whispering the sound to herself, varying in pitch from time to time, as if trying to capture the exact moment again. Like singers picking up a chorus, some of the refugees on the ground repeated: *Shik shik shik*.

'What else can you tell me?' Ninian interrupted gruffly.

The woman blinked. Her hand continued to move, but she stopped her muttering. 'They eat you,' she said. 'The shadows. Just a bit at a time, *shik shik*, they nibble here, the names of flowers, *shik shik*, who cares, the flowers might be different on the other side, then they eat more, the love of your parents, *shik shik*, but who cares, your parents are dead, their love won't save you, but the shadows haven't had enough, they eat more, s*hik shik*, the names of your children, your first kiss, the colours of the sunset, *shik shik shik shik*, and all the while the waves, scratching against the ground, *shik shik shik shik shik ...*'

Ninian was growing impatient; he was about to leave when a young man intervened. He was kneeling on the ground, gnawing on a piece of bread as tough as wood. He stopped eating long enough to say:

'You can't remember what was yours and what was theirs.' His voice was surprisingly clear. By sharing Ninian's knowledge as well as his perception, Isha realised that these were the first refugees Ninian had been able to draw any sense out of. Most people were too far gone to explain what had happened.

The young Sunriser clutched his bread. There were marks where his teeth had scraped off the crust. 'The shadows eat everything and chew it together and spew it back when it makes no more sense.'

He went back to his meal. The woman closed the distance between herself and Ninian, placing a hand on his wrist. He took a step back, but her fingers sank into his arm.

'Do you know you can still hear them when you sleep? The waves, I'll hear them while I die, I'll hear them when I'm dead.' She went back to whispering, *shik shik shik*, and her rhythmic movement with her hand became less fluid, more erratic. Ninian withdrew.

When Isha emerged from mindlink, she was nauseous. She could hear it too, now, in the background of her thoughts, the raspy woman's voice like broken glass, like heavy waves, like shadows drinking at her soul.

It explained the number of refugees in the city. They would never have been able to cross the Shadowpass on their own – the Renegades had helped them. Maybe they had used them, too, but the truth was no big group could have crossed the Shadowpass without someone to guide them.

'Why did nobody tell us?' Lord Daegan asked, glaring at the Sunriser mages.

'My convent and I were running for our lives,' the Wingshade woman said curtly. 'We didn't have time to ask Hawk what she was planning.'

Sir Cintay lowered his face. 'I had no idea the Renegades were willing to wade through the Shadowpass that way. We crossed with Mezyan, but we were never told of the Renegades' plans.'

Or maybe you did know, but they cut that knowledge out of your minds, thought Isha. The refugees who were still sane after the crossing might be systematically cleansed of any useful information by conscientious Renegades – and only a few got overlooked, such as the old woman, who might not make it to the Nest anyway, considering her age, or the young man, who seemed sickly and famished enough to die soon.

Sir Leofric glanced at Isha's hand knotted around his headrest. She quickly let go.

'If I may,' Ninian said, 'I would like to show their encampment.'

As Lord Daegan nodded, Isha braced herself for the mindlink, keeping her hands well away from the chair this time.

It was the mouth of the Shadowpass, snow spread like a hush across the landscape. Her heart tightened at the sight – she had known this place, she remembered it alive with spring, with the lightness of childhood. In Ninian's memory, it was bleak. The Ridge rose high into the sky, casting its shade across the land, over farms and small villages with leafless trees, empty fields. And within the Ridge, like a gaping, toothless mouth, the entrance of the Shadowpass.

The Renegades had cut down the trees they had found – this included not only the forest, but also the nearby orchards. Isha tried to find her foster parents' farm, but she strained in vain; she couldn't turn Ninian's head for him and he wasn't looking in the right direction.

The fortifications were crude but efficient. Logs were piled around the encampment, with guards, both kher and human, doing rounds. In the vision, workers were dragging more trees towards their camp to build a watchtower. It was snowing heavily, but the Renegades kept the grounds clear. The camp indicated they were here to stay. Three walls were made of wood – the fourth was the Ridge itself. They had built their camp around the tunnel that wormed through the mountain range.

Ninian stopped mindlinking and Isha returned to the council chamber. After the black-and-white landscape, the bright colours hurt her eyes. In front of her, Passerine leant forwards onto the circular table. Before the other high mages could process what they had seen, he said:

'They are going to hold the camp while it is impossible for us to travel up to the Ridge, because of the snow. They are going to use that time to get their army across. It doesn't freeze inside the Ridge. The Shadowpass won't be worse because of winter; but we will have a harder time trying to uproot them, if that is what we decide to do. At the thaw, they will march towards the Nest.'

Sir Leofric was playing with a glass pendant hanging around his neck. From this angle, Isha couldn't see what was inside, but it looked like silvery water.

'Surely they'll lack food,' he said.

Passerine shook his head. 'I doubt Hawk would have attempted crossing the Shadowpass if she hadn't gathered the necessary supplies beforehand. She might only have enough to hold out through winter, but when the spring comes, she can always pillage what she needs as she heads towards us.'

'She must have started crossing as soon as Mezyan brought us over,' said Sir Cintay. 'She was never planning to wait for the Nest's answer.'

Or she knew the answer already. After all, it wasn't hard to guess.

Isha had hoped to keep the thought to herself, but Passerine answered her. *Don't be quite so loud.*

Lord Daegan was pensive, his chin pressed into his hands, his lips kissing his knuckles. The blue glow filtering through one of the glass panes highlighted the wrinkles in the folds of his face, coloured the white of his eyes a deep indigo. Behind him, his collarbound could have been carved out of the same alabaster as the stairs.

'Thank you for this,' he told Ninian. It was a clear dismissal.

When Ninian had disappeared behind the glass panes, Lord Daegan turned to his council.

'We will attack the Renegades now,' he said, 'and uproot them before they can pose a threat to us.'

With a finger, he beckoned his collarbound closer.

'You will go,' he said. 'Take down their leader, that woman Hawk.'

The collar lit up. It blazed like heated gold on the verge of melting. Her face impassive, the lightborn didn't react in any way to indicate she had heard or understood what her master was saying.

'Bring me back Hawk's head. Or, failing that,' Sir Daegan added playfully, as if failure was an amusing, improbable notion, 'more information.'

The collarbound didn't protest. She cast her disdainful gaze across the council, then leapt into the air. Despite having seen it before, Isha couldn't help but marvel as the woman shifted into a beam of gold, as wide as the glass wind-paths around them, as stunning as a shooting star, close enough to touch. The council of high mages failed to hide their awe.

Lord Daegan smiled thinly at their wonder.

'As you can see, I have the situation under control,' he said.

* * *

The council meeting didn't end immediately, but it moved on to other subjects. The Wingshade mage, who Isha found out was called Lady Mayurah, wanted to know whether she could shelter her ungifted in the Nest. To nobody's surprise, save maybe the Sunrisers', Lord Daegan said no. When Lady Mayurah insisted that she owed everyone protection, including her apprentices and softminds – the term she used for ungifted – he drily told her she was no longer in her convent to do as she pleased.

'This is ridiculous,' she huffed. 'I have apprentices forced to pay for lodgings in the city, and softminds who haven't been able to find rooms living in the street. What am I supposed to tell them?'

Lord Daegan only shrugged. 'Find money to pay for lodgings, then. I cannot make space appear out of thin air.'

Which meant, Isha supposed, that refugee high mages would soon have to compete for space by giving Duskdweller mages goods – either treasures or skills – that might interest them. If their artefacts were not stolen by khers or ungifted on the street, they would be stolen by mages instead, in unfair transactions for food and shelter. Or maybe they would fight Sunriser mages who already had good lodgings, such as Passerine. She tried not to dwell on that thought.

Once the council meeting was officially over, the high mages divided into small groups whispering together, sometimes even standing silently, their conversation happening only in mind-link. Passerine had gone to find Sir Cintay. When they stood side-by-side, it was clear they came from different convents: Sir Cintay's pointed, angular face and silky, straight hair didn't match Passerine's. It didn't even match Isha's – despite her being much lighter than Passerine, she shared more of his features than any of the Wingshade mages.

She was standing to one side, observing the high mages, admiring how they were framed in yellow, scarlet and green, painted figures conspiring on various canvases. Sir Leofric waved to her, breaking her away from her daydream. She hurried to his side, as was expected of her.

'Do you know, there is a word for apprentices who keep changing masters?' he said, affably. 'I am afraid it isn't a flattering term.'

She focused on keeping her thoughts bland, her words safe. 'No, I imagine it wouldn't be, sir. Thank you for permitting me to stay.'

He studied her carefully. He had a faded scar cutting across his cheekbone.

'Sir Passerine does seem awfully fond of you.'

It was an effort to speak to the lawmage: everything, her features, her mind, her voice, had to be controlled to give nothing away. 'I wouldn't know, sir.'

He hummed, his fingers going back to his pendant. He toyed with it a moment, letting his nails tap against the glass encasement.

'Please enlighten me,' he said. 'What is the tattoo for?'

Before Isha could answer, Passerine was beside her, placing a protective hand on her shoulder. Sir Leofric's smile withered.

'I am afraid Isha's tattoo is, as you can imagine, a trauma that she finds difficult to talk about,' Passerine said.

Sir Leofric's friendly demeanour returned as suddenly as it had faltered. 'Of course! I wouldn't dream of putting your apprentice in a difficult position.' He winked towards Isha, as if they shared a secret, an intimacy.

'Did you know,' he added, turning to Passerine, his voice still airy, 'in some rare cases it is possible for one person to fleshbind *and* mindlink?' He cocked his head sideways. His eyes were sparkling, as if he were the only one with the punchline to the joke. 'I guess it would require diluted mongrel blood and a stroke of luck.'

Isha struggled to keep her breathing steady as the implications of what Sir Leofric said hit her. He was accusing her of being a halfblood, maybe even of practising fleshbinding. But he did so with such an open, guileless smile, that it was difficult to remember that such an accusation could carve a lacunant out of her.

But more than that, he was speaking about something reputed to be impossible, and which Ka had mentioned: someone who could both fleshbind and mindlink. Did this mean he knew where Tatters was? He was the head lawmage, after all. If anyone knew, it would be him.

'I wouldn't know,' said Passerine. 'I have never heard that such a thing was possible.' His tone was polite, but colder than the open council room.

Sir Leofric narrowed his eyes. His body-language said he was annoyed, but his tone didn't. It stayed high-pitched and cheerful. 'Maybe you're right. I shouldn't pry.'

'Curiosity killed the kher, I believe,' Passerine said.

Sir Leofric laughed. It was a sincere laugh, more sinister, somehow, than his fake smiles. 'As long as we agree that it killed something.'

Passerine's hand on her shoulder tensed slightly; enough for Isha to feel it, enough for her heart to speed up.

'I am afraid we have to leave,' Passerine said.

'Don't let me detain you.' The innocent phrase sounded more dangerous in the mouth of a lawmage. Isha felt Sir Leofric's gemstone eyes on her as they left the council.

Chapter Ten

After the council meeting, Passerine and Isha went into Passerine's chambers. Isha was getting used to the strange intimacy of sharing his space. Because there were now two of them, he had purchased an armchair, an antique piece of furniture that smelt of mites and dust but meant Isha had somewhere to sit while he worked at his desk. She had bought him a circular candleholder as thanks, from Tatters' friend the pawnbroker. When it was lit, it warmed the cold stone, replacing the blue winter light. Sometimes, Isha watched Passerine at work, his hand tracing complex, spiralling knots across his papers, never hesitating, as if drawing a maze only he knew the way out of.

'Let's do some training,' he said.

Isha strived to withhold her thoughts while she asked the maids for hot water, prepared leaves for a brew, and served two cups. The exercise had variants – she could either walk or talk or both as she shielded her mind. Sometimes they swapped, and she had to find out what Passerine was concealing, without being perceived by him.

'Tread lightly. Don't push into people's space,' he advised.

She knew this wasn't basic training for a first-year apprentice. Yet it felt as if she had done it before, and if only she could remember how she did it then, the tricks she used, she might be able to do it again. Her progress was slow, but she was conscious it was still faster than what was expected of her.

'If this is done well,' Passerine said, 'people don't even realise that you are hiding something, that there is something to hide.'

It was impossible to apply herself to the exercise today, with Sir Leofric's words still fresh, and the memories Ninian had shared with them running through her mind.

'You are tired,' Passerine said at last. He sounded disappointed. 'We will not achieve anything today.'

Isha would have argued, but she was exhausted. They sat down, her in the armchair and him at his desk, and they drank the fragrant, flowery tea. It was one of the rare non-essential items Passerine had brought with him across the Shadowpass. Outside, the Edge was clouded in mist. Rain slapped at the windowpane.

'The Renegades will destroy the Nest,' said Passerine. 'I don't see how we are going to protect it.'

He was the one who sounded tired. Maybe it was the damp rotting their bones.

The rain was thick and crystallised, a sloppy texture just short of snow. Isha tried to imagine travelling through that weather – Ninian had done the Nest a huge favour, and to do so he had spent days and nights treading mud.

'But nothing can get in the way of a lightborn, can it?' she said, hugging her cup closer. 'With Lord Daegan's collarbound, I'm not sure there's anything Hawk can do.'

Passerine put his cup down on the desk and rubbed his eyes, as if trying to wipe away what they had seen.

'Tatters told you nothing,' he sighed. There was a pause. They listened to the rain outside, to the fire crackling in the chimney.

Passerine seemed to come to a decision. He turned towards Isha. 'You are aware there are more lightborns on the Sunriser side?'

Isha shifted in the armchair. She tucked her legs beneath her, both for warmth and for comfort.

'I know that's where the stories come from,' she said.

'Some people think it's because lightborns are attracted to dawn lights,' said Passerine. There was a wistfulness to his voice. 'Daybreak is beautiful when seen from the Eastern Edge. Here we only have gloomy sunsets, the sun dying again and again, the Ridge hiding any birth of light.'

He placed his hand against the window, watching the rain on the other side. When he removed his hand, its outline stayed on the glass for a moment before fading.

'I don't think it explains the presence of lightborns on the Sunriser side, but the fact is that there are more of them there. And they have a stronger tendency to take human shape.'

Passerine picked up the jug of tea and poured himself another cup, then got up to serve Isha. She was still touched at the way he treated her – like an equal, not like an apprentice.

'Have you heard of the sehwol?' he asked.

She had heard legends, like everyone else. Tales that smelt of smoky fires and long winter nights. Tales which, like lightlures, included the mysteries of lightborns and the dangers in meddling with them.

'They were stolen away by a lightborn as children, and given to the sun,' said Isha. 'The sehwol are sun-touched. You can recognise them by their glowing eyes.'

Passerine went back to his desk. His chair scraped against the stone floor.

'The stories change,' he said. 'They were stolen at birth by lightborns and touched by light. They were born of a union between a lightborn and a human. They are a lightborn in human shape, either by choice or because they were banished or, sometimes, because they were caught.'

Isha felt emotion rise inside Passerine – it was a complex emotion, artfully hidden behind his mental barriers, but it must have been raw enough for Passerine to let wisps of it escape. She couldn't tell what he was thinking, not without prying, not without being noticed. But she could sense the outlines of it, the shape of this diffuse feeling. It was nostalgia, maybe. Sadness tinged with hope, melancholia tinged with happiness. Sun-touched.

'There are too many stories of sehwols for them not to exist,' said Passerine. 'They do. They are lightborns who mingle with humans, whatever the reason. Their eyes don't glow, nor do they shine in the night – those are myths to scare children. But I can assure you Hawk has faced sehwols. And as she has dealt with sehwols, she has an idea of how to deal with a lightborn.'

Isha frowned. The tea was cooling between her hands; when she sipped it, it was tepid.

'They can't be that common,' she said. 'And how much contact would she have had with them, anyway? Enough to fend off a collarbound with instructions to kill her?'

Passerine didn't answer at first. He tapped his fingers against his desk. Their rhythmic sound seemed to match the patter of the rain outside.

'Do you know why collarbounds are so rare?' he asked.

Thrown by the change of subject, Isha shook her head. Passerine put one foot up against his knee and pushed back in his chair, relaxing like a storyteller about to start a long tale.

'There are few collars, and we have no way to make more,' said Passerine. 'That is one reason. But there is another. Most people die if you put a collar on them. The giants' magic crushes their mind.'

She couldn't hide her shock.

'Most humans, anyway,' Passerine amended. 'Sehwols, now, sehwols are different. They have lightborn minds, after all. Light responds differently to gold.'

At last Isha realised what Passerine was trying to say. She found herself shaking her head, incredulous, as if by denying it, she could prevent it from being true.

'The more you consider it, the more it makes sense,' he said. 'Tatters has to be a sehwol. What kind of mind would be strong enough to split itself constantly, even when sleeping, without ever relenting? The best mages of the Nest can hardly do it without becoming lacunants.'

Lal. He didn't think Lal was a parasitic mind, but Tatters' double.

'More importantly, why would the Renegades even bother putting a collar on him, if he didn't have a talent of some sort that required keeping him in check?' Passerine concluded with an easy shrug.

'Wait, wait,' said Isha, putting her cup down at her feet, trying to understand what she'd heard. 'So Tatters has Lal, and he was part of the Renegades, and he has lightborn blood? That's...' She wanted to say: *that's too much*. It felt as if each time she learnt something about Tatters, there was another layer beneath, secrets upon secrets, truth blending with lies. 'That can't be it.'

Passerine shook his head.

'You are thinking in the wrong order. Tatters has lightborn blood, *which is why* he was part of the Renegades, which is how he created Lal.'

Passerine placed his empty cup beside the jug. The sky was dimming, so he went to light the ornate candleholder.

'The Renegades want to win this war. They knew they wanted to win it before they even started it. To win a war, you need a weapon. A better weapon than the other side.' Passerine held one candle and pressed it to the others, spreading small patches of light. 'A man like Tatters doesn't happen by chance. A man with a gift for mindlink and fleshbinding, with lightborn talents, with a collar? Isha, Tatters was *made*.'

Passerine got up, went to the door, and asked the maids to stock the fireplace. Neither of them spoke as they watched the servants bring it to a blaze. Once they were alone once more, Passerine pulled a cover off the bed for Isha to wrap around herself. He pulled his chair close to the hearth.

'Maybe it's easier if I show you,' he said.

He leant back in his chair, expanding his mind. Eyes closed, his face relaxed, he seemed more vulnerable – unguarded. Isha watched him a moment before joining him in mindlink.

She had never been in one of Passerine's memories before – it felt strange to find herself so much taller than usual, with larger shoulders, bigger hands. She was inside a tent that she now recognised as Hawk's. The cloth was patchwork, but red in parts, and dawn light filtered through it. It was winter. The ground was frozen solid, and the rugs on the floor did little to keep the cold at bay.

There was no emotion attached to the memory. It was eerie, like cutting your skin and not feeling pain. Passerine must have been consciously keeping his reactions separated from his mindlink. She wondered how he could disentangle what had happened from how he had experienced it.

He was wearing a leather jacket that chafed at the elbows. Hawk was beside him, holding the collar in one hand, running a finger along it. Its power seemed to react to her touch. Like the sound made by a wet finger on the rim of a wine glass, waves of confused thoughts and desires echoed inside it, spinning as she brushed against them.

'And this will work?' she asked, with the voice of someone who has been disappointed before.

'If he can execute the order, the collar will make him do it,' said Passerine. 'If he has the potential to alight, it will happen. Whatever has blocked him so far shouldn't get in the way of the giants' magic.'

She nodded, then walked out of the tent first. Passerine followed in her wake.

Outside the light was blue and white, and the air colder still. With a start, Isha realised she had seen this scene before – this pale morning, the fires being built, the kher in the corner milking a goat. She had seen it as Tatters had; and there he was, stamping his feet on the ground, looking so much younger than he did now. He was her age or barely older, with a young man's first attempt at a beard growing in wisps across his cheeks.

She knew what was going to happen.

Passerine stood at a distance as Hawk handed Tatters the collar. He held it before him, curious, open, without any trace of dread across his face. The collar was made of a few strands of gold braided together, like the gold woven by maidens in fairytales.

Despite his efforts to conceal it, Isha felt Passerine's trepidation. The whole camp was frozen in place – waiting, watchful. When Tatters lifted the collar above his head, it shone, its glow growing in brightness until it was difficult to stare at. The collar stretched out and out, then descended over Tatters' head.

He seemed relaxed as the collar, this magic that could crush minds, pulsated around his eyes. Isha wondered if they had told him what it might do to him.

Hawk stepped forward. No-one was paying attention to Passerine, standing beside the tent's door. The wind caught

Tatters' black cloak, Hawk's red cape, and slapped the fabrics together, as if clapping invisible hands.

'Is this normal?' Tatters said. His smile was teasing. 'That'd be just like you, to give me a broken one.'

Hawk's smile answered his. From the way they looked at each other, the way their postures matched, it was clear they trusted each other. They shared something that no-one else in the wind-swept camp of smoky, struggling fires, seemed to have – fearlessness. Isha wondered if the realisation was hers, or Passerine's at the time. He was effaced from his own memories, as if he had chosen to remove himself from his life.

'Ready?' Hawk asked.

Passerine watched the collar shrink with nothing but impatience. The moment the gold dulled and touched Tatters' neck, he was reeling, clutching at his head, his expression contorted in pain. Hawk rushed to his side, helping him up. His scream broke Isha's heart – it was so youthful, a sound Kilian would make, and he was begging, he was begging this woman who should have been his friend.

'Take it off! Take it off!'

She was whispering something to reassure him, soothing words and sounds, but he pushed her off and stumbled two steps aside before falling to his knees.

'Give him an order,' Passerine said.

Hawk glanced from him to Tatters, who was pressing his forehead against the stones, shrieking into the ground as if the earth might hear him.

'We should take it off,' she said. 'He can't handle it.'

Passerine reached Hawk before she could reach Tatters – he clasped her hands in his, forced her to spin towards him. Confusedly, Isha perceived that he wanted to know, he desperately wanted to know whether someone born human, bound

233

by flesh, could alight. She didn't know why it was important, but she could sense that it was, more than Tatters, more than anything.

'Give him the order to alight now,' he said. 'If it doesn't work, then we take off the collar. He'll never put it on again afterwards. It's our only chance to do this. Nothing else worked!'

Hawk's face was torn by indecision. It had fewer scars at that time, a softness around the edges that she would lose. She turned to Tatters, who had stopped howling and was now panting for breath, clawing at the ground with his bare hands.

'Alight,' she said. 'That's an order.'

Tatters curled into a ball on the floor, making a noise that didn't sound human. His eyes were squeezed shut. Isha wondered if he was still conscious. The collar blazed and flickered, but Tatters didn't alight.

Disappointment, like a bitter taste on the back of Passerine's tongue. So it wasn't possible. Only pure lightborns could alight.

'That's it,' Hawk said.

This time Passerine didn't try to stop her. She was about to crouch beside Tatters, to remove the collar, when he changed. The tips of his fingers glowed, and the light spread across his body, burning so fiercely it blurred the shape of his hands, of his arms, before spreading to his shoulders and neck. Hawk took a step backwards. For a moment, it appeared as if Tatters had caught fire – or maybe that he had turned into paper, or glass, and sunlight was pouring through his body, casting a haze of red light along his outlines.

And then he alighted.

He became a beam of scarlet light heading towards the sky. He drew an arc, suspended above the treetops – and the silence was what Isha noticed most, the silence now that he had stopped screaming, the shock taking away the breaths from the crowd of

Renegades, a silence only disturbed by the whispers of wind – before crashing back down on the ground.

When he landed, somewhere in the forest surrounding the camp, out of sight, his light went out.

Passerine couldn't hide the warmth that bloomed in his heart – hope. Isha was aware of how strong this must have been, the disappointment first, the elation afterwards, for her to still be able to perceive it, after he had forcefully removed feelings from his thoughts. For some reason, his memory was tinted here with something else, with the image of a blue lightborn, very unlike Tatters, crossing a cloudy sky. It was as if he could see this lightborn rising where Tatters had, burning a cold blue fire, a light unlike any the sun would ever cast.

People were rushing to where Tatters had landed. Shaking himself, Passerine joined them; in a few strides he had caught up to the front of the group. Once again Isha marvelled at how much taller than everyone else he was, how easy it was for him to cover ground, jumping over the roots and rocks of the woodland floor. He couldn't catch up with Hawk, though, who was running with her head low, in the grim way of someone braced for the worst.

They found Tatters unconscious, lying at the foot of a tree, the side of his face bruised. Hawk was immediately beside him, touching his hair, checking him for wounds – aside from the bruise, he was unharmed.

'Let's carry him to your tent,' Passerine said.

A kher helped them, lifting Tatters' feet while Passerine held his shoulders. He wasn't a heavy load.

They put him in the red tent, where a bed had been assembled – it was one of the travelling beds military chieftains used in sieges, made up of pieces of wood that could be taken apart and carried on horseback. For a while there was noise and fuss, four or five people at a time inside the tent, some advising to wake him, some advising to let him sleep, some recommending pulling over the covers, some undoing his black cloak.

In the end Hawk thanked her Renegades but asked them to leave. She let Passerine stay. They stood beside the bed, where Tatters lay swaddled in animal skins, pale and feverish.

'It worked,' she said.

She laughed, as if she couldn't believe what had happened.

'We'll be able to do so much with this.' She elbowed Passerine playfully, and her smile widened. 'So much for us, and so much for you. This is your day as much as his.'

But Tatters is the one who alighted. Passerine's thought, sharp and jealous, was cut off as soon as it started taking shape. Isha wondered how much he had succeeded in hiding from her, and whether this scene might mean something very different had she been able to access all the emotions attached to it, instead of these brief emerging shards.

Hawk bent over, but before she could touch Tatters, Passerine interrupted her.

'Are you sure you want to remove the collar?'

Hawk frowned, her hand still hovering above the gold clasped around Tatters' neck.

'Why not?' she asked.

'Maybe you should wait to see how he reacts when he wakes up.' Passerine was speaking delicately, his deep voice a murmur. 'If he decides he doesn't want to work alongside you anymore, then you'll have lost him forever. With the power he has now – alighting and mindlink – no-one can stop him. No-one can make him do something if he doesn't want to. And the Renegades don't have anything to offer him that he can't take himself.'

Hawk's arm fell back to her side.

'I don't think he'll react badly,' she said.

'But he already has doubts about your methods,' said Passerine. 'And now he is well-placed to lead the Renegades where he wants them to go, not where you want to take them.'

Hawk clicked her tongue against the roof of her mouth.

But you should trust him, Isha urged, uselessly. *He trusted you.*

'All right,' Hawk said. 'Let's see what he says when he wakes up.'

The last image Passerine shared was this: Hawk glancing down at Tatters, a slight crease between her eyes, worried. She had an attractive face, partly hidden by her hair. But she wasn't the confident, fearless woman from before.

Isha blinked, and Passerine's profile overlapped with Hawk's; his features were framed by the fire, hers by the red cloth of the tent. Her skin was dark; his was darker. As Hawk's image faded, Isha was left sitting beside Passerine.

She wanted to ask a thousand questions. Did Passerine regret advising Hawk to leave the collar on Tatters, considering it had ultimately led to him leaving the Renegades? What did Passerine know about lightborns, or want to know, and had he found what he was looking for? Why did *he* leave the Renegades – was it because he had learnt that what he needed was elsewhere? Why was he so emotionally drawn to lightborns, he who never seemed to smile, who never seemed to weep?

But she didn't ask any of these questions. Her head was spinning, and it was late, and she knew they would be unwelcome.

'Was that the first time he alighted?' she asked instead.

She didn't know how to feel about this. She tried to imagine what it would be like to unlock such power within yourself and be locked forever in the collar on the same day.

'No,' said Passerine. 'The Renegades originally discovered Tatters because he'd managed to alight – a chance, freak occurrence. It must have been in his blood, on his mother's or his father's side. After he joined, a lot of Hawk's efforts went towards trying to repeat that feat. And she succeeded. Thanks to the collar, Tatters learnt how to alight swiftly, and often.'

A man who could fleshbind, and mindlink, and alight. A man who was a weapon.

'With him, could we protect the Nest from the Renegades?' Isha asked.

'Maybe,' said Passerine. He brought his hands close to the fire, spreading his long fingers before the flames. His nails seemed to lengthen with the shadows, black lines above the red lights. 'But without him, it's certain we cannot.'

Isha pulled the cover tighter around her shoulders. A cosy warmth was spreading through the room, but her bones felt cold.

'I think Sir Leofric knows where Tatters is,' she said. 'If only you can convince him to let Tatters go.'

Sighing, Passerine rubbed his face. 'I am not sure Sir Leofric lets go of anything. The difficulty is persuading him we're worth his time, without revealing our hand.'

She remembered his cruel, clever eyes; his intent, unhealthy focus. Her spirits sinking, she realised Passerine was right. She wasn't sure there was anything they could do against the head lawmage.

'Give me time,' said Passerine. 'I will find a way.'

* * *

Goldie dragged him through a series of passageways, gripping him by the elbow all the while. Tatters wondered if there was anything he could say that would help him understand what Sir Leofric planned to do and, if he did find out Sir Leofric's schemes, whether it would be of any use to him. In the end, he copied Goldie and stayed silent. He felt worn. Beyond the prison walls, he could imagine a white courtyard, frozen grey shapes, high gates with lacunants shivering in the cold.

They reached a wide corridor with a high ceiling; this wasn't carved out by men, but by giants. It must have been a servant's passage – despite its size, it was undecorated, and the ground was rough. Steps might have been carved here once, but they had been smoothed into an uneven slope.

The humans had filled it with cages. Rows of heavy, corroded structures stood side-by-side. The corridor ended with an ominous-looking door. Tatters assumed that was where they were headed, but Goldie stopped to unlock a cage. A smell lingered, overpowering but difficult to identify. It was sharp like iron but not quite iron. Rust, maybe.

Goldie pushed the cage's door open. It scraped against the floor, a sound like teeth breaking. Tatters noticed lines of dirt on the ground. Thanks to the slope, the mages could clean the place by throwing buckets of water on the floor, so the prisoners' mess slid down the corridor. The lines left behind were black and brown.

Goldie pushed Tatters inside, although there was no need – Tatters went willingly enough. It wasn't as if he had a choice. He stood within the cage, confused as to why Sir Leofric had decided on this change of scenery.

'Enjoy,' grumbled Goldie as he closed the door.

His torch brightening his hair, he ambled out of sight.

A dim light was left behind, from a torch which should have been taken home or smothered, but which was still burning low. Because the cages had no walls, only bars, the torch cast its light inside them. The shadows were long and squirmed like snakes.

He heard them before his eyes adjusted enough to see them. They made a long guttural sound, as would someone clearing their throat. Tatters turned. Two cages up from him, someone groaned. Relieved to find company – more relieved than he would like to admit – Tatters walked up to the end of his cage. He rested his arms against the bars; the rust came off against his skin. He had another whiff of the smell, stronger now. *Metal*, he thought. It was the smell of iron, but strong enough that he could taste it on his tongue.

'May you grow tall,' he said.

His voice echoed weakly off the walls, underlining how small he was in this vast space. He couldn't make out the person in the other cage. They were lying down. Tatters squinted. The silhouette was small, square, solidly built. Dark-skinned, or at least darker skinned than him.

It took him a while to realise their skin was red. When he did, he spotted what he had missed before – the hole in the skull, seeping another kind of red. One stub of horn still stuck out of the iwdan's forehead. It had been broken off, probably with a hammer. It jutted out in irregular shards.

Tatters' breath caught in his throat. 'Idir,' he corrected himself. 'Sorry. I hadn't realised.'

He knelt; it seemed more respectful. When he placed a hand on the ground, it was cold, the kind of cold that was never warm, that has never felt the sun upon it. He noticed how far underground they were, how much earth and stone were above them, how deep into the cliff they had burrowed, like spirits of the dead trying to find a way out of the underworlds.

The stench of excrement and urine mixed with the other unknown smell. *No, not unknown. I know what it is. Not iron. Not steel. I've smelled it before.* But he couldn't place it.

The kher made a sound more like a moan than a sentence. Still, not unlike the scent, it was familiar. It had a rhythm to it. With each repetition, it grew fainter, less coherent.

Tatters managed to untangle the syllables. He had heard those words often – chanted after a victory, whispered after a defeat, screamed across a battlefield, announced solemnly at war meetings. He had heard them so often that, for a time, they had echoed in his dreams. He had feared them nearly as much as he feared a banner decorated with a bloodied hawk.

It was the Renegades' rallying cry.

Through pain,
To victory.

His hairs rose as his eyes accustomed to the gloom – as he understood what had happened. This was someone who had openly showed support to the Renegades and faced the consequences.

Not iron. Not steel.
Blood.

Some of the lines on the ground were still fresh, still seeping.

It took two hours for the kher to die. As he faded, he made those lonely sounds. Maybe he was trying to talk to Tatters. Most probably, he hadn't noticed the new arrival. It was the pain talking, and pain had a deep, wordless voice, as cold and unhuman as the passages dug by giants below the rim of the world.

***

Beyond the row of cages, there was a door. Behind that door, there was a room. Inside that room, there were screams, and the stench of blood stronger than iron, and wet, ripping sounds, which were better left unheard.

Mages didn't often resort to torture. There was no need to rip out people's nails when it was possible to read their thoughts. But one type of creature existed that couldn't be mindlinked to.

No wonder khers didn't work in this part of the prison.

'This will break you,' Sir Leofric had said, with his usual non-chalance.

Tatters sat at the bottom of his cage, the kher's corpse keeping him company. Images flooded his mind, storming it like a wave crashing on a shore, catching walkers unawares. It was the term 'break'. He'd always felt for horses in that way. Why did they need to be broken? Couldn't they just be tamed, like other animals? It sounded so much worse.

He closed his eyes. The kher was giving out a slight smell, not a stench yet, of unloved, unattended death. Tatters lay on his side, shivering, his cloak around him, as he tried to be somewhere else, willed himself elsewhere, despite the kher horn and the smell and the knowledge of that door. Instead, he focused on the past, anything from the past, happy and unhappy memories alike, as long as they took him away from the present.

In the past, Lal still talked to him. In the past, no corpses rotted slowly in the cool underground.

He found that he wasn't in the prison anymore, but curled up underneath a coarse blanket, next to a flickering campfire. He was pretending to sleep, or maybe he was sleeping, drifting in and out of consciousness, catching scraps of conversation as he emerged.

'No, I'm not letting you take control.' Her voice had always been deep for a woman, and it had a rough edge as if she were nurturing a cold.

'I could break him.' Passerine talked smoothly. Through half-closed eyes, Tatters could see them sitting cross-legged before the fire, resting their forearms on their thighs.

'Don't be ridiculous.'

'One day he will do something, something unforgivable, something you cannot overlook, and you will have to admit I

242

was right, and you will hand him over to me. Then, and only then, will he be broken in.'

Hawk looked Passerine in the eye, the flames dancing across her face, shadows drawing scars across her cheeks.

'Tell me, are you still jealous?' she asked. 'Even now?'

And another scene, deeper still in the past, which didn't take place on a normal evening by the warmth of a fire.

It started as he ran desperately through the woods, hearing the clatter of men on horseback behind, certain they could trace him by following his mind, trying desperately to think himself tree, to think himself plant, to think himself animal, anything that would hide his tracks. Lal trailed behind him. He held her wrist too tightly as he dragged her behind, leaving bruises on her skin. Afterwards, that's what he would hate himself for. The circle of yellow marks on her arm.

He tugged her forward to save her life – and his. She couldn't run fast enough. He jumped over fallen trunks, pushed through brambles, half-carried half-hauled her through slippery puddles and underbrush and nettles. The horses struggled to manage the terrain, but they didn't tire. He was exhausted, and his fear was as easy for mages to follow as piss would have been for dogs.

Lal cried that her feet were hurting, begged him to stop. Tatters thought his were bleeding; at least, he slid on something red and slick which wasn't mud as he climbed over a root.

'They'll kill us,' he said. 'They'll kill us if they catch us.'

'I can't run,' she whimpered. 'Fight them, or hide, but I can't run!'

I can't fight them and I can't hide and I can't outrun horses. He would have carried Lal, if he were stronger, if it wouldn't have slowed them down even more.

He reached a clearing and made the mistake of stopping for breath. His lungs, his legs were aching.

The horse's hooves cut into the soft earth, throwing wet clumps of grass aside. It had steam rising from its flanks and white foam down its neck. The lawmage called out: 'I've found them.'

Tatters glanced at Lal, who nodded. As she took refuge inside his mind, her body fell to the ground, suddenly slack. He shielded them both. The lawmage didn't even try to prise his mind open at first. He stood, poking at Tatters' thoughts with his own, enough to keep him busy but not taking any risks. The other lawmages joined him. Soon a semi-circle of horses and riders stood in front of them. The horses were panting, their nostrils dilating as they breathed out clouds of vapour into the night air.

Tatters decided that the first person to strike would be the one to go for, in the hope that he could take one person down before the others closed in. But these were trained men and women, used to hunting down illegal uses of mindlink. They didn't play around. They attacked in formation, all five of them at the same time, from different angles.

Tatters dropped the frontlines of his mind, immediate memories, knowledge, habits. He retreated with Lal into the depths of himself – core sense of identity, unrecognised shames and desires. He felt them rifle through his everyday life, gathering enough clues to prove him guilty, and waited in fear, knowing they would tear down his inner sanctuary next.

You have to alight, thought Lal.

What?

Mum said we are sehwol. She had taken them aside, kissed their brows, and told them they had lightborn blood, that the power to mindlink was a proof the light was strong in them, although she wouldn't say whether the gift was hers or their father's.

If you alight, they won't follow, Lal insisted. It was common knowledge that mages couldn't survive in a lightborn's mind. If he took flight as a pure spirit, anyone trapped inside him would be torn away from their body. At the time, he didn't consider the cruelty of such a fate.

What if you don't follow either?

I'm a sehwol too, she thought. Even in this extreme moment, she was proud and fierce. *If you alight, I'll alight too, and you'll carry me with you.* They were children, really. He was a gangly teenager whom life hadn't kicked around enough, so he didn't know any better. She was a kid who believed she'd never have to become an adult. In a way, she was right.

They ripped his memories. For the first time, but not for the last, he felt the animal terror that grips people when they believe they're going to die.

It was like claws sinking inside his body, in that part of himself where he didn't want to be touched. It was as physical as a hand gripping his guts through some unnameable orifice and trying to unravel him by emptying his stuffing through that hole.

Tatters shrieked. His whole body shuddered and shifted. He could only do it because he was dying.

It turned out that wasn't enough for Lal.

He alighted. He left the ground, and felt minds like threads linking him to the earth, snapping as he broke free. He understood nothing at the time. Everything was light and colour and swiftness and air. He crashed nearly as soon as he took flight.

The rest of that evening, he was unconscious. Afterwards, he pieced together what had happened through the Renegades' stories. Hawk and Passerine had been around a different campfire, staring at the stars. They spotted the sudden rush of red light drawing an arc above the trees only to plummet down again. Hawk asked Passerine, as her lightborn expert, what a lightborn would be doing, so low on the ground, so close to trouble, hardly strong enough to break away from the canopy.

'Is this normal?' she asked.

'Anything but.'

They separated into two groups, one led by Hawk and one by Passerine. Hawk headed for where the lightborn had taken flight; Passerine to where they thought it had landed. Hawk found the bodies. Passerine found Tatters, curled like a foetus between the roots of a tree.

The bodies, he heard afterwards, were in a sorry state. Eyes bulging out of their sockets, tongues stuck at the back of the throat, swollen, blocking a silent scream. Cheeks and foreheads and hands distorted into unnatural positions, as if the skin had been clay, remodelled to make monsters.

The first time Hawk described the scene, she said she'd come upon the bodies of five lawmages, nothing more. Later, she described it differently, and said Lal had been there too, a frail girl in rags, her legs already blue, as cold and hard as if carved. By the time Tatters regained consciousness, all that was left of his first alighting were funeral pyres.

Lal didn't alight. He'd torn her out of her body, as he had the others. The difference was that she was welcome in his mind.

He remembered his mother stroking his forehead, brushing the hair out of his eyes. 'It is such a gift,' she whispered. 'You are such a gift. You are woven with light.'

But his hair was stuck down with sweat and grime, and he was in a place with no light. When he opened his eyes, there was nothing to feel but the cold of carved stone, nothing to smell but flesh decaying.

Chapter Eleven

On her way to the Pit, as she crossed the main courtyard, Isha spotted Sir Leofric overseeing his followers as they were doing drills.

The folk who had been conscripted were assigned a mage who would control them in battle. Sir Leofric trained his people, like all high mages, but rather than teaching mindbrawl in cramped rooms indoors, he gathered them outside, so they could re-enact battle formations.

She paused, watching from the sidelines. She readjusted the bundle she was carrying over her shoulder – it contained gifts for the khers.

Each mage had a small group of ungifted which they manipulated directly: Sir Leofric shared the instructions in mindlink, they made the soldiers move. *Right!* The soldiers turned, eyes unfocused, breathing even, limbs rigid. *Shields up!* With a co-ordination no army should be able to achieve, the shields were raised, lances lowered between them, creating a spiked carapace. *Forward!* Not only did the soldiers walk together, but they all lifted the same leg at the same time, their steps synchronised. Some gestures were jerky, lacking precision, not because the soldiers were unskilled, but because the people puppeteering them were.

Most eerie was the absence of noise. Except for the stamp of feet, the rustle of armour, the clink of metal on wood, the courtyard was silent. The stable hands, calling out to each other or to their horses, were louder than the army.

When Sir Leofric called for a break – for the mages' sake, not for the ungifted – it was even stranger. The ungifted blinked until they could see again. They glanced around, confused at finding themselves in a different position from where they had started. They often stumbled, regaining their balance by themselves, rather than having it dictated to them. When they stretched, when they yawned, it was with the haggard expressions of people who weren't sure why they were tired.

Isha tried to imagine it, on the battlefield. Opening her eyes, to see the dead around her, unsure who she had killed, whose blood was on her hands, why her shield was splintered. Unsure, even, whether she was injured, whether she had walked on a broken bone or with an open wound, before the pain finally hit her. In the courtyard, the discomforts were small: a man noticed he had bruised his elbow, another that he had walked for hours with a stone in his shoe. They made half-hearted jokes about it, noticing too late that they were thirsty, or hungry, or sore.

In the meantime, Sir Leofric gave some advice to the mages to polish their steering. Out of morbid curiosity, she found herself drifting closer. She wondered how the khers would fare if they had to face an army with such uncanny discipline. A twist of fear churned in her stomach.

As Isha inched closer, she heard Sir Leofric speak in his friendly tone: 'You have to let them breathe. Don't hold on too tight. If you are going to take over entirely – which I don't recommend – then remember to *make* them breathe.' He went on to tell an anecdote, which he presented as funny, about rows of ungifted fainting because the mage in charge had forgotten to use their lungs. 'They fell like flies, and she was wondering why!' The mages dutifully laughed along.

Isha had strayed for too long. His attention landed on her.

'My favourite little turncoat!' he said. 'Come over, come over, don't stay skulking under the arches. People will assume you're up to no good.'

She didn't have much choice. She held her packet close, hoping he wouldn't ask to see its contents.

'Have you met the apprentice who cuckolded Lord Daegan yet?' Sir Leofric asked, his tone indicating that this was banter and Isha shouldn't take offence.

The followers played along: they smiled, they gave polite chuckles. Still, Isha couldn't help but sense a tension there, an unacknowledged unease. She bit on her tongue to stop any unwanted words from escaping her lips. She clamped down on her thoughts to avoid giving any secrets away.

'So, any reason why you were eavesdropping?' Sir Leofric continued. The lightness in his voice was deceiving: it was there, Isha was certain, to make her lower her guard, so she would say something damning. He only wanted an excuse to get his hands on her.

From the way he smiled, slowly, as if savouring the moment, she worried he could hear her thoughts – and enjoyed the prospect of a challenge.

'I was admiring your war preparations,' she said. 'It's very impressive.'

'This little display?' His smile soured into a sneer. 'With this clueless bunch, who have only started learning the drill?' The followers, apparently used to the sudden mood shifts, showed nothing but meekness at being rebuked. 'That's nothing.'

His mindlink expanded like a sail filling with wind. The ungifted, who had been resting, all rose to their feet at once.

Their movements weren't as gauche; the jolts had been smoothened. Although they were unfocused, they seemed to look in the direction they were headed. As they lined up, Isha realised Sir Leofric's supervision was firm, but much subtler. Breathing, walking, holding their weapons – he let the ungifted do it themselves. But he was intransigent as to where to stand, where to stride, when to strike.

'Do you know it is the most important skill we have?' he said idly. 'Mages didn't get to rule through duels. Mindbrawl is not what got us here.'

As he talked, he split the ungifted into two groups. He didn't seem much focused on the task at hand as he set the scene, two small battalions facing each other across the courtyard, ready for the clash.

Her heart sped up as Sir Leofric made the ungifted stamp their feet, hit their lances against their shields, in rhythm, as a threat. The merchants and stable hands went quiet at the sight. Some of the soldiers on either side of the courtyard had been chatting before. They might be family, or friends. But they brought their weapons down, the sharpened metal tips pointing at each other.

Worry swathed the mages around Sir Leofric, a dulled fear, of people used to dealing with someone unpredictable, violent. It did nothing to reassure Isha that he wouldn't go through with this little performance, that he would stop before any bloodshed.

'This is what our power is for,' he concluded.

He clicked his tongue. The two lines charged. Weapons held aloft, faces blank and calm, the thunder of feet on wet ground.

'No!' Isha gasped, before she could stop herself.

The silence rang in her ears, replacing the clash she should have heard. The ungifted had paused, mere inches from each other, weapons stilled on their way to each other's faces, lances frozen in front of eyes, shields lifted, everything held in place, a life-size tableau.

'No?' Sir Leofric was glowing. Under his orders, the ungifted took a step back, lowered their blades, and were released. They seemed, at most, confused as to why they had changed position. 'I hope you don't have a sensitive soul, girl,' he said, clearly entertained by her reaction. 'It won't serve you on the battlefield.'

She wanted to get away from him as fast as possible. She muttered some excuse about being needed by Sir Passerine, struggling to hide her loathing. Once he dismissed her, she all but ran from him.

***

Anxiously, Isha crossed the Pit, heading for the central square. She had been invited as a witness, if she understood correctly. Ka wanted her to attend this gathering, during which he'd submit his plan to the iwdan community, so she'd promised to be there.

Reluctant to come empty-handed, Isha had traded her old farmgirl dress for a bundle of wooden toy animals at the pawnbroker's. She had even thought up a pun to go with her present. In the iwdan language, there were several words for gift: a gift that was meant to claim a male to your hearth, like a sort of dowry; a gift that was an apology; a gift that was an insult, which was used to belittle rather than help. What Tatters brought to Arushi's relatives when he visited was a gift that was more of a trade, where someone owed you something in return – a meal, a warm bed for the night, or simply another present when they then visited your tiyayat.

A precious gift, offered in thanks for an act of great friendship, was called a yis, which was the same word as for horse. For a long time, the best gift someone could receive really was a horse, so it made sense for both words to be the same. One of the wooden toy animals was a horse. Isha was hoping to make a pun about bringing a great present and bringing a wooden horse.

It hadn't snowed in a few days, which meant that although the Pit was strewn with frozen puddles and grey piles of packed snow, the tracks between the tents were clear. In the central square, the multiple painted eyes of the fresco were gazing at the gathering below. The women were crowded against the wall; the men had placed themselves in a half-circle before the women, genders distinctly separated. Most people were standing, although Uaza was seated on a rug, brought outside for this occasion. Isha spotted Ka, but he was in the centre of the group of men, so instead she joined the children, who were at the border between both genders, mixed. Apparently they were not part of the rigorous partition.

As she wove through the crowd, she greeted some of Ka's neighbours or relatives with her stumbling iwdan. She could now talk about easy topics, like the weather: *adfer wa yehri, the snow is bad*, was one of her go-to phrases. People usually answered by clicking their tongue and confirming: wa yehri, indeed.

She recognised some children from Ka's hearth. They parted for her, glancing curiously at her bundle as she unknotted it. When the carved animals spilt out, they grabbed them excitedly. She picked out the wooden horse to hand it to one of the smaller children, a little girl called Ayi.

'*Look, I got you a yis,*' Isha said in iwdan.

Ayi frowned and didn't laugh. '*A what?*'

'*A yis,*' Isha tried again. The little girl's frown only deepened. '*Like a yis that neighs, and a yis you give to people.*'

Suddenly, Isha worried the joke would be mistaken for an insult. She hadn't considered it before, but maybe pretending to bring a great present that wasn't that great was in poor taste?

'*Ah, you mean a yis,*' said Ayi, taking the toy from Isha's hand. She didn't sound offended.

Isha couldn't hear the difference. Maybe she'd got something wrong, and the word for gift wasn't pronounced the same? Ayi turned the toy over between her fingers, then put it the right way up, and let out a sound vaguely like a whinny. She made the toy horse gallop on the frozen ground. At least she enjoyed it. The fact that she'd brought presents also helped Isha feel less self-conscious about crouching beside Ayi.

As she settled, she heard a familiar voice behind her:

'A yis. I like it. Since when do you speak our language, soulworm?'

Isha turned around so fast she nearly tripped. Yua was standing there, an amused lilt to her voice, Arushi beside her. Isha couldn't hold their gazes. She hadn't seen anyone from their household since Arushi had kicked her out.

'Tidir,' she managed to mumble, keeping her eyes averted.

Arushi strode past her, towards the centre of the women's gathering. Yua, however, stayed.

'I am curious, you know,' she insisted. She leant over to catch Isha's eye, then said something in her own language, using a complicated turn of phrase – but it included iwdan and a question, so Isha knew what she had asked.

'*I speak only a little iwdan,*' Isha answered. That was another set phrase which had shown its use. She forced herself to lift her chin.

Yua had put woollen decorations on her horns, like mittens, with the tips poking out. She had a human-style scarf, but the kher's loose, armless arrud. Isha had never noticed how much Yua looked like her sister. She shared the same features, the slim jawbone, the nose, even the shape of the eyes. Her hair was longer and curlier. In the same way, her tattoos were longer, more drawn-out, coiled. But she was tattooed in the same places as Arushi: down the arms, across the collarbone, along the wrists. They both dressed in human-style clothes – boots, not the open shoes khers used, for example, with tunics under the arrud.

While she stared, Yua calmly took in Isha's outfit, the brown cape which an apprentice should not be wearing.

'Who taught you iwdan?' Yua asked.

'Ka.' Isha swallowed. 'I'm here to support him today.'

Yua nodded. 'Good luck with that. Sekk iss.' With those words, she joined her sister and her mother. From the way their family was placed, at the centre of the group of women, it was obvious they had power within the community. Uaza and Yua were two longlived, after all, one who had lived for over a century and one who would grow as old, if not older. Their opinions would impact the votes, Isha suspected.

After some shuffling, whispered greetings and reordering, the khers settled at last. Isha stayed off to the side, with the children. On her right were the women, assembled below the battlements, loosely grouped by bloodlines or, in the case of the kher guards, by trade. Arushi had a group of armed women around her, and Isha wondered if, like mages, this meant the guards were her followers and would vote according to what she ordered. Maybe not. Maybe everyone was entitled to their own opinion, whoever led them outside the Pit.

On Isha's left were the men, impatiently kicking the ground with their heels. At the centre was a firepit, unlit, the ashes assembled between a circle of stones. Although it wasn't burning, it served as a focal point to the circle.

When Ka stepped into the empty centre, everyone fell silent.

Ka introduced himself in iwdan. He gave a few ritual formulas which Isha didn't catch, but which she supposed set the tone of the meeting. He had explained to her that decisions regarding the hearth were submitted by the women, but voted on by the men. Decisions concerning outside expeditions were submitted by the men, but voted on by the women. For this reason, his proposal wasn't only his own – he had discussed it with other male khers beforehand, and they had agreed on what to put to the women's vote.

Through keywords and guesswork, Isha caught the gist of his speech. He was talking about the underground tunnels, which meant the iwdan could access the Nest's prisons, and the fact that he suspected Tatters might be down there. Isha also heard something about weapons, and the importance of having someone on the inside.

The proposal he gave in both languages, iwdan and Dusk-dweller.

'Mezyan advised we should arm ourselves in good time before the Renegades arrive, so we can join the upcoming battle against the Nest,' said Ka. 'We should go to the weapons reserves under the Nest and steal them. We can rely on the help of a mage and of the guards. Those who wish to do more could continue to the prisons and free Tatters.'

Isha hadn't realised the expedition would include more than rescuing Tatters, although of course it made sense – why should the iwdan endanger themselves if there wasn't something for them to gain?

Ka stood with stiff shoulders, straight as a rod, his tattoo curling around his waist, the scars of whip marks curling around his shoulders. He had something of Mezyan about him when he spoke: the firmness, the curtness, the clenched jaw. The energy of someone ready to fight.

'Ka tells us you're not responsible for what happened to Tatters,' Yua said abruptly. Isha jumped at being called out so soon into the proceedings. It was unclear, from the kher's tone, whether she believed Ka or not. 'Why didn't you tell us?'

All eyes were on Isha, the real ones, glinting, frowning, and the painted ones on the mural, still, unmoving. She wiped her hands on her shoulder-cape, trying to shed her nervousness.

'I tried to,' Isha admitted. Addressing the audience from her seated position was uncomfortable, but stumbling to her feet halfway through her sentence was, if it were possible, even more awkward. 'But Arushi didn't believe me. I don't blame her. It isn't a very believable story.'

A kher Isha couldn't see properly, standing at the back of the group, huffed and said, 'Arushi is older than her horns, and as hard as them, too.'

Arushi's face stayed expressionless, not rising to the taunt.

'You don't strike me as a liar,' Yua said.

Inwardly, Isha winced. Yua meant it as a compliment, but it showed how little she knew about mages. Isha lied all the time, if only by omission. Trying to be truthful was akin to trying to stay astride two horses – sometimes she attempted it, but most often it was an untruth or a fall.

'Are you happy about being an apprentice?' Yua asked.

Isha clasped her fingers together to still them. She glanced around the gathering, at the children playing with the wooden toys some poor soul had pawned away in despair; at the older khers who seemed to be snoozing; at the expectant, scowling faces of the men; at the fresco which burst with colours and yet was marred, in one corner, with the blood of an iwdan shot by lawmages.

'If you mean do I agree with people cutting your horns, treating you like animals, limiting the places you can go to and work, then the answer is no,' said Isha. 'If you mean do I want to help Tatters, and help you, then the answer is yes.'

Yua's black eyes burnt with inner flames. Her childish horn decorations and the colourful scarf flung around her neck did nothing to dim her fire.

'That's what I wanted to hear!' She clapped her hands. If Ka was embers, waiting for a gust of wind to awaken, his anger and grief contained and condensed, then Yua was an already-bright, already-spitting blaze. 'If we have a mage on the inside, that gives us a good chance. I think we should take it.' Her smile was all teeth.

Isha forced herself to hide her misgivings; this was not the time to feel afraid. This was a time for action.

'It's a stupid idea.' Arushi's voice doused even her sister's contagious enthusiasm.

'This is a question of life or death,' Yua pleaded.

'Yes,' Arushi agreed. 'That's why I'm not putting my life – or anyone's, for that matter – in the hands of someone I don't trust.'

No-one interrupted. Everyone was listening to the argument taking place between the two sisters. Even the children had quietened.

'Consider it, at least,' Yua insisted. 'Can't you see what it means for us, to have someone with mindlink on our side?'

Arushi was standing beside her mother in a leather jacket, high boots, a sword sheathed at her side. It was impossible not to notice that, although Ka and Yua were raring for a fight, she was the soldier here.

'It would be fantastic,' she said. 'If Isha were on our side.'

Yua let out a frustrated huff. She shook her head so hard one of the mittens around her horns threatened to slip off. 'Don't you want to know what happened to Tatters?'

Arushi's chin was bent so low it could have touched her chest; she was breathing hard. Isha knew enough about kher culture to recognise someone considering using their head like a battering ram.

'Don't you dare use his name.' She lifted her fist, and for a moment Isha feared she might punch Yua. But she simply touched her sister's shoulder, briefly, before taking her hand away. 'I have lost him. I will not lose you. And certainly not to the same person.'

They were so alike, the two sisters, with the same determination on their faces, the same frown between their eyebrows. But Yua loved colours and baubles, where Arushi wore nothing unnecessary. Arushi had tired eyes, drawn lips, longer horns. Yua's stubby horns were as high as a child's, and there was something youthful about her face and the way she moved – as if she weren't afraid of falling or hurting herself. As if such things could never happen to her.

'You want to steal weapons from the Nest,' said Arushi, 'and you have found a reckless way to do it. If the mages decide we're a danger to them, they will eradicate us. Even if the Renegades help, like they promised – and that's not certain – even then, they are not here right now.'

'The more people have weapons, the more people get killed.' This from another guardswoman, matter-of-factly. 'The mages see iwdan unarmed, they're worried. They see iwdan with swords, and they start shooting arrows.'

This drew a reaction from the crowd. A few women called out, *We want to fight back* or, *We want to be free.* A few men, although they couldn't vote, joined the debate. *They shoot us whether we're armed or not. They kill us whether we can defend ourselves or not. We want to have a chance, at least.*

'And I want to help Tatters,' Yua added. 'Don't you?'

Arushi bared her teeth at her sister. The debate wasn't limited to the two of them anymore: people were shouting at each other from across the circle, or discussing the situation animatedly with the person next to them. Some of the kher guards behind Arushi were calling out arguments about the danger and the importance of listening to people who knew the mages best. Ka, hands cupped around his mouth, was trying to get something across to Arushi about loyalty.

Taking a deep breath, Isha inched a step closer to Arushi, intending to attempt to persuade her, but as soon as she moved close to the centre of the circle, the debates petered out as attention turned to her. She froze, but it was too late. Everyone was staring at the human mage.

Isha very nearly stepped back again. Still, she struggled against her shyness. Ka had obtained this for her; that she would be heard. She should use it. For him. For Tatters.

'I know whatever we do against the Nest, we'll be taking risks.' She spoke too low, and a few iwdan shouted at her to speak up. Trembling, her voice cracking when she pushed on it, Isha ploughed on. 'People might get hurt. Tatters is an example of that. But things won't change if we don't take risks, if we aren't ready to get hurt.' She lifted her chin and held Arushi's eyes. 'I am so, so sorry for what happened. It's my fault because I'm part of the Nest. But you are also part of the Nest.'

She wondered if this was the right thing to say. Arushi looked like she was biting down on her words hard enough to draw blood. Someone in the crowd snickered.

'But because we're so involved, we're the ones with the most power to change things.' Isha realised, as she spoke the words, that she believed them. That she wanted to make a change. That she could. That she would. 'We have a duty to do so.'

Breathless, her cheeks burning, she took a step back.

'Well spoken,' said Yua. 'Look, we're going to have to trust some people. Isha is trying, at least.'

The conversations resumed. Having said her piece, Isha sat down. When she caught Ka's gaze from across the circle, he nodded. She took it to mean she had done what he'd needed of her. She spent the rest of the debate with the children, uninvolved. The children only half-listened; Isha only half-understood. Everyone was discussing the situation in iwdan. A few men walked towards the centre of the circle, which seemed to be a cue to indicate everyone had to go silent, and made their case in enflamed speeches. A few women did the same. Ganez waved his arms as he argued, but Isha couldn't work out which of his sisters he was supporting. He talked about choosing between blood and soil, but that was all she understood.

As the conversations quietened, Uaza added her opinion in a firm, insistent whisper. Her explanation was long-winded, spoken too low and too fast for Isha to catch even one word, but people nodded and muttered when she was done.

Ka ended the session by placing himself in the centre again, reciting various ritual phrases. To Isha's surprise, the vote happened then and there.

Women lifted their hands. It was varied; this was obviously a divisive subject. At first glance, Isha couldn't tell if Ka had a majority or not. Yua and Uaza both had their hands up.

Grudgingly, Arushi lifted her arm. Before Yua could thank her, before pleasure could light up her face, Arushi amended: 'On condition that Isha is partnered with me at all times, and that she isn't given any important detail beforehand. That way even if she wants to, she can't betray us. And if something happens, I'll eviscerate her myself.'

Ka's deep voice easily carried through the square. 'That's a good precaution.'

Yua turned around to count the votes. As she worked out the result, a smile cut her face like a knife. She pressed her hands together in excitement; despite her childlike gestures, there was an ironclad determination in her voice.

'We're doing this.'

* * *

When the collarbound lightborn – whose name Isha still didn't know – returned, Lord Daegan didn't call for a meeting immediately. But the high mages had seen the yellow flash of light in the sky, and they expected to be summoned. Passerine and Isha were amongst the first to interrupt their training to wait beside the stairs leading up to the council room.

It was dizzying – after being stuck for so long, it all unfolded at once. The Pit had taken their decision and were delving into their planning, which Ka had told her would be ready in a couple of days. And now the first battle between the Renegades and the Nest had been fought. Depending on the outcome, Lord Daegan's power might be strengthened, or easier to contest.

They were, at last, reluctantly, called forth.

'This means trouble,' said Passerine. 'If the news were good, he would have wanted us there to hear it.'

She knew he was right. The climb up the spiral staircase was a long, strenuous one. The council chambers seemed frozen in time, with snow across the table and the chairs. Lord Daegan was standing at one end, his collarbound beside him, as the high mages came out of the maze of glass. The woman was pale, with drawn features. When she turned, Isha bit down on her tongue: there was a bruise blossoming on the lightborn's cheek, and her left eye was puffy.

When Isha went to hold his chair for him, Sir Leofric gave her a wink, which she didn't return.

A problem immediately presented itself, preventing the meeting from starting: the steady trickle of refugees into the city had finally reached its saturation point. There weren't enough seats for all the Sunriser mages.

'There is nothing to it,' Lord Daegan said, apparently unfazed. If anything, this menial matter seemed to please him – maybe the delay suited him. 'Some of you must leave.'

'And how will we decide who gets to stay?' Lady Mayurah asked, from where she had already firmly seated herself, a young female apprentice lingering beside her. 'This isn't only a problem for the council, as you very well know.' It was also, although she didn't draw a list, a problem regarding space in the Nest, rooms for apprentices stranded outside of dorms, food for mages and their followers, and of course – for those convents that sheltered ungifted servants – an issue for their ungifted as well.

Lord Daegan's gaze drifted to Passerine. 'Whoever is most preeminent may stay.'

'In which case,' Lady Mayurah said, not rising to the easy bait, even though her eyes did flit to Passerine, 'Sir Cintay should leave. The Redstone convent is a minor one.'

She held Lord Daegan's glare. She had tied back her jet-black hair, dying the strands of white with henna, so it appeared streaked with fire.

'Sir Cintay is under my protection,' the supreme mage said. 'And welcome, in my name.' His smile hardened. 'Maybe you should fight for your place.'

Passerine intervened. He spoke in Wingshade, Isha assumed – in any case, it excluded most of the Duskdwellers. His voice sounded different in the foreign language, still as deep yet more musical. Whatever he said, it was greeted with agreement from various refugee mages. The Sunrisers mindlinked together, creating a web of images and meaning, effortlessly sharing the council room. Without a fuss, the new arrivals left. There was no need to be physically present when their minds could attend.

'Keep to the Duskdweller tongue, if you wish to be included,' Lord Daegan snapped.

Passerine bowed to him, but it was hard to ignore that his show of meekness hadn't prevented him from doing as he pleased.

Still, the problem was only temporarily sorted. Mindlink could share information, but not bread, not beds. Refugees fighting each other for survival might suit Lord Daegan, undermining all Sunriser mages as they were pitted against each other, but Isha was acutely conscious that Passerine would become a target.

Once everyone was seated, the meeting began.

'We have reached the Renegades,' Lord Daegan said, as if he had personally gone to investigate their encampment. 'And Hawk. But there were ... complications.'

He nodded towards his collarbound. Her eyes seemed to change colour, sometimes as green as Sir Leofric's, sometimes hazel-brown. At the centre of the bruise marking her face, there was a small crescent-moon scar. Without a word – without a sign that she was listening to what he was saying, or even reacting to his order – she mindlinked to the high mages.

She didn't mindlink like a human, with scents and sounds and images kept distinct from feelings, with who the mage was and how they were experiencing the memory separated from what was happening. The point of view kept shifting, as if she were seeing herself from the outside at the same time as she was living through the event, and the memory was layered with meaning – what had happened, what might have happened, what she thought had happened in retrospect.

It was vivid, albeit confusing. It was like having learnt to read music without ever having heard it, and one day listening to an orchestra.

Suddenly Isha was before Hawk – a face that she had seen before, at different points in time, often enough that she recognised her, that she felt as if she knew her. Hawk was weathered, scarred and tanned and scarred again. Her hair was cut short, curling around her ears. She was standing at the centre of her military encampment, with tents and half-built wooden shelters around her, and the looming shape of the Ridge behind.

'I thought someone would come,' Hawk was saying.

Isha could see the camp from above, filled with ant-sized people chopping wood and herding horses – but at the same time she could see Hawk standing before her, as if the lightborn was speaking to her in human form after having landed. For a split second, Isha could even see the scene as if she had witnessed it. She could imagine the lightborn, her long blonde hair cascading down her shoulders, dressed in frosty blue, pale as snow. And Hawk standing in front of her, a force of nature, all muscle and leather and metal, her red cape poking at an angle where her sword's sheath pushed against it.

'Do you want to fight me?' Hawk asked. 'I bet your master told you to.' Renegades were gathering around them, some of them wielding bows, the arrows quivering at their fingers.

Hawk lifted one hand to hold back her troops. 'Have you come to talk? If not, I'd like to warn you beforehand – we're not mages. We have more than mindlink on our side.'

The lightborn shook her head. 'I have not come to talk.'

Hawk unhooked something from her belt and fastened it around her left hand – it looked like a metal glove.

'So be it,' she said.

264

The memory became confused. There were beams of light, and arrows flying uselessly through the lightborn's bright body. Visions flashed past Isha's eyes before she could analyse them, angled so close to the ground that they couldn't be sewn together into a coherent picture. Isha was vaguely aware that khers were rushing over from different places across the camp, and that the lightborn had to swerve to avoid them; they moved in formation, hemming in her movements. No-one was foolish enough to mindlink her. When she closed the distance with Hawk, the leader of the Renegades opened her hand – the glove she was wearing was no glove at all. It was a mirror.

The lightborn bounced off the mirror and slammed into the ground. When she returned to human shape, Hawk punched her in the face, using the pommel of her sword to lend weight to her hand. Pain bloomed across the lightborn's eye and cheek – pain, and shock at such a grounded physical sensation, a sort of surprise, like a child burning her fingers for the first time.

Hawk pinned her against the ground, holding the mirror above the lightborn so she couldn't alight without being reflected.

'Change of plan,' Hawk said, panting from the effort, her breath white with cold. 'Let's talk.'

Two khers grabbed the lightborn – she couldn't alight through them, she couldn't mindlink them. She was such a powerful being, yet she was powerless against them. They held her arms behind her back, forcing her to crouch on the muddy ground, staining her dress from its hem to her knees. The hit across her cheekbone ached, already swelling.

'Don't be rough,' said Hawk. 'Collarbounds suffer enough.'

By now the whole camp was roused; soldiers gathered around. The lightborn was shivering. Her dress was soaked, her bruise throbbed, and there were naked blades pointing towards her throat. Isha felt a pang of sympathy for this woman, far from her home, following the orders of a man she despised, learning to experience pain.

'What is your name?' asked Hawk.

The lightborn held her gaze. 'Nothing a human can pronounce.'

'What does your master call you?'

'Nothing.'

'There is nothing I can call you?'

The lightborn hesitated, then said, 'You can call me Starling.'

It was the most Isha had ever heard the collarbound say. She had a plain voice, which didn't do her beauty justice. If she was akin to a bird, then she wasn't a songbird. Yet she used the name Starling. Isha wondered why Lord Daegan had never told his council what to call her.

Hawk removed the device she had been wearing, not giving Starling a chance to properly study it.

'Who sent you?'

'Lord Daegan.'

Hawk raised an eyebrow. 'Really? What is Passerine up to, then?'

The lightborn was trembling, but she didn't lower her eyes. 'Nothing that I am aware of. Sir Passerine is a high mage at the Nest. That is all.'

Hawk rubbed her nose with the back of her wrist, scrunching her face in thought.

'Where is the eyas?'

'I have no idea.'

Hawk stared at the collarbound for a while, then came to a decision.

'She knows nothing, or she can't speak. Lord Coward must have given her permission to flee so she doesn't die here. Let her fly home.'

A hubbub of protest flared up from the Renegades, but it was clear Hawk expected her orders to be followed. Before the khers let their prisoner go, however, Hawk turned to Starling again.

'I'm curious,' she said, in her gravelly voice. 'This must be your first time away from the sky. What do you think of us?'

Starling didn't hesitate, as if she had been expecting this question, or as if it had been on her mind for a long time. Maybe no-one but Hawk had thought to ask.

'Humans have ugly souls.'

Hawk barked a laugh, unimpressed, maybe agreeing. She waved for her men to stand down. The khers freed Starling, taking a step back. The mindlink stopped abruptly, with Hawk still speaking, shouting some sort of message for Starling to bring back to the Nest.

Returning to the council took Isha longer than it should have. She was shaking, her heart hammering in her chest. Her bones were cold as ice.

'What is an eyas?' asked Sir Cintay.

'I believe it is a kind of bird,' said Passerine.

Isha could hardly breathe. All her concentration was going into keeping her thoughts as unnoticeable as possible, as mundane, as insignificant, as the mediocre apprentice she was.

'Isha?' Sir Leofric was smiling, his chin resting in one hand, his eyes as green as the glass pane behind him, and as lifeless. For a horrifying moment Isha thought he would call her out, that he had noticed, that he knew what the tattoo meant. 'Care to share your insights? I can tell you've thought of something.'

All eyes focused on her. Her mouth was dry, despite the days of rain and tea and snow and rain.

She had to say something.

'Hawk must have sparred a lightborn before,' she found herself answering. 'No, she must have trained with a lightborn before.

That kind of mastery requires practice. She trained with someone, several times, and worked out the mirror technique. Most probably one of the Renegades is a sehwol.'

She focused on her mindlink, as Passerine had taught her. *If done well, this means people don't even realise that you are hiding something, that there is something to hide.* She could feel sweat down her back, sticking her robes to her skin.

Sir Leofric raised an eyebrow. Lord Daegan gritted his teeth, clearly insulted an apprentice was invited to intervene, but unwilling to fight the head lawmage for such a small slight.

'Maybe the eyas is that sehwol,' prompted Sir Cintay. 'Lightborns are often given bird names.'

'Although the Red Scourge wasn't,' Lady Mayurah said. 'It could be him Hawk trained with.'

'In any case, you seem to have made an impression, Sir Passerine,' said Sir Leofric. 'The woman still remembers you. I hope you put up more of a fight than our collarbound friend here.'

They lost interest in Isha, having nothing more to add to her conclusions. When the conversation resumed, thankfully without her, she breathed out a quiet sigh of relief.

Good work. Passerine was so nimble not one of the high mages turned towards them. She sensed he was pleased with her but also that he was poised, ready for action. *Now is our time to act.*

***

The blessing was that whatever lay behind the door was seldom used. The curse was that seldom was not never.

Tatters didn't talk to the other prisoners. He saw them briefly, when they were brought in: khers with their horns broken off hastily, black stumps rising from their foreheads. They were always smaller than their guards, sometimes following them meekly, sometimes kicking and howling as they were dragged through the prisons, cursing the mages in iwdan until they didn't have a voice left with which to curse.

They weren't placed in the cages before they went inside the room. Sometimes they were left in the cages afterwards, if the mages hadn't finished with them, but they couldn't talk then. Sometimes they couldn't even open their eyes.

The only words Tatters heard were the lawmages', when they propped open the door to the interrogation room, maybe to enjoy the draft of cool air from the corridor; when they chatted idly in front of the cages, sharing some candied fruit their spouse had made as a winter treat. Most of the time, he tried to block his ears. He hated their humanity most of all. How mundane those conversations were.

But he caught the name Mezyan a few times, enough to feel a dim, sick curiosity. He gathered, from half-mumbled sentences, that the halfblood was still doing his work as a messenger: he travelled from city to city, village to village, raising trouble along the Sunpath by spreading the Renegades' ideas. Where he'd visited, small rebellions erupted, khers took up arms, most often leading to brief, bloody battles, which the Nest won.

They succeeded, in part, thanks to Starling. From the sky, she had an excellent view. She could tell where Mezyan had been or where he was headed, even though she lost him when he hid in woodlands, or when she was sent elsewhere. He kept avoiding the lawmages, but barely. He never slipped from a village unnoticed. The areas he'd stayed in had soldiers sent out to them before he'd even left. Starling enabled the Nest to view their whole territory like a chessboard, leaving little place for surprise attacks.

Once the unrest was quelled, the main troublemakers were brought to the Nest, so the lawmages could extract information on the Renegades.

Which explained why Tatters didn't recognise any of the people being brought in. The iwdan being targeted weren't city-dwellers, but a mix of rural khers and nomads belonging to the travelling communities that had been deemed illegal under Lady Siobhan's rule. The people most desperate to believe Hawk, most willing to die for the better world she promised.

Through pain,
To victory.

He wondered what they did with the bodies afterwards. They didn't return them to the families, that much was certain. Jewels and magical items carved out of kher bone came to mind. He tried not to imagine the corpses, but he dreamt of them. He tried not to think, but he wondered what they did with the flesh.

He knew he was losing himself because sometimes he heard people screaming even though there was no-one behind the door.

The prison brought back other memories of harsh times. He wished Lal were there, as she had been before, to help him. She had always been stronger than him, or maybe more fiercely attached to life.

He had been younger. He had been angrier. They had been together.

Hawk insisted on sparring with Tatters, even if he alighted against her – especially if he used his lightborn skills against her. She argued that if she could defeat Tatters, she would fear no-one. They would find a clearing, or a patch of flat grass beside the encampment, and Hawk would use her strike-mirrors and her sword, while Tatters fought nearly exclusively with his knife. There was no point in wielding anything heavier that wouldn't stay with him when he alighted. Clothes and small items did, dragged forth by his burning energy, but long blades couldn't follow.

Passerine watched them as they prepared, in the early morning, before the heat was too unbearable.

'He is too reckless to train with,' Passerine said.

Hawk gritted her teeth. She was stretching, the dawn light catching the mirror in her hands, glinting and winking at Tatters. On the other side of the clearing, he didn't stretch – not because he didn't need to, but because he knew it would annoy Hawk. He could see her casting him glances, hesitating as to whether she should force him to warm up, growing more irritated by the minute.

At least that's two of us, Lal thought.

They were just beside the camp; between the trees, Tatters could make out the fire as Mezyan worked to rekindle it. Other Renegades were carrying pots and pans, milking the goats, checking on the horses that had been left to graze, loosely tied to branches and tree stumps. He played with the ends of his scarf, picking at the threads where it had frayed.

Hawk called out to Tatters. 'So this is a sulky day, then, not a snarky day?' When he didn't answer, she shook her head. 'Don't you think you could manage a happy day from time to time?'

Tatters shrugged. He had grown used to the weight of the stana across his shoulders, the way it moved when he did. He didn't marvel as the heavy fabric shifted around him. Like the scarf, the cloak had become part of his identity.

'I'll have a happy day when you're dead,' he answered.

It cannot come too soon, agreed Lal.

Hawk didn't bat an eyelid; she was accustomed to these answers. 'I'm glad at least someone will be enjoying themselves.'

Tatters couldn't help but smirk at that. 'Believe me, I won't be alone. I bet the convents will be rejoicing. We could throw a party.'

With a grunt, Hawk lowered herself into a crouch, one leg pushed out in front of her. Passerine stood beside her, arms crossed in front of his chest, a frown across his features. Without looking up from her stretching, Hawk asked: 'So it's a snarky day, then? Changed your mind?'

'I know you miss the sound of my voice,' he said, before biting his tongue. Lal winced.

Don't, said Lal. *She enjoys it.*

Hawk got up, a smile on her lips. She shook her wrists to unlock them.

'You're not wrong there,' she said, with her easy, simple confidence. Tatters felt like throwing something at her. How dare she pretend they were friends, when he was wearing the collar, and she refused to remove it?

Passerine shook his head. 'That's exactly what I mean.' He didn't seem to notice, or to care, about how his words melted her good mood. 'You don't have the willpower to control Tatters. Because you're not consistent, each time you give him an order, you're wielding wildfire. It could burn you as much as your enemies.'

I have become an item, thought Tatters. *People talk about me as if I'm not there.*

But Passerine is right about this, answered Lal. *We are wildfire. And we will burn.*

Hawk let out a sigh of annoyance and, without forewarning, threw her strike-mirror towards Passerine. He only just caught it, slipping in the dewy grass to reach out. He had to uncross his arms to do so, struggling for balance, and Tatters felt a brief pang of satisfaction. He wished Passerine would fall, but of course he managed to straighten himself.

Hawk threw her hair behind her shoulders, shaking it like a horse's mane. 'Very well,' she said. 'You show me.'

'What?' spluttered Passerine, holding the strike-mirror awkwardly.

Hawk shoved her chin towards Tatters, who stood unmoving, as unresponsive as he could manage.

'You show me,' she said. 'You're always after Tatters as if he's insulted your mother. Well, here you go. Let off steam. Show me how it's done, if you're so sure.'

Mezyan looked up from where the fire was now letting out a thin line of grey smoke. A few other Renegades wandered closer to watch the show. At the time, Hawk and Passerine didn't often argue – although that would become more frequent – and Renegades were used to reacting when Hawk raised her voice.

Hawk turned to Tatters. 'Don't you even think of killing Passerine,' she growled. 'Or maiming him.' The collar glowed gold on sunburnt skin.

'I wouldn't dream of it,' he said.

'Every night, I bet,' she answered. 'And me dead beside him.'

She shook her head as if to clear her thoughts. Any sign of a smile was gone from her face. She had stark, elegant features, which suited her stern expression.

She is square, corrected Lal. *Square jaw, square forehead. All lines and edges. There is nothing soft about her.*

I never said there was, answered Tatters.

He unsheathed his knife as Passerine struggled with the strike-mirror. It was made of two mirrors, cut into crude semi-circles, the upper one with four straps through which to slip the user's fingers, the lower one with a strap for the thumb. Depending on how open or closed the user's fist was, the mirrors were angled differently, and refracted a lightborn accordingly. Although Hawk used them most, they were Passerine's invention.

He pulled the strike-mirror on, keeping one hand free for a weapon. He discarded his sword and, like Tatters, settled for a shorter knife. It would be close-combat fighting, then. Around the clearing, an audience was gathering: Mezyan, looking worried, and a few other khers and humans, tanned by the sun, muscular, wearing bits and pieces of leather armour, high boots strapped at the knees. Hawk was leaning against a tree. A group of women – recent recruits – were sitting together on the wet grass, whispering among themselves. One man had a dog, which he held beside him, to stop the animal from getting excited and joining in.

Haven't they got anything else to do with their lives? grumbled Lal.

Tatters took on a fighting stance. He clutched his knife; the handle, smooth with use, fit perfectly in his hand. Passerine had never been a talker. He placed his feet apart, narrowed his eyes, and waited.

Tatters could play that game. He didn't move. After a while, Passerine closed the gap between them, moving slowly. At the same time, his mind expanded, tentatively reaching out.

I've got this, said Lal.

While Tatters focused on the physical fight, Lal could deal with any mindbrawl. He waited until Passerine, still moving cautiously, was only a few feet away from him – then he pounced.

He threw himself to the side, shifting as he did so into a bright ray of light. He circled Passerine around his right side – his weapon's side, which meant he didn't have the mirrors in that hand. Passerine spun wildly to follow him, and only just had the time to lift his strike-mirror as Tatters came flying at his face.

Shit. Tatters hated flying into a mirror. It sent him bouncing in the other direction, as violently as if a giant had thrown him. He transformed back into a human as he was flung away and rolled on the grass. Before he could get up, Passerine was above him, blade moving swiftly. Tatters snarled and alighted again, staying low on the ground, where it would be difficult for Passerine to block him. Passerine tried anyway, plunging downwards with the strike-mirror, hoping to cut off Tatters' retreat. He ended in a mess on the floor, while Tatters put some distance between them, his light turning the grass to gold.

He returned to his human shape. Passerine was picking himself off the grass and he wasn't; he counted that as a victory.

'I don't see you using all your talents, Tatters,' Hawk pointed out. The fight didn't seem to engage her much; she was busy picking at rust on her sword's blade with her nails. 'Are you playing nice?'

'No, just playing,' said Tatters. That got him an appreciative laugh from someone in the audience.

Passerine got up, securing his hold both on the mirrors and his knife. Hawk lifted a hand to indicate he had to pause. 'Could you please explain to everyone why you're not using a sword?' She never lost an occasion to teach her recruits.

Passerine brushed the dust off his legs.

'A sword is used because of its range, to keep the enemy at a distance.' Although his voice was quiet, it had a musical quality to it, a depth that meant everyone fell silent and listened. Hawk watched her Renegades approvingly as they soaked up his words. 'But a lightborn can close the distance with you anyway, by alighting through anything you put between them and you. In this case, a shield would be useless, for example: if Tatters really wanted to, he could alight through the shield and land on me

275

directly. A sword would slow me down and wouldn't be much use against him.'

If they were taking a break, Tatters might as well use it: he unpinned his cloak and, before he could leave it in a crumpled pile on the ground, Mezyan came to take it from him.

You're as bad as her, you traitor, snarled Lal. Tatters let Mezyan take the stana, and then the scarf. He could have ground them both in the mud, to make a point, but he was the one who had to wear them afterwards.

He turned back to Passerine. Hawk lowered her hand. 'Go on,' she said.

The collar glowed; Tatters was alighting before he could even decide to, heading for Passerine. He bristled, iridescent colours running down his body. Hawk still hadn't learnt that the collar reacted to any order, whatever the context. He circled Passerine, waiting for an opening. Passerine tried to keep Tatters in his line of sight, his strike-mirror aimed towards him. But Tatters was faster. What was the point of having lightborn blood, if he wasn't faster?

He lunged and shifted back into a human as he reached Passerine's weapon hand. He crashed into it with all his weight, pulling Passerine down with him. The strike-mirror bumped his shoulders as Passerine flailed his arm to catch his balance. Tatters shoved him to the ground, holding his arm down, pressing his knee in the crook of Passerine's elbow. He was vaguely aware of the dog barking in excitement.

Now, said Lal.

He attacked Passerine with mindbrawl. He crafted an image of Hawk, with Passerine and Tatters on either side of her, both men wearing a collar. He pictured Hawk giving orders – small things, hardly orders at all, words he'd heard her say to Passerine before, such as 'lead the scouts ahead' or 'bring me my horse' but each time, however modest the instruction, the collar seared white-hot around Passerine's neck.

You're as much a slave as me, he mindlinked.

It was an intricately crafted nightmare, but it wasn't Passerine's — it was his.

He felt the kick connect with his sides before he understood that Passerine had managed to move. He skidded backwards, the strength of Passerine's mindlink spearing him ear to ear.

That's where you're wrong, collarbound.

Passerine was the only person to refer directly to the collar. Because he was the only one to use the word, it carried more weight when he wielded it. They stared at each other from a distance. Passerine had fallen over twice now, and was covered in green stains from the grass, his hair dishevelled, his breathing hard. But he was still standing. He never smiled; not in front of Tatters. He never talked; not idle words. But he clenched his fists, gripping his knife until his knuckles blanched, and Tatters could tell he was furious.

We touched on something, after all, said Lal.

Before Tatters could hold her back, Lal had reached out for Passerine.

Hawk doesn't even need a collar to control you, she mindlinked. *You'll always live in her shadow.*

Don't provoke him. Tatters tried, and failed, to call back Lal. She projected her mindlink, clear and loud, for everyone in the clearing to hear.

You call yourself a bird, but we're the ones to fly, she said. *Maybe we should take your name and start calling you Tatters.*

Hawk didn't intervene, but she put her sword back in its sheath to keep a closer eye on what would happen. As her second-in-command, Passerine was both admired and resented. When Lal spoke, more than one person chuckled. Some helpful soul even explained what had happened to the khers, as they couldn't share the mindlink.

Mezyan stood aside from the group, hugging the cloak and the scarf to his chest. Black and red, the colours of the Renegades' flag, of khers' skins, of Tatters' outfit. The colours with which Hawk wanted to paint the world.

'I will show you how to kill a lightborn,' Passerine announced. He spoke quietly; too quietly for the Renegades assembled around the clearing. Tatters wondered if he was the only person to hear him.

Passerine ran towards him. By instinct, Tatters alighted.

Don't run away, said Lal. *You can fight him.*

Tatters curved, drawing a bright arc of light, and tried to catch Passerine on his weapon side. He closed the distance between them, wondering what he could do to finish this fight, or at least to get Hawk to interrupt it. As he drew closer, Passerine turned to face him with his knife. Tatters didn't have time to change his course; Passerine caught him in the reflection of his blade.

It was a slim piece of metal, catching the sun, only just polished enough to work as a mirror – but it was enough. Tatters felt Passerine's hand twist, aiming downwards, as Tatters hit the blade. Steel couldn't hurt him as a lightborn, but he was reflected at the angle Passerine had chosen. When his back hit the ground, he returned to human shape. Passerine was above him. Before he could pin Tatters down, Tatters alighted. He could see the sky above him, behind Passerine's head, achingly blue, calling to him.

But Passerine moved as he did, placing his strike-mirror above Tatters just as he left ground. Tatters crashed against the mirrors, which he couldn't alight through, and was flung towards the earth, which he also couldn't alight through. He landed heavily, his head ringing as if someone had kicked it, his vision speckled with blue and white patches. Before he could understand what had happened, someone's knee pushed against his chest, and the cold, slick touch of the strike-mirror pressed against his cheek, cutting off his retreat.

And then there was the blade against his neck.

Passerine put his weight into his leg until Tatters found he could only breathe a thin, raspy gulp of air. The knife was touching his skin, just above the collar. Although he wasn't in pain, he could feel something warm welling against his skin, so he knew Passerine had drawn blood.

He looked up. Passerine's black eyes were bright with hatred.

'This is how you kill a lightborn.' When Passerine spoke, he didn't raise one word above the other. The emotion on his face disappeared, replaced by intense concentration.

Maybe he'll kill me. At the thought, Tatters didn't feel fear. He felt a shameful sort of relief.

He heard Hawk shouting, and was conscious of the Renegades moving closer, but Passerine didn't budge. He didn't press the knife any harder, but he kept it licking at Tatters' neck. He didn't seem to be aware that he was being called back. The steel of the knife scraped against the gold of the collar.

Without taking his eyes off Passerine, Tatters lifted his head off the ground. He did so with difficulty, straining his shoulders, pushing into the blade. The pain was sudden, sharp; the blood was now running freely down his neck, pooling at his collarbone.

'Do it,' Tatters whispered. 'Do you think I have anything left to lose?'

Speaking broke the spell. Passerine seemed to realise that he was threatening the Renegades' most precious possession, and that this was something Hawk would never forgive. He removed his knife and got up; air he hadn't known he'd missed filled

Tatters' lungs. When he touched his neck, pain seared the cut. His fingers came back red.

Hawk was growling at Passerine, but Tatters was too light-headed to hear the words. Mezyan was beside him – when had he arrived? – and was holding something against the wound to staunch the bleeding, talking to Tatters all the while.

Tatters couldn't remember what Hawk said, except that she was fuming. And he couldn't remember what Mezyan said, except that it was soothing. What he did remember were Passerine's eyes. A veil had fallen across his irises, but now that Tatters knew it was there, he could still see the hatred once the mask was up.

Don't do that again, said Lal. *He would have killed you.*

I know, said Tatters. *A slit throat is a fast way to go.*

But Sir Leofric wouldn't slit his throat. This time, there was no fast way to go.

Chapter Twelve

After the council meeting, Passerine was tense, humming with energy. They went into his chambers, but from the way he didn't settle, only shuffled and reordered papers on his desk, Isha realised he was bracing himself for something.

One worry was nagging at her, however, and she couldn't help but say:

'We are doomed to lose to the Renegades. With or without Tatters. Hawk knows how to fight a lightborn.'

The meeting had rattled her. She wondered, now more than ever, what Passerine hoped for. He couldn't expect to fight Hawk, not if he had always known of her power.

'I thought so too, at first,' said Passerine. 'When I brought you here, I expected us to hunker down and pray. Still, the Nest changes everything. The Nest brings hope.'

'Does it?' Isha was baffled. She didn't see how Lord Daegan, hanging on to power rather than dealing with the Renegades, would be able to prevent Hawk from wreaking havoc.

'The mages won't help,' said Passerine. He had finished tidying his paperwork, and was ready to set out. But he paused at the door and, to Isha's surprise, took the time to explain: 'I mean the Nest, the building itself.'

She waited for more to come. Passerine let his fingers linger on the doorhandle; she sensed his hesitation. Still, he turned towards her.

'When a lightborn moves in the sky, it is like writing. It has meaning.'

As he said it, Isha could picture it – the elegant arc of a lightborn, like ink trailing from a quill. Meaning drawn in pale shapes against the night sky, when human writing was ink on pale vellum.

'But unlike writing, it doesn't stay behind,' he added. 'It's ephemeral. But now I have found something full of promise, full of potential.'

Isha guessed what Passerine was going to say. She had always admired what the giants could achieve, but she'd never questioned it. Paintings found in the Nest were abstract, colourful pieces which mages interpreted as sunsets or sunrises. Books in the library were filled with complex, interlocking lines, as was the elaborate fireguard before the chimney at the mess. In the council room, Isha hadn't wondered why they'd built a maze of stained glass, why they had drawn bright shapes which, when the light shone through them, glowed exactly like a lightborn would.

'The lines of colour around the council room, and the stained-glass panels, interwoven with iron, are sentences,' said Passerine. 'I can read some of them, although the language is archaic. At least, I am striving to read them.'

Lines of bright light have meaning. And the giants' art is always long, strange lines interweaving. She wondered how she'd missed it. It seemed so obvious now. Of course, it wasn't made to be looked at from ground level – it was supposed to be read from above.

'You mean the giants could write in lightborn?' she asked. 'Or that the giants *were* lightborns?'

'There is a Samudra story,' said Passerine. 'According to them, the giants were brilliant creatures, tall humans who could speak with lightborns and build for them and live with them. But then they started to wither, and grew smaller with each generation, and forgot what they had made. They became human.'

'No, that has to be wrong,' said Isha. 'The giants were brilliant creatures, yes, like tall humans, maybe, but they only grew bigger and bigger, greater and greater, until they outgrew the Nest and alighted.'

'That's not what I was told,' said Passerine.

What a depressing thought. The giants didn't alight. They grew meaner and smaller, became human, petty creatures still yearning for greatness.

'The Nest is a key,' Passerine went on, oblivious. 'The giants had a magic so powerful that we are, to this day, incapable of doing anything against it. If we could read what they wrote for the lightborns, who knows what treasures we might find? We might be able to craft minds into gold. To build walls of magic, as well as of stone. The Nest itself might contain remnants of the giants' minds. One thing is certain: the Renegades cannot fight that kind of magic.'

She tried to let his enthusiasm filter through to her. Maybe ancient words of power lay in wait, carved into the very home where they lived. But even so, Hawk was drawing closer, Tatters was still in prison, Starling had failed to stop the Renegades.

'I'm not sure that knowledge is enough,' Isha said.

'It isn't,' said Passerine. 'We need power to decode, then use, that knowledge. To write the lightborn language is to release its power, but only a lightborn – or, maybe, a sehwol – can write it properly. Which is why I need Tatters to alight and copy out the giants' letters.'

'And that is all you want from him?'

'Starling could do this,' Passerine admitted. 'But it would require sharing the knowledge, however dangerous it may be, with Lord Daegan.'

'So, Tatters can make the magic, but only you can read it,' Isha summarised. 'Are you sure he'll trust you enough to do something without being sure of the consequences?'

Passerine spread out his hands, as if to indicate that was out of his control. 'We are not friends, but we are not enemies,' was all he said.

Turning away from her, he pushed the door open.

'Now, let's show the Nest what we are capable of.' His voice had regained its coldness and confidence.

She fell into step behind Passerine. She soon recognised where he was taking her, although it was a place apprentices seldom used – it was designed for ordained mages. An imposing corridor, which the mages hadn't tried to reduce in size, was decorated with banners as big as a giant's window: some displayed the Nest's heraldry, including the old coat-of-arms, before the gold castle with blue spires; others had personal heraldries from high mages who had done deeds deemed worthy enough of appearing here. The entrance led to the top of an amphitheatre, which cascaded dramatically down towards a central arena.

The arena had served as a court of law since the giants' time, or so it was thought. The stone amphitheatre was seemingly carved out of one huge slab. Legends said the stone was the cliff itself, and that the giants had dug up and carved the rock they stood upon before building the Nest around it. As was customary, the half-circle of stone had been completed with human wooden tiers, to make for more comfortable seating.

Following Passerine, Isha climbed down the amphitheatre. A few people milled about, enough to make a crowd in a smaller room, but forming only forlorn groups in the huge arena. They huddled in bands of ten or so, watching different legal duels taking place at the same time.

Behind the half-circle of the arena there was a window. The stained glass had wrought metal running through the panels like veins. As with most of the giants' art, it was abstract. As with all of the giants' art, it dwarfed the humans beside it. The window took up most of the wall. Before, the colours had melded without any logic as far as Isha was concerned. But now she felt drawn to them, watched them shift when the sunlight shone through; she wondered what had been written there, secret yet in plain sight. The iron lines woven between the glass curled and climbed like vines. There was a pattern, she found, now that she was looking for one.

The duels took place in the central space between the tiers and the window, in the patches of light cast on the floor. Lawmages oversaw the duels, often acting as settlers. More often than not, they separated the opponents by treating each chunk of colour like a different space – the railings between the windows serving as boundaries. People didn't overstep a line, whether it was made of rope or shadow.

When Passerine reached the bottom of the amphitheatre, he gestured for Isha to stop.

'I don't want you to be involved in this if I can avoid it,' he said. 'Take a seat. Enjoy the show. I might need you yet.'

She could tell that behind his focused eyes, his clenched jaw, there was something like a smile, playing at the corner of his lips. He expected this to go well.

She took a seat on the first tier of the arena as Passerine went to speak to one of the lawmages. Normally duels happening here in controlled conditions were linked to legal cases or, more rarely, were done on a dare. Mages could challenge one another anywhere, but a battle overseen by lawmages had an aura of legitimacy about it.

Isha only realised what was happening when Passerine cast his eyes around the amphitheatre and said:

'I want to challenge for rights over the doorgate district.'

It was exactly what he had done when they had first arrived, when he had walked in other mages' territories, disturbing the slim mercury stands that marked their borders. He wanted to lay a claim. She wondered why he had stopped then. Was it because he was worried of her being in the way and getting hurt? Now she was under his protection, no-one could pitch her against him.

From where he was standing, Passerine smiled at her.

Let's ruffle some feathers.

He mindlinked effortlessly. She knew he was talented, but she doubted even Passerine could hold out against a high mage and their apprentices. He wouldn't have one duel to win to gain a district – he would have to beat the whole group, apprentices, mages and high mages. There was safety in numbers, after all.

Isha pressed her fists against her stomach and ground down on the worry building there.

The lawmage chatted with Passerine, polite and professional, trying to discourage him from such a venture. Isha could only hear bits of their conversation, but once it was clear Passerine couldn't be talked out of the duel, the lawmage sent a messenger to fetch the high mage representing the doorgate district.

It was a woman who presented herself, disciples in tow. She had trimmed her black cloak with silver and added a ruby pin to the front of her robe. Her clothes billowed, revealing a slim silhouette, long legs, an elegant neck. Her black hair, tied back into a ponytail, fell all the way down to her hips. Her belt was bleached white, matching the silver of her embroideries, and the tips were dyed red, matching the ruby of her pin.

The woman stopped before Passerine. 'Lady Mathilda, in charge of the doorgate district.'

He touched wrists with her. 'A pleasure, I'm sure.' In the same conversational tone, Passerine added, 'I heard you were having trouble keeping some of your apprentices in line. The rumours say they were threatening to desert you and join the Renegades?'

Lady Mathilda's cheeks flushed. She pinched her lips into a thin, angry line. 'Yes. The troublesome elements have been dealt with.' She copied Passerine, in that she kept her voice soft when she added: 'I'll fight you, Sir Passerine. But what will you give me in return?'

'Why, if I lose against you, or any of your people, I will be at your service,' said Passerine.

Isha eyed Lady Mathilda's followers nervously. She had never dealt with them. They all wore the same belt, white with red tips, but Isha didn't know any red-and-white heraldry.

Lady Mathilda's voice was sweet, but her words were sour. 'I am eager to rid the Nest of Wingshade traitors. I have no wish to be crowded out of my home by spies and failures. I have no need of your services.'

'I am not Wingshade,' Passerine answered. 'But I don't suppose that matters.'

Lady Mathilda ignored him. 'If I beat you, I want you to leave the Nest. You do not belong here.'

The silence that followed that statement was so thick Isha thought she could touch it. She tried to catch Passerine's eye, begging him not to fall for such an obvious trap.

'I accept your conditions,' said Passerine.

Isha bit down on her lower lip. What could she do? The words were spoken. The lawmage made an appreciative sound and went on to deciding where in the arena they would hold the duel. She wondered if she would lose Passerine after losing Tatters and, if so, what she would do then. She could still hear the echo of her mother's voice:

Where is the eyas?

Maybe she would go back to the Shadowpass, to her farm, where the Renegades were building their encampment. There was nowhere else.

Lady Mathilda waved to one of her apprentices, a young man who looked eager but frightened. Isha wasn't too worried about him. Passerine would be able to crush him. But what about the other half-dozen apprentices, and the three mages, who also followed in Lady Mathilda's wake? Passerine would grow more vulnerable with each battle as the fights revealed his weaknesses.

The lawmage was to be the settler. He placed Passerine and the apprentice in a triangle of red light cast by the windows, instructing them not to step outside of that colour. The lawmage closed his eyes first. As this was a public duel, Lady Mathilda and her crew, as well as Isha, and anyone in the arena who cared to, could watch what happened.

Isha entered mindlink, struggling to conceal her apprehension. The lawmage had a mental arena that vaguely copied the centre of the city, including the statue of Lady Siobhan, beneath which the audience could sit or stand. But beyond the square, the buildings and cobbles faded into one uniform grey slope. Isha assumed the opponents were meant to duel in the parts of the plaza which were rendered in detail.

The apprentice placed himself before Passerine. Isha swallowed down her nausea; she wasn't sure if it was from mindlink or from nerves.

'Please,' said Sir Passerine. 'Do the honours.'

The apprentice breathed deeply before closing his eyes. His

outline shimmered for a moment, growing fainter, until he disappeared from sight. Isha searched the settled mind, but he remained invisible, although he probably hadn't removed himself from the fight. She couldn't perceive him at all. It must be a difficult technique, to be able to empty your mind so as to seem absent. It would require thinking about nothing, feeling nothing – something that could only be achieved after hours of meditation. She glanced at where Lady Mathilda was seated, her legs crossed, one foot tapping against the statue's base. This must be her trademark technique.

Suddenly sadness welled, seemingly from nowhere or from Passerine himself: longing for a lost home, horror at being exiled. The illusion was so perfect Isha could believe for a moment Passerine was attacking himself.

The emotions crashed down like a wave, most of them not even linked to images. *The feeling you have when you see a house that has been yours for the last time, knowing it is the last time. The smell of something that reminds you of home when you are far from home. The way a foreign land is like a new piece of clothing, always chafing in odd places. The fear of being cast off twice* – and that fear was so sharp, so well-defined, that Isha couldn't tell if it was hers or the apprentice's creation.

All of this went through Passerine as if he weren't there. It was as efficient as water against a sieve. With a start, Isha realised she had seen this before. This was the technique Tatters had used against Ninian. Crafted imaginings didn't seem able to reach him then – and they couldn't touch Passerine now.

The moment the images were brought to life, Passerine retaliated with a precise sensation of defeat, mingling the Renegades at the Temple with the Renegades crossing the bridge of the Nest, setting its spires on fire. As soon as the apprentice's concentration broke, he became visible – his scattered thoughts first, his shape second. Passerine cracked his mind open like a nut.

If Lady Mathilda was shocked, she hid it well. She gave Passerine a clap when the lawmage announced his victory.

'Interesting,' she said noncommittally.

Two other apprentices went up against Passerine, with as little success. Isha could see Lady Mathilda trying to work out what Passerine was doing. She discussed it with the ordained mages beside her, their mindlink subtle enough that Isha couldn't hear the content of the conversation.

Do it often enough, and people will work out what the trick is. All Isha could think of was what Lal had said. She couldn't even focus on trying to understand the trick itself – she was too scared of what Lady Mathilda might find, or what she might be able to glean from Isha's mind, were Isha to uncover the truth of what Passerine was doing.

I am a liability, she thought. *For people like Passerine, I am a potential leak.*

After the third apprentice lost, Lady Mathilda sent one of her ordained mages against Passerine. All her followers fought in the same way – they removed themselves from the duel completely. It must have taken hours, and discipline, to perfect this technique. There was nothing to grasp, no-one to aim for. They emptied their mind until there were no thoughts for others to read. They only appeared, briefly, when they pounced.

Passerine waited patiently, but Isha knew he was concentrating; his shoulders were tense, his quiet features were taut. In the real world, she imagined he must now be drenched in sweat.

When the ordained mage struck, the hit landed. The mage must have been as surprised as Isha, because she didn't press her advantage immediately. She had crafted a simple image, of a child dying, of Passerine holding the babe in his arms and begging it to live. The emotion was raw, and Passerine's thoughts were rocked. He had cared for a child, worried about her fate – but there was something off. It was as if his thoughts were stilted. Isha could sense his attachment to the child, and even picture her as Passerine helped her up, a young girl with curly hair, dark skin, seen in profile just as she turned, as her tattoo became visible. Her heart skipped a beat.

But still something wasn't right. It was as if the images were seen through a mirror – with the left hand moving when the right hand was lifted, upside-down somehow, overturned. This obviously disconcerted the ordained mage.

The fight lasted longer than with the apprentices, but the same event occurred every time the mage breached Passerine's defences – the thoughts were partly unreadable. Feelings rose, but with no words attached to them, nothing that clarified what they were, what tied them to reality.

Despite being concerned about giving his secrets away, and despite her bafflement, Isha wanted to understand how Passerine did this. He beat the ordained mage, but neither she – nor, from the looks of it, Lady Mathilda – were any closer to working out how he'd managed it.

He must have decided an ordained mage would be able to see through the other technique, Isha decided. *Or it was too costly to maintain. But what's this new approach?* It wasn't something Tatters had ever done. What was even more confusing was that it didn't feel like a mental wall. It was as if the thoughts themselves were corrupted, like a painting spoilt by water.

The lawmage called for a break. When Isha opened her eyes, she was shocked by the size of the audience. The lawmage had included more and more people in the duel without her noticing.

She spotted quite a few high mages, including ones from the council, and mages from across the Nest.

Passerine was sweating profusely, but he was standing straight in his square of light. Isha jumped to her feet when the duel was interrupted, and rushed to the mess to get him a pouch of water, cursing herself for not thinking of this beforehand. When she returned, she had to shove people aside to reach the bottom of the arena. She heard snippets of conversations as she waded through the crowd. 'Apparently Sir Passerine wants to take her district off Lady Mathilda!' 'He's beaten four people already.' 'Was it four? I thought it was six?' 'Lady Mathilda has already lost against him, she's just waiting to see if he gets everyone else.' 'He's duelling on his own, without even one apprentice!'

'Sorry, sorry,' she mumbled, using her elbows to clear a path.

'Hey, Isha, is that you?'

Just my luck.

She swerved to avoid Kilian, but he blocked her way. 'Look, about the other day, at breakfast.'

He was on his own. When Isha checked, she couldn't spot Lord Daegan or any of his other followers.

'Please,' he insisted.

He caught her wrist. She nearly tugged her arm away, but she closed the pouch of water first, to avoid spilling it – in her haste she hadn't even put the cork back in. It gave him time to speak.

'I just wanted to say, I understand. I get it. The Nest is tough at times, but life is tough at times, and we all seem to manage.' He let go of her arm and tried a small, uncertain smile. 'We're lucky we're not the ones with the worst time of it.'

Isha made sure the pouch was sealed before placing it under her arm. 'You think our life is tough?' she asked, keeping her voice level. 'Have a look around you. Our life is a luxury. And other people have a horrible time of it, so we can enjoy that luxury.' She didn't like seeing him sad, his usual cheery demeanour dampened by her harsh tone. But she ploughed on: 'If you want to make a change, make a change. If you don't, keep enjoying your good fortune, for as long as it lasts.' *Which, considering how the Renegades are doing, might not be long.* 'It's none of my business either way.'

She pushed past him. She found Passerine, shoulders squared, talking with the lawmage. He took the water from her and drank in long gulps until he had emptied the pouch. She had also brought him a handkerchief, which he used to wipe his brow.

'Thank you,' he said, returning the two items.

He rubbed his jaw and his neck with both hands. Despite his tenacity, he must be tiring. She wondered, not for the first time, how she had found herself following this man, trusting his judgement, fearing for his life.

'How did you two meet?' the lawmage asked.

Passerine only shrugged. 'Fellow Sunrisers must stick together.'

'I have to agree with that.'

It was Sir Cintay. Behind him, Isha couldn't see Lord Daegan. Still, if Kilian and Sir Cintay were here, it was only a matter of time.

Sir Cintay was thin from hunger, wan from hardships. His black robes hung around his bony shoulders. But he smiled at Passerine, and his smile seemed genuine for the first time since Isha had first met him.

'What are you doing, Sir Passerine? Creating trouble for yourself?' There was nothing but approbation in his voice.

'I am securing us a place,' said Passerine. He spoke so as to be heard by the audience surrounding them. 'After this, I will start taking on followers and apprentices. People who want to join me, please let me know once this fight is over. As you can see from these duels, I have a lot to teach you.' He turned back to Sir Cintay. 'And the means to protect you,' he finished, more quietly.

Isha's ears were still ringing with what Passerine had announced. New followers? Were they going to build an official group? Own a territory? Before she could ask any of these questions, Sir Cintay was taking his leave, the lawmage was asking for the duels to resume, and Lady Mathilda, through gritted teeth, was hissing that a man banned from the Nest would hardly be welcoming followers.

Two ordained mages remained, as well as Lady Mathilda. Biting her nails, Isha joined the audience in mindlink. She kept the water pouch and the handkerchief on her lap; their weight was reassuring. It grounded her back into the physical space when the mindbrawl became too intense.

She watched Passerine duel Lady Mathilda's followers. Both matches were long, but one-sided – although Passerine took time to break his enemies' barriers, it was impossible to hurt him. His thoughts all had the same quality to them, fuzzy, misplaced. Isha observed the mindbrawl closely. She should be able to understand this. She had found out things that mages had missed before, for example when Tatters had hidden his true self from the lawmages.

She could do this. She pressed her fingers to her temples, pushing down until her skull ached, urging herself to put the pieces together.

And then it came to her. It was thanks to an image from Passerine's mind that she worked out the solution. The memory was a sweeping glance across the forest, and then, as he fell, up towards the sky. She didn't know the context for this moment. The thought, like all others, was difficult to read. It was as if the ground, the grass, the trees, the bushes, were all one mush. On the contrary, the sky was divided into lots of little pieces. Each cloud seemed to stand out, the angle of the sun carried meaning, the changes of colour in the ether bore different names.

It was confusing – more than incoherent, it was a different mindset entirely. And that was because, Isha realised, he was thinking in a foreign language.

She had noticed it when learning iwdan. The word yis meant both horse and donkey. She had tried to argue with Ka that they were two different animals, in vain. A yis was a yis, however long its ears. But then Ka had taught her two words for owls, and that they weren't the same animals. An azida and a tmadda apparently belonged to two distinct species. When Isha had asked what the difference between the owls could be, Ka had said: 'You know the little ears of feathers they have? Those are azida. If they don't have ears, they're tmadda.'

'Exactly like donkeys and horses,' Isha had said, and they'd both laughed at that strange similarity.

So, in a kher's mindset, horses and donkeys were one thing, but owls were two different animals. It had struck her as strange, how a language could change how people perceived the world.

This was what was happening with Passerine's thoughts, this was why they felt out of place. Some concepts humans distinguished were grouped together. Some feelings they didn't have words for were expressed. No wonder everyone was taken off-guard. Passerine could understand their language, but they couldn't understand his.

He could read the words of lightborns. That was a language no-one in the Nest could speak.

Her head was spinning with the possibilities. Why hadn't she considered this before? It was like thinking in code. The mage who mastered another language didn't need to put any effort into it, but it took hours of patient studying from the opponent before they even stood a chance of winning. It couldn't be overcome in one duel.

Passerine won his fight against the last mage in Lady Mathilda's group of followers. Isha returned to the real world to see if Lady Mathilda would risk her district, and her followers, by fighting him herself. But she had gone so far now, she couldn't back off with dignity.

In the arena, the tiers were crammed with robes. Bright ones, black ones, it didn't matter, they were clustered together on the first three tiers, with eager mages watching the duel, all of them discussing what sort of secret technique Passerine might be using and spying on each other's minds to see if someone had found out. The room bristled with excitement like a pack of dogs sniffing the air before a hunt. No-one paid any attention to the apprentice squirming at the front row with an empty water pouch on her lap.

A loner had never defeated a coterie by himself before.

When Isha managed to catch Passerine's eye, he gave her a confident nod. Lady Mathilda was standing in front of him, fists clenched. Her face seemed even paler, drained. The rows of mages above her were waiting for the duel, baying for blood. She obviously couldn't back down.

The colours in the windows had shifted as the sun turned, so the lawmage invited the high mages to move, placing them in the centre of the arena this time. He picked a deep blue square. The light filtering through the window coloured Lady Mathilda's belt blue, the tips purple.

'Are you ready?' the lawmage asked.

Passerine merely nodded.

Lady Mathilda relaxed her shoulders, spread her feet apart. Her lips were set in a scowl. 'Yes.'

Before the lawmage could announce the start of the match, however, a bright ray of light flashed above the arena. Everyone stopped to stare as Starling curved in the air and took her human shape beside the lawmage, her golden hair still floating behind her, landing softly on her shoulders moments after her feet landed softly on the ground.

'I have to ask you to stop,' she said.

A voice cracked with age and anxiety boomed: 'What is the meaning of this?'

Lord Daegan appeared at the top of the arena, followed by his Wingshade followers first, Sir Cintay included, and his disciples next, Caitlin included. For now, Isha couldn't see Kilian. They made an impressive group, fanning out on either side of their lord like birds in formation in the sky. Lord Daegan walked down from the summit of the amphitheatre towards the duellists. He took his time. Mages parted to give way, like reeds in a strong breeze.

The silence was of that particular kind that can only happen when a crowd is holding its breath. They listened to the sound of his steps.

When he reached the bottom of the amphitheatre, Lady Mathilda bowed and, to Isha's surprise, Passerine did too.

'My liege,' he said, but it was unclear from Passerine's tone whether it was a greeting, a statement, or a challenge.

Lord Daegan didn't rush his moment. He waited until his apprentices had formed a semi-circle around him, the sheer number of them pressing down on the two high mages. Isha spotted the top of Kilian's head; his hair was so blond it was easy to see from a distance.

'Care to explain what this is, Sir Passerine?' Lord Daegan asked. 'This is not the first time you have caused trouble to loyal members of the Nest.'

Lord Daegan searched the front tiers with his gaze and found Isha easily. His glare pinned her to her seat. When his hands tightened around his ornate cane, the rings he wore scratched against the metal, letting out a grating sound.

'I am following the laws of the Nest,' said Passerine. 'It is permitted to challenge a high mage for their district if one believes one can better control and protect it than them. I have agreed to harsh terms from Lady Mathilda for the right to fight her.'

'It is true,' she reluctantly admitted.

Lord Daegan only frowned at both high mages. He was shorter than them, but the number of apprentices gathered behind him, and the unblinking, quiet presence of his lightborn, were enough to hush the full arena.

'You don't have followers, Sir Passerine. How will you patrol a district and protect the ungifted there?'

This was her cue. Isha's hands were shaking as she put the water pouch down, folding the handkerchief above it. Her movement caused everyone to turn towards her, and their collective eyes were like leeches sticking to her skin, sucking her strength. Still, she straightened and said:

'I am Sir Passerine's apprentice. I will help.'

Lord Daegan's laugh was short; it looked as if he were biting the air.

'You? The two of you will hold a district?'

'I will help too.' The voice was masculine. Isha glanced behind her just as Ninian stood up, a few tiers up the amphitheatre. She had not been expecting him; seeing him at the Nest meant he had not been sent back to the Shadowpass, either by choice or because he was too damaged for war. But here he was now, defying the supreme mage – and, Isha assumed, the high mage he had been affiliated to until now. 'I have only seen one person fight like Sir Passerine fought today,' Ninian said in way of explanation. 'And I want to learn it. I believe he is an asset that the Nest would be foolish to lose.'

He stood alone on his tier, people who might have called themselves his friends gaping up at him. But he crossed his arms and gave no indication that he might back down. In the silence, someone else stood up: Ninian's lover. She saw Ninian throw him a grateful smile before they knotted their fingers together.

'The duel today might sway more people.' Passerine's voice carried easily across the room. His tone, as always, was deep enough to drown in. 'If my liege would simply give me a week, I am sure I can gather enough followers to hold a district.'

This was a taunt if Isha had ever heard one. Lord Daegan bared his teeth in something which could, from a distance, be compared to a smile. He drummed his fingers against his cane. The rings gave out a sharp sound with each tap.

'How will you teach so many when you can hardly teach one?' Lord Daegan spat, his contempt dripping from each word.

'In the precious little time Isha has been with me,' Passerine said, 'she learnt enough to best any of the apprentices who have studied beside you for years.'

Lord Daegan's knuckles were white from gripping his cane. 'Is that so?'

'I can prove it,' Passerine added. Not once did a tremor break the smooth line of his features. 'Isha, you will fight one of his people for me, will you not?'

'Of course.' There was no other answer. She saw the anger glinting in Daegan's eye, the kind of anger that pushed people to kick their dog, beat their spouse, kill their traitor.

'If that is the case...' Lord Daegan turned to his apprentices. Before he could make his choice, someone came forward.

Her auburn hair was brown in this gloomy light. Her hazel eyes were only dull. But even so, her presence was enough to draw attention to her.

'I will do it,' Caitlin said.

Lord Daegan relaxed his hold on his cane. 'Yes.'

Caitlin had an unblemished face, with bones as fine as a bird's. In some ways she wasn't unlike Starling, and that only underlined her elegance, as if she were a step away from alighting. Her robes weren't ruffled, she wasn't damp from sweat after running and huffing in the crowded room. She crossed her hands in front of her, each finger fine and pale, ending with trimmed nails that hadn't been broken by hard work.

She didn't speak, so neither did Isha. The consensus was that two settlers were required for this duel – one for each side, to prevent cheating. Lady Mathilda offered her services to Lord Daegan. Ninian took on the role for Sir Passerine.

Isha couldn't slow her rushing heart, but she could control her breathing, so she focused on filling and emptying her lungs. She went over the techniques she knew that could help her against Caitlin. Making a double. No. That was no good. It was no use relying on a technique that weakened her, that Caitlin was familiar with. Thinking in a foreign language. Was she fluent enough in iwdan to attempt it?

'Are you ready?' Lady Mathilda asked.

Caitlin nodded. Isha wondered what had pushed her to volunteer herself for this fight.

'Yes,' Isha said.

She closed her eyes. The settled space Ninian and Lady Mathilda had created was familiar. The statue of Lady Siobhan was at one end of the cobbled square, the audience gathered around its base. Where the houses should be, the landscape melded into grey mush. Maybe this was the official background settlers were meant to use when legal duels were being fought.

In mindlink, Caitlin was even taller, with long legs like an insect. The settlers were nowhere to be seen, yet their presence was everywhere.

Lady Mathilda's voice echoed around them. 'You may begin.'

Before Isha could decide what would be the best strategy, Caitlin sent her an imagining as perfect as a memory. A man owned mares, and he was sorting through them, basing himself on the symbols branded across their croups. *The smell of the horses' bodies. The charred scent of hot iron against flesh. The knowledge that the mares were docile. The taste of a metal bit between her teeth.*

More shocking than the image itself, however, was the fact that Isha recognised it. Tatters had used it against her during their mindbrawl – during the mindbrawl where Caitlin had been the settler. She had copied his strike.

Maybe Isha should have expected it. But the scene was linked to so many emotions for her – the fact that she had nearly lost to Tatters then, the bitter knowledge that, had he been less tender, had she been less proud, that would have been the end of their duel, and she would never have uncovered his secrets for Caitlin to see. Ultimately, he would never have been taken by the lawmages.

Unable to stop the flow of feelings, she weakened, but she did her best to switch to iwdan. She imagined how she would tell Ka about this, about the surprise when Caitlin hit, explaining it to him in his own language. She hung on to the word yis as if it could save her.

She sensed Caitlin stepping back, confused. She had obviously hit her mark, but she couldn't make sense of what she had uncovered. It was like hitting with a blade, expecting blood, only to see water or milk pouring out of the wound.

Isha pictured herself before the statue, gritting her teeth. Caitlin stood in front of her, lips pressed in a thin line. Everyone had witnessed this. Everyone could see Isha had copied a technique Passerine had done only a few minutes before. A shimmering of mindlink rose from the audience, like whispers.

'That was a dirty trick,' Isha snarled.

Caitlin shrugged her narrow shoulders. 'There are no such things. There are only the tricks that work, and the poor ones.'

Caitlin struck again; she was faster than Isha. This time the image was one of her own, but it was just as brutal as the previous one. *Isha was pressed up against a wall, with someone groping under her robes. Rough hands stroked up her thighs, tugged at her clothes. Half-opening her eyes, she caught a glimpse of sleek black horns, of red skin, of an animal rutting against her.*

But Caitlin made three mistakes. Firstly, it was easier to think in iwdan in an iwdan setting. Despite being caught off-guard, Isha could shield her thoughts behind the barrier of a foreign language. Secondly, Caitlin didn't know khers, or the Pit, well enough. She hadn't drawn the kher's face with enough detail. The curve of his horns was off. She had traced a tattoo around his neck and jawline, but omitted tattoos around his wrists or hips. Isha could easily distance herself from the moment, recognising it for what it was. A fake.

The last mistake was that horn-humping was taboo.

Break apart now, by word of law! The two settlers interrupted the duel, forcing the opponents apart. Isha blinked, struggling to find her footing in the real world. When she came to, Lady Mathilda was reprimanding Caitlin.

'Displays of kher–human intercourse are illegal, as I am sure you are aware.' Lady Mathilda's tone was biting.

Caitlin held her chin high, unapologetic. While the settlers gave out their warning, Isha had a bit of time to gather her wits.

What was notable with that last attack, aside from the choice of subject, was the disgust laced in the imagery. No desire, not even for show, not even to entice Isha into falling for it. Caitlin's aversion was stronger than her capacity to project herself into her mindbrawl. There was a glaring absence of lust.

But the intent had been vicious. Had Caitlin been able to do it right – to project Ka instead of a faceless kher, for example – it might have broken Isha.

I need to get a grip. I can't be a dummy for her punching practice. As soon as the fight resumed, Isha crafted an image to fling towards Caitlin. *There are no such things as dirty tricks, are there?*

She was angry. She had been ready to stand up for Passerine, because he had asked her to, because she owed him that much. But Caitlin's mindbrawl gave away how callous she was. She dared use Tatters against Isha, when she was probably the one who had signed his death warrant. She knew Isha visited the Pit, and had tried to turn that against her, while she paid for her food with baina.

Her offensive wasn't as intense nor as fast as Caitlin's. It took its time. A few people were grunting as they dragged something across the floor. They were walking out of a small door in the walls of the Nest, heading towards the Edge, just after dusk. Caitlin herself was there, and she helped hold their load, hoisting it on one shoulder, feeling something soft beneath the fabric. It was large enough that two people had to carry it. The smell of rotting fruit hung in the air.

They reached the Edge. They were throwing their heavy secret there, into the abyss. Caitlin unwrapped the cloth. Tatters' face stood out, as gruesome as Isha could bear it, battered and bruised, the rot of death already eating away at his eyelids. And with his face, the guilt, the bottomless, pitiless guilt, as deep as the fall over the Edge, the guilt at having killed a man who cared for you.

Because you killed him, Caitlin. Whether you care to acknowledge it or not.

She struck, as hard as she could, as precise as she could stand it. Yet Caitlin managed to disentangle herself from the heaving, dry-retching shame.

They found themselves facing off in the square again. Caitlin didn't seem ruffled.

'I never knew you were so cold. So you don't even worry about what might have happened to him?' Isha didn't care that people were watching them anymore. A sharp pain bit into her chest, around her heart, and she wondered if this was what hate felt like.

'You're too predictable. I knew you would bring him up.'

And with that, Caitlin was upon her again. *Lord Daegan's chambers. The large double-bed, the scented wine. Isha carrying his kher horn, placing it in a cupboard, kneeling on the stone floor. Acting as a servant.* Emotions were built into the vision. Caitlin artfully exploited the moment when Tatters had put on the collar, yielding to Hawk. She was interweaving this trauma – truthful, loaded with remorse that didn't belong to either of them but resonated nonetheless – with what she thought was also a real instance, when Isha had found herself alone in Daegan's chambers. She depicted the humiliation of being worthless even of the most thankless tasks, of being able to belong only when she was enslaved.

Isha didn't try to resist the imagery. Instead she let it settle around her, giving it time to expand and breathe. Once Caitlin had crafted a scene so achingly real it could have been a memory, Isha changed only the person on the floor: she swapped in Caitlin.

You're the one sucking up to Lord Daegan, Isha thought. *I left.*

It was a cheap trap, as mindbrawls went. Turning someone's imagining against them rarely worked, because they usually knew it was false. But Caitlin was too invested. It was the equivalent of a warrior overreaching with a sword, putting too much weight into their lunge – it was easy to use their own momentum, then, to topple them.

A crack appeared in Caitlin's composure.

Through it, Isha perceived something raw, blistering, not shaped for mindlink, not crafted to control and subdue. It was like ripping off a mask of skin, and what was below was exposed and tender.

You were always their favourite, Caitlin seethed. Isha could hear her voice too, younger, a child crying with abandon. *Do you know how long I worked for Tatters? How long I studied beside him? He didn't once glance back at me. He thought I was shallow. And then you drift in, and he has eyes only for you, and he shows you things he never showed anyone, he who never let anyone in – but he brought you to the Temple, to see the khers. He opened up enough that you could hurt him in mindbrawl. And Lord Daegan took you in, and Kilian thought you were fantastic, and Sir Passerine never wanted an apprentice before he had you. Even he thought you were special.*

They all thought you were special.

It should've been me.

Isha had never witnessed a fury this untainted. Caitlin's outburst was contagious; despite struggling to control herself, Isha's own anger rose, her own helplessness, the same useless rage that filled her but which was too great to find an outlet. Both women's fists curled by their sides; both had the same snarl at the back of their throat.

I spent a year toiling to study with Lord Daegan. I earned it. What did you do? Someone scribbled a tattoo on your face.

Maybe Caitlin was trying to knock her over with pure strength of will; but instead, she fuelled Isha's fire.

You have no idea what you are talking about. At last Isha had found the space to interrupt. *Do you know what this tattoo means, really means? It's a symbol. I am nothing more than someone else's legacy. I am nothing else than the punchline in someone else's story.*

You can be whoever you want. I can only be who I was written out to become.

There was more, of course. There was what Isha had lost, memories ripped from her childhood, and the price she had paid, people sneering at her at the gates of the Nest. But she didn't mention it, because in a way Caitlin was right – she had gained from her tattoo, maybe as much as she had paid. Maybe less. Who could tell? She wasn't holding tabs for her life.

They both withdrew from mindbrawl. Isha's hands were shaking, her fingers clenching around the fabric of her robes, twisting the cloth. She wasn't sure she would be able to prepare another attack. She opened her eyes.

Maybe she sensed Isha's gaze on her, maybe she sensed Isha's control of mindlink receding, but Caitlin opened her eyes too. They stared at each other across the stretch of the arena. Caitlin was even paler than usual, the colour of uncooked dough. If Isha didn't know any better, she could imagine that the shine across Caitlin's eyes was unspilt tears.

And yet, even with her hair in disarray, even with her warm brown eyes narrowed into slits, even with her shoulders slumped, Caitlin was striking. Maybe that was why men always assumed she was shallow – because she was attractive.

Sorry, Isha thought to herself. *But I have to win this.*

Caitlin was stronger; she had more practice. Isha thought of Tatters holding out against a group of lawmages, of how he coped when he battled an opponent who was stronger.

Isha strode towards Caitlin and, eyes open, she mindlinked. Caitlin's pupils widened as she tried to block the imagery Isha was sending towards her. While she was focused in the mental world, Isha closed the gap in the real world. Without quite deciding to, without knowing if it would work, she shoved Caitlin back.

She used both hands. Caitlin was slimmer, slighter. She fell backwards.

When she stumbled, she let go of her control on mindlink – for a moment, Caitlin panicked, and tried to catch herself with her hands. While she had the upper hand, Isha crafted an image imbued with truth and insecurities: the picture of Caitlin sprawled on the floor, the bitter realisation that she had lost. She projected it towards Caitlin as she slipped, when she was vulnerable.

Sometimes winning was simply getting the opponent to believe they had lost.

It happened quickly. One moment Caitlin was standing; the other she had crumpled to the floor, her mental defences crumbling with her. When the settlers called for the duel to end, the audience started shouting: a few people were calling out Isha for cheating, others were hooting with laughter. Someone close to Isha cupped their hands around their mouth to holler:

'Catfight! Catfight!'

Other people took up the chant, clapping along or whistling. The apprentices only quietened when Lord Daegan and Sir Passerine joined the settlers. Caitlin got to her feet. She didn't even glare at Isha but kept her eyes downcast.

I'm sorry. Isha couldn't mindlink to Caitlin – not now. But she *was* sorry. She knew Caitlin was right, that the people around her believed she wasn't a force to be reckoned with, that she was a cute face with dreams too big for her.

And Isha knew something else about Caitlin, revealed by her mindlink, something Caitlin hadn't meant to show but had given away nonetheless. Men only saw her as someone to yearn after, and Caitlin hated it. She hated the idea of having sex with a man. Iwdan or mage, it didn't matter, the image was one of the worst she could picture for her enemies. That told a story in itself.

For the first time, Isha considered the fact that maybe being pretty was as much of a curse as being tattooed, albeit a different one.

The settlers went to debate the result of the fight with the lawmage who had been overseeing the duels so far. When they returned, he cleared his throat. The audience fell silent. The high mages stood on either side of him, waiting for his verdict.

'The fight goes to Caitlin, duelling for Lord Daegan,' the lawmage announced.

Both women looked up in surprise. Passerine's face was unreadable.

Lady Mathilda gave Isha a stern look. 'Isha is disqualified for cheating.'

Despite the applause, Isha could tell by Lord Daegan's expression that his victory was bittersweet. Still, he switched to his leadership voice:

'You will not be thieving her district from Lady Mathilda.' There was obvious relief in Lady Mathilda's posture and those of her followers. But the lawmage beside her frowned. Maybe to pacify the lawmage, Daegan explained, 'You have proved you are unfit to teach.'

'I have proved that apprentices who have studied mindlink for less than a year with me can fight toe-to-toe with your disciples,' Passerine corrected, before the lawmage could even decide to express his disapprobation. 'I have followers, and I am ready to

fight Lady Mathilda. I am not thieving. I am obeying the law. Are you about to break it?'

Isha remembered what she had felt the first time she had seen Daegan. Wolves. Mages were grey wolves with sleek fur, who could growl without opening their mouths. They were both bristling.

Someone else got up in the tiers above them. It was Sir Leofric, bright as a flag, smiling his crooked smile.

'It was the question I was about to ask,' he said.

Having the head lawmage challenge the supreme mage was a rare occurrence. The silence was more ominous than the loud shouts of encouragement that had echoed before. Quiet mages were mages who were thinking. Mages who were thinking were mages at their most dangerous.

Sir Leofric is only picking Passerine's side because Starling has failed today, Isha realised. *The council knows Daegan isn't infallible, and that's making them cocky.*

The Nest had always been prone to infighting, but the Renegades had the power to make it worse. It was like putting a lid on a cauldron of hot water: the external pressure meant it could boil over at any moment. Whether she knew it or not, Hawk was already challenging the Nest, if only because she was destabilising it.

Isha could tell Lord Daegan's options were limited. He couldn't oppose a duel between Lady Mathilda and Sir Passerine without a justification, not when the head lawmage was requesting one. He was cautious about his answer; when he spoke, it was without any sign that he was annoyed, or that he was being provoked.

'Unlike the Renegades, I am not merciless,' Lord Daegan said. 'You have put yourself in an impossible position, Sir Passerine, but I will offer you a chance to be redeemed. You will let Lady

Mathilda manage an area she understands well and is best suited to rule. You may instead have the merchants' district, which I originally controlled. I have no use for it, as I am now Supreme Mage of the Nest, and thus rule above all districts, above the whole city.'

A gracious master throwing the dog a bone. It was an insult as much as it was a present, but Passerine didn't seem upset.

'How generous of you,' Sir Leofric said, still grinning. 'We truly are blessed with such a supreme mage.' But the glint in his eye told another story. He was pleased, like an animal that has succeeded in making an intruder back off and that will be more likely to bark and bite in the future, now that he knows the threats serve his purpose.

'This is a gift,' said Lord Daegan through clenched teeth. 'But know your place, Sir Passerine.'

'I will keep it in mind.' Passerine bowed, turned, and headed for the exit, climbing up the amphitheatre of stone. Isha walked beside him.

When people behind couldn't see them, Passerine let his face break into a smile.

'Good work,' he said. 'It doesn't matter who the settler praises. What matters is who is still standing when the battle is over.'

He didn't mindlink to keep his words private. Isha was aware of the people around them, of the fact that anyone who cared to eavesdrop could. His smile faded. He put a heavy hand on her shoulder, and for a moment she didn't know if he was praising her or resting on her.

'In war, there are no settlers.'

Chapter Thirteen

Isha walked to the tavern lost in thought, her nerves thrumming. She had spent the last couple of days at the Nest answering letters and depressing messages from the Ridge asking for soldiers, for food, for help. The local mages described how Hawk was encroaching on the lands around the Shadowpass' entrance, taking over farms and the ungifted there, stealing the winter reserves, sending her forces further and further afield in small, selective strikes designed to keep her army fed.

The Nest had been dispatching soldiers to the Ridge, but travelling in winter was hard, so the reinforcements were slow. High mages were reluctant to trek all the way to the Ridge, preferring to prepare their hometown's defences instead. Most of the time, Isha's standard reply to these desperate demands was a mild promise that, when they could spare the resources, they would be sure to help.

That night, she was so engrossed in her own worries that she didn't notice that the small alley was dark, the torches had been smothered, and the usual ring of laughter had given way to silence. When she entered the Coop, the main room was shrouded in shadows. The innkeeper had placed all the chairs on the tables, had washed the grimy wooden floorboards, and was busy rolling the last empty kegs behind the counter.

'Here you are,' he grumbled. 'Get changed quickly so that I can lock up.' His voice was gruff, but fragile, as if roughened by crying or a cold.

She froze. 'What happened?'

The innkeeper muttered something under his breath. Then, wiping his hands on his apron, not holding her gaze, he said, 'I've been conscripted.'

He lifted a candle, casting long, twisting shadows, and used it to light a second one, so she could find her way up the stairs to the attic. She took it but didn't budge. She couldn't believe what she had just heard. His face, when he handed her the light, was haggard.

'You're going to fight?' she repeated.

A mirthless chuckle. 'I'm not doing anything. Just standing there and letting a mage puppet me around, playing with toy soldiers.'

Each word hit her like a punch, even though she had always known it was a possibility. In truth, it was inevitable that people she knew would be dragged off to war.

'Tomorrow a Sunriser family will be moving in,' he went on, not looking at her. 'Rich folk. Refugee mages, I guess. I'm to hand over the building. It's temporary, they say. Until the end of the war.'

She took the candle and went upstairs to change. She packed her clothes, gathering her belongings into a pile, aware she would no longer be able to store them at the Coop. All the while, all she could think of was the innkeeper's face, which had become so familiar, which had now set into a mask.

Downstairs, he was sitting on a stool, elbows on his knees, head in his hands, staring ahead. She went to stand beside him. Deserted, the Coop was impersonal. Nothing hung on the walls to show who had been there; they had left no mark on the benches, the booths, the tables.

The innkeeper took a deep breath, steeling himself to speak.

'Does it hurt?' he asked. 'When mages control us and make us fight, do we feel it?'

Her mouth was dry. Her mind was blank. All she managed to say was the truth: 'I don't know.'

The innkeeper didn't insist. Isha understood, maybe for the first time, how hard it must be to live as an ungifted, to be subject to the whims of people who could entirely take over your mind, wipe it clean if it so pleased them, make you commit suicide if they chose, to be qualified only by the absence of a gift, rather than by who you were, what you had achieved, what you dreamt of.

The innkeeper didn't have mindlink, but he had other things he had cared for. She glanced around the empty main room, cleaned and cold. The upturned chairs where people should have been, the stools in place of mindbrawlers, the kegs with hollow echoes rather than the hiss of beer.

'You'll have to give me back your key,' he said.

Spirits sinking, she unhooked it from her belt. He fingered the heavy iron key, rust staining his nails.

'I think I'll throw it over the Edge,' he said at last. 'For Tatters.'

Her heart squeezed, a mix of pain and grief and fear clutching her. All she could think of was that she had never asked him for his name. Hours and hours spent at the Coop, and she had been content assuming he'd always be there, that she didn't need to get to know him. It was too late to ask now.

'I think Tatters is alive,' she blurted out, before she could stop herself.

The innkeeper shook his head. He didn't even try to convince her otherwise.

He closed his fist around the rough-cut key. Isha imagined him at the Temple, letting go, letting the mist and the underworlds swallow the warmth, the laughter, the energy of the Coop; letting his hopes for the future, his fond memories of a friend, disappear into the void.

***

From time to time, Sir Leofric came to visit. Tatters had lost his slit of light, and thus the count of days. He didn't know if Sir Leofric's talks were routine or random.

'I am sure you feel sorry for the bloodcows.' Sir Leofric smiled. 'It's your strong suit, after all. But as you can see, I don't need to pity people to control them. So. Are you ready to speak to me?'

I could give him Passerine's name. The idea caught Tatters off-guard. For a moment, he could believe it wasn't his own, but belonged to Lal. When he listened, nothing rose within him, no other voice to help him, no sisterly love. He let himself sink against the iron of his cage.

He could still hear Passerine's words. *One day you will have to admit I was right, and you will hand him over to me. Then, and only then, will he be broken in.*

Maybe it was only a choice between facing old enemies or new ones. Tatters shook his head.

Sir Leofric was losing patience, if he had ever had any. He knelt beside Tatters, staining the ends of his green robes with the grime of the prison.

'You will be mine,' he hissed. 'They always are, in the end. They always beg. You'll be no different.'

Tatters nodded. 'I am sure you're right.' He would have begged, if begging would have made a difference.

Sir Leofric stood up.

'I'm told you aren't eating. Eat, or we will force-feed you. We don't want you to die on us.'

Tatters ate. He threw up most of it afterwards.

He wondered if Arushi had forgotten about him, if Isha had ever cared. If anyone would come for him. He couldn't do this much longer. He would have to give in, or he would die.

* * *

The khers had confirmed this was it. This was the night of their expedition.

As the iwdan had agreed, Isha hadn't been given any details beforehand. Her only instructions were to bring paper or a wax tablet to write on. She'd borrowed sheafs of papers from Passerine, without explaining what she would be using them for. He would try to dissuade her from such a dangerous endeavour.

She met up with Arushi after dusk, when most of the apprentices were sleeping in their dorms. It was the first time she'd worn her normal outfit inside the Nest, and fear knotted her throat. She'd rolled the vellum and tucked it inside her belt, hoping she looked like a scribe rather than a thief.

The moonlight was crisp, white. The stars looked like a spilt bucket of milk: bright lines spread out in splashes across the night. She walked past the stables where the horses were snuffling and sighing, under the stone arches where torches smoked in the frozen air, past the entrance of the Nest, where lacunants huddled under makeshift homes of straw and sticks.

Arushi was standing beside the watchtower's heavy iron door, a bundle of hide and rope under one arm. She had polished her horns until they were the colour of the night sky. Before they went in, she told Isha what was expected of her.

Hearing about her role, Isha felt the urge to back down, to admit she couldn't do it. But then she thought of Ka's father lying on the ground, his head lolling left to right as the butcher tried to tug the horn out of his skull. It wasn't whether she could do this or not – it was something she had to do, no matter what.

'Let's see if Yua's planning holds,' Arushi muttered.

She opened the watchtower's door, stamping her feet, blowing on her fingers, making a show of wanting to escape the cold. Behind her, Isha entered shyly, tugging at the hem of her shirt.

There were two people inside the watchtower: a kher and a human. This was standard practice. Although most of the guards were female khers, a few ungifted also worked alongside the lawmages. This was mostly – as far as anyone knew – to keep an eye on the khers. Lawmages couldn't be expected to take on the more boring guard duties.

A rack of shields was leaning against one wall, and a round table was set in the centre of the tower. Below the table, barely visible, was a trapdoor. Arushi ignored it as she stepped inside, rubbing her arms, swearing against the snow. The kher already there looked up. She had cut her hair short, and had a tattoo curling from her ear down her neck, looping towards her shoulder.

The human was a man in his forties, broad, smiling. He spotted Isha and asked in a booming voice:

'What have we here?'

Isha swallowed, but before she could gather her wits to answer, Arushi said, 'A friend. Said she couldn't sleep. And I remember Tara saying we needed to be four for a game of Foxes.'

The kher, Tara, made a vague sound of approval. The ungifted glanced over Isha once and, to her surprise, laughed.

'I know you, lass. You're the kid who works at the tavern downtown.' He wasn't so much reproachful as amused. 'You shouldn't bring halfbloods in,' he told Arushi. He had recognised

Isha, but it could have been worse – he could have asked whether she was the tattooed apprentice who had no doubt been mentioned to him, even if he had never seen her. Luckily, halfbloods weren't able to mindlink, so now he wouldn't think of her as an apprentice.

Arushi, to her credit, didn't bat an eyelid.

'She was in the scullery already. She works everywhere that hires.'

The ungifted nodded. 'Ah, I remember working for two lords at once. Not an easy task.'

'I didn't want her to be alone tonight,' Arushi added. 'She's had a tough day.'

'Who hasn't?' The ungifted scratched his beard with one hand. Isha thought she would have to find a lie about what kind of 'tough day' she'd had, but he didn't ask her about it. 'Anyway, you know me. Not going to say no to another girl. The more the merrier!'

Isha had expected more resistance, but soon she was sitting at the table with the other three, and they were passing along a jug of diluted wine. Arushi put her bundle in a corner, mentioning a tent that needed repairing. The ungifted mustn't be familiar with the Pit, otherwise he would have known Arushi owned a house, not a tent. Or maybe he assumed she was helping out someone else. As it was, he didn't question her.

The ungifted asked Isha if she knew how to play Foxes. Despite her knowledge of the game being rusty, Isha had played it enough at the farm that she could pick up the rules fast. She couldn't help but pick up on the irony of playing a game where foxes ate chickens, in a place called the Nest, where the mages liked comparing themselves to birds.

Card games were not something mages indulged in. Isha examined the make of the cards, and the ungifted noticed her interest. 'They're beauties, hey?' They were worn at the edges, and some had wine stains, or rips that had been painstakingly repaired.

'They are lovely,' Isha said. The cards were full of life – drawings of trees, of peaches, of animals. Some of them were weirder than others: one had a drawing of rabbit-knights mounted on snails, jousting against each other. There was also a card with plump black chickens running away from a fox. The black chickens were wearing gilded necklaces and rings around their claws.

She won the first round, which made the ungifted bark a laugh.

'The kid is smarter than she looks.'

Isha supposed that was meant to be a compliment. They played for a while, Isha immersing herself in the game to keep her mind off their other projects for the night. Tara was a silent, deliberate player. She didn't seem to mind the cards where khers and cattle were fighting, their horns intertwined, although Arushi gritted her teeth at those pictures.

They played two other rounds before Arushi glanced up from her cards and said, 'Maybe one last game and I'll call it a night.'

'I should be getting back,' Isha agreed. She felt her pulse picking up.

This was her time. Tentatively, her training with Passerine at the forefront of her mind, she reached out for the ungifted. *No-one must notice this.* She kept herself as far removed as she could. *Mages studying his mind mustn't see the change.* She nudged his thoughts towards his bladder, the wine he had drunk, the fact that he needed to go outside for a quick release.

At first nothing happened. Staring through the cards without seeing them, Isha pushed him a bit further. Now. He needed to pee now. This couldn't wait.

'It's your turn,' Tara said. She sounded bored.

'Sorry…' Isha put down a card at random.

The ungifted chuckled with the back of his throat. 'Got a bad hand this time round, did you?' he asked, placing his own card on the table.

They finished the game. Isha was horrified. Had she failed? But just as Tara won the last round, the ungifted got up.

'Need to stretch the old legs outside,' he said. 'Mind holding the fort, Tara?'

'Of course not,' she said, gathering the cards. She shuffled them with the expert movement of someone who has been on guard duty during long winter nights before.

As soon as he was out of the watchtower, Arushi and Tara got up. Isha scrambled to her feet after them.

'You'll need to use the trapdoor,' Tara said. Kneeling, she tugged at the heavy circle of iron which held it in place. She motioned for Isha to push the table; the jug of wine rocked as they dragged it aside.

Arushi grabbed the bundle of hide and rope and put it between Isha's arms. 'Take these,' she said, as she unhooked a torch from the wall. 'We're going to need this too.'

Tara heaved. The muscles down her arms clenched. The trapdoor lifted, a cloud of dust and cobwebs rising with it. A rope ladder hung from it, frayed with age, leading downward.

'Sekk iss,' Tara said. She added something in iwdan for Arushi's benefit, which was too intricate for Isha to catch.

Isha went down the ladder first, gripping her bundle against her chest with one hand. Each step downwards was a step into the unknown. It was pitch-black; she had to feel for the next rung with her feet, not knowing when she would touch the ground. Each time she did so, flailing with one foot in the void, her stomach lifted into her throat. Her arms shook with the strain. The ladder swung from side to side uncomfortably. Each time it moved, Isha wondered if this was it, she was going to ruin a carefully constructed plan by being sick and dropping like a stone.

At last, Isha's feet touched beaten earth. She stepped away from the ladder.

Arushi followed, holding the torch clear of the hemp rope. The fire made her skin glow a wine-deep red.

'This is a one-way entry,' Tara said. For the first time, she sounded worried.

'If Ka is right, there is another exit,' said Arushi.

The trapdoor shut above them with a thump; dust fell across their shoulders and their hair, making Isha cough. She imagined Tara upstairs, putting the watchtower back in order, and the ungifted returning, thinking Isha and Arushi had simply left for the night.

Arushi moved her torch in a large circle, lighting up the walls of the cellar. It was a storeroom. There were broken and rotting shields, lances resting against the walls, racks of swords like soldiers standing to attention. Isha unrolled the hide, as Arushi instructed her to, and went up to the weapons.

'Swords only,' Arushi whispered. 'One-handed, otherwise they'll be too long. Try not to take broken ones. Blunt is not an issue.'

Isha started packing the swords – as many as two women could carry on their backs. She placed the blades inside the hide and then wrapped them together, securing the load with rope. Above them, they sometimes heard the thud of a chair hitting the trapdoor, nothing more.

Arushi manoeuvred the torch into a hole in the ground to keep it upright as they worked. Skipping the small talk, she explained the rest of the plan to Isha.

They didn't have a map. Yua, Ka and some other khers had also entered the tunnels from the entrance off the cliff-edge and were trying to join them to help carry weapons. The difficulty was finding the link between the Nest's official underground and Ka's entrance. Chances were both webs of tunnels were linked – but how, where?

'Which is where fleshbinding comes in use,' said Arushi. 'When sharing sensations, iwdan have an idea of where the other person is. I'm going to fleshbind with Yua, and her with me, and we'll try to find each other.'

'I just tag along then?' That sounded easy enough.

Arushi scoffed. 'You're drawing the map. So that we can come back to this place with more people.'

With those words, Arushi hoisted her load onto her back, leaning over awkwardly to retrieve the torch. When Isha pulled the swords over her shoulders, the rope bit into her skin, as if trying to reach her bone. The weight nearly toppled her. Once she had found her balance, she unrolled the vellum. She had no idea how to draw a map on the fly, but it would be a waste of breath to say so.

Arushi followed the circular wall, away from the trapdoor, until she found a corridor leading away from the disused store-room. They headed out into the unknown.

They didn't have any landmarks to go by. Arushi guided them through half-carved, half-built tunnels, which slowly deteriorated. Despite being wrapped tightly, their loads clinked as they walked. At each intersection, Arushi would stop, bringing her torch close to Isha so she could unfurl the long sheet of paper against the moist walls and struggle to draw cramped, imprecise lines.

It was slow progress. Arushi often found herself up against a dead end, forced to backtrack. Isha's map was a mess of criss-crossing lines; each time they retraced their steps, her work became more confusing.

They reached a cave that humans had converted into a room, paving parts of it, scraping most of the mud off the sides. One wall didn't quite reach the ground, leaving a crack big enough to crawl through if the person went down on their belly.

Isha had to lie down and slither on her elbows to the other side. They got the bundles across by rolling them, Arushi pushing on one side of the hole, Isha tugging on the other. Then Arushi handed her the torch, holding it horizontally, letting the fire lick at the damp. At last Arushi crossed the passageway herself. Her horns made it more difficult for her to fit through the narrow gap; they scraped at the stone as she forced her way through, bending in a way that made Isha's teeth hurt.

When they got up on the other side, they were covered in filth. The rope chafed against Isha's wet hands, tearing skin. The map was sodden. She was sore, and tired, and cold. But she noticed the lines of bruises the bundles had left near Arushi's neck and she didn't complain.

From then onwards, the caves were natural formations. There was no trace of a human hand, only undisturbed stalactites growing like babies' teeth, water dripping quietly over stone. Footsteps.

Isha braced herself by instinct, and she felt more than she saw Arushi tense, her free hand flying to the pommel of her sword.

'They can't be far now,' a voice said.

'Fleshbinding isn't made for this.' Another person, clearly frustrated. 'I have no idea how close my ucma is, only that she's in this direction.'

Arushi and Isha relaxed together, and both noticed they had at the same time. Isha couldn't help but smile, and Arushi relented enough to nod.

'Seshaq, they would be easy to sneak up on,' Arushi whispered.

For a second, Isha entertained the idea of trying to jump out at Yua and Ka – but then Ka called out: 'Arushi? Is that you?'

'Yes, but thank you for blowing my cover if it hadn't been,' she answered, maybe more loudly than necessary, laughing.

They went to greet the other khers. Aside from Ka and Yua, there were a handful of men, whom Isha didn't know. Both sisters hugged, which Isha hadn't been expecting; Yua dirtied her clothes with Arushi's mud, squeezing her hard. Despite their situation, Yua had a woven bracelet around one of her horns, probably plaited by one of the children of her tiyayat. It was garish, a tasteless mix of pink and orange, but it was so typical of her that it touched Isha nonetheless.

'You made it,' Yua said. She tapped the bundle on her sister's back appreciatively, listening to the jangling sound that came from it. 'And you've brought us these.'

Ka smiled at Isha. 'Congratulations.'

'Yes.' Arushi put a grimy hand on Isha's shoulder. 'Thank you. I won't forget what you did for us today.' She gave out compliments like she gave out threats, as if there was no need to make a big deal out of it. The fact that it was true was enough.

There was a bit of banter between the khers, some of it in iwdan, and Isha recognised it for what it was: relief. They complained about the cold; Yua teased her sister about the state of her clothes; Arushi scolded Yua about chatting while they were supposed to stay low-profile. They handed the weapons to two of the men, who would start bringing them back to Ka's cache. The others would follow Arushi and Isha back to the derelict storeroom.

'Now your map comes in use,' Arushi pointed out.

Isha tried to smile, although nerves clogged her throat. They sneaked through the narrow passage again, Yua the only one to be able to slide comfortably through, wiggling in the mud like a worm. It was a long trek. Isha paused often, holding the map open with her elbow, following the lines with her finger. The khers waited and stared. The gazes were bored at best, unfriendly at worst.

'I think I'm getting the hang of this,' she said, to break the silence, maybe to convince herself.

'Get the hang of it quickly,' Ka grumbled. 'The longer we stay here, the more at risk we are.'

They crawled and slithered and shivered and, excruciatingly slowly, progressed. To her relief, she was able to find the store-room again.

Immediately, the khers fanned out, the men taking over, starting to rope bundles of weapons, getting to work to carry as much as they could in one trip. Exhausted with anxiety, Isha stood below the trapdoor, listening for any signs that someone was coming down. Seeing a group of tough, muscular men piling weapons in their arms was a different experience to gathering a couple of bundles with Arushi. The threat felt more tangible. Scarred iwdan collecting weapons they would use to kill.

As he was searching through the room, Ka stopped abruptly. Isha froze, her heart speeding up by habit. Had he spotted an intruder? Her mind expanded to find the foreign presence. There was no-one but them. Ka was running his fingers along a tri-angular wooden frame. It was a crossbow, the string long-broken.

The last time Isha had seen one of those was inside the Pit, when humans were shooting at Ka's family, after his father's death. She had no doubt he was picturing the same scene. He hesitated, then pulled the crossbow over his shoulder.

'Arushi, it's now or never,' Yua announced. 'We need to find Tatters. Who is coming with us?'

Ka glanced up at the question, his fingers still playing along the length of the crossbow.

'I'll come,' he said.

'Me too,' added Isha.

The other khers ignored them. Obviously, saving a human wasn't their priority. Isha felt uneasy knowing there would only be four of them.

Yua broke the moment by clapping her hands. 'That's decided then. Let's get going.'

Their goodbyes to the other men were solemn, quick.

They went in the opposite direction to Ka's entrance, relying on Arushi's knowledge of where the overground prisons were, hoping the underground cells would be in the same area. The corridors looked less worn here; the ground was still beaten earth, but the walls had obviously been restored by humans. In places, they were built with the creamy sandstone the giants used to make the Nest. They paced the tunnels in grim silence. At each intersection, Ka and Arushi hesitated. It was clear they were advancing with guesswork.

'We're too far to feel Tatters,' Arushi admitted. 'We're going in blind.'

'That might take too long,' said Yua. 'Two of you have flesh-bound with him before. We can do two teams.'

'I'm not sure that's a great idea,' Arushi complained, rubbing at the marks on her shoulders. But now Isha knew enough about the two sisters' dynamics to recognise this for what it was – for all her quibbling, Arushi couldn't say no to her sister for long.

'It's one of my ideas,' said Yua. 'It's fantastic.' She barely paused for breath before giving out instructions. 'I'll be with Ka; he can guide me towards Tatters, and I can guide him towards you. You'll be stuck with the soulworm, though.' But she said so with a smile, nudging Isha with her elbow. Isha tried to smile back.

At the next crossroad, they peeled off into different directions. Trying to ignore the worry coiled around her heart, Isha kept in step behind Arushi as the grimy, roughly hewn sandstone gave way to wider, cobweb-strewn hallways. The ceiling was streaked with smoke-lines from past torches.

Arushi put a hand on her wrist. Isha heard it the moment Arushi touched her, drawing her attention to it. Footsteps. Again. Heavy, lazy footsteps, dulled by tunnels that didn't carry an echo. She trained her eyes towards the sharp bend in the corridor – was the darkness there lighter, maybe, not quite as deep, a distant glow turning the blackness into grey?

Arushi walked backwards. Silently, Isha copied her. They were too late. They had barely tiptoed back, both of them still staring at where the sound was coming from, when the light became clearer. Shadows cut the bend in front of them, as if eager to see what was on the other side. Before Isha could think to run, someone strode into their line of sight.

'Arushi? What are you doing here?'

The lawmage had blond hair, a deeper shade than Kilian's, the kind of curls people have in fairytales that they can spin into gold. If he washed it, it would be beautiful. As it was, it hung in strands around a face marked by age, smallpox and drinking.

Isha recognised him immediately. It would have been hard to forget the man who had arrested Tatters. He was alone.

'May you grow tall, Varun,' Arushi replied, giving no sign that anything was wrong. Varun eyed her suspiciously. 'I was escorting this apprentice, and I believe we got lost.'

Once his attention was on Isha, his scowl only deepened. 'Not the first time you've been hanging around trouble,' he said. 'Why aren't you wearing your robes?' Then his interest shifted to the map tucked in her belt. 'What are you carrying?'

He took a step closer. Isha took a step back. His lips curled into something which wasn't a smile, but which was victorious, like a snarl before a predator pounced, knowing he had a catch.

Arushi moved faster than either of the mages. One of her hands went to cover Varun's mouth, while the other hit his temple. She put all her weight into it, grabbing the pale hair as she slammed his skull against the wall. Isha felt the shock in her bones as Arushi knocked his head between her fist and the stone. He slid to the floor, and the kher let herself fall to her knees with him, still holding on to his face to prevent him from screaming. There was no need. He was unconscious.

When Arushi let go, strands of hair were caught between her fingers, and a patch of blood stained the wall.

The head of guards was calm, but breathing fast.

'Why didn't you mindlink him into silence?' Her angry whisper was so loud it echoed across the corridor.

'I can't just mindlink a lawmage into keeping quiet!' Isha answered, struggling to keep her voice low.

'If you can't, no point in getting involved,' snapped Arushi. 'And if you can't wipe his memory of what just happened, our cover is blown.'

Isha's hands were shaking. 'I can't wipe out his memory. I have no idea how to do it.'

'Really?' Arushi didn't seem impressed. 'The only other way to keep him quiet is to slit his throat. Varun is Sir Leofric's right hand. If he knows something, we're finished.'

'Give me a minute.' Isha knelt on the floor, trying to ignore the shivers going through her. She wondered why her teeth were chattering now, when they should have betrayed her before, when Varun was closing in on her. The horror of nearly being caught was sinking in, and she had to bite down on her lower lip to stop her jaw from rattling.

'Isn't it easier if he's unconscious?' Arushi asked. 'It's not like he can defend himself.'

Isha motioned for Arushi to be silent. The kher went to check the corridor beyond the bend, keeping watch.

Closing her eyes, Isha projected herself towards Varun. His thoughts were unsettled, sifting through dreamlike images, unfinished ideas lying like strands of broken thread in the tapestry of his mind. She had never preyed on someone unconscious. It was like breaking into someone's house; it was private, it was theirs, and yet she had the key to everything and could wreck what she wanted.

His memories were scattered, linked by theme rather than the linear passage of time. They were difficult to navigate, and more difficult still to isolate – this round was linked to other rounds, other lonely nights checking the prisons one last time before going to bed. This recollection of Arushi was mingled with all the other times he had seen her. For Isha it was even more confusing: he had imagined her before seeing her, and the picture of what she might look like overlapped with what she actually looked like.

She unearthed the memory of a prisoner; a man, worn, aged, unshaven. Hollow eyes, but a glint of defiance still inside them. Tatters. She gasped, loud enough for Arushi to hear. Dimly, she was aware of Arushi unsheathing her sword.

Before anything else, she compared Varun's mental map to their network of passageways. The two didn't quite overlap, and she was uncertain whether she'd interpreted his thoughts correctly, but still she indicated where, according to her best guess, Tatters could be found.

She then tried to destroy Varun's memories of meeting them in the corridors. She felt like someone soiling another man's sheets while he was away from home. She wondered if the Renegades who had forced her to flee, who had broken her and her foster family, had shared the same qualms when they tore through her mind.

She couldn't take any chances – but each time she pulled away one event, others followed, closely woven together, and the task was as hard as trying to burn certain threads in a tunic while sparing the others. When at last she finished her gruelling work, she knew she had destroyed more than she had meant to.

'So?' Arushi asked.

Isha nodded, but she felt nauseous, and moving made her head swim. *I have done to another man what my enemies did to me.*

'He's seen Tatters,' she managed. Swallowing back the taste of bile, she indicated the map. 'Here.'

The expression on Arushi's face was a complicated one, and not one Isha cared to stare at.

Arushi crouched beside Varun. She untied his belt and slid the ring of keys off. As she was doing so, she abruptly folded over, gasping. Her torch rolled on the floor, sputtered, and died. In the pitch blackness, Isha rushed to her side, assuming Varun had regained consciousness and attacked her – but the lawmage wasn't moving. Isha found Arushi's hand, pressed to her side, as if to staunch a cut.

'Yua is in pain,' Arushi hissed, jumping to her feet.

She was running before Isha had a chance to gather her bearings – she just had time to grab her hand. They left the dead torch where it had fallen. They sprinted through tunnels, bumping into each other as Arushi kept changing directions, scrambling wildly for a phantom pain she could feel but couldn't pinpoint, for a sister she could sense but couldn't see. Never had mindlink seemed such a wasted talent as it was right now: Isha could see nothing, feel nothing, hear nothing, and mindmagic seemed a useless ability to have, compared to the capacity to tell whether a loved one was close or far. As it was, she could only fumble behind the kher, scraping her skin raw against the gritty sandstone, bashing her shins into irregular rocks, holding on to Arushi.

They heard the screaming before they reached them. It was a man's voice. Ka.

He was shouting abuse in iwdan. As they rounded a turn, Isha smelt the stench of blood and excrements, and half-slid, half-fell over someone spread across the floor. She landed flat on her hands. Someone kicked her aside; someone else tried to grab her, their hands slick with something which wasn't water. She found herself screaming too, struggling against whoever or whatever it was that was trying to catch her. At last her mindlink served her: there was another human consciousness here, a mage. Their presence was like a beacon.

'*Everyone dive down,*' Arushi barked in iwdan.

Already on the floor, Isha flattened herself further. Abruptly, the other mage's mind disappeared. There was a wet, sickening sound; someone panting; and a hot wetness spreading across the floor.

Further down the corridor, Isha spotted lights dancing on the wall. People were coming. When she reached out in mindlink, she counted at least half a dozen guards. Briefly, she saw through their eyes: lamps rather than torches, weapons rather than empty belts.

Then the bell started ringing.

It was a small, handheld bell, the sort used to announce the change of guards. Someone was raising the alarm.

'This way,' Arushi whispered. 'Ka, can you walk?'

His voice was muffled, strained. 'Yes.'

They held hands, stumbling away as fast as they could. They groped for the walls, for footing, for each other. At first they were headed nowhere, only away from the sound. As the noise decreased, and their panting could be heard more clearly, Arushi slowed.

'Has anyone got a light?' she asked. 'I can't... I can't feel everyone.'

'Give me a moment,' Ka muttered.

They listened to the metallic sound of clasps opening and closing, the scrape of glass on stone, the choked click of a fire striker. At last, a spark, and the wick caught.

Ka was squatting beside the lamp, a cut running down his forearm, as if he had tried to parry a sword strike with it. His arrud was ripped, soaked in blood, although the wound seemed shallow. He was breathing hard.

Arushi took one glance at their group and her face fell. 'Yua isn't here.' It was a statement, not a question.

There were only three of them. It was then that Isha noticed Arushi's sword. It was splattered with blood. Arushi looked across the cave again, searching with her eyes, as if she hoped against hope to find Yua there.

'I can't feel her,' Arushi said. 'She must be unconscious.'

'What happened?' Isha asked.

When Ka spoke at last, his voice seemed to come from far away.

'We failed.'

Chapter Fourteen

Sir Leofric had won. That was what it boiled down to.

Tatters had tried everything he could think of. He had tried mindrambling, but the kher horn prevented him from tricking his mind into believing it was somewhere else. He had tried reciting Hawk's poetry, to force himself to focus on something else. He had tried coiling into a ball and pressing his fists against his ears, like a child.

In the end he gave up. He could hear them. Even if he couldn't hear them, he could imagine them. *Maybe I was always blind to other people's suffering. Maybe I always tried to look away, and now I can't.* He slept, sometimes. It was the only respite he could find. In his dreams he could speak to Lal, but when he woke their conversations faded, and he wasn't even sure whether he'd heard her voice, or if he was steadily growing mad.

He had slept today, because he woke as a lawmage kicked open the cage next to his and shoved someone inside. In his corner, Tatters hugged his knees. He heard the person stumble, then crash to the ground. They mumbled something, maybe a swearword, and crawled away from the front of the cage to rest against the wall at the further end.

The lawmage left, taking the light with him. For a while no sound but hoarse breathing broke the silence. If Tatters wanted to, he could imagine it was someone snoring, sleeping peacefully. But he knew full well the person was awake, and that their breathing hadn't been roughened by a winter cold.

'Hey.' The voice was high-pitched, juvenile.

Tatters wondered if, one day, his mouth would stop tasting like bile. *Are they killing children now?*

'Hey,' he answered.

It was the first time a prisoner had been able to communicate. He waited.

'Do you have water?' the voice asked.

Tatters had a jug. He picked it up and brought it to the bars separating both cages. It was too large to fit across.

'If you come closer, I can pour the water in your mouth,' he offered. 'From across the bars. I can try, at least.'

He heard shuffling. Without a torch, deep beneath the ground, he couldn't even make out his hands. He worked out where the other person was by groping at the edge of the cage until their fingers met. After using the bars to help himself up, he lifted the jug above where he hoped the person was sitting.

'This might not work perfectly,' he warned.

'Tatters?'

He dropped the jug. It clattered to the ground, and he felt a shock of cold water over his feet.

'Shit,' he said. He knelt to retrieve the jug, sticking a hand inside it to find out if there was still water inside. There was, but not much. He sat clasping it to his chest, trying not to shiver. It was like hearing a ghost.

'We've been looking for you,' said the voice.

Where had he heard it before? It was coarse, changed. Even if he had known it, hearing it here, amongst memories of sobs and sighs and screams, it sounded like no-one or nothing.

For all he knew, madness had struck at last, and this voice belonged to the shadows.

'Well, I was here,' he answered.

The person exhaled slowly, as if letting go of something. It turned out they were letting go of hope.

'If Arushi didn't find you, she won't find me.'

'Yua?' Tatters couldn't believe it. 'Is that you?'

She didn't answer. Maybe she was too exhausted to waste breath.

'Do you still have some water?'

'Yes.'

He poured it across to her, as best he could. The sound of her trying to drink broke his heart. They sat side-by-side, each in their cage. He listened to her breathing, not knowing what had made it so laboured. He thought of her short stubby horns. The lawmages wouldn't have needed to break them to keep her under control: they weren't enough of a threat.

The mages didn't know that short horns, even on an adult, meant the kher was in the first third of their life, and should be taken care of, should be forgiven their mistakes.

'You know what happens to people here,' said Yua. It wasn't a question.

He told her the truth.

'So, this is how I die,' she said when he had finished.

He wished he could tell her that she would survive this, but he didn't believe she would. He extended his hand through the bars of his cage until he found her hand. The nails were broken; the skin was slick and hot. He didn't squeeze it so he wouldn't hurt her. But he held her hand, and she held his. She turned towards him; he could feel her warmth.

'What happened?' he whispered.

Her voice was stronger now that water had soothed her throat.

She told her side of the tale. When he heard that Isha had tried to help, that she had sided with the khers, Tatters felt a knot in his throat, a physical relief. *I know who my friends and foes are, at last.* Had they talked, maybe, before their fight, before the lawmages, they could have... But there was no point dwelling on the past.

'Why haven't they killed you?' Yua asked.

'They don't want to kill me. They want to break me.'

And they will. And they have.

Hawk had wanted to break him, too. But people forgot that when they broke someone, all they had afterwards was something broken. It was of no use to anyone. The fun was in the breaking. The aftermath was shards of glass they had to wipe away, so no-one got cut.

'I don't mind if they kill me,' Yua said. 'As long as they don't break me.'

But the mages would try – they needed to extract information out of her, who she had come with, how she had found the entrance to the prison, how many accomplices she had. Each word she'd give them would condemn more iwdan to the same bloody fate.

It came to Tatters like a lightborn flying across the night sky.

'I can help,' he found himself saying.

I am sure you feel sorry for the bloodcows. It's your strong suit, after all.

He swore that, one day, somehow, Sir Leofric and his kind, the ones who treated others like objects, who played with lives, would be dragged before justice. He could have forgiven anything they did to him. He never cared enough about his own suffering. But he wouldn't forgive what happened here, in this place below the Nest, what happened to the forgotten, to the lost, to the missing.

He took his hand away from Yua. His palm was sticky with her blood.

'Yes,' he said. 'I will help.'

***

Isha was out of bed late. Her night had been fitful, filled with whispers. Once she'd finally sunk into sleep, even the Nest's bell couldn't wake her. But as soon as she came to, she got ready to leave – she was reduced to wearing her robes, as all her other clothes were caked in mud. She needed to go to the Pit, to check on Arushi, to see if maybe, against all odds, Yua had returned. She hadn't eaten and she hadn't slept enough, but she ran down the staircase of the Nest, skipping the human steps, her feet thudding on the stone of giants.

She was so intent on reaching her destination – and on not twisting her ankles – that she didn't notice Kilian until she nearly crashed into him, skidding to a halt mid-stride.

'Ah, Isha, I was looking for you.' He must have come out of the mess. His hair was ruffled and golden.

'May you grow tall and all that,' she answered, pushing past him. 'See you later.'

'What? Wait!'

She heard him stumbling behind her, trying to catch up. She slowed down. She couldn't have him hounding her all the way to the Pit.

'What is it?' she asked, fighting down her annoyance.

He couldn't hold her gaze, so instead he toyed with his sleeves. For the first time, she noticed he wasn't wearing his yellow belt. The robes hung loosely around him without a rope to hold them in place.

She had forgotten how much he looked like someone out of a painting: sky-blue eyes, wheat-blond hair. In the Nest, where the stone was grey, the stairs were grey, the robes were grey, the heavy winter air was grey, he stood out like spring.

'Well?' she repeated.

Kilian chewed on his lower lip. 'I thought about what you said. About making a change, and being the lucky ones, and doing other people's dirty work.'

Isha wondered if he realised how slow he was being. She wanted to hold him by the shoulders and shake him. *Someone might have died.* She waited, but she could feel her legs aching to run, her heart speeding up in anticipation. *And her sister will think it is my fault. Again.* Before, Kilian was someone she could relax with. Now she she knew he could only afford to be happy because he wasn't aware of what was happening.

'I want to train with you and Sir Passerine,' Kilian said. 'I told Lord Daegan as much.'

He lifted his eyes towards her at last, and she could see the jet-blue of the irises blooming with hope, with pride, with fear. He must have gathered all his courage to face down Lord Daegan, and it couldn't have been easy, to tell his master he was betraying him for a rival.

'Great.' She didn't know what else to say. *Thank you, but this is too late?* 'Well, you can meet up with us in the training rooms at the usual times. Ask the servants to dye you a new belt or something. Now I really have to go.'

She was sorry for him as he deflated, his chest caving into a sigh. But when she turned away, he slipped from her mind, and all she could think of was Yua, the silly bright ornaments she put in her horns, and she ran out of the Nest and towards the city, ran until her lungs burnt, until her feet ached, until she thought she would collapse.

REBECCA ZAHABI

She ran until she reached the house, standing in the middle of the Pit like a statement. Arushi was sitting across the threshold, shivering in the cold. Her eyes were empty.

She had been waiting all night for her sister. That much Isha knew without mindlink. If she was still waiting, then Yua hadn't returned.

Isha stood, catching her breath, heart still pumping uselessly. There was nowhere else to run. Around them, the Pit was going through its morning routine: women were outside with shovels, packing the snow along the walls of the half-built houses and around their tents, to hem in the warmth with ice. The children had brought the dogs outside for a run; barks and peals of laughter echoed across the streets. Male khers without much to do either joined the children, carrying the younger ones on their shoulders, or worked on the murals, painting during the brief span of daylight.

Isha went to sit beside Arushi, on the hard wood of the threshold, in the biting cold. She didn't have anything to say. Everything was bright in the pale winter sun – the snow seemed to sparkle. Every wet surface glinted. There was birdsong, trill and gleeful, from the birds who had missed the dawn chorus.

'I didn't know birds sang in winter,' Arushi said.

Her face was blank. Her sword was unsheathed across her lap, as if she expected to rise and fight someone. Isha knew it wasn't good to have naked metal in the damp air with snow melting around it. Arushi looked like she might sit here, motionless, until the blade rusted away.

Isha tried not to notice how lovely the day was – the sun, the crisp, cold sky, as if the world had been rinsed and polished during the night. The beauty of it ached all the more because Yua wasn't there. How could birds sing, how could the kher down the street whistle a tune, how could children laugh, when

Yua hadn't returned, and they didn't know what had happened to her?

Arushi ran her finger along the length of her blade, her nail catching against the iron. It was as if a careful blacksmith had sanded down her expression, taking all emotion away from her features. Isha recognised that emptiness. She had seen it on refugees, on mourners at the Temple, on her foster father at the farm.

It was a face set in grief.

When Arushi spoke, her voice was softer than Isha had ever heard it.

'Ganez asked me why I didn't stop her. Why I didn't prevent her from doing something so foolish.'

'It's my fault,' Isha found herself blurting out. 'I should never have agreed to it, I shouldn't have tried to convince you. You were the only cautious one, and we all pushed you to do this. I should have known what mages were capable of. I should have been the one to stop her, us, all of us. I should have thought this through.'

Arushi didn't answer, didn't argue, and that, in itself, was enough to silence Isha. She had never seen the kher so quiet. They sat together without a word. Whenever someone's footsteps came their way, they both looked up. It was never who they were hoping for.

'They had prisons down there, prisons for iwdan only.' Arushi spoke so low she might have been talking to herself. 'I'd heard stories, of course. But I didn't think they murdered us in secret.' Arushi pushed her thumb against her sword, as if she were considering cutting it. 'I always assumed the Renegades were our enemies,' she whispered. 'But if the Nest is killing my people, they might be our only hope.'

Isha thought of the black-and-red flag. Of knowing who were friends and who were foes. Of making choices. How did someone know beforehand whether their choice would be the right one – whether choosing the collar would mean they could alight, or whether it meant they would never be free again? Whether they would save their people, or lose their sister?

What do we do, if it is the Nest? she wondered. *How do you fight the land on which you stand?*

The muted sound of horns hitting a hard surface pulled her from her daydream. Arushi had slumped backwards, horns scraping at the wall. Tears were pooling in her eyes, spilling down her cheeks, meeting below her chin.

'Do you think I'll ever see my sister again?' she asked.

Isha couldn't answer. She turned away so Arushi wouldn't see her cry. She had no right to it.

***

Then Isha had to go back. It was as simple as that. She stayed with Arushi for as long as she could, but she belonged to the Nest, not to the Pit, and she couldn't wait with the khers, she couldn't weep with them.

When Isha picked herself up from the threshold, Arushi still hadn't moved. Although it was only early afternoon, the sun was already setting. Snowflakes stuck to Arushi's shoulders.

'You should go inside,' Isha said. 'You won't be much use to your family if you fall ill.'

'I am no use to my family anyway,' Arushi answered.

Isha wanted to reach out, but she couldn't find the words to breach the distance between them. At that moment, Arushi looked like the head of guards – silent, focused, protecting her house with her weapon drawn. The snow was starting to fall harder now, flecking her hair with white, as if she were ageing before Isha's eyes. She was staring ahead of her, with the look of someone who couldn't see.

Isha tore herself away. If she lingered much longer, with this snow, she would have trouble returning to the Nest. She wiped the lines of tears from her cheeks.

The walk back was a dreary one. The snow was falling thicker by the minute, and soon Isha had to drag her dripping robes through the mush and mud blocking the path. Thankfully, a man let her climb on the back of his cart, hanging behind the wares, which turned out to be shields painted with the Nest's crest, in precarious piles, covered by a canvas sheet waterproofed with beeswax. Her wet robes slapped her ankles as the cart rocked, the horse panting, putting all its weight into its collar, its ears pressed far down in its mane.

They were in view of the bridge when she heard someone calling her name. It was faint, but the top of the river had frozen, and the sound of the water crashing over the Edge was dulled somewhat, letting voices carry further than they did in spring. She squinted at the figure on the bridge, braving the weather, walking towards the city.

'What kind of fool leaves his Nest now?' grumbled the cart driver.

The fool was Kilian. His shoulders sagged in relief when he was close enough to recognise her.

'I thought it was you,' he said. 'Thank the lightborns, thank the skies. Thank everyone.'

He was as dishevelled as she must be, his hair plastered to his skull by the damp, his robes soaking up snow, his too-short sleeves showing wrists red with cold.

'What are you doing out here?' she asked. 'You'll freeze to death.'

She put out her hand to help him onto the back of the cart – she could do that for him, at least. His hands were like ice. He had trouble gripping the ropes holding the shields in place. The cart driver clicked his tongue. The horse barely went faster than they would on foot, and the bumping up and down was making Isha's head spin.

'I was looking for you,' said Kilian. 'I mean, everyone is sort of looking for you right now. But I knew you'd gone out, so I thought I'd try to find you.'

His teeth were chattering, but he was doing his best to hide it. He gave her a brave smile. She could see he was faking it, but the smile was warming all the same. It told her he forgave her for being brusque, that he cared enough to come out in this weather, that he wanted to be by her side.

'All right,' she said, 'I'm listening.'

'Apprentices are talking about Sir Passerine's duel with Lady Mathilda, and about changing masters. Everyone's discussing his offer to join him. Lots of Sunriser mages have decided to band with him.' The wind blew his hair away from his face, and he looked older, somehow, without his blond curls in front of his eyes. 'You should be there. You're the only one who knows Passerine, who can tell people what it's like studying with him.'

They didn't say much for the rest of the ride. The white air coming from their mouths mingled as they breathed. As soon as they reached the gate, before the horse stopped, Kilian jumped off. He stumbled, struggling to keep his footing with numb toes. Still he put his hand out and, because he had taken hers before, she let him help her down.

Dimly, she noted the dye from Kilian's shoes was finally coming off. He left green footmarks in the snow.

'Everyone's chatting in the mess,' Kilian said, rubbing his hands up and down his arms, stamping his feet. Glancing down, he saw the dye was leaking. 'This isn't my day, is it?' He shook his head and did his best to ignore the shoes. Aside from the footsteps, the dye was also staining his skin. Isha could see his ankles turning a shoddy brown-green.

They walked with such long strides they might as well have been running. Kilian didn't seem willing to slow the pace. He still didn't have a belt, so he hugged his robes closed, shivering as the cold cut through the gap between the fabrics. Their feet squelched.

Outside of mealtimes, the mess should have been empty. Today, however, the apprentices had gathered in clumps, by affiliation. A shouting match seemed to be taking place. Two groups were facing off: a couple of newcomers and small-rank followers, including Wingshade apprentices, clearly the underdogs; and a group with golden belts, the supreme mage's followers. Caitlin included. Of course.

Isha guessed what was happening at a glance. It was the way they were gathered around a table, as if defending it. It was the experience from having been unaffiliated, and having nowhere to eat. It was the same argument the council kept having, in a room too small to accommodate everyone.

She was too exhausted to be polite. 'I can't believe this. Are you fighting about where to sit?'

Everyone stared at her. She was conscious of her damp, frizzy hair; her wet cheeks. She wondered if her eyes were puffy from crying, or if they would mistake the traces on her face for someone suffering from a cold.

They were bickering about tables. About place. About territory. Would mages never learn? Who cared about the seating plan?

'Was I always this shallow?' she asked aloud.

Her robes, heavy with water, were weighing down on her shoulders. She considered wringing them, but decided it would be too ridiculous.

'You're not shallow,' mumbled Kilian behind her.

She had their attention now. Both groups had been stumped by her intervention, but the second one especially, the misfit team – the people who, she supposed, wanted to join Passerine – were lapping up her words. She had to pick them with care.

Because we're so involved, we're the ones with the most power to change things. We have a duty to do so. There was no point in challenging Arushi if she wasn't ready to stand up for the iwdan now. There was no point in facing Caitlin in a duel if Isha couldn't persuade apprentices to join her – to join Passerine, for now, but maybe also to change, once they had joined.

She wanted to make a difference. She could do it. She would.

'Forget the stupid tables,' she said. 'That's not what's important. I'll tell you what is: people suffer for us. Do you know who makes your clothes? Who goes hungry so you can have food? Do you care? Are you happy to know that the money you use is harvested from people's corpses?'

In some ways they must know. They must have seen a serving maid cry, or the butcher returning with his gruesome goods, but never face-on, always as an aside to their lives. They were worried about how their families coped without them. They were worried about their social standing within the hierarchy of the Nest. They were worried about their future working for the lawmages. They didn't have time, or energy, or faith enough to risk their comfort – and for what? For the sake of someone else?

'We're the only ones who can do something,' Isha found herself saying. The ungifted were busy working to feed their families; the refugees had a hard enough time rebuilding their homes. The khers would get slaughtered. 'We're the ones who can make a difference. For the ungifted, for the khers, for the downtrodden, for everyone who needs help.'

Her voice softened. 'So, what's your excuse?'

She wasn't even angry. She was disappointed. Disappointed at herself. Disappointed at the Nest, which had promised to be so much more.

'I'm not like you, Isha,' muttered a young girl, an apprentice Isha didn't know the name of. 'What can I do? I'm a nobody.'

'Everyone is a nobody. Until they aren't.'

Caitlin scoffed, but her lightness felt forced. Her reaction was late, like someone who was taken off-guard in a brawl, and who was slow to unsheathe their weapons. 'Easy for you to say. With your tattoo and your precious Passerine to protect you. If we do anything, we'll get kicked out of the Nest. End of story.'

Isha found her hands closing into fists. Maybe other apprentices had thought the same, each generation that came, but then they had convinced themselves that the world was this way. Maybe it was because people had decided that nothing could be done that nothing was being done.

We couldn't have done anything before. But we can do something now.

'You don't realise what you're saying.' Caitlin's voice cut like a whip. She glared at the apprentices around her, and Isha felt her mind, overbearing, strong, as it pressed down and imprinted her beliefs in their souls.

Before Isha could protest, Caitlin sent her a message. *You're not the first one to speak up*, she warned, *and, if you're not careful, you won't be the first one to die for it, either.* Isha was taken aback by the intensity of her mindlink.

'You are leaving,' Caitlin ordered.

Unlike Caitlin, she was caught in a turmoil. Grief and fear for Yua. Adrenaline from running, both to and from the Nest.

She was in no state to have an argument, and yet she knew that she couldn't back down.

'No,' Isha said. 'You can leave, if you can't stand talking. Here's the truth: if we band together, they can't kick all of us out. If we work together, they have to account for us. If we rely on Passerine, that's one high mage who's not afraid of standing up to Lord Daegan, and who's on our side.'

She took a deep breath, looked as many people as she could in the eye, and ploughed on:

'If you want to do your own thing, do your own thing. I'm not here to force your hand. If you want to be a part of the Nest's traditions, there's plenty of mages who'll take you on. But if you're fed up with how things are, and if you're ready to give a bit of yourself for others – for people less lucky than you are – then, yes, you're welcome.'

Welcome to the clan of nobodies, who are neither Renegades nor mages, who stand nowhere – but that doesn't mean I stand for nothing. She didn't want to give out an ultimatum, so she kept quiet. But something must have come through, from her tone, from her posture, because a couple of apprentices agreed through mindlink.

She turned to Caitlin. 'Do you want to fight me over this? Again?'

Caitlin bared her teeth. Isha could image her arching her back and hissing like a cat. 'I'll pass,' she said. 'Everyone's free to make their own mistakes.'

For once, it was Caitlin who left the room first.

Without having decided to, simply because it was necessary, Isha escorted a large group up to Passerine's chambers, guiding them to the high mage so they could officially join his ranks. She knocked at the door, explained the situation to him, and stepped back.

She stood aside with Kilian as the apprentices presented themselves. She knew Passerine well enough to notice that his aloof, taciturn front was in fact unease, a form of shyness when faced with this many people. Still, he welcomed them.

'I can't believe he's got so many followers already,' she said, trying and failing to do a quick headcount.

'Honestly?' said Kilian. 'I'm not sure they're Passerine's followers.'

They watched the small crowd make its way to the high mage one by one, formally requesting to join him.

'I think they're yours,' Kilian concluded.

Chapter Fifteen

Tatters would never forget the night of Yua's passing. He would dream of it until he died.

Luckily he might die soon.

It must have been dawn by the time Sir Leofric and an unknown lawmage strode into the cell. Tatters pushed himself into the furthest corner of the cage, huddling his knees against his chest. He didn't care to ask why Goldie wasn't there today. His head was still ringing with her hysterical laughter; his flesh was still crawling with her pain. When he closed his eyes, he could see a huge mouth stuck too close to him, with broken teeth jutting out of the gums and the stench of rotting meat breathed across his face. He opened them again. Sir Leofric was still there.

Sir Leofric took out his small bone cane and placed it underneath Tatters' chin. He used it as a lever to force Tatters to look him in the eye.

'Do me a favour, get up before I kick you to your feet,' said Sir Leofric.

Tatters unfolded. Every inch of him ached. He hadn't done fleshbinding like this in years. When he stood up, the soles of his feet burnt as if he were walking on embers. When he folded his arms across his chest, he felt the fat finger of the torturer as it ran across her ribcage, counting the bones.

In his mind, he could hear Yua shouting through the door. *You cannot hurt me. You cannot hurt me.* Her voice still rang, like the echoes of a bell, although he knew she was dead.

Sir Leofric waved to his henchman. The brute sprung to attention.

'His wrist,' said Sir Leofric.

The man caught Tatters' forearm and tugged, forcing him to stumble closer.

'Spread out your fingers,' said Sir Leofric.

Fear, cold and leaden, ran through Tatters. He uncurled his fist, certain that Sir Leofric would smash it then and there, with the knob of his cane. They stood before each other, Sir Leofric with his polished boots and a handkerchief down his sleeve, the henchman smelling of sweat and puke and excrement, the stench you picked up from working in the prison – and Tatters. He was shaking. It must have been from exhaustion.

Sir Leofric took out his white embroidered handkerchief to hold Tatters' hand in his. Gripping Tatters' index finger, he pushed hard against the nail, and Tatters felt searing pain, as if his flesh was tearing. He howled and would've collapsed to his knees if the henchman hadn't held him upright, dragging him back to his feet.

Sir Leofric wiped the grime off his hands. There wasn't any blood. He hadn't done anything, after all, but touch Tatters' finger. He hadn't even twisted it; most of the pain had been residue fleshbinding.

You cannot hurt me. She had laughed, in the end. It was a desperate laugh, manic, gleeful. It was the laugh of someone who was already dead. Maybe there was nothing to do but laugh. She couldn't feel anything, after all, but she could see what they were doing to her. She must have known, before Tatters, when she was going to die.

All he could do was hold on and wait for her to go.

The lawmage looked from Sir Leofric to Tatters, clearly puzzled at how violently their prisoner had reacted. 'What was that about?'

Sir Leofric put the handkerchief back inside his sleeve before tucking the cane under his arm. 'One of our men thought fleshbinding might be involved.'

It was enough for Tatters. He listened to the rest of Sir Leofric's drone distractedly. They knew. He stood, swaying on his feet, coming to terms with the fact that he wouldn't escape. He couldn't get out of the kher horn. He couldn't get out of the cell.

So, this is how I die. He listened to Yua's voice and repeated her words for himself.

He wished he could talk to Lal one last time.

'She didn't tell them anything. She wasn't reacting to physical pain. She laughed them off at the end. He had never seen anything like it. He thought she was particularly resistant – he misjudged her endurance and killed her.'

'Do you think it's linked to what happened to Varun?' the henchman asked. 'If a mage helped her, could they have wiped her memories of their plans?'

'Oh no,' Sir Leofric said, waving as if to dispel such silly ideas. 'Only fleshbinding can influence a kher.'

'And it's him?' When the henchman shook Tatters' shoulder, the rest of Tatters followed. He focused on breathing as lashes like flames went down his spine.

Sir Leofric squinted at Tatters. 'Yes. Do you know why he reacted like that?' He plucked his cane from underneath his arm to tap Tatters' nose with it. It was a friendly tap, which someone might grace a child with. 'The body remembers the fleshbinding. The nails remember being ripped out; pull against them, even lightly, and the pain returns. The flesh doesn't lie.' Sir Leofric's tone was playful. But the way the cane lingered on Tatters' face reminded him of how a handler might use a stick on a dog: show it to the animal first, hit afterwards.

'Why did you do it?' asked Sir Leofric. 'What is a kher's life to you?'

It wasn't worth it – but Tatters thought of Yua laughing through the night, Yua the longlived, Yua who was nearly a child by kher standards, who should have had many more years of innocence and laughter in front of her, Yua who sang when she cooked and put bells in her horns – and he did it nonetheless.

Tatters lifted his head. 'You know why you'll never ascend?' His voice was a croak, but he held on to it and spoke despite the rawness in his throat. 'Because of that question you've just asked.'

Sir Leofric's fingers tensed around his cane. Tatters thought he would hit him, smash his nose, watch the blood run down the carved piece of ivory, red on white. Sir Leofric's knuckles paled, but he didn't lift his stick.

'What would you know about ascension?' he hissed.

Tatters didn't want to laugh, but he did. It was nerves. He could hear Yua laughing with him. His laughter hurt his ribs, tore through his lungs. He struggled to speak. He wasn't even sure what he wanted to say – frighten Sir Leofric with an image of the collarbound prophet? He wouldn't survive this. He nearly didn't care.

'Enough.' Sir Leofric pressed his hand across Tatters' lips. The sudden scent of perfume filled his nose, the smells clinging to the glove, soap and herbs. 'Shut up.'

Sir Leofric didn't seem fazed. Maybe he was used to prisoners breaking in front of him.

'Now, *Tatters* . . .' Sir Leofric spoke the name with distaste. 'I hope you are listening.'

Tatters nodded. It was such a low nod it might have been a bow.

'The punishment for interfering with the executioner and, in your case, preventing the Nest from accessing crucial information, is to be hanged, drawn and quartered. Not exactly a torture per se, but I've been led to believe it is unpleasant. Obviously, because you have the dubious gift of fleshbinding, we won't be able to do this. Your death would be quick – I'm guessing the axeman would take care of you.'

Sir Leofric paused for a moment, pensive, as if toying with an idea. But in the end, he sighed and shook his head.

'I would make you a lacunant, but I am sure you have another trick up your sleeve. I will not risk taking off those shackles to find out.'

Tatters wished Lal was there – but Lal was silent, as she had been for weeks, since the kher horn had muted her. Not only would he die before hearing her voice again, he couldn't even remember her last words. The touch of Sir Leofric's cane against his cheek brought Tatters back to the present.

'But you're lucky. Do you know why you're lucky?'

Yua had tried to smile when they had come to fetch her. He had this lingering image of her face, afraid, brave, looking back over her shoulder at him. *I am lucky you were here, Tatters.*

When he didn't answer, Sir Leofric tapped his cheek with his cane, as a warning. He could probably, if he hit hard enough, break Tatters' jaw.

'I am listening. Why am I lucky?'

'You are a slave,' said Sir Leofric. 'You're property. As such, you're not responsible for your crimes. Only your master is. But I am not waiting any longer.'

A short silence. Tatters opened his mouth, and Sir Leofric touched his lower lip with his cane. The smooth bone was strangely intimate.

'Before you say anything,' said Sir Leofric, 'if you lie, you'll die. If you stay quiet, you'll die. No second chances.'

Tatters swallowed. He licked his lips and tasted blood. He could say Passerine. Whether Passerine would help or not, he wasn't sure. He might. But if he did, it would only be to take Tatters out of prison and reignite the collar, binding him forever as a slave. Whether he returned Tatters to Hawk or not, Passerine knew enough about the collar to activate it.

He wouldn't be able to cross the Shadowpass again. He wouldn't be able to break free of the yoke of the collar twice. He would be dragged into the upcoming war, and he would witness more blood, he would smell more fires where bodies were smouldering. He would see more people like Yua – young, bright, hopeful – die. He would kill some of them. He had before.

'You always thought you would win, and I would beg,' Tatters said quietly. 'Well, you've won. I won't beg.'

He held Sir Leofric's bright eyes.

'Kill me, if you must.'

***

The maids brought herbal tea to Passerine's chambers. Leaves floated in the earthenware jug; vapours from the boiling water filled the room with the scent of bergamot.

Passerine was sitting at his desk, working at the headache that was trying to fit all his Sunriser followers into the merchants' district without pushing the ungifted residents out. The tip of his quill made a soft, scratching sound. As he toiled, Isha sat on the armchair beside the fire, resting, listening to the sound of the vellum rustling. If she closed her eyes, she could imagine it wasn't Passerine beside her, but Hawk, writing her poetry with quick, broad strokes. It was a fantasy, of course. Hawk had never visited the farm long enough to stay and write. The heat from the fire touched her cheeks like a mother's hand.

They were waiting for a guest.

She thought of a man who could both fleshbind and mind-link. Of the fact that Varun was Sir Leofric's right hand. Of the memory of Tatters' face, lit up in Varun's thoughts. He was alive. She knew he was alive. Yua was missing, but she hoped there was still some way they could save her. Him. Both of them.

A knock at the door.

Passerine stopped writing. Isha placed her cup down on the floor beside her armchair and, because it was her duty as an apprentice, she went over to welcome their guest.

'May you grow tall,' she said.

It was Sir Leofric. He was wearing his usual green robes, a deep colour like the underside of fronds, like foliage growing low on the ground, far from the light. In contrast, his undyed belt stood out as poor and frayed.

'May you grow tall,' he echoed. 'I was invited by your master.'

Isha bowed her head and let him in. Passerine went to touch wrists with Sir Leofric, who answered his greeting before sitting on the armchair. Passerine returned to his desk. Once she had poured the lawmage a cup of herbal tea, Isha stood.

She held her cup between both hands. She focused on its warmth, trying to ignore the fact that it was colder here, away from the fire.

Sir Leofric tapped his fingers against the armrest, glancing across the room. Isha knew he was comparing it to lusher chambers, with enough space to fit multiple apprentices, a bedroom annex, and furniture to spare. Passerine didn't hang tapestries on the walls. The carpet wasn't decorative; it was there to prevent the cold from seeping through the floor.

For a while Sir Leofric didn't speak, only sipped his tea. Passerine waited, one hand resting against his half-written notes; black hand white nails, black ink white paper.

Sir Leofric turned to Isha first.

'You have an interesting way of fighting,' he said. 'Where did you learn to mindbrawl that way?'

She wasn't sure if he meant 'mindbrawl' or 'shoving people to the floor when you mindbrawl'. There was only one answer an apprentice was expected to give:

'All I know, I learnt from Sir Passerine. But any faults that remain are mine, and mine alone.'

Sir Leofric listened to her formal, meaningless reply. A thin smile tugged at the corner of his lips.

'Of course. So, why did you invite me here?'

By instinct, Isha clamped down on her thoughts to keep them blank. Sir Leofric studied her, his head cocked to one side, but whatever he was hoping to get out of her, he didn't succeed. He shifted his attention to Passerine. His eyes, like his clothes, belonged somewhere far from the sun.

'We are living in troubled times,' Passerine said.

'Lord Daegan is a strong supreme mage,' Sir Leofric answered. He finished his cup of tea and waved to Isha to pour him some more.

'That is true,' Passerine said. 'But I can't help but wonder – what will his lightborn do when khers are at the gates, screaming for blood? If the Renegades fight not like mages, but like beasts, will his power protect us?'

Isha got up to fetch the jug of tea. Breathing deeply, she made sure her hands didn't shake. Sir Leofric watched her all the while, steady as a snake.

'What happens when the Renegades kick you to the floor before they mindbrawl? Or when they use khers as weapons in their war?' Passerine asked.

'I don't know. Do tell.' Sir Leofric's voice was pleasant enough. He crossed his legs as he lounged back in the armchair.

'A collarbound who can fly is an asset. A collarbound who can fleshbind might be a better tool.'

Passerine spoke casually enough, but the atmosphere in the room changed. Isha tensed. From the corner of her eye, she noticed that Sir Leofric, despite his efforts at seeming relaxed, had stiffened. He made a show of stretching, like a cat taken by surprise, buying time with his long, lazy movements.

'I wonder,' Sir Leofric said, picking at something underneath his nails, 'what someone with such a collarbound could gain. And what he would give the people who helped him.' He let his hands fall back into his lap, where his slim cane was resting.

'Now is not a time for mages at the top of the Nest to fight.' Passerine's voice, in contrast to Sir Leofric's light tone, seemed deeper still. 'And, maybe, the idea of one leader for such a large flock is one that is growing outdated.'

Isha bit down on her lips to stifle a gasp.

'A council of high mages – including the head of the lawmages, as is only proper – would offer better leadership.' Passerine's expression, as always, was unreadable. 'Maybe a council implies too large a group. A triumvirate would suffice.'

A triumvirate. Three leaders, then: Daegan, Passerine, Leofric. This was a lot more than Isha had expected. Passerine had never told her that he hoped to rule the Nest, with or without other high mages.

Sir Leofric's eyes gleamed, bright as emeralds. 'What an interesting idea. You always surprise, Sir Passerine.'

Passerine bowed his head; it wasn't clear whether he was acknowledging what Sir Leofric had said or thanking him. The more Isha considered it, the more she understood the logic of a shared leadership. Passerine would stand for the Sunriser convents, and maybe for the khers. He would represent a new, less traditional way to be a mage. Sir Daegan could unite the more old-fashioned followers. And Sir Leofric represented justice, a neutral settler, even if he was anything but.

'I have something that might be yours,' said Sir Leofric.

'I thought you might,' said Passerine, keeping his tone as affable as Sir Leofric's, as if they were only discussing misplaced wares.

'Would you care to check if he is yours?'

The lawmage was lively and lithe, as if he were inviting Passerine to a dance, not a trip to the prisons. Isha swallowed through clenched teeth. Her head was ringing. She tried not to hope, but hope tore her heart until it ached.

'Yes,' said Passerine. 'I would.'

* * *

Tatters curled in a corner of his cage, closed his eyes, and pretended the stone at the back of his neck was the sturdy wall of the tavern, and the distant sounds of prisoners moaning were laughter. He didn't know for how long he stayed unmoving, thinking of Yua, imagining conversations he would never have with Lal. He waited for them to come back and kill him.

When he heard their voices, when the door of his cage creaked, he didn't open his eyes. If he was going to die, he could do so without having to see Goldie's face again.

'Yes, it's him,' said a low voice. It was the voice of a ghost. It was Passerine.

Tatters looked up. There was Sir Leofric, resting on his cane, an unamused smile playing on his lips. And Passerine, wearing the full black robes of a high mage, towering above him, the light streaming from the torch behind him.

Tatters got to his feet, grabbing the bars of the cage to help himself up. Part of him realised he wouldn't die. Another part of him realised he would be given back to Hawk, by Passerine, on a plate. He wondered if it was worth running.

They stared at each other for the first time since Tatters had crossed the Shadowpass. Passerine's eyes were as deep as water at the bottom of a well, at the bottom of the worlds.

'You idiot,' said Passerine.

Tatters couldn't say he disagreed.

Passerine nodded to Sir Leofric, and dropped a purse of coins in the lawmage's hand.

'For your troubles,' he said, 'and as a promise for more.'

'A pleasure, I'm sure,' said Sir Leofric, smiling at master and slave.

He tied the purse of money to his belt before moving towards Tatters. Instinctively Tatters backed away. It was only when the lawmage unhooked the key from his belt that Tatters understood what was happening. He felt numb as Sir Leofric unlocked the kher shackles and pulled them off his wrists.

Lal was glowing inside him, like the embers of yesterday's fire.

I am back, brother. It's been a long time.

'I am taking you home,' said Passerine.

TO BE CONCLUDED IN VOLUME 3:
THE LIGHTBORN

Acknowledgements

Thank you to the usual suspects, for helping me through thick and thin, blank pages and messy edits. I hope you recognise yourselves, but just in case:

My thanks to my agent, Alice Speilburg, and to Marcus Gipps and the rest of the Gollancz team. Thank you to the peer group – we're still going strong, guys, after all these years! I hope soon it's your books I'll be seeing in print and asking you to sign for me at events. Thank you to my family and loved ones, who know how precious they all are.

Last but never least, Nicolas, for everything.

Credits

Rebecca Zahabi and Gollancz would like to thank everyone at Orion who worked on the publication of *The Hawkling*.

Editor
Marcus Gipps
Claire Ormsby-Potter

Copy-editor
Abigail Nathan

Proofreader
Patrick McConnell

Editorial Management
Jane Hughes
Charlie Panayiotou
Tamara Morriss
Claire Boyle

Contracts
Dan Heron
Ellie Bowker

Audio
Paul Stark
Jake Alderson
Georgina Cutler

Design
Nick Shah
Rachael Lancaster
Joanna Ridley
Helen Ewing
Tomás Almeida

Finance
Nick Gibson
Jasdip Nandra
Elizabeth Beaumont
Ibukun Ademefun
Sue Baker
Tom Costello